# SYMPHONY

# OF

# DREAMS

CYNTHIA ROGAN

ISBN: 1470162636
ISBN-13: 9781470162634

Library of Congress Control Number: 2012904545
CreateSpace, North Charleston, SC

*To Granny*
*who taught me everything she could*
*by simply being the wise woman she was.*

*To my daughters*
*who keep me grounded.*

# *ACKNOWLEDGEMENTS*

The occupation of writing leads to much alone time but the finished product is never accomplished solely by the author. It takes a village to raise a book. For me the better part of that village was made up of other authors, editors, readers, critique groups, and those closest to me.

I would like to thank Robert Brazeau, Darlene Ensor, Janine Hollingsworth, Karen Parker, Robynn Sheahan, Kathi Teese, Dianne Tighe, Russell Turney, Lyda Woods, Leanne Zinkand, the extended members of HayWire Writers' Group, Margo Kelly, the members of Oregon Rogue Authors' Guild, and Catie Faryl (for the cover art).

Your contribution of time, effort, and love, helped make *Symphony of Dreams* a reality.

Special thanks to my daughter, Stacy Tanzi, whose belief in me and the story kept me focused and encouraged—no matter what.

# PART ONE

# CHAPTER ONE

IT WAS HARD to be five years old and feel inclined to keep a secret. Even if that secret was just a dream.

The rusty spring on the screen door whinnied as Symphony pushed up her short sleeves and stepped outside. At nine-thirty in the morning, she was already coated in a thin layer of sweat. From the porch, she eyed the dark green car in front of her house. It looked just like the one in her dream. "Or was that one black?" she whispered, squeezing her eyes shut, trying to see it in her mind. "Green," she decided, inching toward the stairs.

A flock of starlings flapped away, having had their fill of ripe blackberries in the side yard. Startled by the ruckus, Symphony darted back to the house and ducked behind the screen door, as if the thin piece of mesh could protect her from the danger that car could bring.

⌘　⌘　⌘

In a household of six, being the first one up on Saturday morning was a quiet blessing. Symphony had turned the television to her favorite cartoon, making sure the volume was low. She didn't want to wake anyone up, especially Daddy. The thought made her stomach ache.

*Maybe he's at work.* She slipped behind the closed drapes and looked out the front picture window. Daddy's car was gone, but there was a strange one in its place. The car, itself, wasn't unusual. It just didn't belong at her house. The man in her dream had been driving it. Symphony stared through the glass, chewing her fingernails, waiting for the man to appear behind the steering wheel.

Soon after Mama's slippers scuffed down the hallway, the aroma of percolating coffee called Symphony from her vigil. She rambled into the kitchen. "Mama? Do we have comp'ny?"

Mama's long, brown hair was pulled back in a ponytail. It swished back and forth, as she worked at making breakfast. "Comp-a-ny," she corrected, her back to Symphony. "No. Why?"

"Well, whose car is here?"

"Oh," Mama said, turning around. "It's ours. You were already in bed when Daddy brought it home last night. You like it?"

Symphony gave Mama's knees an extra long hug.

"I guess that's a yes." She stroked Symphony's short blonde hair. "We'll take a ride in it later, okay?"

Knowing Mama was awake seemed to renew Symphony's courage. And if it *was* their car, it couldn't belong to him. Still, she had to see it to know for sure. "Can I go out and play?"

"After breakfast," Mama said.

But, after breakfast came bath taking and teeth brushing. When Symphony was dressed she asked again, but Mama was firm. "It's Saturday, honey. You know the rules. Your room has to be cleaned first."

Daddy came around the corner. "Don't ask again," he barked, "or you'll spend the whole day inside. You hear me? Now go on." He nudged her shoulder. "Do what your mother said."

Symphony glanced up at his hard, black eyes. "Yes, sir." She went straight to her room, closing the door behind her.

Her older sister, Dani, had already made her own bed and was curled up on top of the floral spread reading a book about Dick and Jane. After five years of sharing a bedroom, Symphony knew one thing for sure—Dani never picked up anything on purpose. Sometimes, she would even sleep on top of the covers just to avoid making her bed the next day.

"You have to help too," Symphony prodded.

Dani didn't even put her book down. "You have to help too," she mocked. She turned a page and stretched into a more comfortable position.

"You do! Mama said!"

"*You* wanna go out," Dani snipped. "*You* finish."

Half an hour later, Mama was checking all the best mess-hiding spots.

Dani batted her eyes at Mama. "I don't know how our room gets so dirty. Let's try and keep it clean this time, Symphony."

Symphony cut her a look but didn't say a word. An argument would only keep her in the house longer.

"Well, I guess you can go outside now," Mama said, following Symphony to the living room. "Stay in the yard, okay."

Now, after everything Symphony had done to get out of the house, she couldn't seem to make it off the front porch.

She wriggled out from behind the screen door and peeked around the corner. The noisy birds were gone. "It's *our* car," she declared, clenching her fists. "Mama said so." She jumped down the steps and snapped a dandelion puff off at the base. With closed eyes, she made a wish and blew the seeds into the sweltering air. They floated above the ominous sedan, refusing to land anywhere near it.

She stole a few steps closer, pausing to pick up a tiny set of angel wing shells lying in her path. After tucking the treasure into her pocket, she flitted sideways toward the unsuspecting vehicle. At the trunk, she stopped and held her breath, waiting to see what would happen.

When she was sure lightning wouldn't strike, she put her finger in her mouth, pulled it out, and wiped a wet stripe onto the shiny new car. Against the dark green paint, it made a rainbow of purple, blue, and copper just seconds before drying in the hot Alabama sun.

She tried the spit trick again. This time her finger wasn't wet enough. For the moment, she gave up painting rainbows and walked backward to the driver's door, dragging one heel of her saddle shoe through the crushed shells that made up their driveway.

On tippy-toes, she strained to see inside, but the window was too high. She pushed the button on the door handle. When it didn't move she squeezed with both thumbs, groaning, "I think I can, I think I can." This time the door fell open, freeing the expanding heat inside. The blast sucked the sweat right from her pores. She stepped back to breathe and glanced toward the house. Mama and Daddy never allowed her to play in the car. But, this wasn't really playing. She just needed a better look.

On the inside, the car was different. *The man's seats were light green.* These were tan. Relieved, she slid her palm across the slick upholstery. *So, it was just a dream.*

At least that's what Daddy always told Dani when she woke up scared. But, Symphony didn't have nightmares about monsters like Dani did. In fact, she couldn't remember ever having a bad dream—before last night.

She had opened her eyes to a dark room, her throat aching with a scream that wouldn't come. The nightlight was burned out so she flipped on the lamp and forced herself to look at her sister's bed. Dani was right where she was supposed to be. But, in the dream, they had been in a car with a man they didn't know.

Now, satisfied that this was not the same car, Symphony closed the heavy door and hopped to the road on one foot. The Japanese honeysuckle by the ditch was in full bloom. She plucked a flower from the vine and pulled it apart, licking the honey-sweet nectar from its long yellow pistil.

Miss Ida Stalls drove up, her powder blue convertible raising dust as it stopped in front of Symphony's driveway. "J'all get a new car, honey?"

Symphony nodded. "Uh-huh. Daddy brought it home last night."

"It *shore* is pretty."

"Thank you, ma'am."

"Tell your mama I said hey."

Miss Ida looked like she should be on the cover of a magazine, and she always smelled like flowers. Symphony watched her park at the end of the road and wrestle brown Piggly Wiggly sacks from the car to her front door. Mama said all the single men in Mobile stood in line to buy her dinner. *So, why does she have to buy groceries?*

When Miss Ida went inside, Symphony walked under the carport and sat on the cool concrete steps where the memory of the dream caught her alone once again.

She tried to remember what the man looked like. He hadn't turned his head once. The whole time, his nose had pointed like an arrow toward wherever he was taking them.

Using her shirt, she wiped the sweat off her face.

His hair was black. And long for a man. And it looked wet. *But Uncle Gray's is like that too. Mama says he uses too much grease.* He wore glasses, and they were shiny—*like Granny's spittoon. And his cheeks went in instead of out, the way Mama's do when she smokes a cigarette.*

In the dream, Dani was sitting by the door, Symphony in the middle next to the stranger. Inside, the car was hot but the sisters shivered as they looked at each other.

*We have to get away.*

Symphony was staring at the floorboard, trying not to cry, when something shifted below Dani's feet. Scooting closer, she used the toe of her shoe to lift a flap that covered an opening almost as large as the entire passenger floor. The road rolled beneath it as the driver accelerated once again.

*We can fit through.*

As the car slowed to a stop at the next intersection, Symphony glanced at the man. He was still looking forward.

*You go first. Just slide out.* She thought it. Dani heard.

Holding Symphony's hand, Dani pushed herself down through the hole. After one more look to make sure the man wasn't watching, Symphony leaned over and Dani pulled her, head first, to safety.

The girls lay still beneath the car, in the center, away from the tires. When the light turned green, the stranger drove on.

⌘   ⌘   ⌘

At preschool the next Monday, Symphony and her friend Davy watched through the activity room window as mothers drove into the circular driveway to pick up their children.

"We could fit under a car. And not get hurt, either," Davy assured her, raising his eyebrows and crossing his arms. "A lot of it duddn't even come close to the road." He reached for the doorknob. "Wanna try?"

"No." Symphony shook her head and backed away. "Mama'd be really mad."

"Not if we don't get hurt," Davy told her. "You only get in trouble if you get hurt."

Davy was the only person she'd told about the dream. Their daddies rode to work together and the families had been friends for as long as Symphony could remember. She knew Davy would believe her and, most important, he wouldn't tell.

5

"Maybe it was one o' your uncles."

"No it wasn't!" She stomped her foot and glared at him. When she turned back toward the window, Mama was pulling their new car into the circle. Symphony ran to her cubbyhole and grabbed her newest drawing. She couldn't wait to see it taped to the refrigerator. "See ya tomorrow."

This was Symphony's favorite time of day. With Dani still in school and the little sisters asleep in the back seat, she got to sit up front with Mama. Most days, the two of them talked the whole drive home without interruption.

"Look, Mama," Symphony said, leaning toward the driver's side. "I made you a new picture."

Leesa, the baby, started to fuss.

"Just a minute, sweetie." As Symphony waited, drawing in hand, Mama reached into the back seat to prop up the baby's bottle.

Leesa held it with both hands and was quiet.

"See, Mama. I made it just for you." Symphony pushed the picture toward her mother once more but before Mama could look, they turned a corner, the bottle shifted, and Leesa began to cry again. This time Jeanne, the two-year-old, woke up, wailing.

The bottle was re-propped but Leesa's contentedness lasted only a moment. Jeanne, grumpy at the shortness of her nap, grabbed the baby's bottle and flung it into the front seat, drizzling Symphony's artwork with formula.

*Mama won't like it anyway.* She let the drawing drop to the floor and stepped on it as she got out of the car.

Later, while Mama cooked supper, Symphony crept into the kitchen. Aside from the gurgling boil of dinner, the house was quiet. Her two little sisters were taking another nap and Dani was practicing her reading.

"Mama."

"Yes, sugar," Mama said, glancing over her shoulder.

"Today at Tiny Tots, me and Davy—"

"Davy and I."

"Um, Davy and I, we laid down under a car, away from the wheels, and it drove over us. And we're okay. See." Symphony held both arms over her head and pirouetted.

Mama dropped the spoon into the pot of stew she was stirring. "What?"

"If you get right in the middle and lay real still, it can roll over you and not even touch you."

"Symphony Ann Weber!" Mama knelt down and took Symphony by the shoulders. "Never go near a car without a grown-up. You know that. Where was Miss Ruby?"

"Um." Symphony stared at her feet. "In the bathroom . . . I think."

"You could have been run over. Why would you do that?"

"I'm sorry, Mama." Symphony braced herself for a spanking, but the tears in Mama's eyes smacked the truth out of her. "We really didn't. We just said we wanted to."

"You made that up?" Mama stiffened and let go. "Why?"

"I don't know," Symphony said, turning her face away.

"Go sit on your bed until I call you for supper."

"But, Mama, I—"

"Go, young lady. And you stay away from cars. Do you hear me?"

Symphony stared in disbelief. Mama had never been this mad at her. She slumped away to her room.

"What'd you do?" Dani asked, grinning.

Symphony shrugged and lay down, pulling her pillow over her face. *Davy's wrong about the getting hurt thing. Maybe that's just if you're a boy.*

# CHAPTER TWO

IT WORKED. PERHAPS because no one had told her it wouldn't.

*The stranger drove them past the park as Symphony stared out Dani's window.*

*I'm dreaming.*

*The reminder steadied her as she watched for the red light at the corner. As soon as she saw it, she closed her eyes and focused her thoughts on one word—Stop.*

*Right in the middle of the dream, the car halted. Everything froze: the mockingbird just above the power line where it always landed, the woman in the crosswalk who looked at them as she passed, the small boy watching through the park fence. Dani wasn't even trembling anymore.*

*Symphony sat still, waiting. In this part, the man always coughed. His silence told her it was safe to move. She turned, rose to her knees, and tried to lean over in front of him, holding tightly to the steering wheel. If I could just see his face . . .*

Seeing his face was all Symphony could think of since she and her family returned from their summer vacation at Granny's. As usual, the four hour trip to Granny's side of Alabama had felt more like a day. But, with Symphony's mind full of what ifs and how tos, the ride home went quickly.

While in preschool, the dream had bothered her three times. In first grade, it showed up as soon as she stopped worrying that it would. This year, in second grade, the nightmare had established more of a pattern, waking her at least once a month. But it didn't scare her the way it had at first. Not since she discovered she wasn't the only one whose dreams played over and over again. When her grandpa was alive, he had the same problem. Now, Uncle Gray did too.

⌘   ⌘   ⌘

That summer morning, her youngest uncle, Austin, had sent her in search of gold. Just before noon, after digging for hours in the cool dirt floor of Granny's barn, Symphony wandered over and handed him the flaky golden nuggets she had found.

"They're not gold," Austin said, handing them back. "Them're just rocks."

Symphony held them out in a stream of sunlight. "Are you sure? They're really shiny."

"Yep. What you got there's just fool's gold."

"Well, I'm gonna keep 'em anyways, just in case." She shoved them into her pocket.

"Suit yourself," Austin said.

For the first time, Symphony noticed the heap of wood and chicken wire piled next to him. "Whacha makin'?"

"A cage," he said, bending a nail with his hammer to hold the wire in place.

"What kinda cage?"

"Rabbit. I've gotta trap it 'fore it ruins the rest of the garden. You should see what it's doin' to the beans and carrots."

Symphony imagined a soft white bunny with a pink nose. "If you catch one, can I hold it?"

Austin shook his head. "Not a wild rabbit. That thing'd scratch you up. Then it'd bite ya. Besides, we'll prob'ly feed it for a few weeks, then skin it and cook it." He looked up at Symphony and grinned. "If you want, I'll save you the fur."

She crossed her arms to match her sudden change of mood. "People don't eat rabbits!"

"Sure they do," Austin said with a smirk.

"They do not." She hesitated, wondering if he was right. *Why would anyone eat a bunny?* There was nothing cuddly about chickens or fish. Cows were too big and pigs smelled bad. But bunnies . . . She put her hands on her hips. "I'm gonna go ask Granny!"

"Go ahead," he called after her as she marched up the back steps. "She'll tell you. They taste just like chicken. You've prob'ly eaten rabbit before and just didn't know it."

Symphony let the screen door slam behind her and headed down the hallway, Austin's laughter nipping at her heels. As she neared the kitchen, the sound of voices stopped her and held her in the hall.

Granny cleared her throat. "I just don't know why you have to—"

"I'll tell you why," Uncle Gray said. "'Cause, when I pass out, I don't have the nightmares."

*Nightmares?* Symphony leaned against the wall, waiting for the next word.

"I know you didn't ask for this gift, Graydon." Granny's voice was soft and sad, as if she were making a wish for something she knew she couldn't have. "Your papa said his started when he was only three or four. He fought it too—till he was nearly grown. But then something happened. One night, he and a few of his friends—I won't tell you who—got their teenaged hands on a jug o' whiskey and snuck off down to the river to drink it. Two of 'em got to arguing and kept it up till one of 'em said something real mean. Your papa told me he'd seen it all in a dream. He knew what the next words would be and that they would make the first boy mad enough to draw a knife. So, he did the only thing he could. He interrupted before those words could come."

Granny paused.

"I need to get some sleep, Mama," Gray said.

A chair scraped the floor. Symphony tiptoed back three steps.

"Hang on," Granny said. "You need to hear the rest of this. It'll just take a minute."

The chair slid again. Symphony tiptoed closer.

"Your papa welcomed the dreams after that. He even practiced talkin' to himself while he was dreaming, learned to slow 'em down so he wouldn't miss anything important. Did I ever tell you? He knew I was pregnant with you before I did."

"Yeah. That one must have been more like a nightmare," Gray said.

"No it wasn't."

For a moment, neither of them said a word. Then Granny continued. "Look, son. I know you're not happy about it, but there must be a reason this is happening. Promise me you'll at least try to slow 'em down like your

11

papa did. Maybe once you see what the dream is telling you, it'll give you a rest. Want lunch before you go to work?"

"I'm not hungry," he said. "I think I'll take a nap."

Symphony hid in the bathroom as Gray walked down the other end of the hall. She washed her hands, splashed cold water on her face, and gazed at herself in the mirror. *Uncle Gray has dreams like me.*

She was starving by the time Granny called her to the kitchen for lunch. Right in the center of the table, piled high enough to topple, was a platter of fried chicken. Carefully, Symphony turned it, searching for a drumstick.

Uncle Austin walked in, grabbed the top piece and took a bite. "Oh, Mama," he said, flopping into a chair, "you outdid yourself this time." He held the unfamiliar-looking piece out to Symphony. "Try it," he whispered, grinning. "I'm tellin' ya, it tastes just like chicken." He put it on his plate and made bunny ears with his hands, all the while nodding at the mound of poultry.

"I'm not really *that* hungry, Granny," Symphony said. "Could I just have a tomato sandwich?"

⌘　⌘　⌘

From that day forward, Symphony waited for the dream, hoping to slow it down as Papa had done with his. She wanted to see everything: the car, the man, where they were. With no one to tell her how, she experimented. No matter what she tried, she could only change her *thoughts* in the dream, not what happened.

One night, while in the midst of it, she felt the heat of the stranger next to her. Wanting to escape for a moment, she closed her eyes. She imagined riding her bicycle, the handlebar streamers fluttering, the cool breeze on her face. Then, she took her feet off the pedals and felt the bike coast, the speed drop, the wind ease. When she opened her eyes again, everything in the dream was in slow motion.

Since she believed the man's face was the first detail she needed to see, she stood, turned around, and pressed her back against the dashboard, squeezing as close to him as she could. She got a glimpse, but within seconds, his cold, dark eyes glared back, erasing his features from her mind.

12

A shiver of terror ended the dream well before she and Dani made their escape.

Tonight, with the dream paused, she tried another angle, but between the man's rigid form and the steering wheel, she couldn't get close enough. *I'll have to get out of the car.* She stretched over Dani to open the door. Just as she did, a loud noise jolted her awake. There it was again. *What is that?* The phone was ringing. *In the middle of the night?* She reached over and turned the lamp switch but the light didn't come on.

There were footsteps in the hallway, then a crash and "Ow!"

"Mama?" Symphony called out, just as lightning flashed.

It lit the house long enough for Mama to find the phone. "Hello," she said. "No. The power must have gone out after I went to bed. I think I just broke my toe. Are you still in Charlotte? Okay. Well, do you know where the transistor radio is? No. You took it last time you went fishing. I guess we'll just have to do without it, then. A flood warning? What about the hurricane? But you have the car. How am I gonna—Shoot. I lost him." She hung up the phone. "Daniele, Symphony. Get up and get dressed."

Dani groaned.

"No arguing," Mama said. "Just hurry."

Symphony watched through the bedroom door as a strobe of lightning helped Mama find her way to the kitchen. Minutes later, she was back, carrying glorious candlelight across the living room. She made her way to the phone and dialed.

"Hello. This is Maisy Weber. 1451 Dogwood. Is the hurricane supposed to hit Mobile?" She paused. "But I don't have a car right now. My husband's out of town. And I have four daughters. Is there anyone who can—Okay. I'll hold on." In Mama's silence, the winds grew louder, first whispering against the house, then smacking the windows with small branches and debris. "Thank goodness," Mama sighed with relief. "How long? Okay. We'll be ready."

She hung up the phone. "Girls!"

"What's wrong, Mama?" Symphony asked.

"Everything'll be fine," Mama said, sounding as if she were trying to convince herself. "Are you two dressed yet?"

"There's a *her-cane?*" Symphony asked.

"Yes," Mama said. She lit another candle on their bedside table. "Pull your little suitcases out from under the bed. Pack three changes of clothes. Don't forget panties and socks."

"Where are we going, Mama?" Dani asked, her short, brown hair a mass of tangled curls.

"To your school for now," she replied. "Stay away from that candle," she added, hurrying out of the room.

"What about Daddy?" Dani called after her.

Mama stopped and turned around. "He's still in North Carolina, far away from the hurricane."

Symphony pulled both suitcases out from under the beds.

"But how will he find us when he gets here?" Dani asked, yanking hers away from Symphony.

"You hurt my finger," Symphony said, spinning toward Dani.

"Girls, please! Just do what I asked you to do. Without fighting. I have to pack for your sisters. Someone's coming to drive us to the school. We have to be ready." Muttering, Mama limped away.

Within minutes, there was a knock on the door. Mama rushed to open it, carrying Jeanne, half-dressed, on her hip.

A man and woman held fast to the porch columns, their yellow raincoats slick and shiny in the car headlights. Mama glanced at their volunteer badges. "I'm so glad you're here." At the wind's insistence, they stepped inside.

"Daniele, Symphony," Mama yelled. "Blow out your candle and c'mon." As the girls came out of their bedroom, Mama pulled a shirt over Jeanne's head. "Just let me get the baby and we can go."

"Wait," the man said.

Mama turned back toward him.

"I'm sorry, ma'am." He rubbed his forehead and looked away. "We can only take two this trip."

"What?" Mama gaped at him.

"There's two other families in the car," he said. "We don't have room for all five of you."

"But . . ." Mama's chest seemed to cave in. "I told the operator how many and . . . That's okay," she said. "We'll wait for the next car."

"What if you all won't fit in the next car?" the woman asked. "Then what?"

Mama couldn't speak. Jeanne squirmed to get down. Leesa screamed from her crib. The wind threatened to blow them all over. The man reached around Mama and closed the door.

"Are these the oldest two?" the woman asked.

Mama nodded.

"Let them go with us. I give you my word, I'll stay with them until you get to the school. It's just for a few minutes anyway." She handed Mama a piece of paper with two names scrawled on it. "Just ask for us when you get there. The other car should be here shortly."

"Girls." Mama squatted to Symphony's eye level. "These people are with the Red Cross. They'll take you to the school where there's a shelter. Your sisters are gonna have to ride with me in the next car. Okay."

"No, Mama," Symphony begged. "I wanna wait with you."

"You can't, sweetie," Mama told her. "Go on. I'll be right behind you."

Each volunteer led one of the sisters down the stream of headlights toward the car. Symphony stopped resisting after the first three steps until a bolt of lightning turned the sky silver, revealing the vehicle her sister was stepping into. *It's his car.* "Dani!" she screamed. "No!" But a gust caught her warning and fed it to the storm. Dani disappeared into the front seat.

The woman tugged at Symphony's arm. "C'mon, honey," she shouted over the roaring wind. "We have to hurry."

But Symphony stiffened, refusing to take another step. She jerked, trying to pull her hand from the woman's grasp, but in an instant, another gust slapped them both toward the car.

Within moments, Symphony was inside. She glanced at the four grownups crammed into the back seat, counted three sleeping children in their laps, and scooted closer to Dani as the woman squeezed in next to her and slammed the door. *Mama and the little sisters would never have fit.*

The driver pulled the car away from the house. "My name's Bob," he said with a smile in his voice. "And this is my wife Norma."

"I'm Daniele," Dani said. "And this is Symphony." She squeezed Symphony's hand. "She never gets scared."

But tonight, Symphony was terrified. The hood of the driver's raincoat was covering the side of his face. All she knew for sure was that he was someone she didn't know driving a car she didn't feel safe in. She stared straight ahead at the windshield wipers as they batted back and forth at raindrops and debris. *What if Mama doesn't come?* It wouldn't be the first time Mama hadn't been able to keep a promise. *What if it's him?*

As the storm threw a tantrum outside and the adults in the car softly spoke back and forth, Symphony squeezed Dani's hand and closed her eyes, hoping for sleep. Lately, she'd been able to see bits and pieces of her dreams in real life. Maybe if she had a dream about Mama doing something tomorrow, she'd know things were going to be okay.

⌘　⌘　⌘

She awoke in the school lunchroom with Miss Ida Stalls and Dani standing over her. "You all right, sweetheart?" Miss Ida asked. "I brought you some peanuts and a bottle of *Co-co-ler*. Why don't you sit up a take a little drink, okay?"

"Where's Mama?" Symphony asked, looking around.

Dani sat down on the cot where Symphony had been sleeping. "Miss Ida can tell you."

"They're fine, honey," Miss Ida said. "They couldn't get over the bridge, that's all. So they had to go to the high school. But don't you worry. I'll stay right here with you till we get to go home, okay." She looked at both girls and smiled.

"See that policeman over there?" The officer looked in their direction and Ida winked. "He was nice enough to radio someone at the high school to make sure your mama got there okay. Plus, I had him tell her I was here with the two o' you so she didn't worry so much."

The lunchroom was crowded with evacuees. Symphony glanced around searching for a window. She couldn't tell if it was night or day. *And what about the her-cane?* If the wind was still blowing hard, she couldn't hear it over all the people.

"Miss Ida," she asked. "Why do they call it a her-cane and not a him-cane?"

"I don't know, sweetie. They name 'em after women too. Someone told me once that it's 'cause hurricanes are unpredictable, and so are women. Funny. I can almost always tell what a woman'll do in a given situation. But men. Who knows?" She looked up and waved at a red-haired man. "Well look who's comin'," she said.

"Who?" Symphony asked.

"It's Bob," Dani said. "The man who brought us here last night."

Bob smiled when he saw Symphony sitting up. "Hey, honey," he said, tousling her short blonde hair. "Norma and I were worried about you. We felt real bad about having to leave your Mama and sisters behind. But you're all safe anyway, even if you aren't together. You think you'll ever be able to forgive ol' Bob?"

Symphony studied him in his yellow raincoat. The hood was down, showing his orange-red hair. On his right cheek was a mole the size of a horsefly. *It's not him.* She let out a breath and gave him her biggest smile.

# CHAPTER THREE

FIVE MONTHS HAD passed since Daddy's promotion.

"I didn't expect it this soon," he told Mama at dinner the night he found out. "But whether we're ready or not, I can't turn down the job. I'll be making three-hundred dollars more a month."

Mama beamed. "What do you mean, 'ready or not'? Of course we're ready. When do you start?"

"July first," he said. "There's one condition, though. And you're not gonna like it."

She raised an eyebrow. "Don't tell me we have to move again."

"We do. But not back to Chicago. It's too cold. This time we're going to Florida."

Mama slumped in her chair. "I thought you'd decided to wait for Wally to retire. They've already offered you his position and next March isn't *that* far away." She paused for a moment, watching Daddy's face. "Besides, if you took Wally's job we could stay here. We've been here for six years. The girls are in school. I hate to uproot—"

"God dammit, Maisy!" He pounded the dinner table, his eyes as hard as his fist. Iced tea sloshed out of his glass. Mama flinched. Dani and Symphony stiffened. The little sisters whimpered and began to cry.

"It always comes down to this, doesn't it? I'm sick of you putting these kids before me." He stood up, shoved his chair against the table, and stomped away. The front door slammed. The car started. The tires crunched as he backed out of the long shell driveway.

The room grew quiet. Four pairs of eyes watched Mama as she wiped a tear with her napkin. She carried Daddy's plate to the sink. When she returned, her expression had relaxed. "Finish your supper, girls."

Soon, they were all chattering, taking advantage of Daddy's absence to act silly at the table. They kept it up until Mama was laughing so hard she had to use her napkin again to wipe her eyes.

That June, as soon as school let out, they packed their things. Four men in brown cover-alls carried the beds, the couch, even the refrigerator, into a huge green and yellow truck. When the house was empty, Miss Ida Stalls glided across the lawn, carrying with her the essence of a lily field. Her platinum hair was puffed up high on top, even though strands of it hung straight past her shoulders. The deepening of their friendship was the only good that had come out of last year's hurricane.

With sad eyes, she surveyed Symphony and her sisters. "Lord, I'm gonna miss you girls like all get out. You're the closest thing I've got to nieces." She planted a kiss on top of Leesa's head and handed her a rag doll. The three-year-old's eyes brightened as she clutched the soft toy to her chest. "Now if this baby starts to cry 'cause she misses me, you just give her a big ole hug, okay?"

And for my favorite little redhead, I have a story about a little red hen." She handed Jeanne a book and scooped her up with a groan. "Next time I see you, you're gonna be too big for me to pick up." Ida gave her a squeeze and set her back down. "Let your sisters read this to you on the way to Florida," she said, "and if you listen real good, pretty soon you'll know it by heart. Why, you'll be readin' 'fore you even start school."

As Jeanne began to look at the pictures, Dani cut in front of Symphony. "Will you come see us at our new house?"

Ida stooped to hug Dani. "Titusville's a nice little town. I drive right by it every time I go to Miami. I'll get the phone number from your mama. I can let y'all know when I'm comin' through." Her eyes teared as she kissed Dani's forehead. "You were so little when you came to live here. Now, look at you. You're growin' up so nice."

"I know." Dani gave Symphony a smug look. "Now, Mama lets me—"

Symphony didn't hear the rest. She walked away, waiting for them to finish their good-bye. She was standing behind the moving van, watching one of the men lock the huge double-doors, when Dani tapped her on the shoulder.

"Miss Ida wants to see you. And Daddy says hurry up." She smirked at Symphony and ran back toward the house, yelling, "I told her."

Symphony took her time crossing the yard. "I don't wanna say bye, Miss Ida."

"Okay, sweetie," Miss Ida answered. "But let's at least sit for a minute." She led the way to the rusty, old swing set in the side yard. "'Member what you told me last time we were talkin'?" Ida said, squeezing her fanny into a child-sized seat.

"About the kids at school?" Symphony asked, sitting in the second swing.

"Yeah," Miss Ida said. "Well they're wrong. And here's the proof." She pulled a photograph out of her shirt pocket and handed it to Symphony. "Here's a picture of one of the most beautiful people I know. Only this person isn't just beautiful on the outside. Inside, she's even prettier."

For a moment the picture hung limp in Symphony's hand. Then she raised it to her eyes. "But this is me," she said, breaking into sobs. "You're teasin' me too, Miss Ida."

"Oh, honey." Ida pulled the chain on Symphony's swing, drawing her close. "You've known me most o' your life. Have I ever teased you or lied to you?"

Symphony shook her head.

"I meant what I said, Symmie. There's a kindness that comes from deep inside you. You *are* one of the most beautiful people I know. Promise me you'll never let anyone make you believe you're not."

⌘　⌘　⌘

They had skipped the summer week at Granny's, arriving in Florida on June fifteenth to a new neighborhood packed with kids. But none of them were Symphony's age. While the rest of her family made friends, Symphony spent her time moping around the house watching the blades of the fan spin, eating everything she could get her hands on.

⌘　⌘　⌘

It wasn't that she was hungry. She'd had plenty to eat at supper. Then, afterward, there was dessert—coconut cake. But Mama had only given her a sliver.

Now, at two-thirty in the morning, Symphony opened the refrigerator and stood in the triangle of light, searching. *There.* Leaning over, she reached to the back of the bottom shelf and scooped a finger full of gooey coconut filling. She sucked her finger clean, tasting only the blessing of her decision as the buttery sweetness flowed to some empty place inside her. *It's my birthday.* She lifted the cake plate and set it on the counter. *And this is my cake.* As quietly as possible, she slid the silverware drawer open and picked up a fork.

⌘　⌘　⌘

Symphony stared into the dresser drawer at her last clean pair of shorts. She slipped her feet through the leg holes and pulled them up. The zipper would only close half-way. She let them fall to the floor, wadded them into a ball, and threw them back into the drawer. *I'll just wear a dress.* But the ones she tried were too tight around the middle. The clothes she'd been wearing when she got out of school didn't fit anymore. The heat of central Florida must have shrunk everything. Everything but Symphony.

Two weeks before Symphony was to start third grade, Mama made her try on every outfit she owned. Nothing fit. Symphony was excited about the prospect of getting new school clothes until nothing in the store fit right either. Inside the cubicle she tried on dress after dress as Mama and the sales clerk discussed her dilemma.

"We should try the baby-doll-style dresses," the clerk said. "They'll flatter her shape. And I have a couple of A-lines too, in the *chubby* section. One's a sailor dress. She'd look real cute in that one, I think."

After two painful hours of changing from one outfit to another, she and Mama left the store with the beginnings of Symphony's new wardrobe. Aside from the sailor dress, everything she would be wearing to school was printed with vertical stripes. "Aw, Mama. Why didn't you let me get the one with the big roses on it?"

"Because," Mama replied, "the ones we got make you look thinner."

The next week, Mama took her to the doctor.

"She's always been a little husky," Mama told a nurse in a crisp white uniform. "But the bulk of this came on so quickly . . . I just want to make sure there's nothing . . . physical."

After the nurse recorded Symphony's weight, they walked down the hallway into a tiny room that smelled as if someone had spilled a bottle of alcohol.

"Go ahead and strip down to your panties," the nurse said. "And sit right up here." She patted the exam table and pulled a starched white sheet from a shelf beneath it. "You can cover up with this. Doctor Hall will be in shortly." She left Mama and Symphony there to wait.

As soon as Symphony undressed, the doctor came in, wielding a cold stethoscope and lots of questions for Mama. When he and Mama finished talking, he looked at Symphony. "We need to get you on a diet."

*Diet?* She'd heard the word before. It always sounded like a bad thing. But that day, she found out a diet was just two lists: a short list of foods she should eat and a long list of foods she shouldn't. Cake was on the second list along with most of her favorites.

⌘　⌘　⌘

For months, she'd eaten exactly what Mama told her to. Her clothes were loose again, but she was hungry all the time—sometimes even when her stomach was full.

But tonight was her birthday. And the sliver of coconut cake was just enough to make her want more. Standing in front of the refrigerator, she took another forkful of cake, claiming her rightful birthday piece, and then some. When her tummy began to ache, she placed the fork in the sink and looked up to discover Daddy watching.

"Well," he said, shaking his head, "are you sure you had enough?"

Symphony felt fire rise in her cheeks.

"Go back to bed, Symphony."

"Yes, sir," she said, glad it was too dark for him to see how red her face was. As she turned down the hall, she caught a glimpse of Daddy throwing the rest of her birthday cake into the trash.

*Mama's gonna be so mad at me.* She fell asleep hoping she would awaken to discover it had all been a dream.

By the time she got up the next morning, Daddy was gone.

Mama didn't say a word about the incident. She just left the mayo off Symphony's mustard-laden, olive loaf sandwich, washed a tennis-ball-sized apple, and filled the thermos with watered down skim milk. Symphony glanced at the celery and carrot sticks, wishing she could take cookies like everyone else. She peered into the trash. There was the cake. *It wasn't a dream.*

At lunch that day, Greg Stanton stared from the next row of tables, faking a smile one minute, then crossing his eyes at Symphony when no one else was looking. On the first day of school, he'd called her Symphony Weigh-big.

It's Weber," she had corrected him. When he said it again, she realized he was saying it wrong on purpose. Over the last month he'd begun to call her the ugly nickname in front of some of the other boys. Today, she turned away from him and focused on the girls gossiping around her.

As usual, Tally Brewer led the conversation. "My Aunt Wanda started getting fat like that and she went on a diet."

Symphony looked across the table in response to Tally's statement. *Does she mean me? I'm already on a diet.*

"Who are you talkin' about?" asked the girl next to Symphony.

"Mrs. Walker," Tally answered, rolling her eyes. "I don't know how you couldn't notice. She used to be the prettiest teacher here."

*Used to be?* Symphony felt as if someone had shut her inside a box. The beating of her heart echoed in her head as she measured the meanness of Tally's words. "She's not fat."

They all stopped talking and turned toward Symphony.

Symphony's cheeks burned. *I said that out loud?* She glanced around at the others. Some of them looked shocked at her willingness to differ opinions with Tally. Others just seemed to be waiting for what she would say next. "She's not fat," Symphony repeated. "She's gonna have a baby."

"Oh, she is not!" Tally argued.

"Did Mrs. Walker say so?" a girl asked from farther down the table.

"No." Symphony stared down at her lunch. "I just know." And that was the truth. She hadn't known this morning, but as Tally Brewer had bad-mouthed Mrs. Walker's spreading figure, Symphony wanted to help. The words just came.

On the way out of the lunchroom that day, two girls smiled at Symphony. It was the first time anyone had been nice to her since the beginning of school.

She rode the bus home, sitting by herself in a seat for two as Dani laughed and joked with her friends in the back. At school, Dani always ignored Symphony. But that was all right. The two of them shared a room at home. Most of the time that was too much.

Seven people got off at Symphony's stop that afternoon. As the bus pulled away, a girl with freckles and curly black hair walked up to Symphony. "I heard what you told that blabbermouth today at lunch," she said. "I'm Therese. We just moved into that green house on the corner. Think your mom'll let you ride bikes or somethin'?"

Symphony beamed all the way home. "Mama," she said, walking into the house. "Can I ride my bike till dinner?"

"That's fine. But no television until your homework's done. How was school today?" she asked, slicing an apple for Symphony's snack.

"It was okay." She glanced up at her mother. Mama's middle was growing again, just like Mrs. Walker's. *Not another sister!* Symphony munched on the apple, considering the possibilities. *It could be a boy this time.*

# CHAPTER FOUR

IT'S NO WONDER folks who live in the southernmost regions of the Bible belt are known for their religious inclinations. Summers have taken them as close as the living can get to the heat of hell and they are sure they want no part of it.

⌘ ⌘ ⌘

Symphony awoke at daybreak to the hiss of the percolator boiling over. The scent of frying ham and browning biscuits lingered just beneath the smoky aroma of coffee grounds burning in the flame of the gas stove. She could hear Mama and Granny talking softly as they huddled together in the kitchen. For a moment, she lay still, lulled by the sound.

In the dim light, she looked around. She and her three sisters were still where Granny had kissed them goodnight—in the biggest bedroom, all four of them tucked into one double bed. With a grin, she slid out from under Jeanne's arm and down the side of the bed until her feet touched the cool linoleum floor. Without so much as a breath sound, she tiptoed toward the kitchen where she waited just outside the door for the right moment.

On the other side of the wall, Mama sighed. "She's just a regular kid. I haven't noticed anything out of the ordinary."

"But Maisy," Granny said, "isn't she always findin' things you lose? Like your car keys and your lipstick. And, if I remember right, once there was a twenty dollar bill."

"I still think she's just an observant child. And if she was like Papa or Gray, wouldn't she be having nightmares by now?"

"Mornin'," Symphony said, stepping into the doorway.

Mama set an empty baby bottle on the table. "Come here, sugar." She pulled the eight-year-old close, but not too close. Joe, Symphony's baby brother, was asleep in Mama's lap.

Granny kissed Symphony's forehead. "Good morning, sugar." She tugged at her thin, brown housedress, smoothing the wrinkles as she shuffled to the oven and pulled out a pan of biscuits. "Want me to put cheese in some of these?"

"Yes." Symphony answered before Mama had a chance. "And tomato," she said, eyeing a plate of sliced tomatoes. "And, please can I have some coffee this time?"

Granny looked over the top of her glasses. "I'll make it real light, Maisy." She opened the refrigerator and pulled out a bottle of milk.

"All right," Mama said. "But don't expect it again tomorrow, young lady."

"I won't." Symphony crossed her heart. "I promise."

Granny handed her a cup of cream-colored coffee and a biscuit with cheese and tomato on it.

"What else is going on around here?" Mama asked. "Gray didn't come home last night. Is he back on graveyard?"

"No. He's still on swing shift," Granny grumbled. "He's just got a new girlfriend. Probably roll in sometime this afternoon for a nap." She paused and shook her head. Her stiff, grey curls, permed into place, didn't even budge. She adjusted her glasses, smiled at Symphony, and changed the subject. "Maisy, have I told you what's goin' on with the Munfords?"

"Uh-uh." Mama blew on her coffee.

Symphony latched onto the tail of their conversation. She knew who the Munfords were. *We drive by their store every time we come here.* Her eyes met Granny's so she turned her head. She had learned the hard way that looking like a ping-pong spectator could get her sent outside to play, so she stared at her breakfast, her ears trained on every word.

"You knew Rachel Munford's sister got married a few years back and moved to Cullman, didn't you?" Granny paused, running her finger around the rim of her cup.

Mama nodded.

"Since then, Rachel hasn't heard from her. Not once. So, a few weeks ago, out of the clear blue, Rachel gets word that her sister's real sick and they don't know if she'll make it or not. Well, Harold has no idea what's goin' on because he's running the store that day."

Granny picked up her coffee and took a sip.

"By the time he finally gets a chance to take a break, he goes up to the house and finds the boys alone with Talbott, the oldest. On the kitchen table is a note from Rachel explainin' that she'll be back, soon as her sister's better. That's it. Three-and-a-half weeks she's been gone, and those Munford boys are runnin' wilder every day."

"She hasn't even called?"

"Not according to Harold. And I'm startin' to wonder whether she's comin' back. You went to school with Harold Munford. He wasn't the nicest boy." Granny put a hand up, blocking her lips from Symphony's view. "And between Harold and those boys, I wouldn't be surprised if Rachel didn't even look back."

A picture filled Symphony's mind: A man, a woman, and three stairstep boys. She slathered a buttered biscuit with Granny's plum jelly and dipped it into her coffee before taking a bite.

"Hmm." Mama stared off into the distance, wearing a puzzled expression. "I'm anxious to hear how that comes out." She walked to the stove and, balancing the baby on one arm, refilled her coffee cup. "It's supposed to be pretty today. I think we'll ride out to Fredonia to see Aunt Eunice."

Symphony scrunched her eyebrows. "But, Mama, I'm s'posed to help Granny in the garden."

"Shhh, Symphony. You'll wake your brother."

"Pleeeez!" She groaned, slumping in her chair. "I promised."

Mama set her coffee on the table and sat down.

"Can't I just stay here? Please?" Symphony walked over to Mama's chair and fidgeted until Mama looked at her. "Can't I see Aunt Eunice next week?"

Mama paused. "I guess so." She softly swatted Symphony's behind. "Go on now. Get dressed."

Granny winked at Mama. "I'll meet you on the back porch, Symphony. Make sure you grab those two buckets. The biggest one's for me."

Ten minutes later, Symphony yawned as she walked to the garden, the empty pail bumping her shin with every step.

With Granny on one side of the row and Symphony on the other, they began with the speckled butter beans, picking, bent at the waist. There was no need to rely on watches to know the time. As the sun advanced closer to its noon position, it baked their skin and the clicking of the grasshoppers in the adjacent field became a whirring roar. When Symphony's bucket was nearly full, she heard the slamming of car doors and stopped to look up.

"Behave yourself," Mama called.

"I will," Symphony yelled, waving as their car drove out of sight.

At the end of the second row of butter beans, she and Granny dumped their buckets into grocery sacks and moved on to the purple hull peas. Symphony fought with the first few. They just wouldn't let go of the vine.

"Don't pull so hard, honey," Granny said. "You'll break the plant." She stepped over the bean bush and put her sun-spotted hand around Symphony's to teach her the motion. "Pulling harder isn't always the answer. Some things you have to feel your way through. See here, now. Take hold of the bean up close to the vine where it curves like a hook. Then, turn it the other way like you're trying to break the hook. It almost always comes right off. If it doesn't, it's probably not ready. So just leave it and I'll get it next week."

"He's mean to her, Granny."

"Who, honey?"

"Mr. Munford. He hits her . . . I think."

Granny stood up and straightened her hat. "What makes you say that?"

"When you and Mama were talking, that's just what I was thinkin', that's all. Sometimes I think the right thing and sometimes I don't."

"Did you happen to see Mrs. Munford in that thought?"

"Ah-huh."

"What'd she look like?"

"She had long black hair with a line o' white in it."

Granny's eyes widened. Symphony had never met Rachel Munford.

The butter beans were set aside for later but the purple hull peas were for dinner. With the mercury a hair below one-hundred degrees, Granny and Symphony sat in the shade of the apple tree, staining their fingers as they broke open the hulls to get at the peas inside. "Just shut your eyes and hold real still," Granny said, her lap covered with a huge aluminum bowl half-full of the peas they'd just shelled. "You'll feel it. Soon as a breeze comes up."

"What's it like, Granny?" Symphony was almost nine, but she still lacked the patience to wait for the wind on a day this warm.

"It happens when you think you're hot as you could ever get. That you can't sweat anymore than you already have. Then, God'll blow you a kiss and the minute it hits your sweaty face, you feel so cool you could almost shiver. But you have to wait for it, and you've been a wiggle-worm since you got outta bed."

Granny leaned over and picked up a shiny silver can filled with tissue. She discreetly spit tobacco juice into it, wiped her mouth with a handkerchief, and set the can back down. "Why don't you go play for awhile? Run off some of that energy."

So Symphony went in search of Randy and Barry, her cousins who lived next door. During the summer, they played at Granny's while their parents were at work. She found them in the side yard, shooting marbles with the three Munford boys.

"Aw," Talbott Munford complained. "I don't wanna play marbles with no girl. What about Hide and Seek?" He winked at the other boys and they winked back.

When it was Symphony's turn to be *it* they disappeared. She checked every spot she could think of. "Olly, Olly, oxen free," she called. But they were gone.

Giving up the search after only a few minutes, she opened the screen door next to where they'd been playing. She didn't want to tell Granny the boys had tricked her. Besides, it was too hot to run anymore. So she leaned back in the swing on Granny's screened-in side porch and squeezed her eyes shut, waiting for the breeze that would bring the kiss of God, all the while wishing she had a paper fan to speed up the process.

*I could be riding in the car with the windows down.*

It was her last thought as the wind picked up and lulled her to sleep.

In the dream, five boys stood on the riverbank. She could see their backs, hear them arguing.

*"I've waded in this spot a million times. Daddy told me the current wasn't bad between Breakneck Rock and the little dam. That's where we are. And it's hot. I'm goin' in! Rest o' you wanna sit here and melt while I cool off, that's just fine with me."* The tallest boy stepped closer to the water's edge. The smallest one followed.

*"Wait a minute, Daniel."* It was Randy's voice. He took hold of the younger boy's arm and pulled him back. *"Talbott's just jokin' Your daddy didn't say that. You know there ain't no safe place in the Chattahoochee. Not around here. 'Cept the backwaters, or maybe some places where it pools off to the side."*

*"You callin' me a liar?"* Talbott growled.

*"I bet Mama'll take us to Langdale pool when she gets off work."* Barry's voice squeaked whenever he got anxious.

*"Let's just go home, Talbott,"* Daniel whined. *"Please."* He tugged his older brother's arm, but Talbott jerked away, knocking the four-year-old into the water.

*"Daniel!"* Talbott screamed, diving in after his brother.

Randy grabbed Barry by the arm. *"Run straight to Granny's. Start hollerin' for Uncle Austin soon as you see the house. He'll get here fastest."*

Randy led Marcus, the middle Munford boy, away from the water and sat him down behind a nearby tree. *"Don't take your eyes off this path. Soon as you see help comin' you yell out, 'We're here.' Okay?"* He picked up the longest stick he could find and ran back to the water. Talbott was diving under again.

⌘ ⌘ ⌘

"Symphony?" Granny shook her awake. "You're havin' a bad dream, sugar."

Wrapped in a cocoon of oily sweat, Symphony opened her eyes and looked around, shocked that the scene had changed.

"You kept sayin', 'We're here.'"

"Oh, Granny, I was so scared. The littlest Munford boy fell in the river. And Randy and Barry were there, too. And Talbott tried to get him out, but—"

"Close your eyes again," Granny ordered.

"Are you mad at me?"

Granny sat down next to her. "No, sugar. I just need to know where the boys were in your dream. Can you tell me what it looked like?"

"They said it was Breakneck Rock."

"Graydon! Get up," Granny yelled before she was even out of the swing. "I think the boys are playin' down on the river. I need you to go get 'em."

Uncle Gray rumbled to his feet, his nap on the couch cut short. He ran to his car as Granny called for Austin.

Symphony gazed through the screen door as Uncle Austin raced across the property and into the dense brush on his way to the Chattahoochee. Gray revved his engine and drove off, leaving her wondering who would get to the boys first. "It's just a dream," she said aloud to remind herself. *I bet they aren't even at the river.*

"Symphony," Granny called from the kitchen. "Let's have a glass of tea. Then you can help me re-dress the scarecrow. Birds are starting to land on him."

Symphony joined Granny at the table.

"And, while we're outside, I think I'll cut myself a fresh switch," Granny said, setting down two full glasses.

"A switch?" Symphony asked, bewildered. "For me?"

"No, child. You're not in trouble." Granny kissed the top of Symphony's head and sat down. "You couldn't be farther from it."

⌘　⌘　⌘

"I wish they'd get back," Granny said to Symphony as they buttoned a red flannel shirt over the scarecrow's two-by-four frame. It had been almost an hour since Austin and Gray left for the river.

Just then, Austin came around the corner. "Hey! That's mine," he said, reaching for the shirt.

Granny slapped his hand. "Now, Austin. You outgrew this shirt ten years ago, but not before you nearly wore it to death. Are all the boys okay?"

"I'm tellin' you what," he snorted. "That Talbott Munford is just about as stupid as he is mean. Randy says he's been tryin' to get 'em to go in the river ever since this heat wave started. Today, when Talbott walked to the edge o' the water, Daniel tried to stop him and ended up fallin' in."

Granny gasped.

33

"Time we got there, Talbott had him up and was tryin' to swim toward the bank with him. Hot as it's been, I'm surprised how high the river is. Current's still movin' pretty good, too. I took the rope with me. Gray reeled us in like he was catchin' the biggest Chattahoochee trout ever. Daniel's pretty waterlogged, but he's all right. What made you think to look there Mama?"

Symphony blushed.

Granny studied the redness of Symphony's cheeks then turned back to Austin. "We just couldn't find 'em anywhere else."

Austin lit a cigarette, took a long drag, and held it in his lungs for a moment. "You know, I don't think I've ever seen Talbott back down from a chance to argue but when I told him to get in the car, that little shit didn't say a word. He was quiet till we started gettin' close to his house. Then he said, 'Since we're all okay, you don't have to tell my daddy.' I told him, 'Yes, I do.' After that, he just got madder by the second, tryin' to make me feel like I was tellin' Harold just to be mean. When we pulled up in front of the store, he grabbed me by the shoulder and said, 'Please, Mr. Austin. You don't know what he'll do to me.' You know, Mama, I almost changed my mind. But then I looked at little Daniel. His daddy needed to know. So I went in first to give Harold the news while Gray stayed in the car with the boys.

"I'll tell you what. Talbott was lucky more than once today. His daddy was in a damn good mood. Rachel had just called to say she's comin' home tomorrow.

"Oh, Harold was still steamin' when Gray brought the boys in, but before we left I reminded him that Daniel might have drowned if it hadn't been for Talbott. When that didn't calm him down, I told him I'd be back later to check on the boys."

Austin was the smallest baby Granny had given birth to. Under four pounds. But he had thrived and now, in his mid-twenties was a whopping six-foot-four, two-hundred and something pounds. You had to be an idiot to make him mad.

Austin shook his head. "Lord, Lord, Mama. This could've turned out a whole lot worse."

"I'm just glad they're all in one piece," Granny said. "But Randy and Barry better hurry up and get over here. The longer they take, the stronger my switchin' arm gets."

"Gray took 'em to cut their own switches. I hope that's okay. I'm sure they'll be here directly."

Randy and Barry arrived, looking at their feet, ready for their punishment. Granny squeezed them in a relieved hug. "You keep those for your Mama and Daddy," she said, pointing at the switches they'd cut. "I'm gonna use the one I picked while I was worried. What were you thinking going to the river today?"

The boys must have known it was better to keep their mouths shut.

"What would have happened if your uncles hadn't shown up?" she asked, nettling their bare legs. "Go find a quiet place to think about that!"

Randy and Barry spent the rest of the wordless afternoon under a tree waiting for sundown. On occasion, one would shoot a marble to the other out of sheer boredom.

⌘ ⌘ ⌘

Granny was in her chair under the apple tree with her eyes closed. She opened them as Symphony walked toward her. "Hey, sweetie," she said. "Let's sit here for a minute before we go into the hot kitchen to start supper."

"Okay." Symphony pulled a lawn chair close to the outdoor rocker.

"Can you feel that?" Granny asked, fanning hard with a folded newspaper.

"Feels good." Symphony smiled, sinking back into her seat. "Granny? You said you'd tell me later why you needed to know about my dream."

"Yeah. That's what I was just thinkin' about. See, I know someone who has dreams that really happen sometimes. That's why I had Gray and Austin go to the river today. Do you know anyone whose dreams come true?"

Symphony wiped the sweat from her forehead, pushing aside her short, sun-bleached bangs. "Parts of mine have, a few times." She chewed her fingernail and began swinging her feet.

"That's what I thought," Granny said. "Why don't you tell your mama?"

"'Cause." Symphony looked away. "I don't want 'em to be real." *I hope the man in the car never comes true.* "And I don't know anyone else who talks about that kinda stuff. They'd just think I'm makin' it up."

Granny lowered her glasses. "Look at me, Symphony."

The tone of Granny's voice, calmed her. She stopped kicking her feet, dropped her hands to her lap, and focused her gaze on her grandmother.

"You know how some people can sing like angels and some can play baseball and others can grow anything they plant?" Granny paused.

Symphony nodded. "Yes, ma'am."

"Well, what if your dreams are somethin' like that? Like a gift for you to use to help other people. I won't make you tell your mama but I want you to think about it. And if you ever need to talk to me, you just write me a letter or have your mama call. Okay?" She groaned to a stand, walked over and kissed Symphony on the forehead.

At that moment, Symphony knew that part of Granny's heart lived in hers. They would always be together, no matter how far apart they were. "I love you, Granny."

"I love you too, sweetie. Now let's get that meal goin'."

⌘ ⌘ ⌘

Aunt Lena and Uncle Henry gave Randy and Barry a good talking-to, then decided the boys had been punished enough. The two freshly cut switches were stored on top of the refrigerator to be used at a later time.

When dinner was done and the sky hazed over with the brown shade of evening, the children came to life again, filled with the giddiness only the relief of dusk can bring to a summer day. And as darkness fell, the air thickened with lightnin' bugs, turning the night into the celebration of a day well spent.

# CHAPTER FIVE

"MAMA," SYMPHONY SAID at dinner. "Miz Shepherd says we all have to bring a chicken heart to school tomorrow. And it's s'posed to be cooked. Do we have one?"

Mama tilted her head and stared at Symphony, one eyebrow raised. "No. We don't. How long have you known you needed it?"

Symphony wrinkled her nose and shrugged.

"I wish you hadn't waited till the night before to tell me." Mama looked at Daddy and shook her head. "If I don't go right now, everything'll be closed. Do you mind if I leave the kids here? I'll bathe them when I get back."

"How long will it take?" He rattled the ice in his empty glass.

As if entranced by the sound, Dani stood, picked up the green tea pitcher, and filled Daddy's glass.

"I'll go to Winn Dixie," Mama said. "Probably twenty minutes there and back, and five in the store. No more than half-an-hour."

Daddy picked up the baby from his high chair. "Go ahead." He had been a sergeant in the army and wasn't shy about giving commands. "Daniele. You fill the tub for Jeanne and Leesa, and sit with them while they take a bath. Symphony. Put supper away and start the dishes."

Dani swept her dark, wavy hair behind her shoulder and glared at Symphony. "Thanks," she mouthed, rolling her eyes.

First, Mama had bought Dani a bra. Now, she was allowed to shave her legs and wear lipstick. *She thinks she's so great since she started seventh grade!* Symphony returned the glare.

Dani helped the little sisters down from their chairs. "Come on. Let's find your pajamas."

Symphony stood and began clearing the table, raking the scraps into the trash and stacking the dirty plates and cups next to the sink.

Daddy watched the older girls for a moment. As soon as they started following his orders, he put Joe on the floor and headed for the living room. Joe, who refused to crawl like other babies, followed on his hands and feet rather than on his knees. With a throaty baby laugh, he passed Daddy and made his way over to a basket of toys in the corner.

Symphony pulled three small bowls from the cabinet and filled them with leftovers from the serving dishes. *Where'd Mama put the foil?* She stuck them into the refrigerator uncovered; knowing that overnight, they would change into rock-like substances no one would ever eat.

She could hear the little sisters laughing as they played in the tub, and Joe babbling his *toddler-ese* over the sound of the television in the den. Everyone else in the family seemed to be having fun. She felt cheated, but the feeling peaked and died in an instant.

One night just after the school year began, Symphony had realized that when Mama did the dinner dishes, she was usually alone in the kitchen. Daddy, who was still elated over finally having a son, would watch the baby. By that time of night, the little sisters had been bathed and were ready for bed, playing in their room. Dani would offer to watch them. Symphony knew her older sister was just avoiding real work but, to hear Mama talk, Dani was the only one who did anything at all.

The first time Symphony volunteered to help with the dishes, Mama seemed surprised but grateful. After the first week, it became a habit. Every night, as soon as Daddy got up from the table, Symphony started scraping food off plates. So what if nobody thanked her? During the twenty minutes it took to clean the kitchen, she had Mama all to herself. They could talk about anything.

Tonight, Symphony took her time, holding off the actual dishwashing until Mama got back with the chicken heart. But when Mama returned,

Daddy quickly changed the plans. The little sisters were now clean and running around in their pajamas.

"Daniele, I want you to help Symphony with the dishes tonight," he said. "Give your mother a break."

Mama shook her head. "It's a nice thought," she told Daddy, "but I'm sure they both have homework to do. Don't you, girls?"

"Here we go again," Daddy said. "Just once, I'd like to sit down with you before you're ready to fall asleep."

It sounded like the rumblings of war.

Mama gave in.

"Shit," Dani said as she walked into the kitchen.

"You're not s'pose'ta say that!"

"Everyone in junior high cusses. What're you gonna do? Tell on me?"

"No."

Dani must have noticed Symphony's disappointment because, for once, she backed off. "If you wash, I'll rinse, dry, and put away."

"You don't have to help if you have homework," Symphony said.

Dani pulled a dishtowel out of a drawer. "I do, but prob'ly not as much as you. That's why I hated fifth grade," she said. "Just be glad you don't have Mr. Johnson. He picks his nose and eats his dandruff. I stayed sick to my stomach the whole year. I don't think I finished lunch even once. At least Miz Shepherd is nice."

"Yeah. But every night I have millions of story problems and reading to do." Symphony washed a glass and set it in the sink for Dani. "Last year I used to be able to watch TV."

"Everyone says she gives too much homework. But I've never talked to anyone who had her that didn't like her. Every year, she lets her class read *The Black Stallion*, and she spends a whole week on Leonardo daVinci." Dani began to rinse the dishes Symphony had washed. "He painted lots of stuff, sometimes even ceilings and made sculptures and all. But he drew machines hundreds of years ago that people couldn't even make till this century. I bet you'll like that part of her class."

"Right now, we're on the human body," Symphony said, placing a soapy plate in the sink for Dani to rinse. "Tomorrow, we're gonna cut open a chicken heart to see the different parts that hold blood."

"Yuck. I think I'm gonna throw up. Let's talk about somethin' else," Dani said.

"Like what?"

"Like Tracy Tucker. He's this boy in Social Studies and Monday, he smiled at me. Then today he walked with me to class."

It was the first time Dani had told her a secret. She was usually only nice when she woke up from a nightmare and didn't want to sleep alone. The rest of the time, Symphony was just another slice out of the attention pie, and Dani didn't like to share.

Symphony was still awake at ten-thirty, reading with a flashlight beneath the bedspread, when Mama conducted her nightly mosquito search. As usual, she flipped on the light and groaned at the abundance of blood-sucking insects. Whipping out the fly swatter, she began to smack. "*You* got someone," she said to the first bug as it became a red splat on the pastel green bedroom wall.

Symphony lay still, hoping Mama wouldn't notice the glow of the flashlight but as soon as the switch was turned off she turned it right back on.

Mama pulled the sheets back. "What on earth are you doing up so late?" she whispered.

"I'm sorry, Mama. I just have three more pages to finish."

"I knew I should have helped you with the dishes tonight. We'll do them together tomorrow, okay." She kissed Symphony on the forehead. "Now, hurry, or you won't be able to keep your eyes open in school tomorrow." She darkened the room once again and closed the door.

The next day, Symphony got all the answers right on a pop quiz. She was the only one in class who passed.

"We should study together from now on," her friend, Therese, said as they rode home on the bus that afternoon. "My dad says if my grades don't get better, he's puttin' me back in Catholic school. How'd you know all that stuff on the test, anyway?"

"I don't know," Symphony answered. "While I'm readin' I just try and guess what Miz Shepherd'll ask us about. That's all."

"Really. Maybe I'll try that. You wanna come over for awhile? No one's home but me."

"I can't today. Mama's takin' me to get new shoes," Symphony said.

"Well, if you'd rather get new shoes than be my friend."

Symphony looked down at her worn saddle shoes.

When she looked up again, Therese was grinning at her. "You thought I was serious?"

"Yeah," Symphony replied.

"My mom's right. You don't have enough fun," Therese said. "See if you can come over tomorrow after school, okay?"

When Symphony got home, Mama was just washing the remnants of a cookie off Joe's face. "Girls, Symphony's here. Let's get ready to go to the shoe store," she said. "And I don't care if you just went pee. I want you all to go again before we leave."

After taking turns in the only bathroom, they piled into the crème-colored 1959 Bel Air station wagon, Dani and Joe in the front, Symphony and the little sisters in the back.

Mama sang and the girls tried to follow her lead. *"There was a man and he was mad, so he jumped into a pudding bag."* They turned left onto Barna Avenue and drove past the old country club. Someone had painted it sky-blue. Symphony wished they could live there. *I bet we'd all have our own bedroom.*

*"The pudding bag it was so thick that he jumped into a walking stick."* The sun was shining. Mama was smiling. The girls knew the tune and some of the words. *"The walking stick it was so narrow that he jumped into a wheel barrow."*

Each time the singers stopped to take a breath, the baby bounced around, tooting the little horn on his car seat.

*"The wheel barrow began to break so he jumped into a chocolate cake."* They drove past the junior high school where Dani was in seventh grade. Then, they passed the shopping center where the old Woolworth's still served ice cream sodas.

*"The chocolate cake became so rotten that he jumped into a bag of cotton."* The elementary school sat on the right next to a huge park. Its large oak trees offered welcome relief from the searing afternoon sun. In the shade beneath them, children played as mothers half-watched, half-chatted.

*"The bag of cotton caught on fire and blew him up to Jeremiah."*

There, along the side of the road, between the elementary school and the park sat the car from Symphony's dream. The strange man was behind the wheel, his nose, like an arrow, pointing forward.

"*Poof*," the others sang, laughing. It was their favorite part of the song.

Symphony pushed her face against the window and froze. For a moment, the scene stole her breath. With only enough air in her lungs to whisper, she said, "Mama." But the word was lost in the finale. She slumped back in her seat recalling the lie she had told Mama about the car at Tiny Tots. *She'll never believe me. But what if he—* "Mama! Please, Mama. Stop!"

"Symphony Weber. What is the matter with you?"

"Just stop, Mama. Please stop!"

Mama pulled the car to the side of the busy road.

"I need to show you something."

"Where, Symphony? What?" Mama demanded.

Symphony was shaking. "Outside," she answered, beginning to cry.

"Dani, make sure everyone stays put!" Mama said, getting out of the car. She walked over to the sidewalk by the park and opened Symphony's door.

"Come here, sugar. What's wrong?"

"There's a car back there, Mama. I had a dream about it—and the man sitting in it took me and Dani. But we got away. Every time I dream it, we get out. Through the floor. If it's just a dream, why's he here? What if he takes us?"

Mama paused. With a puzzled expression, she studied Symphony's eyes.

"Mama, please. I promise it's not a story like when I made up the car thing at Tiny Tots."

"Tiny Tots? You mean that whole thing about lying under a car?" She tilted her head and looked at Symphony. "That was at least five years ago. Is that when you had this dream?"

Symphony nodded. "The first time."

"Tell me where he is."

Without turning to look, Symphony began. "The car looks just like our old one. But the seats are green. See it? It's back there by the fence."

"Yes, honey. I see the car. But I can't see the seats. Tell me, what does the man look like?"

Symphony described him, from his slicked-down hair to his pointed nose. Even the clothes he was wearing.

"Okay, sweetie. Get back in the car. Lock the doors and sit still. I'll be right there."

Symphony watched through the rear window as Mama strolled down the sidewalk to the corner, acting as if she were going to throw something into the trash can next to the man's car. She pretended to drop the imaginary garbage instead, and bent over to pick it up. Symphony's heart pounded as Mama looked into the man's windows.

Then, in a flash, Mama had unlocked her door and was back in the car sitting behind the steering wheel.

"Move over," Jeanne said, pushing Leesa away from her. "You're squashin' me."

"Stop it!" Leesa yelled.

"You wanna sit by the door too, Leesa?" Symphony asked. Once the little sisters were separated, the car was quiet again.

Mama looked in the rear view mirror. "Okay, girls. I need to walk up to the corner to use the pay phone. Keep the windows up and the doors locked no matter what. You hear me? Use the horn if you need me."

The girls nodded.

Mama locked her door and briskly walked to the end of the block.

Dani turned toward Symphony, a question in her eyes.

Symphony shrugged.

"You'll tell me later, right?" Dani asked.

Symphony blushed and shrugged again. Finally Dani was starting to treat her like a sister instead of a rival. But that might change if she knew about the dreams.

Mama dialed the phone, talked for a few minutes, then walked back to the car. "All right," she said, sitting down. "Because you were all so good, I think you deserve a Popsicle." She drove to the closest convenience store, a block away, on the opposite side of the street. "Lock your doors and roll up the windows. I'll be right back." She started into the store but stopped and leaned against the car.

Symphony turned around on the seat to see what had snagged Mama's attention. Two police cars had pulled up at the park and the officers were walking over to the stranger's car.

Dani looked at Symphony. "I've got goosebumps," she said. "You have to tell me everything when we get home."

Symphony looked down at her own trembling hands. She would tell Dani something, but not everything. Not yet. "Okay." She turned again and saw the stranger get out of his car and run, dodging traffic to cross the street. One policeman chased him. The other moved down the avenue until there was a break for him to cross, too.

Mama got into the car and slammed her door. She turned the key and put the car into reverse. But by the time she was ready to move, she couldn't take her foot off the brake. The man was standing behind them.

Still staring through the back window, Symphony watched as the policemen caught up with him. He moved around to the side of their car where one of the officers grabbed him and cuffed him, pressing his face against the window.

"You," he growled, glaring at Symphony.

After five years of trying, she'd finally gotten a good look at his face. Immediately, she wished she could forget it.

# CHAPTER SIX

THE RIDE HOME had been quiet. Without a word to Symphony, Mama went straight to the kitchen. As the aroma of pork chops filled the house, Symphony sat in front of the television, absorbed by the news.

"Just minutes ago, Roscoe Stanley, a man wanted in connection with the disappearance of three Alabama children, was taken into custody outside a local convenience store. Authorities believe the person who anonymously reported his whereabouts may have additional information. They're requesting that this witness come forward for—"

Jeanne walked into the room, her auburn hair rubber-banded into a ponytail on top of her head. She looked like a rooster as she strutted over to the TV and turned it off.

"Hey! I was watching that!" Symphony jumped up to turn it back on.

"You have to help set the table," Jeanne said with a smirk.

"Who said?"

"Mama." Jeanne turned and left the room, her attitude still showing.

Symphony plopped back down on the stiff sofa cushion and sat in silence for a moment, thinking about what the reporter had said. There were three missing children. *Where did he take them?* She rose from the couch with a shudder. *Roscoe Stanley.* For five years that man had haunted her. She took her time walking to the kitchen, mentally attaching the pointed nose and slicked-back hair to that name.

Dinnertime seemed the same as it did any other night of the week. Mama calmly told Daddy about her day, including how Roscoe Stanley had approached them at the convenience store. Symphony watched in wonder as Mama omitted the parts about the dream and the phone call to the police. It was clear. Mama didn't want anyone to know, not even Daddy.

For once, Dani kept her mouth shut. But at bedtime, she closed their door. "You have to tell me," she said, her dark eyes wide. "Mama didn't say anything to *Daddy* about the phone call she made." Dani slipped off her deck shoes. They thumped against the floor. "Who else are you gonna tell? Besides, you know all kinds of stuff about me."

"Okay." Symphony squeezed her eyes shut so she didn't have to see Dani's reaction. "That man at the park today—I've been dreaming about him since Tiny Tots. But in my dream, he kidnapped us—me and you."

When Symphony opened her eyes Dani's brown eyes had turned black. "God! I hate you sometimes." She crossed her arms. "If you didn't want to tell me, you shoulda' just said so." She pulled down her covers, slid into bed, and turned her back to Symphony.

Symphony stomped to a stand and put her hands on her hips. "I'm tellin' you the truth!"

The bedroom seemed to shrink around them. For the next few days, it was too small for them both to be in there at the same time, unless they were sleeping.

⌘　⌘　⌘

*Symphony was alone, standing in the center of Boynton Park. A clown leaned against the wrought iron fence. He was handing out a cluster of balloons, one by one, to a crowd of children. She studied the childrens' expressions as she approached, smiling at a boy who walked toward her. "This one's for you," he said, passing the string to her. As he walked away, she glanced upward. His offering was not a balloon after all. It was a string tied to the floating head of Roscoe Stanley. It slipped from her fingers and drifted away, the face shouting "You!" as it moved out of sight. She glanced at the clown and his bunch of balloons. All of them had the same face.*

She awoke to Dani tugging at the covers.

"I had a bad dream, Symphony. Can I sleep with you?"

Relieved to be awake, Symphony turned onto her side and slid over to make room.

That was the end of their argument.

The balloon dreams shook Symphony awake each night for several weeks. Then they stopped. One day, during breakfast, she began to wonder how long it would be before something replaced the Roscoe Stanley nightmare. For some reason, without it, she felt she was missing something important.

"Try not to worry so much, honey," Granny told her on the phone one Sunday. "When you're meant to know something, you'll see it or hear it or dream it. That's the way your Grandpapa did, whether he wanted to know it or not. And the gift does your Uncle Gray the same way."

But the anticipation Symphony was feeling, reminded her of something that had happened in the past.

Their old neighbors had three boys who were always throwing rocks and chasing cats with their bicycles. When they played helicopters in the summer, their rotors were strings tied around June bugs. On top of that, they were always borrowing Symphony's kick ball but would never let her play. For almost a year, she'd wished they would move. She even said it in her prayers on nights after the boys had been particularly ornery. And they moved, all right.

In their place came the Booths—four girls—and all of them biters.

Leesa was the first to come home from their yard engraved with the Booth brand—a logo of twelve tiny teeth in a purplish-blue circle. The next day, it was Jeanne. By the time the Booths had lived there a month, all four of those girls had cut their teeth on someone in the neighborhood. Dani and Mama had even seen Mrs. Booth bite her husband's arm during a front-yard shouting match.

*What if nightmares are like neighbors? What if, when a bad one goes away, the new one's even worse?*

⌘    ⌘    ⌘

What Granny said was true. The dreams came when they wanted to. The fact that Symphony was older now didn't seem to matter. At ten, she had no better knowledge of how to use the information bestowed upon her than she did at age five. For a while, her sleep was filled with visions of other kid's test scores or presents being opened on birthdays and holidays that hadn't come. On occasion, she would dream about something that seemed important, like Mrs. Jones, their straight-laced music teacher, kissing Mr. Babcock, the man around the corner who wore a black leather jacket and rode a motorcycle.

She began predicting pop quizzes for her friend, Therese.

"Mr. Norwood thinks I'm cheating," Therese said one day after school. "He watches me the whole time we're taking a test. And yesterday, he started asking me questions out loud, in front of the class. He couldn't believe I knew all the answers. I couldn't believe it either."

Symphony shook her head. "You used to just read the chapters," she said. "Now, you study them."

"Just 'cause you tell me when I need to. There's nothing wrong with that—is there? How do you always know, anyway?"

"It's like I just remember it. Only no one told me in the first place."

"Weird," Therese said, with a perplexed stare.

"But you can't tell anybody," Symphony said. "If you do, I'll get in trouble."

"Okay. I won't. Hey, Mark Powell sat next to Martha at lunch today. On purpose. She said he tried to hold her hand on the way back to class, too."

"She stopped liking him weeks ago," Symphony said.

"I know. Maybe he'll move faster next time someone writes him a letter and dots all the *i*s with hearts."

⌘　⌘　⌘

Bam!

*Was that the front door?* Symphony got out of bed and peeked into the hallway. It looked like everyone in the house was still asleep. *Didn't anyone else hear that?* She inched her way to her parent's bedroom where she found Mama sitting on the side of the bed.

"Com'ere, sugar," Mama said. "It's okay. Your father just got called in to work early, that's all."

48

Symphony kissed her mother and headed back to bed, stopping on the way to pee. As she sat on the icy toilet seat, she decided Mama wasn't being completely honest with her. *Who buys insurance in the middle of the night?*

The next morning, she wasn't exactly truthful with Mama.

"Could you take me and Jeanne to school today, Mama? I need to see how to get to Candy's house just in case I get invited to her birthday party this weekend."

"Symphony, honey, let's just do that on the day of the party."

"No, Mama. I wanna walk to the party like some of the other girls. It's just a couple blocks away. I think it's the pink house on Niagara Street. Please?"

"Oh, all right," Mama said. "Wipe the oatmeal off Leesa's face and find her something to wear while I get Joe ready."

"Okay."

Symphony was right. It was the pink house on Niagara she was looking for, but it wasn't so she could go to a weekend party. It was because of the dog in the front yard.

Mama dropped them off at school early and Symphony walked straight to Mr. Tucker's classroom. "I saw Patches today, Mr. Tucker," she said proudly.

"Patches?" The teacher's eyes widened. "Where?"

"He was tied up at the pink house on Niagara Street."

"But he just went missing last night. How did you know?" Mr. Tucker asked.

"Mama drove me to school this morning and we passed by there. He's a real cute dog," Symphony said, forgetting that she'd never seen Patches until her dream, the night before.

⌘　⌘　⌘

Mark Fitzpatrick arrived at the school's clinic fifteen minutes before last recess. "I feel like I'm gonna throw up," he told Mrs. Lathrop, the nurse. He lay on the cot as she took his temperature.

"Well, you don't have a fever," she said. "And I hate to send you home this late in the day. Just rest. Let's see how you feel in a few minutes."

"Mrs. Lathrop," the office secretary buzzed through the intercom. "We need you right away. A student in room thirty-eight is having a seizure."

49

The nurse handed Mark a stainless steel basin. "I have to go." She unlocked a door at the far end of the room and blocked it open. "The teachers' lounge is right through here," she said. "If you need anything, just ask someone to find me." She breezed through the clinic door, into the hallway, and was gone.

Mark closed his eyes and turned onto his side. He was almost asleep when the recess bell sounded and teachers began arriving for their breaks.

"I still can't believe it," a female voice drawled. "When Frank, here, told me at lunch today that the Weber girl had found his lost dog, I was shocked."

"What's so odd about that, Natalie?" another woman asked.

"Well, I was the only person, besides him, who knew Patches was missing. Besides, Symphony had never even seen the dog before."

"What do you mean? She had to have seen him, otherwise how did she know which dog she'd found?"

"Precisely," Natalie replied. "And how did she know his name?"

A man cleared his throat. "Did it occur to either of you that we may be dealing with an exceptional child—perhaps someone with E.S.P.?" he asked.

"E.S.P.? Frank Tucker! I can't believe that's your explanation," the second woman said.

As Mark listened, he forgot his stomachache. His luck had just changed. Quietly, he sat up on the side of the cot, rose, and walked out of the clinic without saying a word to anyone. This was his chance to be the one talking rather than the one being talked about.

He hit the hall just as recess was over, and eased his way through the crowd toward one of the most popular girls, Darla Terry. "I heard Symphony Weber used E.S.P. to find Mr. Tucker's dog," he said.

"Do I know you?" Darla jabbed. But she turned and repeated the information as if she'd read it in the Bible. Each girl in her group passed it on to someone else.

"Symphony Weber? Who is she?"

"You know. That fat girl in Mrs. Evans' class."

"The one with the blonde hair?"

"Uh huh."

The story was volleyed from noisy hallways to the low voices of restrooms and back again.

The Straight "A"s Club seemed to think it gave Symphony an unfair advantage.

"She gets good grades and so do all her best friends. Did you ever notice that?"

"I'll bet she knows the questions before she even takes a test."

"That's cheating."

From around the water fountain, flowed another opinion.

"You know what? I think it's all a lie."

"Yeah. I think she's making it up just to be popular."

"Really? How could *she* be popular? Look at what she wears."

A group of boys huddled in the bathroom, laughing, as they discussed the question: Does E.S.P. mean she can see through my clothes?

Therese moved through the crowd, hearing "Symphony," here and "Tucker's dog," there, with an occasional, "E.S.P.," thrown into the dialogue. As she approached her classroom, she stopped to listen to several students who had gathered just outside the cafeteria to discuss their concerns.

"She has to have special powers."

"Do you think she's a witch?"

Therese rolled her eyes and shook her head.

"Yeah. Remember how I touched her that one time and she shocked me?" a short, curly-haired, brunette said as she chewed her nails.

"She probably did it on purpose."

"She's from Alabama, you know," said the only boy in the crowd. "Those people still practice voodoo and stuff," he reminded them.

"Don't you mean New Orleans?" the nail-chewer chided.

"Oh yeah," he replied. "Then she must be from New Orleans."

Therese pushed up her sleeves as if preparing for a fight. "No, she's from Alabama." Her pale blue eyes turned icy as she glared at them. "And she's a nice person. You all should just shut-up!"

A blonde with glasses piped up. "Well, I still think they oughta kick her out of school."

Greg Stanton walked by with his usual band of buddies. "I warned you guys. That girl's a freak. Somethin' about her gives me the creeps."

When the bell rang, the students carried the story back into classrooms. Forced to quiet down, they continued the discussion by way of notes.

"Watch what you say about her. If she's a witch, you'll be sorry."

"I don't know. Every time I see her, she's bein' nice to someone."

"Watch what you say. If people think you like her, you'll get treated as bad as she does."

By the time the rumors found their way to Symphony's ears, she was a fat, evil freak.

"Just ignore 'em, Symmie," Therese said on the bus after school. "Don't let 'em make you feel bad."

Symphony gazed at her friend. The only one who had ever called her "Symmie" was Miss Ida Stalls. Suddenly, she felt warm all over.

"I've never heard you say a bad word about anyone," Therese continued. "And you don't go around hurting people, either. Are you all right?"

"Yeah," Symphony said. "I guess I've never really fit in. I oughta be used to it."

"It's Friday. See if you can spend the night at my house."

Just before supper, Therese's mom showed up at the Webers' in a full-length sky blue peasant dress. Her honey-colored hair hung loose, passed her shoulders, and trailed almost to her waist. "We'd love to have Symphony stay overnight, Maisy," she said, walking over to admire a family portrait. "They can make as much noise as they want. Clay works third shift tonight and nothing bothers me. What do you say?"

Recently, Mama had replaced her long, straight ponytail with permed curls. Next to Collette, her hair appeared even shorter. She washed her hands and, in the absence of a dishtowel, dried them on the butt of her pink shorts. "I really should ask her father," Mama said after a short pause. "But I don't know how late he'll be . . . Oh, I guess so. Yes, go ahead," she said. "How 'bout a glass of tea, Collette?"

"I'd love to," Collette replied, "but I left a casserole in the oven so I'd better take the girls and run. Maybe next week? Sometime during the day?"

"That'd be great," Mama said. "Call me before you go to bed, honey. Can I have a hug?"

Symphony hugged Mama and kissed her cheek. "It'll be fun," she said, smiling.

And it was.

Collette let them paint using sponges, toothbrushes, forks—anything they thought might make the design they wanted. They turned up the stereo and listened to the same songs over and over again. Then, after Collette went to bed, they ate chocolate ice cream and made up funny stories about people who weren't nice to them. As they sat around the table, Therese pulled two cigarettes from her mother's pack of Marlboros.

"Have you ever smoked?" she asked, sounding rather worldly for a ten-year-old.

"No," Symphony said.

"Wanna try?"

Within seconds, they both had a cigarette between their lips and Therese was lighting Symphony's.

"Now when I put the match up there, you breathe in," Therese said.

Symphony inhaled. Her mouth burned. Her throat burned. She began to cough. Her head got fuzzy.

Therese lit her own without coughing. This was not her first time.

"Aren't you s'pose'ta blow out?" Symphony asked. "I always see people blowing smoke out."

"No," Therese said. "You have to suck the smoke in first. Then you move the cigarette and blow it out."

"Are you sure?" Symphony asked, doubting her best friend's tobacco savvy. "Why would so many people do it if they had to suck the smoke in?"

"You don't have to finish it. Just put it out in the ashtray. What do you wanna do now?" Therese asked, blowing a smoke ring.

Symphony smiled. Right now, she wasn't fat, or evil, or a freak. She was just a regular girl spending the night with her best friend. And she hadn't had a best friend since she said goodbye to Davy in Mobile three years ago. "I don't know," she said. "Whatever you wanna do."

# CHAPTER SEVEN

SIXTH GRADE HAD been in session for one month—long enough to establish the school year's pecking order. Darla Terry, who seemed to have a crush on her own reflection, was third in line for head hen. That was, until Monday morning, when some of the lower chickens began sharpening their beaks and Darla, despite her brand new penny-loafers and stylish skirt, was forced to step down.

By Friday afternoon, she was just the odd girl in a group of five. As her four best friends paired off and whispered to each other behind open palms, she wandered over to the shade beneath a stand of longleaf pine trees where Symphony and a few of her friends met daily during recess.

"What's *she* doin' here?" Martha asked.

"Looks, to me, like she's combin' her hair," Therese said.

Symphony looked up from the book she was reading and grinned. When any of them got too serious, Therese seemed to think it was her job to make them laugh.

Today, Martha was immune to it. She rolled her eyes at Therese. "You know what I mean! It's not like we bother her when she's with *her* friends."

"I know," Therese said, with disgust. "Most o' the time if you say hi to her she just looks at you like you're crazy. But now that *they* don't want her around, we're good enough? That's just—wrong."

Darla halted a few steps from Therese. She closed her compact mirror and stopped combing her tangle-free, wavy, black mane. "Symphony, can I talk to you for a minute?" she asked, eyeing the rest of the group.

"Sure." Symphony closed her book and walked over to the next tree with Darla.

The other girls remained silent, inching closer to the whispered conversation until it ended and Symphony joined them once again.

Joanie sat cross-legged on the ground and picked up some pine needles to braid. "What'd she want?"

Symphony shrugged. "Just someone to talk to, I guess."

Therese put both hands on her hips. "But why you?"

"She was prob'ly just hopin' you'd tell her what's gonna be on Monday's Social Studies test," Martha said. "I can't stand it when people do that to you."

"Un-uh." Therese gave Symphony a questioning stare. "She's looking for new friends. Look how hers are actin'."

Symphony glanced back at the school to avoid Therese's eyes. "Did the bell just ring?" she asked. "I'll race you to the sidewalk." And she took off running, afraid that one more second with her friends might loosen the secret she'd just been asked to keep.

⌘ ⌘ ⌘

On Friday nights, Mama didn't make any of the kids take a bath and Dani and Symphony got to stay up until eleven o'clock. Sometimes, just to celebrate the weekend, Mama would say, "Let's leave the supper dishes till morning."

It was one of those Fridays.

After the little sisters and Joe were in bed, Mama, Dani, and Symphony crowded around the television hoping Daddy would wake up from his nap on the couch and stumble off to bed so they could turn the channel to something silly. But Mama began to yawn and soon, as Daddy snored, she settled in her chair watching *The Wild Wild West*. The girls, giving up the wait, kissed their mother goodnight and went to their room.

Dani closed the bedroom door. "That show is so boring. I don't see why we can't just get another TV. Then maybe *we* could pick a show *we* want to watch, for a change."

"We wouldn't need another TV if Daddy would stop fallin' asleep on the couch," Symphony said.

"Yeah? Well, I'm not gonna wake him up and send him to bed. Are you?"

Symphony pulled her lavender bedspread down and fan-folded it, making sure that, when she was finished, its purple, turquoise, and pink ruffles hung like a princess ball gown at the foot of her bed. Then she put on her pajamas and fell back onto the cool, white sheets. She closed her eyes, thinking about the day.

"Dani?" she asked.

Dani was reading, as usual. "Yeah?"

"You go to school with David Terry, right?"

"Ah-huh," Dani replied without looking up from her book.

"Is he nice?" Symphony sat on the side of the bed, swinging her legs.

"I guess. Why?"

"Oh, I just made friends with his sister today."

"Darla?" Dani spat. "I met her at a birthday party last year. She's mean to everyone. You better be careful."

"She was really nice today. The girls she usually hangs around with are mad 'cause she wants to be friends with me."

Dani put down her book. "Really? Did she say anything about why David's been so quiet lately?"

Mama knocked, then opened their door. "Lights out, girls. I love you."

⌘ ⌘ ⌘

"Dammit, Maisy!" Something heavy struck the kitchen countertop. "How the hell are you gonna go back to bein' a nurse? You can barely keep the diapers washed out."

Symphony wrapped the pillow around her head and played possum. It was Saturday morning. Daddy almost never worked weekends anymore. That meant two whole days of tiptoeing around the house, trying not to make him mad. The very thought made her stomach hurt.

He pounded the kitchen table.

Symphony let the ends of the pillow go and listened.

"Well? Say something!" he hissed.

"I wouldn't have to work full time," Mama said, "maybe just a few hours a week."

"And what? This god damned house is gonna clean itself?"

"I could work while the girls are in school. Then, we'd just need a sitter for Joe. I think it would help."

For a moment, all Symphony heard was the squeak of the refrigerator opening.

"You really think your going back to work will help our marriage?"

The refrigerator closed with a bang. Seconds later, a glass shattered.

"God dammit! I'm goin' *out* to eat. I *pay* for our food. I shouldn't have to cook it, too. By God, Maizy, you'd better pull out of this—and pretty damn soon, you hear me?"

The door slammed. The car engine revved. The house was quiet again.

Symphony and Dani rolled over to face each other.

"Should we go out there?" Dani asked.

"I don't know. 'Member, last time she wanted to be by herself." Symphony picked up a blue crystal vase from the night table and peered into it as if it were a kaleidoscope, momentarily altering the color of her world. "Maybe we should just stay in here and pretend we didn't hear anything. She feels better if she thinks we don't know."

"She does not! Where do you get these stupid ideas? And you say 'em like you read 'em in a science book or something. I'll bet he made her cry again." Dani threw back her sheets and was out the bedroom door before Symphony could defend her words.

"Mornin', sugar," Mama said, blowing her nose.

"Are you okay?" Dani asked.

"I just can't seem to get everything done these days, that's all. I wish I could—" Mama started to sob so hard she couldn't talk.

Symphony felt like someone was standing on her chest. She went to the kitchen and put her arms around Mama. "We can help you more, Mama. Just tell us what to do and you can go sleep for a little while. We'll do whatever you want. I promise."

"Yeah, Mama. Whatever you say," Dani agreed.

Their kind offer seemed to upset Mama even more. "I'm sorry," she choked, and shuffled down the hall into her bedroom.

Dani turned the hot water on over Friday night's dirty dishes. "I hate him!"

"Me too," Symphony said. "I hope he stays gone all day and all night." *But he won't.*

Together, the two sisters cleaned the kitchen. When Jeanne woke up, they fed her breakfast. Then Leesa. Then Joe. In between picking up toys and trying to keep the noise level to a minimum, Dani and Symphony took turns tiptoeing down the hallway to listen at Mama's door. Mostly, there was no sound at all, but sometimes, they could hear her crying. After lunch, when Symphony heard Mama sobbing once again, she pulled Granny's phone number from the bottom of her panties drawer.

"Granny, please don't tell Daddy I called you, but I'm worried about Mama. She can't stop crying."

Late Sunday afternoon, Gray's gold '55 Chevy pulled into the driveway. Granny was first to the front door, followed by Gray who set two suitcases on the living room floor as Daddy watched, a baffled look on his face.

"Where's Maisy?" Gray asked, crossing his meaty arms, the tattoo on his biceps showing bigger than ever. "I can only stay an hour or so. Then I'll head home so I can make my graveyard shift tonight. I'm telling you what! It's gonna be a long eight hours back to Alabama." He yawned. "Mama'll be here for a while."

"When was all this arranged?" Daddy asked, puffing out his chest. "It's the first I've heard of it."

"I've just had Maisy on my mind," Gray said. "And you know me. Once I get something in my head . . . Besides, Mama wanted to come help out for awhile."

Granny put her hands on her hips. "Young'uns are a lot o' work. Even with an automatic washing machine. Maisy has to get worn out sometimes. I've got just under five months 'fore the garden has to go in. If I'm gonna visit, now's the time."

"She's taking a nap," Daddy said. "Why don't I go wake her up?"

Gray stood at the hallway arch, blocking Daddy's path. "Why don't I . . . since I can't stay for long?"

"Suit yourself." Daddy threw his hands up in the air and backed away.

Gray knocked on the bedroom door. "Hey, Sis," he called. "It's your favorite brother."

There was a pause. "Austin?" Mama said, laughing as she opened the door.

Gray threw his arms around her and lifted her off the ground. "You're still a brat."

"You put me down," she chuckled. "right now, *little* brother."

"Watch your head, sis," Gray said, carrying her through the kitchen doorway. "And close your eyes. I brought you a surprise." He set her feet back on the floor right in front of Granny, who had taken a seat at the table.

Mama's eyes filled with tears as she hugged Granny. "What are you two doing here?"

"We just got to missin' you," Granny said. "I was hopin' to stay for a little while."

"You know how bored she gets waiting for spring." Gray stepped back, smiling as he watched Mama's relief at the sight of Granny.

In Gray's presence, some of Daddy's steam seemed to escape. But even after Gray left for the long drive back to Alabama, Daddy was on his best behavior. Granny's visit eased Symphony's stomach ache, which usually lasted all weekend, every weekend.

At bedtime, when Symphony had brushed her teeth and said her goodnights, she paused outside the door to her room. Daddy was in there talking to Dani.

"It wasn't your mother so it had to be you or Symphony," he whispered in a low growl.

Dani leaned against her headboard, looking terrified. "It wasn't me, Daddy," she said softly. "I wouldn't do that. And I don't even know Granny's phone number."

Daddy turned and walked out. Stopping in the hallway for a moment, he lowered a scowl at Symphony.

The inside of her belly burned like the time she'd spilled lemon juice on her scraped knuckle. *He knows.*

In the past, when Granny was visiting, Dani and Symphony took turns sleeping on the floor so that Granny could have a bed. This time, Symphony made a pallet with four doubled quilts and insisted that Dani stay where she was. Each evening, after the house was quiet, Symphony moved to a different spot on the floor. On the nights she caught Daddy glaring at her during supper, she made sure to sleep under Granny's bed.

One morning at breakfast Granny studied Symphony's face. "You're startin' to have raccoon eyes," she said, running her finger along the dark circles. "I don't think you're gettin' enough sleep on the floor. Why don't you switch with Daniele for a few nights?"

Symphony was far more comfortable moving her pallet at bedtime so Daddy couldn't find her. He knew she had called Granny. She had deliberately betrayed him. *What's the punishment for that?* Fear was keeping her awake at night. Sleeping in Dani's bed would make that fear even worse. "I'm okay," she said, hoping Granny would let it drop.

For weeks, Symphony's sleep had been so fragmented, she couldn't finish a dream. One day in the lunchroom, she nodded off for a moment and was startled awake by a woman who sounded like she was talking through gritted teeth. "You sass me again and it'll be the last time. Now I said, find him and bring him back home."

Symphony glanced around the cafeteria. *I don't see anyone yelling.*

Then a boy whined, "Ow, Mom. What'd you have to hit me so hard for?" He sounded familiar.

The woman raised her voice. "It's your fault he got lost in the first place. If you'd o' been watchin' him like I told you to, he'd be right here, wouldn't he? Now go."

Symphony hurried through the rest of her lunch, tossing the celery sticks into the trash so she wouldn't have to take them home. She wanted to get to the restroom before she went back to class. If anyone else had heard a woman yelling during lunch, the girls in the bathroom would be gossiping about it. They might even know who the boy was.

But she didn't glean any information from the bathroom that day, even though Tally Brewer was there. That girl wouldn't have survived two minutes as a spy. *I'd never tell Tally anything. Before you've even finished what you're saying, she's looking around trying to decide who to tell first.*

So Symphony listened, peed, and went to class. She sat down and opened her desk, searching for her spelling book. Instead, her eyes were drawn to a folded note with *Weirdo Weigh-big* scrawled across the front of it in red letters.

*Greg Stanton!* He was the one who made up that awful name. She turned around to look at him. He smirked back, the way he always did. Anyone could have put that note in her desk. She glanced up and down the rows then unfolded the piece of paper. In three-dimensional block letters, it read, "You're a freak!"

Students were still filing in from lunch. She walked to the back of the room and stood in the aisle next to Greg. "Did you put this in my desk?"

He stared at her. Without a word, he rubbed the back of his hand along the front of her skirt. Then he pressed it between her legs.

She didn't flinch. She didn't say stop. She just froze right there by his desk until the sound of scraping chairs and Mr. Thompson calling the class to order, shook her. Symphony carried the note back to her desk and sat down.

Five minutes into a study session, trembling and feeling like she was going to cry, Symphony asked to go to the restroom. Twenty minutes later, Darla knocked on the stall door.

"Symphony? Mr. Thompson sent me to find you. Are you okay?"

"Yes," Symphony sniffled from inside. "I just don't feel good."

"Do you need to go home?"

"No. I'll be okay." She wiped her eyes and opened the door.

"You've been crying." Darla went to the sink and turned on the faucet. "Here, splash some cold water on your face. Wanna talk about it?"

If she told anyone how Greg had touched her, he would deny it. And since everyone liked him, they would call *her* a liar. Not only would she be known as the fat girl who seemed to know things she couldn't explain, but she would be the girl who accused Greg of touching her. *Forget it.*

"It wouldn't help," Symphony said. She dried her dripping face with a paper towel and returned to class. As she opened the door, every student in the room turned to stare. Alone, she would have felt like running back to the bathroom. With Darla next to her, she walked to her desk, sat down, and opened her book.

She turned to look at Greg. His face reddened. *Maybe he thinks I told her. I hope he does.*

# CHAPTER EIGHT

IT WAS SEVEN-THIRTY on a Thursday evening. Mama had taken Joe with her to the grocery store. Jeanne and Leesa were in the bathtub guffawing their way through a wet washcloth fight that left almost as much water on the floor as there was in the tub. In the kitchen, Granny piled dishes in the sink, smiling and humming to the laughter as one might to their favorite song. Dani, who was in her room trying to study, would occasionally stop and shake her head in irritation.

Symphony, tickled by the hilarity of the water war, took some dirty towels from the hamper to clean up the mess before Mama got home. "Can you guys be a little quieter?" she asked, closing the door to the bathroom. "Daddy's gonna get mad." She turned toward the toilet to squeeze water out of a towel when, "shlopp!" one of the sopping weapons hit her butt. Then, "shlopp!" A second hit her shoulder.

"Hey!" She turned around wearing the meanest expression she could muster but couldn't fight the giggle. A moment later, she was on her knees catching the tub-water in cupped hands, splashing it into her sisters' laughing faces.

Daddy walked into the kitchen just as Granny started washing glasses. "I can't believe Maisy's raising such lazy daughters. Daniele! Symphony! Get in this kitchen and help your grandmother!"

"I'll be right there," Symphony called when she heard her name. She glared at the little sisters and tried to sound serious. "You're gonna get in trouble if you don't be quiet," she said, hoping that would scare them enough to settle down. "And take your bath, you guys. Leesa, wash that shampoo out of our hair before it dries." After washing her hands, she hurried into the kitchen.

"Coming, Daddy," Dani said, her voice nearly singing with delight. She scowled, slid a piece of paper between the pages of her English book, and threw it across the bed harder than she meant to. It bounced against the wall with a thump, giving voice to her frustration. She was lucky. Daddy didn't hear it. By the time she danced into the kitchen to help, she had forced a thin smile.

"I was just giving the girls a night off," Granny explained to Daddy as Dani and Symphony joined them. "I'll be finished in no time."

"I can help, Granny," Symphony said. "Dani has homework, though. Don't you, Dani?"

"Tons," Dani said with a "what the heck?" look.

"I can help by myself. Is that okay, Daddy?"

He had already turned and headed through the doorway to the living room. "That's fine," he called over his shoulder.

"I'll pay you back," Dani whispered, returning to her English book.

"I wanted to do the dishes with you anyway, Granny." Symphony picked up a dishtowel and began drying. "I can't believe it's already time for you to go home."

"Aw, honey." Granny pushed her glasses down for a better look. "I've been here nearly three months." She bent over and kissed the top of Symphony's head. "Your Mama's okay now. I helped her get some things caught up. And she's rested a little more since I got here. So she's ready to take her house back. And two women in charge of the same house never works for long. Soon, I'll just be in the way."

"No you won't."

A year ago, Symphony would have cried and pleaded with Granny not to go, but being eleven was tough. Acting like you did when you were younger only made you look like a baby. She stared at the dishtowel afraid that one glance at Granny would make her eyes tear up. "I wish you could stay forever," she said, drying another dish. "I like it better when you're here."

Granny looked at her and smiled. "Well, at least you'll get to sleep in your own bed again."

Symphony was terrified.

Granny turned back to the sink. "You know, you can call me any time," she said, her voice low and quivering. "About anything. And this summer, let's see if your Mama and Daddy'll let you spend some extra time at my house."

"Really?" Symphony picked up the plate Granny had just rinsed.

"Sure." Granny cleared her throat. "Now tell me what's goin' on with those dreams o' yours. Have you figured out who that boy is yet? The one who's in trouble with his mama?"

"No," Symphony said. "I've only had the dream three times and the first time doesn't count 'cause I didn't see 'em. That was the day at lunch when I just heard 'em talkin'. In the real dream, all I can see is his mother. But it's like I'm lookin' through a curtain with a hole in it so I can only see part of her."

"Hmh." Granny shook her head and gazed out the window for a moment. "I'll bet you can see more if you look hard enough. Maybe you should keep some paper and a pencil in your nightstand. Then if you remember somethin' when you wake up, you can write it down. And you've already got that little flashlight in there. You're all set."

Mama came in from the grocery store carrying Joe, who had dozed off on the way home. "Sshh," she said, going straight to his room. She laid him in bed, took off his shoes, and covered him up, clothes, dirt, and all. With Joe taken care of, Symphony helped Mama bring in the groceries.

Daddy, who was still watching television, turned up the volume to block the additional commotion.

Mama moved on to her next project—getting Jeanne and Leesa to bed, as Granny and Symphony put the groceries away. When the kitchen was spotless, they turned out the light and went to their room.

Dani gasped as they walked in. "You scared me half to death," she huffed. Shivering, she put her book down on the bed.

Symphony moseyed over and picked it up. "This is that 'Rebecca' book. Isn't it scary?"

"It's for a book report," Dani said. She grabbed it from Symphony and opened it to her marked page. "And I don't get scared like I used to."

Symphony rolled her eyes. *Yeah! Not as long as Granny's sleeping in our room.* She suspected her sister's newly found courage would disintegrate when it was the two of them in the dark once again. "Granny?"

"Yes, sugar?"

"Can I help you pack?"

"No thanks, sweetie. You better get back to your homework. It'll be bedtime before you know it."

Granny took dresses off hangers and folded them into her suitcase. Symphony sat on the end of the bed studying her spelling list. By tomorrow night Daddy would finally be able to do what he'd been forced to put off for months—punish her for calling Granny in the first place.

⌘   ⌘   ⌘

That afternoon, Symphony had sat alone on the bus, her stomach aching, while Therese shared her seat with another girl. All the attention from Darla had weakened their friendship.

Gray came during school hours to take Granny home. For the first time in months, Symphony was without her protector. By the time she got off the bus, she had the deep blues.

At home, her bedroom was deserted. The closet seemed empty without Granny's dresses. She put her books on the bed and sat down. There, on the night table, Granny had left a small jar of honeysuckle hand cream. She opened it and dabbed some on.

Smelling like Granny seemed to make her feel better.

"Symphony," Mama called. "Darla's on the phone."

⌘   ⌘   ⌘

"Thanks for not telling anybody," Darla said, as Symphony sat on the floor going through stacks of forty-fives. "If I'd said anything to Rose or Sandy or Maddie, the whole town would know about David by now. And they'd all think it was true. Everyone wants to believe bad stuff about rich kids."

"You think so?" Symphony asked, making a small pile of the records she wanted to hear.

"I know so. Kids say stuff about me all the time, don't they? That's why I've been friends with the same girls for so long. I never thought they'd talk about me. But look how fast they x-ed me out once I started hanging around with you."

Symphony looked away. "I'm sorry," she said, feeling like she was ruining Darla's life.

Darla opened a jewelry box filled with notes from her old friends. "It's not your fault." She unfolded one and began tearing it into tiny pieces. "They'd have done the same thing once they found out David was arrested. I'm just glad nobody's heard about it yet."

"But David didn't do it," Symphony said, looking up at Darla. "The police'll know that soon."

"They still think he did it. They say he has a 'history.' So what if he stole a lighter and some rubbers from Ideal Drugs last year."

Therese had told her about rubbers a couple of months ago. The thought of David using one made her face blaze. "Taking something from the drugstore is bad," she said, "but breaking into someone's house is a whole lot worse."

"Why did he have to pick that night to sneak out? That was so stupid. If anyone broke into the Robinsons', it was those jerks he was with."

Symphony was convinced the other boys hadn't done it either.

On David's instruction, one of them had brought some beer from home, the other, a pack of cigarettes. In her dream, there was a full moon. David and the other boys were sitting in the bushes by the junior high drinking and smoking as they smashed eggs against the brick walls of the school.

⌘ ⌘ ⌘

The girls fell asleep around midnight. Symphony awoke after two, her bladder ready to burst. She still couldn't believe Mama had let her spend the night at the Terrys'—especially without Daddy's permission. Across the room, the moon beamed between pink satin drapes painting the white carpet with a wide stripe of silver light.

It was a relief to sleep here, where it felt like nothing bad could ever happen. *I'll bet she never has nightmares.* However, Symphony didn't want to get up and wander around the unfamiliar house in the middle of the night. Hoping the urge to pee would subside, she turned over and dozed off.

Within the hour, she was awake again.

She stared around at the bedroom walls. Everywhere she looked, there were pictures she hadn't noticed in the daylight. Each nightstand was blessed with a vase of black-eyed susans accented with just enough lavender to sweeten the air. But satin drapes, fresh flowers, and all the paintings in the world didn't change the fact that she needed to pee. And there was no way she could wait until morning.

She crept toward the door, opened it, and peered into the hall, first one way and then the other. *Now where's the bathroom again?* Turning left, she inched down the dimly lit corridor to the first door. It was shut. *I know there was a bathroom right next to Darla's room.* She turned and doubled back, passing the bedroom and proceeding forward to the next door. It was closed too.

Symphony stood still for a moment trying to recall what she'd seen earlier. *I'm sure it's that one.* She headed back to the first door. When she got there, she stopped and leaned her ear against it. *Silence.* She put her hand on the doorknob. *Woosh.* Inside, the toilet flushed.

On tiptoes, she rushed to Darla's room, waiting as whoever it was did their sleepy shuffle back down the hall. After a door clicked shut and all was quiet, she made her way to the bathroom once again.

The stream seemed to go on forever. When it stopped, she sat for a moment in thankful relief. *Ereeeek.* Somewhere outside, a floorboard creaked. She listened for a moment. *Nothing. Probably just my imagination.* Her heart-beat slowed. She opened the door and started out, running straight into David.

He pushed her face against his chest and walked her back inside. She watched, terrified, as he shut the door and locked it. He bent over until they were nose to nose, his blue eyes glaring fire. Then his expression soft-ened. He flashed his dimples. "I'm not gonna hurt you, if that's what you think. I'm not like that. But my sister says you know stuff about the night I got in trouble. You better tell me everything."

Symphony was trembling. "You didn't do it. That's all I know."

"Look," David said. "I've heard about some of the other things you've done. Finding that teacher's dog, knowing how movies are gonna end, telling your friends what questions'll be on a test. So tell me, how do you know about that night?" His eyes were angry again.

She looked down at the floor. "I had a dream."

"Okay," he said. "Tell me about it."

So, she shared the dream about the other boys and the beer, cigarettes, and eggs.

"That's it?"

She nodded.

"Nothing about M. T.?"

"M. T.?" she asked, confused.

He dug his fingers into her arm. "You better be telling the truth. 'Cause I could hurt you if I wanted to." He let go and opened the bathroom door a crack, glancing into the hallway before leaving.

The moment he was gone, Symphony locked the door and slid down to the floor with her back against a corner wall. *Why can't I just be like everybody else?* Her eleven-year-old demeanor fell apart and she began to sob softly, afraid of attracting anymore attention.

She awoke feeling like she had pins and needles in her butt, still sitting on the bathroom floor. The thin line of light beneath the bathroom door gave her the courage she needed to go back to Darla's room. Crawling between the sheets, she closed her eyes. Granny was gone and she was afraid to be at home. She'd lost her best friend, Therese. And now, she was afraid her life was about to change again, all because of something that was supposed to be a gift.

While she was asleep in the bathroom, she had dreamt of David and M. T., and there was no way she could keep it a secret. With what she had to do, Darla would never speak to her again.

For the first time in her life, she fell asleep not caring whether she ever woke up.

# CHAPTER NINE

SYMPHONY OPENED HER eyes just long enough for a glimpse at the clock. It was almost noon. She had been feigning sleep for hours as Darla snored from her bed. By now, they had avoided breakfast with the rest of the Terry family.

Her mind replayed a scene from dinner the night before. David had beamed those nicest-boy-in-the-world dimples from across the table more than once. Looking back, she realized there'd been nothing in his behavior to warn her.

She turned onto her stomach and wrapped the pillow around her head like a cocoon, hoping she could sleep for a while longer. Mama wouldn't be there to pick her up until two-thirty.

She must have dozed off because the delicate knock on the door sounded like a start gun. She shot out of bed and scrambled into her robe.

"It's nearly two-o'clock, girls," Mrs. Terry exclaimed, walking into the room. She had a delicate appearance, every hair in place, never without her makeup. But Symphony noticed she always had a strange scent on her breath. "I can't believe you two are still asleep. How late did you stay up?"

"Not that late," Darla yawned. "I guess we were just tired."

"Well, you'd better get up and get dressed." She looked at Symphony. "Your mother will be here any minute. You don't want to keep her waiting."

So, the girls got dressed and nibbled on oatmeal cookies until Mama arrived. Each time the conversation swayed toward a serious topic, Symphony asked a question about clothes or make-up, Darla's favorite subjects.

Darla was always saying stuff like, "If I were you, I'd cut my hair short," or, "I'd wear powder blue every single day," or, "I'd stop eating bread for a year." Then she'd smile and shake her head. "You're just so cute. I'd absolutely kill for your face. If you were a little thinner, all the boys would be after you."

When the Webers' car pulled into the driveway, Symphony grabbed her overnight bag and headed out the door. "Thanks, Darla," she said, squeezing into the back seat with the little sisters. Before the car started for home, Jeanne leaned over and put her arm around Symphony. "Daddy had to work at his-ami," she whispered.

Symphony grinned, wondering who had passed the story down. As a youngster, when Daddy said, "Miami," Symphony said, "your-ami." Now, it had evolved to *his-ami.*

Jeanne smiled back and leaned against her the rest of the ride.

At home, Symphony found Dani sprawled across the living room couch, talking on the phone. She watched for a moment waiting for Dani to notice her. When that didn't happen, Symphony tapped her sister's shoulder. "How long is Daddy gone for?"

"Would you mind holding on for a minute," Dani asked the person on the other end of the line. She put her hand over the receiver and snarled, "Can't you see I'm on the phone?"

"Sorry," Symphony huffed, walking away. *It wouldn't've taken her any longer to tell me.* But Dani's eyes were sparkling and her cheeks were red. It only took a moment for Symphony to realize why. *She's talking to a boy.*

Symphony followed Mama out to the clothesline. "Jeanne said Daddy's in Miami?"

"Just for the weekend," Mama said. "Mr. Barker asked him to do a class for some new agents."

"So he'll be home tomorrow?"

"Ah-huh." Mama answered, her voice breathy as if her thoughts were somewhere else. She took a towel from the line and shook it with a snap before folding it and stacking it on top of the others in the basket. "Did you have fun at Darla's?"

"It was all right," Symphony said, careful to give the answer that would keep Mama from asking for more details. "Want help with that sheet?" Mama handed her two corners and they folded the stiff sun-dried sheet right there in the backyard.

⌘ ⌘ ⌘

"Let me and Symphony make dinner tonight," Dani said. She nudged Mama into Daddy's favorite living room chair and turned the television loud enough to drown out the sisters and Joe playing in the hall. There, in the blue-gray light of an *I Love Lucy* rerun, Mama put her feet up and began to chuckle.

Together, Symphony and Dani planned their perfect Saturday night dinner. The dye in the hot dogs turned the boiling water red. The macaroni and cheese was prepared according to the directions on the box, but it was mushy anyway. Brown sugar and cinnamon were stirred into a can of applesauce and heated until the kitchen smelled like one of Granny's pies.

"Can we have candles, Mama?" Symphony asked. "Just at the table?"

Mama nodded. "Is supper ready?"

"In a minute," Symphony said. They were having trouble getting Joe to sit still. Jeanne and Leesa were fighting over who had the most applesauce.

"Don't you want the candles lit?" Symphony scolded as she returned to the kitchen. "We can't light 'em till you guys quit squirmin' around."

"Put your hands in your pockets," Jeanne said, turning to Leesa and Joe.

"You're not my mama," Leesa said.

But, Joe put his hands in his pockets and those at the table grew still and quiet. Symphony switched off the light.

Dani pulled two candles and a box of matches from the flashlight drawer. She lit the candles and called Mama in from the living room.

Mama appeared in the doorway, looking like a queen, smiling like she'd finally remembered how.

"Voila!" Dani said, beaming. "Dinner is served."

They told funny stories as they ate, sitting around the table until the candles burned out. No one seemed to be in a hurry to finish.

For the first time since Granny had come to stay, they left the dishes for the next morning. Daddy, after all, would not be home until sometime Sunday.

"Who was that on the phone today?" Symphony asked when she and Dani were under the covers and the lights were out.

"None of your bees-wax," Dani snipped, turning toward the wall.

"You don't have to tell me but I know it was a boy."

"You don't know anything," Dani said. But her voice turned up at the end of the sentence, as if it were a question.

"Okay," Symphony replied, not wanting to ruin a good evening. "I'm glad we cooked supper tonight. But the best part is that, even with Granny gone, Mama seems okay. Did you see how hard she was laughing? Maybe we should get up in the morning and do the dishes."

"You can if you want. I'm gonna sleep in."

The instant Symphony closed her eyes it was as if a film of the night before was running on the inside of her eyelids. She felt the fire of David's glare. Her stomach churned. *He has to stop before someone gets hurt.* But she didn't know *how* to stop him.

*I just wanna sleep.* But the images in her mind kept her awake. When the next scene drifted into her thoughts, she forced herself to describe it in one sentence. Then, she broke the sentence into words, and those words into letters and spaces. She tore apart each image that followed, dismantling her anxiety as well. Soon, she was sleeping.

That night was a dreamless one. She awoke as soon as it was light and wandered into the messy kitchen. Jeanne, still wearing her green flannel pajamas, was sitting at the already-cleared table.

"What are you doin' up?" Symphony asked. Jeanne loved her sleep. "You already cleaned off the table?"

Jeanne's shoulder-length, auburn hair poked out in all directions. "Daddy's comin' home today. And Granny's gone."

Symphony pulled a chair out and sat down, looking at her little sister. In the eight years they'd been sisters, she'd never noticed that their eyes were the same shade of dark brown. But Jeanne's held a far away gaze. She always looked lost, like someone who had been dropped off at the wrong place and had no idea how to get where she belonged.

Symphony thought of the last time Daddy had made Mama cry, the reason Granny had come to visit. "Just 'cause it happened once," Symphony said, "doesn't mean it'll happen again." She patted down Jeanne's unruly strands, stood, and walked to the sink. "It'll be okay."

Jeanne was quiet for a moment, then she looked up at Symphony. "You think so?"

"Yeah." Symphony turned on the water and began putting glasses in to soak. "Why don't you pull a chair over and help me with the dishes."

Through two sink loads the girls were almost silent, as awkward strangers, unsure of what to say to each other. But as Symphony washed the dirty pots, Jeanne asked a question that made her stop what she was doing.

"Why doesn't Daddy like us?"

"Who?" Symphony asked, knowing full well what the answer was.

"Me and you," Jeanne said, that same lost look on her face.

It was not the first time Symphony had considered the question. Daddy played with Joe any time he got the chance. At six, Leesa was still allowed to climb into his lap. Dani got to take his shoes off when he took a nap and never got yelled at for talking to him at supper. It seemed the only time he talked to Jeanne or Symphony, they were in trouble.

She wanted to lie to Jeanne, to say, "He likes us too." But when she opened her mouth, "I don't know," were the words that came out.

Jeanne's shoulders slumped. She stared into the bottom of the sink as if there was a better answer there.

"But *I* love you," Symphony said with a smile. And for the first time in her life, she realized she did love her little sister—ornery or not.

"Well I love you, too," Jeanne answered.

⌘　⌘　⌘

The sun burned off a thin layer of frost and the day turned glorious. The rest of the morning, Symphony stayed outside with Jeanne, watching Leesa and Joe play in the backyard. In the afternoon, she dodged two phone calls from Darla and walked down to Therese's house.

Therese met her at the front door with a question in her eyes.

"Hi." Symphony mumbled, studying the gardenia bush at the corner of the porch.

They stood there for at least a minute, neither speaking. Their eyes never met. Then Collette drove up and carried a sack of groceries in from the car. "Hi, Symphony," she said. "I haven't seen you in a while. Why don't you come on in?"

Therese held the door open.

The girls stopped in the kitchen, poured glasses of iced tea, then went to Therese's bedroom and locked themselves in.

Therese crossed her arms. "So tell me. Why's Darla Terry so great all of a sudden?"

"She's not." Symphony sat down on the bed, focusing on the huge green tumbler full of tea. "She just needed my help, is all."

"And that means you can't do anything with me?" Therese slammed her glass down on the dresser and crossed her arms again. "I mean, you never even call me anymore."

"I'm sorry," Symphony said, looking into her friend's eyes for the first time that day. "I guess I'm not used to having more than one friend at a time. But you're still my best friend. We can tell each other anything, right?"

"Yeah. Don't forget, I'm the one who kept your secret before the rest of the school found out," Therese said.

"Well, here's a new one. You know the lake behind Overlook Terrace?" Symphony asked. "There's alligators in it."

"That's no secret," Therese said. "I've seen 'em. Haven't you?"

"No. Mama won't ever let us get that close. But, anyway, you know the island out in the middle?"

"Ah-huh."

Symphony's throat tightened. She thought of the night she'd spent in the Terry's bathroom and began to shiver. Tears ran down her cheeks.

Therese bent down to hug her. "What's wrong? Why are you shaking?" She reached to open the door. "Do I need to get my mom?"

"No. Wait. I think I'm okay." Symphony paused for a moment. "Have you ever heard anyone call that Empty Island?"

"Yeah."

"Well I haven't. So, when David said, 'M. T.,' I thought he was talking about someone's initials. I didn't know he meant Empty Island until I had the dream."

"You had a dream about David—Darla's brother?"

"Yeah. See, he's in trouble. That's why Darla wanted to be friends with me. I mean, I think she really likes me now but I'm not sure she did at first."

"Why's he in trouble?"

"I'll tell you everything, but you have to promise not to talk to anyone else about it—unless I say. Promise?"

"I promise," Therese said.

⌘　⌘　⌘

Symphony felt lighter as she walked home from Therese's until she rounded the corner and saw Daddy's car in the driveway. Inside, the house seemed to have changed colors, as if a tint of grey had been painted over every wall, every piece of furniture, even the people who lived there.

She suffered through supper, listening to Dani go on about how *she* had made the meal the night before, and what was happening at school the next week, and how report cards were coming out soon and what her grades would be. Four-year-old Joe threw a fit and had to go to bed early. Leesa was able to charm Mama and Daddy with her cute, yet elaborate, tales of life in the first grade. Jeanne picked at her food, that far away look in her eyes. Symphony stretched her leg out and bumped Jeanne's foot. They looked up at each other and smiled, which got them through the rest of the meal.

That night, Symphony lay in bed wondering if Daddy had forgotten how mad he was at her. For a moment, she was afraid of what he might do now that Granny was gone. Then she began to think about Jeanne. *Is she scared, too? Or is she just sad?*

Funny thing was, the more Symphony worried about Jeanne, the less she worried about herself.

# CHAPTER TEN

THERESE'S MOM, COLLETTE, smoothed the wrinkles out of her ankle-length peasant dress and leaned against the back of the sofa. "We have to do something," she said, tapping a cigarette end over end in her palm. "But I'm not sure what that is just yet."

Symphony had tried to talk to Mama about her predicament but couldn't get three words out before they were interrupted. She thought about calling Granny, but Daddy seemed to be home whenever Symphony was. As the week progressed, she began to panic. She didn't want to lose Darla's friendship but she had to find a way to stop David.

"Talk to my mom," Therese encouraged. "She's cool. She'll know what to do."

So, after school on Thursday, Symphony blurted out the details surrounding Empty Island. Therese was right. Collette accepted Symphony's dreams without question and began searching for a way to ease the burden David Terry and the dreams had dumped on Symphony's shoulders.

Symphony sat on the ottoman in front of the sofa, her heart beating wildly as she awaited the solution. She knew, somehow, Therese's mom would find one.

"Wait a minute." Collette sat straight up, a gleam in her eyes. "All I have to do is make a phone call." She lit the cigarette she'd been holding and threw the match into an ashtray. "As long as I don't give any names, there's no way they can trace it back to Symphony."

The two girls looked at each other and grinned.

"A phone call." Therese shook her head. "Why didn't we think of that?"

Collette took a puff of her cigarette but there was no smoke when she exhaled. "Just to be on the safe side, I think we should use a pay phone," she suggested, striking another match. She took another fruitless drag, pulled the cigarette out of her mouth and examined it. "There's a crack in it," she said, stuffing it into the ashtray. "It makes me so mad to break one. They're thirty-five cents a pack!" She looked at the clock in the kitchen and pulled her long blonde hair into a ponytail. "Oops. I'd better get dinner going."

"Can I be there when you call the police?" Symphony asked.

"I think you should be," Collette said. "See if your mom'll let you go to a movie tonight. We'll do it on the way home, when it's dark." She walked over to the table and picked up an open newspaper. "Hmmm." Her eyes grazed the kitchen counter from one end to the other. "Well, shoot!" She moved some magazines off the coffee table in the living room. "Did either of you see what I did with my cigarettes?"

They shook their heads.

"Damn! It was a brand new pack, too."

"I'll walk Symphony home now," Therese said. She opened the sliding glass door and stepped into the back yard with Symphony close behind. As they walked between the bushes that marked the corner of the lots, Therese pulled a pack of cigarettes from her pocket.

"Is that what your mom was looking for?" Symphony asked with an accusing tone.

Therese grinned.

Symphony put her hands on her hips. "Why are you sneakin' around? I thought she didn't care if you smoked."

"She didn't," Therese said, "before I started doing it all the time. Now she's changed her mind."

"Just talk to her," Symphony said. "She'll understand. Look what she's doin' for me."

Therese lit up and took a few puffs. "Yeah. Well, it's different when she's your mom." She held the cigarette toward Symphony. "Want some?"

Symphony rolled her eyes. "Are you kidding? Don't you remember last time? I nearly threw up."

The girls meandered down the path leading to Symphony's street, arriving at the Webers' just as Mama was finishing supper.

"You're so lucky," Therese said as they stood outside the kitchen door. "I wish my house smelled like this right now. *We'll* probably have T.V. dinners again."

They stepped inside where Mama stirred the ham and butterbeans, opened the oven to check the cornbread, then flitted across the kitchen to work on the salad. It was the perfect time to ask.

"My mom was wondering if Symphony could go to a movie with us tonight. It's the early show."

A "yes" was always easier if Mama was busy or if the inviter asked. In this case, with both those conditions met, the outcome had to be positive.

"Is your homework done, Symphony?" Mama responded without looking up.

"I don't have any today," Symphony replied. That was mostly true. None of today's assignments were due until Monday.

Mama stopped tearing lettuce, and studied Symphony's eyes for a moment. "Well, all right then. But I don't want you fussing around when you get home. You have to promise to go straight to bed or the next time, the answer'll be no."

⌘　⌘　⌘

The movie was one of those mushy, dancey, sing-songy shows that didn't really seem to have a storyline—not one Therese or Symphony were interested in, anyway. They sat in the theatre using a mini-flashlight to practice their sign language—something a guest speaker at their school had begun teaching them. At the moment, they were shaping mostly four-letter words using a card the speaker left behind. This led to an occasional spurt of laughter, which resulted in a shushing from the woman behind them and eventually drew a glare from Collette.

On the ride home, they stopped at the pay phone by Boynton Park. The same phone Mama used to report the whereabouts of Roscoe Stanley. Symphony shivered as they got out of the car and made their way into the circle of light offered by the corner streetlamp. She glanced at the Barna Avenue traffic, hoping no one would notice them. As Collette placed the call, Symphony was thinking about Roscoe Stanley, how he'd glared at her through the car window that day. She pictured David Terry in the bathroom a few nights before, his scowl melting into a terrifying smile.

Collette winked at Symphony. "I need to speak with an officer, please. No, it's not an emergency. I'd rather not give my name if that's okay. Thank you. I'll wait.

"Maybe you two should get back in the car," she said, lighting a cigarette. "Symphony's freezing and I may have to wait for a—Yes, sir. I'm here." She turned her back toward the girls.

"Well, you see, I was visiting a friend last weekend, someone who lives on Overlook Terrace. I couldn't sleep and I didn't want to wake everyone in the house up, so I decided to take a walk. I thought maybe that man-made lake would be pretty in the moonlight. You know the lake I'm referring to? Yes. That's the one. Well, I heard something splashing around, so I shined my flashlight at it. I was hoping to see an alligator. And I did. But a gator wasn't what made the splash. There were three teenaged boys inside the fence and I couldn't believe what they were doing."

She paused for a moment, listening. "Well, in my opinion, this *isn't* boys being boys and I don't think you'll call it that once you hear the rest of it."

"One boy was standing on the shore with his arms out like he was ready to dive in. While he waited, another one reached into a box and pulled something out. I couldn't see anything at first. But I heard it. It was a kitten. And there were others in the box, too. The poor little things were crying. Just then, the moon came out from behind a cloud and I watched as that boy threw a tiny, defenseless kitten into the water. That's when the alligator showed up. Well, as soon as they had the alligator busy, the boy who was waiting, dove in and started swimming like crazy toward that island in the center. I should have yelled at them, but I was out all by myself in the middle of the night. I *know* I didn't handle it properly. That's why I'm calling you now."

"That's right. There were three of them and for all I know they're out there doing it right now. No one should treat an animal like that. It's terrible. But those boys! If they keep this up, sooner or later a gator's gonna get one of them."

"No, I can't leave my name. I don't want to cause trouble for the person I was visiting. I just thought the police should know what those boys are up to. Maybe you can stop them before it's too late."

"That would at least give me some peace of mind. Thank you, officer." Collette hung up the pay phone and picked up her keys. "Well, they're sending a patrol car. He says they'll keep an eye out for anything suspicious."

By the time Symphony got home, she was breathing easier. She didn't fuss around at bedtime. She kissed Mama goodnight and slid under the covers. Within minutes, she was asleep.

⌘　⌘　⌘

Symphony couldn't see herself but viewed the dream as if she were standing outside a window peeking through the hole in the curtain which, it seemed, had grown larger since the last time she looked through it.

*The woman inside trembled and stretched the sleeves of her sweater until they covered her hands. She folded her arms across her chest. "I told you not to come back without him."*

*"But, Mom," the boy protested.*

*"A paddlin' ll get you out there lookin' again." She stood and crossed the room, her back toward the window. As she moved away, the moonlight found her empty chair and the liquor bottle on the table next to it. She stopped at the refrigerator and felt around on the top where her eyes couldn't reach, smiling when her fingertips found what she was searching for. She picked up a wooden paddle and slapped it against her palm. Behind her, the front door slammed. The boy was gone.*

*The eye of the dream climbed upward where the moon hung in the sky like a hook waiting for Merlin's robe. The focus paused for a moment, then slid back toward earth. On the street in front of the house, the boy was walking alone, shining a small flashlight, its beam only one foot ahead of him. He seemed taller than the boys in elementary school—more like the kids in junior high.*

*Inside the house, hands trembling, the woman lifted the liquor bottle to her lips. She took a swig and pushed the dark curly hair out of her face, revealing a jagged scar above her right eye. "Tell me to call the police," she sneered. "Lazy little bastard. But I told him, didn't I? Pfff. Call the police!" She shook her head and took another gulp.*

Symphony opened her eyes in the darkness. This dream always came in pieces, like a puzzle, and this portion was new. *Who is he? Why is his mother so mean? And why can't I see the whole dream?*

"What's the matter?" Dani whispered from her bed on the other side of the room.

Symphony, absorbed in her wondering, couldn't hear anything beyond her own thoughts.

A moment later, her older sister was standing over her. "Are you okay?"

"Oh! Yeah. I was just having a nightmare."

"You were walkin' around, too," Dani said. "To the window and back. Once you even went into the living room. I was scared you'd wake Daddy up. You were standing there looking out like the curtains were open. For a minute, I even thought you were gonna go outside."

"I haven't ever walked in my sleep before, have I?"

"Shh." Dani lowered her voice even more. "Not that I remember."

"Sorry about wakin' you up," Symphony said, turning over.

"You sure you don't want to talk about the bad dream?"

"It's not like one o' yours. My dreams never end with a monster, just a question."

"If you say so." Dani said, crawling back under the covers.

⌘　⌘　⌘

On Friday, Mama refused to let Symphony spend the night with Therese.

"Why?" Symphony demanded.

"Esther and Ron are coming over after supper for Scrabble and dessert. I told them to bring the boys, too."

"The Guttmans?" Symphony said with a tone of disgust.

Three months ago, when the Guttmans moved in down the street, they were just another family with three rough sons. But as soon as Mama discovered they were from Alabama too, she and Mrs. Guttman became instant friends. Often, when Symphony came home from school, Mama and Esther were sitting at the kitchen table, drinking iced tea, their conversation so juicy Symphony was skedaddled to another room before she could taste one morsel of it.

Mr. Guttman, worked for the space program at Cape Canaveral. When he and Daddy got together, they usually formed a huddle of two around the mailbox where they talked for hours. If any kids ventured by, they were shooed away.

Although the three Guttman boys were in the same grades as Dani, Symphony, and Jeanne, none of the girls had made an effort to get to know them and that Friday wasn't the best time for a first visit. The phone calls from Dani's secret boy had stopped, so she was in a bad mood. The only board game they had all the pieces for was Monopoly, and Symphony hated that game. On top of that she was irritated about not being able to spend the night with Therese. But Jeanne, well, she was fine. For once, she was being treated like a big kid. Leesa and Joe were banished; sent away to be children.

All three of the Guttman boys were covered in freckles, but the taller they got, the more space there seemed to be between dots. At one card table, Dani and Symphony sat down to play Monopoly with Ronnie, Jr. and Ray. Lucky for Jeanne, Bobby brought his *Go Fish* game.

"It's a baby game," Ray said, rolling his eyes.

"Is not," Bobby argued.

"Well, Monopoly's boring," Jeanne said. Bobby agreed. So they took the table farthest from the television. Symphony longingly stared at the *Go Fish* table, wishing she could play the "baby" game with Jeanne and Bobby.

"Girls first," Ronnie, Jr. said, his blue eyes glinting as he arranged the money into proper stacks. "Pick your game piece."

Dani fluffed her long, brown waves, smiled at Ronnie, and picked up the silver dog. "Thank you ever so much," she said, sounding a bit like Scarlet O'Hara.

Ray reached his grimy, boy hands across the table to collect his token. "I call the race car."

Symphony stared at Ray in disbelief. *Hey, I'm a girl, too.* Perhaps if she gave Ronnie the same look Dani had . . . She tried and waited.

"I'll be the battleship," Ronnie said, grabbing the boat just as Symphony reached for the shoe.

"C'mon, Symphony," Dani said. "Just pick one."

Symphony had won a few games using the shoe as her token, but the thimble reminded her of Granny. She picked it up and stuck it on the end of her little finger. Ray looked over at her and grinned. At that moment, she realized how cute he was and suddenly, she no longer minded playing Monopoly. She set the thimble down on *Start* and waited for her turn.

There was nothing subtle about the way Dani was acting. She was a stream of giggles the entire evening, twisting her hair around her finger every time she talked to Ronnie. She even laughed when he took possession of her two railroads. If anyone else had tried that, she would have been furious.

The television blared as Mama and Mrs. Guttman, with almost identical heights and haircuts, carried Kool-Aid and cookies into the room.

"What do you want to watch now?" Ronnie asked, ready to change the channel as soon as *Tarzan* was over. "*Hogan's Heroes* or *The Man From U.N.C.L.E.?*"

"I vote for *Hogan's Heroes*," Symphony said. "The U.N.C.L.E. show makes me sleepy. I can't even say their names."

About that time Joe ran into the living room to get a cookie. When Dani saw him, her face turned bright red. She jumped up and started toward him, standing between him and Ronnie. Joe seemed to think Dani wanted to play. With a chortle, he began running circles around the two card tables with Dani in pursuit. Bobby took one look at him and began to laugh.

Once Symphony saw Joe, she realized what the problem was. Somewhere, the four-year-old had found a bright white sanitary napkin and was wearing it over his crew cut like a bonnet. Ronnie saw him and glanced back at the T.V. before he grinned. Ray looked away from Symphony but as soon as his eyes met Bobby's the brothers began to howl.

"Joe," Dani said through gritted teeth. "Give me that right now, or I'm gonna go get Daddy."

He stopped and let his fine bonnet fall to the floor.

"Now, get a cookie for you and Leesa, and go play," she scolded.

She picked up the pad and, barely holding it between her thumb and forefinger, carried it down the hall to the bathroom trash.

When she returned Bobby asked, "What was that thing on his head, anyway?"

For a moment, the older kids stared at each other. Everyone in the room was silent. Then Bobby looked at Jeanne and began to crack up. "I laughed so hard I farted," he said.

That remark eased the tension and they all burst out laughing again. After a few minutes, they settled down to finish their games, which continued until midnight.

⌘　⌘　⌘

In the morning, the whole Weber household slept in. The phone rang around seven-thirty. Symphony could hear Daddy stomping down the hall to answer it. "She's still asleep," he said. "Who's calling? Okay, Darla. I'll tell her when she gets up."

"God dammit, Symphony," he grumbled on his way back to bed. "Tell your friends not to call this early."

Symphony waited as long as she could stand to wait, which was almost half-an-hour. Hoping Daddy had gone back to sleep, she dialed Darla's number and spoke quietly into the phone. When Darla answered, she sounded like she was crying.

"Darla, it's Symphony. Is everything okay?"

"You said he didn't rob them," Darla yelled into the phone. "You were supposed to find a way to prove it."

"What happened?" Symphony asked, trying to sound innocent and ignorant.

"I figured you'd already know—I mean, with your *abilities*," Darla jabbed. "He snuck out again last night. The police arrested him. Now what's he gonna do? My mom's been crying since they came."

"Are you sure it's for that robbery thing?"

"What else could it be?" Darla demanded.

Symphony chewed her nails as the silence on the phone line chipped away at their friendship. *I should'a just stayed in bed.*

# CHAPTER ELEVEN

DAVID TERRY'S GROUP of follow-the-leader daredevils disbanded. As soon as the story hit the local paper, public outcry accused the unnamed teens of animal cruelty and demanded they be severely punished. Amid the more than one-hundred reports of missing pets, no law on the Florida books allowed for the boys' criminal prosecution. They were sent to a juvenile facility for breaking curfew and trespassing. After a week, authorities thought they'd learned their lesson and they were sent home. The next day, Mr. and Mrs. Terry sent David to live with his uncle in Vermont.

Darla employed a campaign of sleepovers and parties to buy her way to the center of the popular girls once again. Symphony never made a single guest list. In fact, Darla seemed determined to prove that her friendship with Symphony had been an illusion from the beginning. Once she was back in her position as third from head hen, her small group of chapstick-toting, perfume-wearing guerrillas bombed Symphony with cruelties if Darla so much as yawned in Symphony's direction.

Most days Symphony felt like the punch line of a joke everyone understood except her. She pretended not to hear, tried to look away, but it was tough—especially on those days when her clothes felt tighter than usual.

One day she wore a new outfit and Sandra Dixon said, "Nice dress Symphony." When Symphony thanked her, Sandra responded with a smirk.

"Yeah. It's just like the one my aunt dropped in the Salvation Army bin over the weekend."

A few days later, Symphony walked by a circle of girls. "Hey, Symphony," one of Darla's friends called out. "I heard Doug Archer say he loves you." Then she turned to the others and in a volume loud enough to be heard in all points of a football stadium, said, "Well, actually, he said he loved bacon."

The giggles were the hardest to take and Symphony began to shrink at the sound of them even when they weren't intended for her. Therese came to Symphony's defense whenever she could but they weren't together every minute. When Symphony was alone she braced herself for the next mean word, the laugh, the joke. The only time her heart slowed to a normal beat was when she was at home, locked inside her bedroom.

Winter arrived and it was the coldest central Florida had seen since the Webers moved there. On the frostiest mornings, the sprinklers s*chook-ta, schook-ta*-ed wherever an orange tree was in danger, transforming the groves and yards of Titusville into palaces of magical icicles—keeping the citrus safe in the freezing temperatures.

Christmas came in its splendor and excitement, and left behind an emptiness which had been fed by too much wild anticipation. After the first week of Christmas vacation, Symphony, who had managed to regain some of her positive attitude, left her room each day, allowing for some fun with Therese. Just before break was over, Therese's father delivered the biggest surprise of the holidays.

"He won't talk to me about it," Therese said on Friday afternoon. "My mom's even mad at him and she never gets mad."

"But your grades have been really good," Symphony said. "Why's he making you do it?"

"Because I won't stop smoking. He says I'm too young but *he* started smoking when *he* was ten. Besides, everybody smokes."

"What does he think? That Catholic school'll make you stop?" Symphony wanted to scream! *Why can't you just quit?*

"It doesn't matter." Therese picked up a pen and one of her white tennis shoes. "There's nothing I can do about it. He's already signed me up. I'm starting there on Monday."

"This Monday?"

"Yeah." Therese finished drawing a picture of a nun on the bottom of her sneaker. "I can't believe he's making me do this." She drew a thick mustache just above the nun's upper lip and colored it in.

"Well I'm mad, too!" Symphony's eyes were beginning to sting. She stood and turned her back to Therese, hoping she could hold her tears until she made it home. "I've gotta go."

"Hang on. I'll walk you half way." Therese pushed her foot back into her shoe and ground the picture of the sister against the floor. "I just have to find my coat."

"I can't wait," Symphony said, rushing out the door. "I have to hurry."

At home, she passed the living room where the television blared with Mama's stories. The little sisters were in the kitchen arguing over whose half-an-apple was the biggest. Joe kicked his yellow ball down the hall.

"No kicking in the house," she said, stepping over it. Without speaking to another soul, she walked into her bedroom and locked the door. She picked up the blue crystal vase from the bedside table and lay down, staring into it. From that vista, it was impossible to see any other color.

School returned to what it was before Therese's family moved in. For a while, Symphony, Martha, and Joanie still met for recess but the three of them always ran out of things to talk about. As soon as they did, the conversation turned to the subject Symphony most preferred to avoid—Darla Terry.

"I'll see you guys later," she would say. "I have to go to the bathroom." Sometimes, she pretended to have a library book to return. Then, one day, she didn't go to the tree at all. When she looked, Martha and Joanie weren't waiting for her, either. In the clearing, boys chased each other. The older girls congregated in the corners of the playground, having serious conversations. Symphony sat in a swing as younger kids ran circles around her. Being alone wasn't so bad. It was better than being teased.

⌘  ⌘  ⌘

Dani was rarely home before dinner. In junior high, she had been stricken with club mania and had meetings almost every day after school.

Under the guise of doing homework, Symphony would stretch out on the bed and squeeze her eyes shut. Once her lids grew tired she relaxed them until a grayish-blue fog was all she could see. Eyes closed, she concentrated. Droplets of mist danced around and reorganized into patterns, sometimes forming colorful designs that swirled like an internal kaleidoscope. More often, a word or scene would appear, filling Symphony with pieces of puzzles that rarely fit together. Each afternoon, she locked herself away, hoping to use her gift to find an end to the daily torture she was enduring, but whatever she saw always involved helping someone else.

⌘ ⌘ ⌘

It didn't matter where Symphony was or what she was doing, she felt like an extra part that didn't seem to fit anywhere. School became a dreaded chore, and her grades plummeted.

Evenings, when her family was together, she would look up to find Daddy glaring at her. He still hadn't punished her for calling Granny and she was growing tired of wondering what he would do or say, and when. She tried to steel herself against his cuts and digs but they always came when she was least able to ignore them.

"You know, you don't have to eat every scrap on your plate," Daddy said one evening at dinner.

Instantly, Symphony's eyes grew wet. She had been sneaking comfort from the kitchen between meals and it was beginning to show. Her middle had expanded. On top of that, her breasts were growing so quickly, they felt like two lumps of fat on her chest. Buttons were popping. Zippers wouldn't close. She turned away from Daddy's look of disgust.

Mama frowned at him.

"What?" he said, "She practically licks her plate."

Symphony grabbed the roll of fat across her waist and squeezed so hard, her hatred of it left a bruise where her thumbs had been. The anger faded to frustration and that gave way to realization. *Are people watching me eat?*

So, she changed her eating habits. From that point forward, she ate less at mealtimes and increased her private snacking. Cleaning the kitchen after dinner gave her first pick of the leftovers. Some of the tastiest tidbits never even made it to the refrigerator. By the time she turned the kitchen light out each night, she felt full and relieved that she had control over at least one part of her life . . . what she ate.

By June tenth, school was out for the summer. On the fifteenth, Mama drove Symphony halfway to Granny's. Gray and Austin met them just south of Valdosta, Georgia, and took her the rest of the way.

"Listen to your Granny," Mama said, kissing Symphony goodbye.

"I always do," Symphony said, getting into the back of the gold and white '55 Chevy.

"We'll take good care of her, Sis," Austin said. "Don't you worry 'bout a thing. And to keep her busy, we got a job lined up for her at Manley Davis' chicken farm. She's in double digits now so Manley says she can be a gutter."

"Austin!" Mama said, rolling her eyes. "Don't you get her goin'." She bent down and looked through the window at Symphony. "I love you, sweetie. Have Granny call me when you get there, okay?"

"Okay, Mama."

Gray waited for Mama to drive away before he pulled back onto the highway. Austin continued to go over the details of Symphony's summer job.

"Really?" Symphony asked. "A real job?"

"You betcha," Austin said with a chuckle.

"What's a gutter?"

"Oh. You don't know? Well, that's where you pull all the guts outta the chicken. It's not too bad bein' they're already dead 'n all."

Symphony's eyes opened wide. "Do I have to? Can't I just feed the live chickens or something?"

"Okay, Austin," Gray said. "Knock it off." He looked in the rearview mirror at Symphony. "He's just pullin' your leg, honey. He wouldn't tease ya if he didn't love ya."

"That's right," Austin turned to grin at her. "Hey, are either of you gettin' hungry?"

"I am," Symphony said. She hadn't eaten since breakfast.

At that very moment, they passed a road sign. Gray looked at Austin. "Let's fill up at this Sinclair station and pick up some Co-co-lers and peanuts. Then, we can wait and have supper at Ezell's. You all right with that, honey?"

Everybody knew Ezell's hushpuppies were the best God ever created. "Okay," she said.

Three hours later, they were sitting on the front porch of the restaurant waiting for a table to empty. Once inside, it was worth the wait. As country music wailed in the background, a waitress in a red gingham dress set three quart-sized glasses of sweet tea in front of them. Then, she brought a serving bowl of coleslaw and another heaped with still-steaming hushpuppies. Symphony bit into the crispy, deep-fried outer bark. "Um." The oniony cornmeal center was just moist enough. "Yum." By the time their dinners arrived, they were well on the way to stuffed-dom.

Austin continued to eat long after Gray and Symphony stopped. "There's only one thing tastes better than fresh catfish you caught yourself," he said. "That's fresh catfish someone else cleaned and fried for you."

An hour later, they pulled into Granny's yard. Symphony was the first inside, carrying the leftovers. "I hope you haven't eaten, Granny," she said with a smile when she found her grandmother in the kitchen.

Granny peeled back the aluminum foil and peeked inside. "You stopped at Ezell's?" She turned the oven to three-fifty, set the food on a pie pan and slid it onto the top rack.

"Yep," Austin said, poking his head into the room. "I tried to get Gray and Symphony to leave you a couple more fish but they were just too hungry."

"It wasn't Uncle Gray and me."

"I know, sweetie. I've been feedin' Austin since he was a baby. He never gets full." With the food out of her hands, Granny grabbed Symphony and gave her a huge hug. "We better call your mama and tell her you're here. How was the ride up?"

Symphony giggled. "I could just listen to Austin and Uncle Gray for hours."

"Well, if you stay the full month, I'm sure you'll have your fill of both of 'em."

⌘　⌘　⌘

As it turned out, Manley Davis didn't even *have* a chicken farm. Austin had just made it up, which was a relief to Symphony. Besides, at twelve, she couldn't have a real job anyway. Granny let her sleep in for a few days but, before the week was over, Symphony was up before daylight helping with chores. The weather was cooler than normal for the end of June which meant more energy for play in the afternoon.

Her cousins, Randy and Barry, had found two soap barrels during the school year and stored them in Granny's shed. One day, when they bored of playing tag and good guy-bad guy, they remembered the thick-sided cardboard barrels and, taking Symphony along, they pushed them up the highest hill on the school grounds.

"Hold this one while I get in," Barry ordered. "But don't let go till I say." Randy and Symphony held it still. "Geronimo!" Barry hollered. Then, he squealed like a girl all the way to the bottom.

"Wanna be next?" Randy asked Symphony as Barry pushed his barrel back up the hill.

It didn't look like fun to Symphony. "No," she said. "I'll just watch for awhile."

Once her cousins had taken the ride several times and were too dizzy to do it again, Symphony decided to try. Reluctantly, she slid into the barrel.

"Make sure you keep your arms inside," Randy said, giving her a push.

"And bend your knees to help hold you in!" Barry shouted as Symphony started down the hill in the cardboard cylinder.

She wanted to laugh but her body wouldn't let her. As the barrel picked up speed, her mind filled with the swirling blue-gray mist she always saw when she tried to concentrate on her gift. From that mist appeared the most beautiful boy she'd ever seen. The corners of his pale blue eyes crinkled as he smiled at her. Then she saw herself a few years older. His arm was around her shoulder. She felt warm, safe. Then—

*Thunk!* The barrel stopped at the bottom of the hill, bumping against the base of a small pine.

"Symphony?" Randy and Barry ran down the hill toward her. "Are you okay?"

And when she didn't answer... "Symphony!"

She slid out of the barrel and grinned. "I wanna go again!"

⌘　⌘　⌘

The three of them spent many afternoons at the schoolyard on that hill. Sometimes while Symphony was dizzy, she saw the beautiful boy. Other times she didn't. But his image was permanently etched into her heart and mind. He was something to look forward to. A promise that she wouldn't always be alone, that life would get better.

July sizzled. For the Fourth, they had a fish fry in Granny's back yard and made strawberry and peach ice cream with the hand-cranked freezer. Austin had fireworks, mostly firecrackers and cherry bombs. Symphony hated the loud ones so when the bottle rockets and sparklers were gone, she went inside with Granny to clean up the supper dishes.

"You know, sugar," Granny said, raking scraps into the pig's bucket. "I haven't heard you talk about one single dream the whole time you've been here. Are you still having them?'

"Yes, ma'am." Symphony turned away from Granny and began clearing the rest of the table. "But sometimes I wish I wasn't. Ever since I tried to help Darla…"

Granny pulled an apron over her head and tied it behind. "Now tell me what happened. Who's Darla?"

Symphony told her the story of Darla and her brother. "I tried to help her and I tried to help her brother. Then, everybody was mean to me. So what I've been doin' is trying to find a way to use it to help me sometimes. Then I don't have to worry so much about people like Darla and her friends. See, Granny, if I always knew where they were then I could go another way and I wouldn't run into them."

Granny's eyes were glistening with tears as she listened to Symphony. "I'm so sorry you're havin' such a hard time, baby, but you have to understand. Your gift isn't *for* you. It's for you to give to others. If you start tryin' to use it for yourself, there's no tellin' what'll happen. I know it's hard to be your age and have to think about something in a grown-up way, but try and look at your gift like this: Imagine God gave you a mirror and when he shined the sun on just you, you held that mirror in such a way that it made the whole sky light up. Then, suppose one day, you got tired of holding the mirror that way and just decided to look at yourself instead. Well, because you were so busy looking at yourself, the whole day would be dark for everyone else. How long do you think it'd take God to give that mirror to someone who didn't mind holdin' it just right?

"I just wanna be like everybody else, Granny." Symphony sat down at the table and buried her face in her hands.

Granny sat down next to her. "Well, baby, you're not like everybody else. You have something special."

Symphony looked up and shook her head. "I don't wanna be special!"

Granny patted her shoulder. "I know when those kids get to actin' like jackasses you're wishin' you were just like 'em. But you're not. You could never be a jackass—not even if you worked real hard at it."

"I don't wanna be that, either."

"Good. Just be who you are, baby. Just be who you are."

# CHAPTER TWELVE

THE SUMMER NEITHER dragged nor rushed by. It took its time like a stream of poured honey, each day more golden than the ones that had passed.

Symphony and Granny began their gardening each morning as soon as it was light, and finished before noon. Sometimes, they just weeded and watered. After lunch, if there was nothing to snap, jelly, string, shell or preserve, Symphony often went fishing with Gray or Austin. The rest of the day was spent building up a sweat playing games with Randy and Barry—all of which involved running.

The week after the Fourth of July, Mama called. As Granny talked to her, Symphony stood close by trying to piece together the conversation, using the only side she could hear. Just as she was about to give up and move on, Granny handed the phone to her.

"Are you having a good time, sugar?" Mama asked.

"There's so much fun stuff to do here, Mama. I been thinkin'. You should let me bring Uncle Gray and Austin home with me. They take me fishin' whenever I want."

Mama laughed.

"When'll you be here? We usually come in July. Don't we?"

"Well, that's what I called about. We'd planned on next week, but something happened at your father's job. It seems he can't take his vacation until the middle of August."

"Can't you come without Daddy?"

"Your father and I talked about that. He'd rather I wait until we can all ride up together. But if you're homesick, I could ask Gray to meet me in Valdosta like he did on your way up."

"That's okay, Mama. But could you give Therese Granny's address so maybe she'll write me a letter?"

"I'll have Daniele take it to her today. You need anything else?"

"Can I talk to Jeanne for a minute?"

For a moment, there was silence on the line. In the background Mama said, "Say hello so she knows you picked up."

"Hello?" Jeanne said in a meek voice. She and Symphony had never talked to each other on the phone and she didn't know what to say.

"Hey," Symphony answered. "Is Daddy home right now?"

"No. He's still at work."

"Good," Symphony said, relieved that they could speak without the fear of him overhearing. "Is he being nice?"

"Sometimes. I wish I was in Alabama with you."

"I wish you were here, too. Maybe they'll let us both come next summer. Remember what I told you before I left. If you're reading, Daddy kinda ignores you. So read a lot, okay?"

"Okay."

"And you can borrow any of my books you want. They're in that big box in the bottom of my closet. Dani'll show you where."

"Thanks, Symphony. Mama wants the phone back. I miss you."

She wasn't ready to let Jeanne go. "Miss you more. And I'll be home before you know it."

"All right, sweetie." Mama was back on the line. "We need to get off this phone or the long distance bill'll be through the roof. Are you sure you're all right staying? I mean, it's almost another month."

"I'm sure, Mama. I miss you guys sometimes, but mostly I'm havin' fun. Love you."

"I love you, too, sugar. Bye, bye." With a click, Mama was gone.

For a moment, Symphony was down-hearted. *There's nothing wrong at Daddy's work, he just doesn't want me home.* Then, she glanced outside where Randy and Barry were rolling the cardboard soap barrels up the hill across the street. "Granny? Can I go play now?"

"Drink a big glass of water first," she called from the rocking chair in her bedroom. "It's pretty hot out there today."

"Yes, ma'am," Symphony answered. She was thirsty. After two glasses, she could hear the water sloshing in her belly as she walked to Granny's room and poked her head through the doorway. "Did Mama tell you I'm stayin' till the middle of August?"

"Yes she did. And I told her I couldn't imagine the rest of the summer without you. I don't know what I'm gonna do when I have to send you back for school."

"I love this summer," Symphony said, skipping down the hall. "See ya later, Granny." She let the screen door slam behind her. "Wait for me." She crossed the road and the field in a flash, headed for their favorite barrel-riding spot. As she ran, her shorts slid down on her hips. She pulled them up and kept going. When they slipped again, she was irritated. She tucked the top of them into her panties, but that only held for a second or two. She stopped, undid her ponytail, gathered up the loose section of her waistband and tightened the rubber band around it. Then, she blasted toward Randy and Barry, not slowing until she reached the top of the hill.

"You're 'bout the fastest girl I ever saw," Randy said.

*Then why am I always the last one picked for dodgeball?*

⌘ ⌘ ⌘

Symphony wiped beads of perspiration with the back of her hand. "Granny, there's something wrong with my shorts." She swept her damp, blonde hair behind her ears. "Do you think you can fix 'em?"

"Give 'em to me tonight and I'll see. Could be the elastic's worn out."

But worn out elastic wasn't causing the problem. *It* was all those afternoons spent racing and climbing with her two country cousins who knew just how to alleviate boredom over a long, hot summer. *It* was the fact that Granny needed her help in the garden every morning. *It* was the day-to-day happiness that comforted her outside of the kitchen. And *it* wasn't a problem. *It* was a solution.

If Granny noticed Symphony was shrinking, she never said a word about it. She just dusted off her old pedal powered sewing machine and took in a seam or two, until Symphony's shorts stopped falling down.

The night before Mama, Daddy, and the rest of the kids arrived in Alabama, Granny closed herself up in the sewing room for what seemed like forever. Every half hour or so, Symphony would ask, "Can I come in, Granny?"

"Not yet, child. Give me just a little bit longer."

When the door finally opened, Granny poked her head out. "Close your eyes," she said, beaming at Symphony.

Symphony did as she was told.

Granny moved toward her, limping in shoes that always fit at breakfast, but were too small by sundown. The floor groaned and shifted. Then, Symphony smelled the sweetness of her grandmother's snuff.

"Okay, you can open 'em now."

Granny stood right in front of her, holding a brand new dress. It was turquoise, Symphony's favorite color, and printed with a busy pattern of small black paisleys, each with a lavender center.

Granny grinned. "The fabric looks just like you. Well, what do you think?"

"I love it, Granny." It was a beautiful dress. Pretty, but not in an elementary school way—more like something the girls in junior high would wear. She stared at it for a moment in awe. Then her lip began to quiver.

"Aw, sweetie, what's the matter?" Granny asked.

"I think it might be too small."

"It's not. I measured it by the shorts you've been wearin'. You'll see. Go try it on."

Symphony took the dress into the bathroom and laid it over the towel rack. Slowly, she took off her blouse. She pulled down her shorts and let them fall to the floor. She opened the zipper, pulled the dress over her head, and smoothed it against her body. If anything, it was a little loose. *Granny's right!* But would it still fit when it was zipped up? She opened the bathroom door. "Granny, I can't get the zipper all the way."

"Come here. I'll do it." As Symphony approached, Granny's smile seemed to grow. "Turn around a minute."

Symphony gritted her teeth and crossed her fingers. When the zipper was zipped, the dress hung just right, the way a dress should.

Granny gave her a nudge. "Let's go look in the full-length mirror."

The two of them walked to the corner of the bedroom where Granny stood gazing over Symphony's shoulders. "You're so pretty. You look just like your Mama did at your age. "

Symphony couldn't remember ever hearing those words spoken about her. She stared at her thinner image for a moment before her smile crested. *This dress is like magic!* "Thank you so much, Granny."

"Oh, girl." Symphony and Granny turned to find Austin watching them from the hallway. "Look at you! Those boys in seventh grade won't know what hit 'em."

Symphony blushed. "You think so?"

⌘   ⌘   ⌘

The next afternoon, the rest of the Webers arrived.

Mama hugged Symphony for a long time. "I missed you." Other than Jeanne, no one else made much of a fuss. Although, on occasion Symphony would look up to find Mama or Dani staring at her.

She was glad to see most of her family but their weeklong visit seemed an imposition on her life there with Granny. The house was too crowded and the days seemed to disappear before she got to play in the afternoon. And one on one talks were out of the question. Someone else was always sitting next to Granny.

On Symphony's last night in Alabama, Granny pulled her aside to the porch swing where she'd had the dream about the boys and the Chattahoochee. "You've had a happy summer," she said. "Not too many dreams and lots of time away from worry to rest and heal your spirit."

"Granny?"

"What, sweetie?"

"I don't wanna go home."

Granny sighed and began to rock the swing back and forth. "I wouldn't trade this summer for anything, baby. But you're ready to go home. That light's back in your eyes. You're stronger than you were when you got here and, if *you* know that, other people'll see it, too. You've got a big year comin'. Junior high. Some days'll be good and some won't. But no matter what, remember this: you don't have to be like everybody else to be happy. People who are different make some of the biggest and best things happen.

So, go back to Florida tomorrow and know that I'm gonna miss you somethin' terrible." Granny put her arm around Symphony. Symphony leaned against her.

"I love you, Granny."

They sat there, the chain of the swing groaning as they rested in the moment. Then Symphony sat up and looked at Granny.

"Ya know, I was thinkin'. If we do this again next summer, can Jeanne come too?"

Granny chuckled. "We'll have to see about that when it gets closer."

⌘　⌘　⌘

The ride home was excruciating. For eight grueling hours, Joe fussed. He was tired of sitting still, but refused to sleep. Jeanne and Leesa argued over everything from crayons and coloring pages to who had to pee the worst. Dani and Symphony lay in the back of the station wagon. As Daddy cursed at Mama for telling him the wrong way to turn, and at the kids in the back seat for fighting and complaining, Dani shared every juicy morsel of gossip she'd heard while Symphony was in Alabama. Most of it involved people Symphony didn't even know.

They pulled into the driveway about seven in the evening. Mama threw some hotdogs on to boil and they called that dinner.

Afterward, as Dani and Symphony unpacked their suitcases, Symphony looked up to find Dani gawking at her.

"What?" Symphony asked.

"I could tell you'd lost a little weight but . . . I think you're skinnier than me," Dani said, stuffing some of her clothes into a drawer and the rest into the wash pile.

"Nunh-uh." Symphony checked her sister's expression and was happily surprised. Dani seemed serious.

"Yeah-huh! Try a pair of my shorts. Here. How 'bout these stripedy ones. I don't really like 'em."

Symphony put them on. They zipped and buttoned with room to spare.

"See. I told ya." Dani giggled. Not because she was excited about Symphony's weight loss, but because, more than anything, Dani enjoyed being right.

Sometime during the night, Jeanne tapped Symphony on the shoulder. Her eyes were worried. "I had a bad dream. I was scared to wake up Mama or Daddy."

The house had been closed up for the trip and was still hot inside, like a Dutch oven. Symphony was already drenched in sweat. She shifted over to make room. "You can sleep with me." When Jeanne had settled into slumber again, Symphony moved to the hard terrazzo floor. At least it was cool.

She awoke in the morning, ready to call Therese. When she realized it was only six o'clock, she moved back to the bed, which was now a tolerable temperature. Just before eight, when she heard Daddy leave for work, she got up and went to the front window. A mist of rain was falling on one side of the yard, but the other side was still dry as if an invisible wall stood between the two sections. The shower hovered for a few moments, then stopped completely.

She walked to the refrigerator, opened it, and looked inside. There was a strangeness about the action. It seemed foreign, unnatural. She closed the refrigerator and went to the television. As she turned it on, the same feeling washed over her. If she were in Alabama, she would be helping Granny in the garden just about now. She walked outside and turned on the hose. She watered the flowers and bushes, then the lawn. By the time she was done, everyone in the house was awake and breakfast was ready.

At ten, she called Therese.

"I can't believe you're finally home," Therese said. "Are you as excited as I am?"

"About being home? Yeah. I miss my granny, though."

"No, silly. About junior high."

"I'm a little nervous about it," Symphony said.

"Didn't you get my letter?"

"You wrote me a letter?"

"Well, yeah!" Therese said. "So I guess you didn't get it. You're not gonna believe this."

"Believe what?"

"My dad changed his mind. Now he's decided the kids in Catholic school get in more trouble than the ones in public school. So he said I can go to Parkway next year."

Symphony laughed. Starting junior high with Therese would make the change a whole lot easier. And it did.

⌘　⌘　⌘

Symphony had never been so thin. Her sun-bleached hair, which Mama usually kept short, fell straight past her shoulders. As she got ready for the first day of school, she studied herself in the mirror and smiled.

That morning, Parkway Junior High was complete chaos. Symphony, wearing the dress Granny had made, sat with Therese as seventh graders from five different elementary schools poured into the auditorium. There, they were stirred together and sent forth to find classes and get to know each other. For Symphony, junior high was truly a fresh start. All of her classes were filled with total strangers. But that fresh start didn't apply to everything. As soon as school started, her dreams began again.

None of the other students knew it but Elaine, one of the girls in Symphony's Science class, was sick with something called cancer of the blood. She'd lost her hair and wore a wig. In Symphony's dream she was an old woman with lots of grey curls.

Symphony still dreamed about dates for the occasional pop quiz. As usual, she knew everyone's score before tests were ever taken. And on the best nights, the eyes of that beautiful boy would smile at her as she slept.

But more often than not, she dreamed about the boy whose mother drank the whiskey, the boy who was sent out after dark to find his little brother, the boy she had been trying to identify since the dream first began. One night, she envisioned herself being picked up by a large bird that flew over the boy as he walked away from the house. When he turned his flashlight toward the road in front of him, the bird set Symphony down a few inches behind.

She touched the boy's shoulder. He turned with a glare.

"Whadda ya want, Weigh-big?"

It was Greg Stanton.

# *CHAPTER THIRTEEN*

SYMPHONY FROZE IN the dream just as she had that day in class when Greg Stanton rubbed his hand against her crotch. His hardened gaze seemed to hold her. Like a rat swallowed tail-first by a snake, all she could do was wait.

Her heart pounded as she remembered the beginning of the dream. The woman had threatened to hit him. Fear sent him back out into the dark night. She studied his face. *He's scared too.*

He seemed to read the change in her expression. His blue eyes softened. He swept his dirty blonde hair to the side and surveyed the vacant street. "I can't find him," he said, beginning to walk ahead. "He isn't anywhere."

"Who?" Symphony called out.

He kept moving.

She ran to catch up. "Wait!" But when he stopped and turned his head to look at her, he had Mama's face.

"Wait? Don't you dare take that tone with me, young lady!"

Symphony opened her eyes. "Mama," she said. "I musta been dreaming."

"I don't care what your reason is. This is the third time I've called you two this morning. If you miss the bus, you're both losing privileges. You hear me?" Mama stepped into the hallway. "Tell me to wait," she grumbled, disappearing in a slap of flip-flops.

Dani lay silent, the covers pulled over her head. She seemed to have missed the entire episode. Symphony flipped the radio on and out flowed The Beach Boys' *Sloop John B*. She turned up the volume.

Dani shot out of bed, each hair pointing in a different direction. "What time is it?"

"We're runnin' late," Symphony warned. "Mama says if we miss the bus we're in trouble."

"Shit." Dani dashed for the door. "I get the bathroom first."

"Girls," Mama shouted from the kitchen. "You have twenty-five minutes till the bus comes."

Three weeks into the school year, Symphony was still very fussy about the outfits she wore. Before bedtime, she would mix, match, and lay her clothes out. This morning, that gave her an advantage over Dani. She got dressed, carried her school books to the table by the front door then stood outside the bathroom doing the full-bladder dance as she waited for Dani to finish. After a few moments, she knocked. "How much longer are you gonna be in there?"

"I don't know," Dani groaned. "I have a huge pimple right on the end of my nose."

"I'll bet it's not that bad. Let me see." It was really a ploy to get Dani to open the door, and it worked. Dani stood poised in front of the sink, her dark curls and brown eyes, wild. She was poking at the bright red spot with the point of a diaper pin. Symphony rushed past her to the toilet. "If you stop messin' with it, it probably won't be so red."

"How would you know, miss perfect complexion?"

Symphony squeezed between Dani and the mirror to wash her hands. "Aren't you gonna eat breakfast?"

"I doubt it." Dani wiped a small glob of toothpaste onto the tip of her nose.

"Well, I am. Mama made eggs and toast. Can't you smell it?"

"I don't have time," Dani said. "You'll understand when you're older."

Symphony shrugged. "I'll come back after I eat."

By the time breakfast was over, Dani had washed the toothpaste off her nose. "How does it look now?"

The bump was still red, but it seemed smaller.

"Wow. I didn't know toothpaste could make a pimple shrink," Symphony said, stashing the remedy for sometime in the future. "Here. I brought you a piece of toast."

"It's coming around the corner, girls," Mama hollered from the living room.

Dani and Symphony grabbed their books and ran for the bus.

⌘ ⌘ ⌘

That day, during fourth period, the fire alarm sounded. "I'm sure it's just a drill," Elaine said to Symphony as the students in their class formed a line and exited the building. "My mom says the only reason they do it is so if there ever is a fire, we'll all think it's just a drill. Then no one panics."

"That kinda makes sense," Symphony said, following along behind. They stood in orderly rows on the basketball court, along with the other seventh graders awaiting Principal Robertson's permission to re-enter the building.

"Symphony!" a girl shouted from somewhere in the crowd.

Elaine adjusted her shiny black wig and tapped Symphony on the shoulder. "I think that girl in the green skirt is calling you. See her?" She pointed a few lines away.

Symphony peeked between the students crowded onto the blacktop. She finally spied the color green. Above it, she found Joanie's smiling face. "Hi." She glanced around. "Where's Martha?"

"Way over on the other side," Joanie answered. "She's not in any of my classes this year."

"I haven't seen either one of you since sixth grade," Symphony said. "Look for me at lunch tomorrow. Okay?"

"Okay. Jeez, I miss you. I'm flunking all my pop quizzes."

Symphony laughed.

"What'd she mean by that?" Elaine asked.

"Uh." She leaned her head to the right. "We, um, used to have a kind of study group."

"Her name's Joanie, right?" Elaine gently tugged at the right side of her jaw-length wig, then pulled a compact mirror out of her pocket and checked the results. "She's in my Social Studies class. She seems nice."

"She's really sweet." Symphony caught herself staring at Elaine and looked away. She couldn't stop thinking about the blood cancer that was supposed to be a secret. The sorrow must have shown in Symphony's eyes because Elaine asked "Are you upset about something?"

Symphony knew, sooner or later, she'd have to find a way to tell Elaine about her dreams. It wasn't right to let someone go on thinking they were dying when you had seen them at seventy. But she couldn't tell her yet. For the first time in Symphony's life, she fit in. She wasn't about to risk becoming the freak she'd been in elementary school. *Maybe I'll tell her next week.*

"Good afternoon," Principal Robertson's voice boomed from a megaphone.

"Great fire drill today, students. We beat last year's fastest time, but I'd still like to trim a few minutes off the total. You did a pretty good job of staying in order. Now let's see if we can do as well on the way *back* to our classrooms."

Lines of students filed into the school just as the bell rang.

"Hey, Weigh-big," someone shouted above the buzz of the crowd. Symphony, positive it was Greg Stanton, looked straight ahead, refusing to acknowledge his meanness. Just outside the boy's bathroom, someone shoved her from behind. She grabbed onto the person in front of her to keep from falling.

"Hey! Whadda ya think you're doin?" The boy turned with a scowl but as soon as he saw Symphony, his whole posture changed.

"I'm sorry," she said. "Someone pushed me."

"Who?" he asked, glancing around.

"I didn't see," Symphony said, "but thanks for keeping me from falling."

And then he smiled. For a moment, she just stood there. Something about him reminded her of the beautiful boy in her dream. But it wasn't him.

"You know who that was, don't you?" Elaine asked dreamily as they gathered their books and left for fifth period.

"No. But he's cute."

"His name is Riley Owens. He's a ninth grader." Elaine turned right and Symphony turned left. "See you tomorrow, Symmie."

*Symmie?* The nickname caught her by surprise and she smiled. "Bye."

Over the next month, Elaine and Symphony began talking on the phone every day. At first, Therese was jealous. That was resolved the night the three of them met at the public library to work on an English project. Before they'd been there an hour, the librarian booted them out. They couldn't stop laughing. From then on, they spent every spare minute together and one day, over a slice of pizza, in the middle of a crowded mall, Elaine told them about her leukemia.

"It's not that I think I'm gonna die or anything," she said. "But, it makes everything else seem not as scary, you know? Like when I wear my purple striped skirt with the green flowered blouse. Who cares if some girls say it doesn't match? And if someone has to tell a jerk they're a jerk, I'll do it. What are they gonna do? Kill me? I try not to do dangerous stuff though, 'cause it makes my mom cry. I wear this wig for her too, even though I hate it. It makes my head sweat. Even when it's cold out. My hair's almost two inches long now. Wanna see it?"

"Right here?" Symphony glanced around. It was noon on Saturday and the food court was packed.

"We could go into a bathroom stall," Therese said.

"Nah!" Elaine pulled out her mirror and made the sides of her hair even. "Maybe by next year I'll look like a girl again, even without this thing." She put the mirror away and stared at Symphony. "How did you know?"

Symphony almost choked on her orange soda. "Know what?"

"That I'm sick."

"I didn't know."

"Yes you did. Sometimes you look at me just like my mom does. No one else knows. So how did you?"

Therese and Symphony glanced at each other. Symphony shrugged. "If I tell you, you have to promise not to say a word to anyone else, no matter what."

"Okay. Well, tell me on the way to the car," Elaine said. "My mom's probably here to pick us up by now." She took the news of her grey curls like a girl who had believed in miracles all along.

⌘　⌘　⌘

At school, Riley Owens began to appear wherever Symphony was. "How ya doin', little sis?" he'd ask. "Anyone givin' you trouble?"

111

"No." And no one was.

"Well, they *better* leave you alone," he'd say, and disappear down one hallway or another.

His protective presence lasted for the rest of the school year. If Darla Terry or Greg Stanton wanted to make Symphony miserable, they didn't try it with Riley around.

But when eighth grade arrived, the story changed. As soon as it became obvious that Symphony's bodyguard had moved on to high school, the old Whispering Hills terrorists began to target her again but with less success than they had previously enjoyed. This time, Symphony had a small army of her own friends, some of whom were popular kids from other schools.

The fat jokes didn't work anymore. Symphony was too thin for them. So Darla tried the wardrobe shaming that had worked in the past. Symphony began trading clothes with some of her wealthier friends. Then, Darla started rumors that one boy or another had a crush on Symphony but she made the mistake of using the name of one of Riley's younger friends. Soon, the rumors stopped.

The next few times Greg Stanton called Symphony, "Weigh-big," in front of a group of boys, no one joined in. In fact, from what Symphony heard, a few of them even voiced their disapproval. He stopped singling her out. But every time she ran into him, he would either smirk or scowl at her. And he always called her Weigh-big in the dream.

One Saturday, she and Elaine spent the night at Therese's house where they could stay up as late as they liked. The next morning, the phone rang early, while it was still dark outside. It rang for a long time before Collette answered.

"Hello." There was a long pause. "Oh, no. I'm so sorry. Should I wake her up? Okay. Is there anything I can do? Well, I'll make sure she's ready. All right. Bye, bye."

Symphony felt a pain in her heart. Something was wrong with someone she loved. She closed her eyes hoping to fall back to sleep, to awaken and find it was just a simple dream. But she couldn't stop listening.

Therese's father met Collette in the kitchen. Coffee was brewing, cups clattered lightly against saucers. As the two adults whispered back and forth, an occasional word or phrase found its way to Symphony—fire— stopped drinking—go up there—service—brother—married today—

bury—instead. She knew from the words that Uncle Gray was gone. *But . . .* She deflated.

Gray had stopped drinking. And he'd finally found someone to love— Sue. Symphony had met her over the summer. Sue and Gray were always laughing about something. *And that time I saw them kiss . . .* It was like they melted into each other the moment their lips touched. Their wedding was supposed to be Sunday. *Today.*

A tear ran down the side of her face. She slid out of bed and got dressed. Down the hall, she found Therese's parents drinking coffee at the kitchen table.

"Morning, sweetheart," Collette said. "Did you sleep all right?"

"Is something wrong?" Symphony asked.

"Your mama needs you at home." Collette stood and picked up her car keys. "Here, let me drive you."

"It's light enough outside. I need to walk."

"Give me a hug, sweetie," Collette said. She wrapped her arms around Symphony and held her tight for a moment. "Call us when you can."

Symphony cut through the backyard. With one last glance at Collette, she started down the street.

It was a grey morning. She made her way home slowly, noticing the mist as it dripped from the leaves of trees onto the sidewalk in front of her. She wondered if every living thing felt sad when someone or something died.

⌘　⌘　⌘

The ride to Alabama was quiet. Even Joe seemed to know it was best to find something to do other than complain. Daddy rubbed Mama's shoulder and called her "Sugarfoot" whenever he spoke to her. Dani and Symphony colored with Jeanne and Leesa, fed them snacks to keep them quiet, and wrote notes back and forth.

Just when it seemed they would never get to Alabama, they turned the corner and there was Granny's house. Uncle Austin and Granny were in the side yard under the apple tree. When Symphony saw them, she felt her stomach sink. She ran to them, sobbing.

Panic pounded in her chest. Uncle Gray's nightmares had finally stopped. She wondered what would happen to stop hers.

The next few days seemed surreal: the mourning, the tears, putting her fishing buddy into the ground and covering him with hard red dirt. But the toughest part was watching Granny cry.

When it was time to go back to Florida, Mama and Joe stayed. "Just for a week or so," Mama pleaded with Daddy. "I called Esther Guttman. She'll help out around the house. And Collette offered to help with the girls."

"Stay," Daddy said, "for as long as your mother needs you." But during the ride home, he began to show himself again and without Mama there to buffer them, his ugly words struck cruel blows.

Mrs. Guttman came in during the day and straightened up the house. Collette was there in the afternoons until Daddy got home. The evenings were hell. After a few beers, Daddy would sleep on the couch as the girls tiptoed around him. If they woke him while doing the supper dishes, he took off his belt and threatened to use it. If they argued with each other, he used it. The first Friday around midnight, the refrigerator door slammed.

"We're out of goddamn salami!"

Dani and Symphony scrambled out of bed.

The bedroom light flashed on. Daddy's bulky frame wobbled in the doorway. "You two. Get over here."

Both girls rushed to him. Dani got there first.

His eyes were angry, red. "Who finished the goddamn salami?" he bellowed, his breath thick with the smell of liquor.

"I don't know, Daddy," Dani said. "I don't think any of us like sala—"

He backhanded her, knocking her face against the door frame. Immediately, her eye bruised.

"I should have known I wouldn't get a straight answer from either one of you. It was probably the fatty who ate it, anyway. Go back to bed. Ungrateful little . . ."

He stumbled down the hall into his room and slammed the door.

"Get some ice," Dani said.

Symphony returned moments later with a popsicle. "There weren't any open ice trays and I didn't want him to hear me. Here. Put this on your eye. I'll check the little sisters."

Jeanne and Leesa were awake, whimpering beneath the covers of Jeanne's bed.

"Sshh," Symphony said as the three of them tiptoed down the hall. "Leesa, you sleep with Dani. Jeanne, get in my bed."

When the little sisters settled down once again, Dani's dry sobs broke the silence.

"Why did he do that?" Symphony whispered. "He's the one who ate it."

"Because he can," Dani whispered back. "Because he can."

# CHAPTER FOURTEEN

GIVING DANI A black eye must have shaken Daddy up. There was no way he could take it back and his early morning, "I'm sorry but . . ." hadn't made the bruise go away.

He didn't tell them to lie about what had happened but, when Therese showed up at their house the next day, the truth just wouldn't form into words. Dani was sitting on a swing when Therese walked into the back yard.

"No one answered the door so I just followed your voices. Whatcha doin'?" When she saw Dani her eyes widened. "Oh my gosh! Is that a black eye?"

"Yeah," Symphony said, picking up a rubber exercise cord. "We were fighting over this and it slipped out of my hand." She looked away, hoping Therese didn't notice the embarrassment rising in her cheeks. Symphony had never lied to her best friend.

Dani glanced at Jeanne and Leesa who were perched on the slide, taking every lesson they could from the situation. "I'm hungry," she said. "Let's go get some lunch."

"Wait." Therese hurried over to the swing. "Let me see." She grimaced. "Does it still hurt?"

"No. But I don't wanna go to school on Monday. I look awful. And everyone's gonna ask me what happened."

"Couldn't you cover it up—put make-up on it or something?" Therese brushed her finger lightly over it. "Let's ask my mom to take us to the drug store."

"You think some pancake make-up would hide it?"

"My mom'll know what to do. She used to do make-up for actors in plays."

By Sunday night, Collette and the girls had found the perfect way to make the black eye disappear. "Now, tell me again. How did you do this?" she asked, applying a thin coat of white lipstick to the discolored area.

"Mom," Therese protested. "She's already told you twice."

For the rest of the time Mama was in Alabama, Collette and Mrs. Guttman hovered close by. They alternated. One night, all four girls would have dinner with the Guttmans, staying until everyone's homework was done. Then, Esther walked them home for baths and bedtime. The next evening, the process was repeated, only this time it was at Therese's house. As for Daddy, he got leftovers, but he didn't complain. In fact, he didn't utter a foul word for at least a month.

Mama and Joe stayed with Granny a total of three weeks. By the time they took a Greyhound home, Dani's black eye had healed and Symphony had begun to eat her way into forgetting it. Mama, oblivious to the trauma in her absence, was happy to see everyone—including Daddy.

With Mama and Joe back home, Symphony wasn't as restless. Dreams came every night, sometimes more than one. A few of them were terrifying, but they were all confusing—especially the one about her.

*She was young, maybe six or seven, walking down a dirt road lined with huge oak trees. Just ahead, she could see a clearing. In the center was a small blue lake. She glanced at her reflection in the water, then stripped to her underwear and waded in. The padding of fat that had plagued her throughout elementary school was back, the concentration of it around her waist. When the water was up to her hips, she dove in, emerging a few years older. Her breasts had grown and she was thinner. On the shore, her clothes were gone, but there was a new outfit. She put it on quickly, eyes searching for whoever had left it. But she was alone.*

*The sun rose higher overhead and the road grew dusty. Around the next curve she found a large brimmed hat with a shiny lavender band. She put it on and, feeling lighter, strolled on, humming as she went, stopping only when the road forked.*

*To her right, stood Greg Stanton. "Help me," he demanded.*

*On the left, the beautiful boy's smile beckoned her. She started toward him.*

*"Weigh-big would have helped me," Stanton growled, but as she stepped away from him he grew silent.*

*The beautiful boy was right in front of her. Twice he stretched his arms toward her, but she was out of reach. The third time he tried, she took off her hat and held it out. He grabbed it and tugged her closer. "For me?" he asked with a grin. He put the hat on and held her hand. When Symphony looked up, it had become a baseball cap. Together, they passed the fork in the road. She gazed at the spot where she'd left Greg Stanton and wondered when they had turned around?*

*The air seemed cooler and the sweetness of springtime rode on the breeze. The fields were dotted with flowers in bloom. They stopped on the roadside and he broke a sprig of Forsythia for her. She gazed into his pale blue eyes for a long while before she realized she was staring again at the cool lake in the clearing. When she looked up, he was gone and she was holding the baseball cap.*

⌘　⌘　⌘

Throughout seventh and eighth grade, there had been intermittent rumors about Symphony's psychic abilities. Once in a while someone she knew would ask her whether so-and-so liked them or whether she knew what questions would be on this or that test.

"Sorry," Symphony would answer. "It doesn't work that way. I have to dream about something to know it." That was a lie, but individual predictions required a great deal of concentration and left Symphony feeling used. Besides, her friends had done a good job of making light of her abilities and she didn't want to call attention to them.

On occasion, she found it necessary to corner someone and advise them with statements such as, "Don't ride your bike after school for a while," or "Stay away from Hearth Street," or "Your mom needs your help. Talk to her." Those recipients of her gift usually seemed grateful afterward. But then, there was Jason Bender.

In a dream, Symphony had seen his mother crying as she searched in desperation for a lost earring, part of a set her grandmother had given her.

"It's in the litter box," Symphony told Jason. "The cat buried it in there."

In the lunchroom the next day, Jason confronted her. "You're a witch," he yelled. "The earring was just where you said. And now my dad made Mom throw it out. He says you get your power from the devil."

119

Symphony shrunk in her chair.

"Well if that's the case," Therese said, raising an eyebrow, "then you'd better be nice to her."

"Yeah," Elaine agreed. "*If* you want to keep all your body parts." She cackled as Jason walked away.

"Thanks, you guys." Symphony sat up, red-faced. "But did you have to throw in the body parts thing, Elaine? What if he tells his dad?"

But there was no slip from the principal's office requesting Symphony's presence, nor was there an angry phone call to her parents. So, she stopped worrying about it and decided to be a bit more cautious about who she helped in the future.

⌘　⌘　⌘

The rain bulleted sideways making puddles in the windowsills. Dani was away at a slumber party. Symphony lay in bed soaking in the perfume of rain on baked earth as she read the book she'd smuggled into her room earlier.

"You gotta read this!" Therese had said, handing her the condensed version of *Joy In The Morning*. "Some of the parts are kinda—well, you know. Your mom probably wouldn't let you read it." Symphony was still waiting for a question and answer session similar to the one Therese had gotten at the start of her first period. Mama had improvised on Symphony's big day, giving only a crash course on how to use a sanitary pad and a lecture on the importance of hygiene. No egg, no sperm, no sex, no where babies come from. Elaine and Therese had filled her in on the details in advance. Until then, the closest she'd come to the subject of reproduction was a glimpse of two dogs stuck together on the front lawn.

*Mama and Daddy had to do that at least once to get each of us. Yuck!* But, apparently some people did it just for fun, although Symphony couldn't imagine why.

⌘　⌘　⌘

She dozed off, awakened just before midnight by the silence of the house. The evening rain had rinsed the dirt off the screens, then stopped, leaving cooler air and brown pools on the floor below the window.

Symphony unlocked the door and opened it a crack. The living room was dark and quiet, no dusty blue television glow. She slipped down the hallway into the bathroom and grabbed a dirty towel to clean up the puddles in her room.

Returning to the bedroom, she locked the door, blotted some of the water out of Dani's soaked bedspread, dried the floor, then settled back down with her reading. Moments later, the rain began again and its gentle tapping weighed on her eyelids. She hid the book inside her nightstand drawer and turned out the light.

*"Didn't you hear me?" A girl with dark hair was standing in the middle of the street shouting at Symphony. "I called you a liar."*

*Suddenly, the sky was blue-black and lightning began to flash. She noticed the smell of sulphur, followed by an odd smoky odor. Symphony wrinkled her nose. There was a strangeness in her chest. She looked down. Blood was dripping from her heart.*

She sat up gasping just as lightning flashed outside the window. She thought about the dream for a moment, turned on the lamp and wrote down the details of it in her nightstand notebook. When she finished, she was still wide awake. She pulled out *Joy In The Morning* and read until she fell asleep with it open on her stomach.

⌘　⌘　⌘

As the end of eighth grade approached, Symphony began to outgrow her clothes again. Her rise in weight seemed to put an awkward distance between her and many of the friends she'd made at Parkway. She wanted to stop snacking, but the harder she tried, the more frustrated she became and the more food she'd sneak. She had planned on spending the summer with Granny but Mama thought it would be too much.

"Not this year, sugar. Your granny still needs some time to adjust to Gray being gone. So does Austin."

"Maybe she needs us to keep her from thinkin' of Uncle Gray, Mama. That would be better, wouldn't it?"

"Some things you just have to get used to, honey. There *is* no easy way. Your granny needs time to think about him—to find a way to keep living where he used to live too. You understand?" There was almost always kindness in what Mama said and did. That's why it was so hard to complain to her.

"But, Mama, I know just how to help her in the garden." Symphony paused, hoping that would change Mama's mind.

Mama just smiled.

"I'm even gettin' pretty good at helping her can stuff." Symphony waited. "And Jeanne doesn't have to go this year. It could just be me."

"No, Symphony," Mama said. "Now drop it." She sealed her decision with a glare. "We'll visit Granny as a family in July. You're not going for the whole summer."

Then and there it was decided. Symphony would be miserable.

June wasn't so bad. Daddy was sent to West Palm Beach for a month to help his company set up a new office. Symphony spent a lot of time on the phone and she slept at Therese's or Elaine's at least one night a week.

The house across the street was sold and by the time the Webers got back from their two weeks in Alabama, a family had moved in.

"They've got three boys, Maisy." Mrs. Guttman shook her head. "Another three boys on this street? God help us all."

Mama laughed. The Guttman boys were always pushing the limits on what their mother told them to do. Sometimes they acted as if they were deaf to her vocal range.

For the next few days, Dani, Symphony, and Jeanne spent every spare minute peeking between the curtains, hoping for a glimpse of the new neighbors. Later in the week, they were packed door to door in the family station wagon, headed out to do some school shopping, when they interrupted a street game of kickball. The teams parted to allow the Webers through. Although the oldest girls nearly broke their necks trying to get a good look, all they saw were the backs of six boys.

It did appear that none of the new boys were old enough for Dani and that turned out to be a good thing. By the time the Westhills had been there a week, Dani had a Friday night babysitting job.

Mr. and Mrs. Westhill left for dinner at six-thirty. Mama sent Symphony over at seven with her sister's plate. A small boy answered the door wearing denim overalls, a matchbox car in his fist. He eyed Symphony with suspicion. "Who're you?"

"I'm Daniele's sister, Symphony." Ever since seventh grade, Dani had insisted everyone outside the family call her Daniele. "What's *your* name?"

"Cody. How old are you?" He turned back to the obstacle course he'd set up for his tiny, red race car, leaving the front door wide.

"Almost Fourteen," Symphony answered, stepping inside. "I'll be in ninth grade this year."

Dani was stretched out on a furry blue chaise lounge, watching the Westhill's color TV. "Come on in," she said, standing to take her supper from Symphony. "You've gotta try this chair. It's really comfy."

Symphony leaned back into the fluffy blue chair. "Oh, my gosh! I could sleep here."

Just then, a gush of music blasted from behind a closed door at the end of the hall. "Can I tell 'em to turn it down again?" Cody asked.

"Yeah," Dani said.

He ran down the hallway. Seconds later he was running back, dodging an airborne pillow. The volume of music doubled. "They won't."

"Tell 'em to come here," Dani said.

Soon, one of the older boys followed Cody into the living room. "My mom said you're not here to babysit us. Just Cody."

Another joined them, tousling Cody's hair. "C'mon. It's Iron Butterfly," he said. "You have to listen to it loud or—" And then, he looked at Symphony. "Hi."

"Hey guys. This is my sister, Symphony. Symphony, this is Mack and that's Bo. They're goin' to Parkway next year."

"What grade?" Symphony asked.

"I'm in seventh," Bo said.

"Eighth," Mack answered. And then Symphony was glad she hadn't spent the whole summer with Granny. Mack smiled at her. His pale blue eyes crinkled at the edges. She'd seen him before. Her beautiful boy had just moved in across the street.

# CHAPTER FIFTEEN

NINTH GRADE CAME with its own set of growing pains. Within Jr. High's eldest burned the need to appear grownup. It was a desire that overrode mere academics. On top of that, the criteria which defined maturity seemed to be based on rebellion rather than responsibility, defiance over deference, and an outspoken confidence in your own rightness.

The kids who were into sports separated themselves from the other students. Mostly they were guys, constantly accompanied by a few envied girls who managed to move, without visible effort, from one hunk to another. Some of the more intelligent boys stopped cutting their hair and traded in their Clark Kent glasses for brass frames in either round or rectangular shapes. Each day seemed to find them more intent on disproving their IQs.

Girls, aside from the beauty queens and the football groupies, let their hair grow long and straight. They wore longer, fuller skirts and, as soon as the school allowed, blue jeans.

"No daughter of mine is wearing dungarees to school," Daddy shouted when Symphony started out of the house one morning dressed in a pair he had discarded.

"But, Daddy, the principal said—"

"I don't give a rat's ass what the principal said. *I* have the last say around here, and *I* say no."

"Yes, sir." She went back to her room. Those jeans were the first comfortable pair of pants she'd had since her last weight gain. Besides all of her friends had promised to wear denim that day.

Daddy was waiting when she stepped out in some brown corduroys. "That's better," he said.

She walked right by him with the jeans stuffed neatly between the pages of her notebook. He couldn't stop her from putting them on at school.

"My parents wouldn't let me," Elaine apologized.

"My dad said no, too," Symphony said. "But he didn't have a good reason so I changed when I got here."

Therese just laughed. "I don't understand why they're making such a big deal out of this. You'd think we'd asked to wear the emperor's new clothes."

As usual, Therese had a remark to break the tension and, chuckling, the three girls went to their homeroom classes. The rest of the day was pretty average except for the fact that Symphony ran into Mack on his way to the office.

"Did *you* know you weren't allowed to smoke in the bathroom at this school?" he asked, nodding toward the teacher who was escorting him down the hall. "Nice jeans."

Symphony was surprised. "You smoke?"

That weekend, she and Mack talked alone in the street.

"Do you smoke?" he asked.

"I did once." She looked down at the ground. "But I was thinking of trying it again."

It was suppertime and Daddy whistled for her. Not a regular whistle but the supersonic "fweeuuuwheet" that pierced eardrums up and down the street each time he called his kids home.

"Doesn't that bother you?" Mack asked.

Symphony cocked her head at him.

"Your father calls you the way most people call their dogs."

"Oh, that," she said, "I hate it," although she'd never given it much thought.

Mack pulled a rubber band out of his pocket and gathered his sand-colored hair into a tiny ponytail in the back. "I heard him yelling at you the other night."

Symphony blushed and looked away.

126

"My dad can be a real jerk sometimes, too. See if you can get out of the house later. After dinner. If you can, I'll try to meet you at the other end of the street. I wanna show you something."

"Okay." Something warm and mushy moved inside Symphony. She joined her family at the table and ate as quickly as possible, avoiding eye contact with her parents and Dani, only involving herself in conversation with Jeanne, Leesa, and Joe. But mostly, she spent her time wondering. *Does he like me yet? How am I gonna get Mama to let me go out? What's he gonna show me?*

"Your Granny called today," Mama said. "Austin ran off and got married."

"To who?" Dani asked.

"Camilla Waters. None of you know her yet. I met her after Gray's funeral. They make each other laugh just like Austin does with all of us. But she knows how to put her foot down, too." Mama grinned and took a sip of iced tea. "She's good for my little brother."

Symphony laughed. As big as Austin was, it was always funny to hear Mama call him little. "When did they get married?" A picture of Uncle Austin flashed in Symphony's mind. He had his arm around a woman who, next to him, looked tiny. Her hand was balled up into a fist. She pretended to punch Austin in the stomach as he grimaced.

"Yesterday," Mama answered. "Symphony, Daniele has plans tonight and I told her you'd do the dishes so she can get ready."

Symphony panicked. "But, Mama. I wanted to—"

"Please, Symphony," Dani was serious. "I'll do them for the next three days."

It was Dani's first car date.

"Of course she will," Mama said. "Won't you, Symphony? It's what sisters do."

*There's no way I can meet Mack if I do.* "Yeah," Symphony answered. *Maybe if I hurry.* She stood and took her plate to the sink, then glanced around to see who else was finished eating.

"Sit down," Daddy ordered. "You don't clear the table while everyone's still eating. What the hell's wrong with you?"

"Nothing," Symphony said. "Sorry." She flopped into her chair next to Jeanne and looked away from Daddy, fearing he would see the frustration in her eyes.

"You're cruisin' for a bruisin'," he boomed. "Look at me."

She glanced at him and away, but she wasn't quick enough. He must have seen a flicker of what she was trying to hide.

"Get over here." Daddy slapped his palms together. His eyebrows scrunched together. His irises changed from dark brown to black.

Symphony knew what was coming.

"It's okay," Dani said. "I'll do the dishes."

"I'll help," Jeanne offered.

They all knew what was coming.

"Look at me!" He exploded.

Symphony felt the glare in her eyes. She looked at the floor, trying to focus on thoughts that would calm her down—flowers, Austin getting married, the sound of Joe's laughter—but she didn't have enough time.

"God dammit! I said—"

She faced him.

"Don't you ever look at me like that again. You hear me?"

"Yes sir."

As the rest of the family looked on, he grabbed her arm, jerked her around, and struck her open-handed on the rear, again and again and again.

She flinched as she felt the first blow sting and burn, the next as the heat increased. After the third, he couldn't hurt her anymore than he already had, her butt was numb.

"Now, you can do the dishes," he said with one final smack. "I think we're all finished eating."

Although everyone else left the room, Daddy remained, watching as Symphony cleared the table. She avoided his eyes and took his plate last, hating the weight of it, just because it was his.

"You think I don't notice the way you're slamming things around? If you break one, you'll pay for it. And I don't mean with your allowance, either."

She slowed her movements but her thoughts raced against him. *You hate me? Well I hate you, too! I HATE YOU!* Screaming it would have felt better. But what good would come of that? She still had to live with him. Finally, he joined Mama and the others in the living room.

With clenched teeth, Symphony washed the dishes, stopping for a moment to listen when Dani's date came. She watched through the kitchen window as the boy opened Dani's door, wishing she was with them as they pulled away. She rinsed the sink full of soapy dishes.

By the time she was finished, the numbness of the spanking had faded to pins and needles. It was getting dark outside. *Too late to meet Mack.* She went to her room, locked the door, and let tears wash the venom from her eyes.

Monday, back at school, Symphony waved at Mack as he walked the other way down a corridor headed for class. He smiled and nodded, his hands too full to wave back. The gym teacher had given a new girl the locker next to Symphony's. "Name's Lilly," she said. Her reddish-brown hair was woven into two braids banded together at the back. "Hey, what happened to your arm?" Lilly's huge dark eyes widened as she moved closer for a better look.

Symphony hadn't noticed the thin bruise lines that wrapped around her arm where Daddy had grabbed her. "It's nothing," she said.

"I've had those kinds of bruises, you know what I mean?" Lilly frowned. "I think I saw you when I was movin' in with my aunt over the weekend. Do you live on Overlook Terrace?"

"Yeah."

"You should come see me sometime. My aunt and uncle are super nice, you know what I mean? And they don't mind if I have company. Besides, I don't have any friends here yet and if I can make some, it'll make me wanna stay, you know? Do you smoke?"

"Not right now. But I'm thinkin' of starting again," Symphony said, remembering her first cigarette with Therese. *Maybe it'll be easier now.* After all, she was a few years older. "C'mon. If we don't get outside, the teacher'll come lookin' for us."

Lilly didn't mention the bruise to anyone. It wouldn't have mattered if she had. Daddy had grabbed Symphony's arm and spanked her. *Who cares?*

⌘　⌘　⌘

The next weekend, Symphony got another chance to talk to Mack.

After dinner on Saturday, Mama and Daddy went shopping for a new car and left the kids at home.

"Mack's out front," Symphony told Dani when she saw him in the road. "Do you mind if I talk to him for awhile?"

"Go ahead," Dani said, "but don't stand out there. If Daddy comes home and sees you together, he'll get mad."

"Hi, Mack," she said, meeting him in the center of the street. "Is there somewhere else we can talk?"

"Yeah," Mack answered, a mischievous glint in his eyes. "I wanted to show you a place I found. It's where I go when my dad gets mean."

They walked to the corner and cut through the driveway of the vacant house where the Hightowers used to live. In the backyard, they climbed the fence and followed a path into the woods. About five steps in, hidden by a clump of bushes and some broken tree branches was a small green rowboat. The word "Freedom" had been painted freehand on the side.

"Well?" he said. "Whadda ya think?"

"It's a boat," Symphony said.

Mack handed her the oars. "Here. Can you carry these?" He dragged the Freedom down the path toward the water. "Come with me and I'll show you the rest."

She caught up with him just as the wooded area opened to the shore of a lake. Glancing across the water, she recognized Empty Island in the center. "Don't you worry about gators?" she asked.

He squinted at her and grinned. "Why? Are you scared?"

"Well, maybe a little."

"C'mon." He nodded toward the lake. "My mom works for the county. They told her all the alligators were moved last year. There aren't s'posed to be anymore in here. Bo and I haven't seen a single one."

"Okay," Symphony said. "As long as the gators are gone."

"Good. What I wanna show you is on the island. Get in."

Mack placed the oars in the boat and held it still until Symphony settled in the front, then he pushed it away from shore and slid in. Facing her, her took the oars and began to row. "Wait'll you see," he said. "You're gonna love it."

Not once did she wonder how he knew whether or not she would love something. Although the two of them were nearly strangers, Mack's appearances in her dreams had made her comfortable with him in a way he hadn't earned. Because she could see them together in the future, she trusted him today.

⌘ ⌘ ⌘

Dani was standing at the picture window when Mack and Symphony disappeared behind the vacant house. Now, the sun was going down and they still weren't back. Dani paced from one end of the living room to the other, glancing, on occasion, at the end of the road where she'd last seen her sister.

Just as she began to chew the nail polish off her thumb, Jeanne walked into the living room. "Symphony's not back?"

"No. And I don't know whether to be mad or worried."

Jeanne twisted a strand of her red hair around her finger. As she and Dani checked the street in front of the house, a strange new station wagon pulled into the driveway, followed by a black Volkswagen.

"Shit!" Dani said. "It's Mama and Daddy. Now what do we do?"

"If they ask," Jeanne said, "just say she's at Therese's and offer to go get her."

"What if I get caught lying?"

But Jeanne had the answer. "Say Symphony *said* she was going to Therese's. Then if she's not there, she's in trouble, not you."

"Wow," Dani said. "Where'd you learn to think like that?"

"I guess I'm just scared enough of what Daddy'll do." Jeanne turned and went to her room.

⌘ ⌘ ⌘

The rowboat reached the island. Mack hopped out and pulled it to shore. They trudged inland about twenty steps where the sandy area ended, then turned left toward the corpse of a lightning scarred tree.

"We painted red spots on the pines so it'd be easier to find. So watch for those. And keep an eye out for snakes," he said, scanning the ground ahead in the failing light. "We'll just be here a minute. I want to make sure you know how to find it. In case you need a safe place."

The next paint spot led them right, into a thicket of spindly oaks. Just past the thicket was a small clearing. "Here it is," Mack said, pointing to a canvas tent fully set up on the floor of the woods. He unzipped the flap and they crouched under the entryway. "There's some cans of food over here, and these blankets'll stay. There's even some matches if you need to build a fire or light a candle. Cool, huh? I wanted to stay and have a smoke with you, but it's startin' to get dark so we better go." Mack followed Symphony out and re-zipped the tent.

⌘ ⌘ ⌘

"Oh my gosh!" Dani said, bouncing in place like a cheerleader on hot coals. "I can't believe we have two cars. Can I get my learner's permit now?"

"You sure can," Daddy said. He was in a wonderful mood—a grand provider who had bought two new cars in one day. "That's one of the reasons we got them both."

"Which one should we ride in first?" Mama asked.

"The Volkswagen," Dani said.

"No. I wanna ride in the black car," Joe argued.

"The black car is the Volkswagen," Jeanne said. "Now, shut-up."

"Jeanne Weber! Watch the language," Mama scolded.

Amidst the bickering, Leesa managed to get her vote in. "I wanna go in the Volk, um Volks, um, the black car, too," she said.

"And Symphony, which car would you like to ride in?"

Dani and Jeanne looked at each other.

Mama walked to the house and called through the front door. "Symphony?"

She turned toward Dani with a confused expression and asked, "Where is Symphony?"

# CHAPTER SIXTEEN

THE SUN SANK and hid behind the curve of the earth as the Freedom carried Mack and Symphony away from Empty Island. The trip over had been exciting. But now, on the way back, tension was thick.

Symphony couldn't stop worrying. *What if Mama and Daddy are home?* She shifted her position in the boat and reached over the side to trail her hand along the cool water.

"Don't," Mack snapped.

The sharp edge of his voice surprised her. She jerked her hand back inside the boat. "Why?"

"Didn't you see that cottonmouth?"

"No." She gasped and shivered as the thick brown snake wove its way through the mud-colored water right where her hand had been just moments earlier. "Are you sure that's what it is?"

"Just look at it. Not many snakes can keep their whole body on top of the water like that. But you shouldn't be sticking your hand in the lake, anyway. There's garfish in here, and terrapin, too. Either one'd be happy for some finger food."

"I didn't know." Silently, she examined her hands, relieved to find them still intact. "I thought since the gators were gone it'd be safe."

"Nope. You *are* from Alabama, right? As much as your daddy loves to yell, you'd think he'd have taught you the important stuff, too."

She felt the fire rise in her cheeks.

"In the south, you always have to pay attention to the water."

Symphony watched the moccasin slither lazily toward the row of houses on the other shore. "That snake just went into Spencer's back yard," she said. "Joe plays there sometimes. I'm gonna have to tell Mama about it."

"What're you gonna say? 'I was in Mack's boat out in the lake and—' Don't worry about it. I'll tell my mom I was messin' around back here and saw the snake. If I know her, she'll have me knocking on doors right after breakfast tomorrow."

When they reached the bank, Mack hopped out of the boat and pulled it onto the slippery mud. "Here. You carry the oars and I'll drag this back into the bushes."

Once the Freedom was hidden, they made their way up the path and over the fence.

"Why don't you hang back just a little," he said. "Let me see if your parents are home." He left her on the back patio and stole carefully through the side yard, coming to rest behind an unkempt camellia bush. "There's two cars in your driveway. But neither one of 'ems yours."

"Oh, no!" *Daddy's gonna kill me.* "I can't just walk up the street."

"No, you can't. Look's like your whole family's standing out front."

"Lemme think." Her face was sweating. She wiped it with the back of her hand. "I know. I'll run around the block and go over the Theodore's fence into my backyard. The back door's always unlocked when we're home."

"Okay. And I'll give you a few minutes before I start up the street."

Symphony ran. She rounded the corner and kept moving toward the center of the block. Every thump of her heart and pang of nausea reminded her why she didn't run more often. She climbed the chain-link fence at the Theodore's just as she had planned, slipped over into her own yard, and cruised through the back door just as Mama called, "Symphony?

Symphony ran all the way through the house and out the front door.

"There you are," Mama said. "We were just taking a vote. Which one of the new cars would you like to ride in first?"

Symphony's breathing was still too rapid from the run. "They're both ours?" she asked, trying not to pant. A pearl of sweat ran down her nose. She wiped it away and studied the shiny black Beetle. It was so different from the other cars they'd owned. "This one." She slid her fingers along the chrome door handle. "It's a Bug, right?"

"Yep," Daddy answered. "Everyone pile in."

And they did. All seven of them were packed into a space no bigger than a phone booth. Mama and Daddy sat in the front seats. Dani, Jeanne, and Symphony sat in the back. Just behind them, Leesa and Joe squeezed into a small storage area.

Daddy backed out of the driveway and into the street. As he let out on the clutch, the car lurched forward and stalled. "Ah, dammit," he said. He started the ignition again just as Mack walked by.

"Cool car, Mr. Weber." Mack grinned and looked into the back seat.

"Thanks, Mack," Daddy answered. "Been fishing?"

"No sir. Why do you ask?"

"Your pants legs are wet. Thought maybe you were wading."

"Oh," Mack said, pausing long enough for the silence to become awkward.

Symphony's cheeks glowed. In a panic, she reached down to feel her pants. They were dry aside from a few splatters of mud. Her heart and breath began to slow to a normal rhythm. When she looked up, her eyes met Mack's.

"I better go in," he said. "I'm sure my mom's wonderin' where I went. You all have a nice night." As Mack turned and walked toward his house, the Volkswagen putt-putted up the street and into the dusk.

Dani and Jeanne shot questioning looks at Symphony as she sat between them "Where were you?" Dani mouthed.

"What took so long? Jeanne whispered in her ear.

Symphony didn't answer, but put her finger to her lips and smiled.

After they circled the neighborhood a few times, Leesa began to complain. "Mama, I've got pins and needles in my legs. Can someone else sit back here now?"

"I'll tell you what," Daddy said. "If you'll sit back there quietly for just a few more minutes, we'll take the other car and go get ice cream cones. Okay?"

Leesa didn't even answer. She just sat still until they returned to the house and moved into the new station wagon. That night, anyone who'd seen them could easily have mistaken them for a happy family. From Daddy to Joe, everyone was beaming.

⌘ ⌘ ⌘

"Where'd you go?" Dani asked as she and Symphony got into bed at the end of the day. "And what'd you do? You were gone forever."

"We were just talking." Symphony said, keeping the evening boat ride to herself. Mack had invited her into his secret haven. Their relationship had begun. She turned out the light and fell asleep thinking of how he'd saved her from the snake, the way he'd helped her get home undetected, and his smile—the one that seemed to erase anything bad.

⌘ ⌘ ⌘

Sunday morning, soon after the Webers were awake, there was a knock at the door. When Jeanne answered it, Mack was standing there, his hair wet and combed to the side as if he'd just gotten out of the shower. "May I speak to your mom for a minute," he asked in a soft voice.

"Mama," Jeanne hollered," Mack's here."

"Good morning," Mama called. "What are you doing out and about so early?'

"Well, yesterday after dinner when I was messin' around down by the lake, I saw a huge cottonmouth go into Spencer's back yard. My mom thought it would be a good idea to let everyone know that there's a poisonous snake around. I've seen Joe playin' over there sometimes."

"Thank you so much," Mama said. "Maybe Spencer will have to come over here and play for awhile."

"You're welcome." Mack smiled. "Well, I have to tell everyone on that side of the street. See you later."

"What a nice boy," Mama said after Mack walked away. "He's got kind eyes, too."

"I don't think so." Daddy walked into the kitchen shaking his head. "If that boy's awake, he's up to something. You can almost see the wheels turning. He's headed for trouble. I'd guarantee it."

Sunday afternoon, the phone rang. "Symphony, it's for you," Mama hollered from the kitchen.

"Who is it?' Symphony asked.

"Sounds like Elaine." Mama basted the chicken, slid it back into the oven, and left the room.

"Hello?"

"Hey, Symphony. Whatcha doin?"

"Hey, Elaine. I was just reading the comics. It's boring. Plus my dad's home."

"Ask your mom if you can come over for a while. I'll call Therese, too."

"I doubt if she'll let me," Symphony said. "You know how weird she is about Sunday dinner."

"I really need to talk to you guys."

"What's wrong?"

"I could have my mom call your mom, but I'd rather not ask her right now."

"I'll be there in a few minutes," Symphony said, hoping Mama would understand.

She hung up the phone and went to the laundry room where Mama was putting wet clothes into a basket.

"You were right. It was Elaine. Something's wrong, Mama. She wants me to come over. Is that okay?"

"Now, Symphony, you know how important Sunday dinner is."

"I know. And I reminded her that you might not let me come. But she says, if you don't, she'll have her mom call you even though she doesn't really want to ask her mom for anything right now."

Mama stopped what she was doing and turned toward Symphony, her light brown eyes revealing just a hint of sadness. "Okay, sweetie. She bent slightly and kissed the top of Symphony's head. "Just make sure you're home before dark."

A soft rain began to fall as Symphony trudged to the corner of the street where Therese was waiting. Together they finished the walk to Elaine's.

"What did she tell you?" Therese asked in a somber tone.

"She wouldn't really say much."

"What do you think it is?"

Symphony started to bite her fingernails but remembered she was trying to stop. "I'm too scared to think about it."

137

"Me too. I can't believe your mom let you skip Sunday dinner."

"Me neither."

Just then, the Westhills drove by. Mack and Bo waved.

Symphony smiled and waved back. "They're pretty nice."

"You think so? Did you know they've both been in the principal's office three times since school started?"

"Three times?" Symphony tried to act nonchalant. "I knew Mack got in trouble once for smoking in the bathroom. But you can't hold that against him. You used to smoke, too."

"I've been meaning to tell you." Therese stopped in the middle of the street. "I started again."

"I've been thinking about it," Symphony said.

Elaine met them on the porch. "I saw you coming. I was hoping we could just go over to the dunes and talk but since it's raining . . . I know. Let's sit in my dad's car."

They all got into the back seat and closed the door. For a while, no one said a word.

"I've never been in here," Therese said. "This is nice. Is it leather?"

"No, I'm sure it's that Naugahyde stuff," Elaine answered. "I'm glad you guys came over. I've been stuck in that house all weekend with my parents. Mom's been crying. Not in front of me or anything but I can tell. My dad's just been quiet. It's driving me crazy."

"What's wrong?" Symphony asked.

Elaine just sat there, breathing. Therese closed her eyes and whispered a Catholic prayer. Symphony waited, hoping for the best.

Finally, Elaine broke the silence. "It's back," she said. "The leukemia is back."

Therese put her arm around Elaine's shoulder and they both began to cry.

"But the worst thing is, the doctor says they don't have anymore treatments that'll work. The only place that can help me is in Tennessee. A hospital called St. Jude." Elaine began to sob. "I told my mom about your dream, Symmie. I told her how I was an old lady. I told her that sometimes when you touch my arm, you can see me old, like that. But, I know she doesn't believe it. She just ran out of the room. She's afraid I'm gonna die. So, I don't wanna go, but I have to."

Symphony took hold of Elaine's hand and squeezed. She closed her eyes, hoping for a glimpse of the elderly Elaine, but it didn't come. "When are you leaving?" she asked.

"Sometime this week."

The three of them held each other and cried until every window in the car was fogged up. The rain came down harder, tapping on the roof above them. They sat back and listened, breathing in, breathing out, until there was a knock on the window. The front door opened and Elaine's dad stuck his head in. "Are you girls okay?"

Elaine nodded.

"What say I take you all down to Krispy Kreme for some hot chocolate and maybe a donut or two?"

"Thanks, Dad," Elaine said.

"Good. I'll just go see if your mother wants something." He closed the door.

"I wish my father was more like yours," Symphony said. "You're lucky, in that way."

"I know." Elaine smiled. "I'm gonna miss you guys so much."

Symphony took her hand again. "I don't know what it'll be like around here without you."

"But you'll come back," Therese said, "after St. Jude."

"And we can send you letters while you're there." Symphony closed her eyes and concentrated. No old lady.

Between the rain and the cocoa and a donut or two, the girls seemed fine until they had to say goodbye. Therese and Symphony wrote their addresses on the inside of a matchbook cover before they got out at Therese's.

"Come see me after school tomorrow," Elaine invited, "if we haven't left yet."

"Thanks, girls," her father said. And with a sad wink he drove away.

"Wanna stop in for a cigarette?" Therese asked.

"Maybe tomorrow," Symphony said. "I've got something I need to do."

She found Mama in the kitchen cleaning up after dinner. "Hey, sugar. How did things go at Elaine's?"

"Mama, can we call Granny?"

"I'm sorry, Symphony. I just got off the phone with her about an hour ago. She asked to speak with you but—"

"I need to talk to her, Mama. Please."

"Well, sugar. I guess I can call her back but why don't you talk to me first? Maybe I can help."

"You can't, Mama. You don't believe in dreams and stuff. But Granny does. I have to know if you dream that something doesn't happen, then later, can it happen anyway?"

"I'll call your grandmother right now." Mama dialed the number and sat guarding the kitchen door. As Symphony explained the situation to Granny, Mama watched, her heart visible in her expression.

"And you're absolutely positive it was Elaine in the dream?" Granny asked.

"Yes, Granny, I'm sure," Symphony said, barely able to hold back her tears. "But now they're saying there's nothing they can do. And when I touch her arm, I don't see the old woman anymore. Have you ever known a dream to change like that?"

"I'm sorry, sweetheart. Life is always changing on us."

Symphony began to cry. "So what you're saying is that she could still die, even though I had that dream? That's not fair, Granny! I told her she would live to be old. God, I hate this stupid gift."

"As you get older, you'll learn how to use it. Before long, you'll be glad you have it."

"I don't think so. I hate it. I have to find out how to make it go away."

She hung up the phone without saying goodbye. As she started toward her room, Mama grabbed her, spun her around, and wiped the tears from her eyes. "You do what you can to help Elaine stay happy," she said.

"I can't even do that, Mama. They're taking her away to St. Jude's."

"When?" Mama asked.

"Maybe tomorrow."

Mama hung on to Symphony until the tears came easy and ran out. "Now, go splash some water on your face while I make a few phone calls."

Mama called Granny to make sure she was okay. She called Collette to see if Therese could skip school the next day.

"Since the girls don't have to get up early tomorrow, why don't they just sleep here tonight?" Collette offered.

"Great idea," Mama said. "I'll bring some snacks when I drop the girls off."

Elaine's father agreed that a small slumber party "will probably make things a little easier on all of them."

So Mama and Symphony picked up Elaine. They stopped at the grocery store to load up on goodies. Within the hour, the girls were at Therese's house for what turned out to be an all-nighter none of them would ever forget.

# CHAPTER SEVENTEEN

M AMA HANDED THE last soapy plate to Dani. "You can afford to be a little more tolerant," she scolded. "Symphony won't be this upset forever. Let's just give her a few more days." She pulled back the kitchen curtains and stared out as the moon brightened in an otherwise empty sky. "Elaine's parents must be terrified." Mama shivered and closed the window as if the breeze were the problem. "Let's talk about something else," she said. "How was school today?"

⌘　⌘　⌘

Elaine and her family pulled out of Titusville on Monday after the slumber party ended. "They'll probably be in Memphis in a couple days," Collette told the girls. "But don't expect to hear from Elaine right after they get there. I'm sure she'll be really busy for at least a week, with doctors and tests and all."

On Tuesday, whispered rumors of "leukemia" spread through school like a virus, turning people who had seldom spoken to Elaine into her *best friends*. "Have you heard from her?" almost-strangers would ask. Symphony and Therese would shrug and shake their heads.

That afternoon, Mack caught Symphony as she walked home from the bus. "I'm sorry about your friend," he said.

"Saying, 'sorry' makes it sound like she's dead—and she's not." Symphony glanced at his face and realized she'd hurt his feelings. "I didn't mean . . . I mean . . . It's just hard." Tears stung her eyes and she turned away. "Thanks." She took a few steps up the driveway.

"Wait," he said. "I just wanted to tell you. If you ever want to get away, you can use Freedom."

Symphony stopped and faced him. "I'd probably sink it and be eaten by snakes and garfish days before anyone even missed me."

"Seriously." No smile played across his lips. His eyes had lost their sparkle. "That's why I took you there. So you'd have a safe place." Mack looked at his feet. "I hear him when he's mad. And I know what it's like." He pushed up his shirtsleeve revealing a circular bruise that was just beginning to yellow. "When mine makes that much noise, he's usually doin' this, too."

Their eyes met again.

"So don't forget about the boat," he said, "just in case, you know?"

"I won't. Thanks." The warmth of his concern eased her as she went inside to do her homework and help with supper.

"Mama," she called as she stepped through the front door.

"I'm in here."

Symphony followed the sound of her mother's voice to the living room, where she was folding clothes in front of the television.

"Did I get any mail?"

"No, sugar, I'm sorry." Mama snapped the wrinkles out of a towel and looked up from the soap opera she was watching. "I'm sure she'll write just as soon as she can."

"*If* she can," Symphony mumbled and moped away.

She missed Elaine's matter-of-factness. And whenever something bad happened, Elaine could make her feel as if it had no more effect on her life than dropping the string of a helium balloon. And, sometimes, she said the funniest things with the most serious expression.

Symphony and Therese kept a close watch on the mail and jumped each time the phone rang but, after ten interminable days, neither of them had heard a word.

Lately, being at home wasn't so bad. Daddy seemed to be ignoring her. But that wouldn't last forever. She knew that one night soon he would walk through the door after work and his fuse would be burnt. Then—blam! That would be the end of her break.

⌘　⌘　⌘

Greg Stanton still floated atop the popularity pool. Shortly after the first of the year, Parkway's ninth grade class elected him President. Darla Terry didn't waste a minute becoming his girlfriend. As a couple, they were a perfect picture: Greg with his surfer-boy tan and short, dirty blonde hair; Darla, always in the current fashion, her shimmering, black hair cascading down her back. They promenaded through the hallways whenever the opportunity presented itself, Darla doing that parade-float-beauty-queen wave with one hand, holding tightly to Greg with the other.

Seeing them together was like a double assault on Symphony. She did her best to ignore their glares and stare past them into the crowd but, if no one else was around, they would walk straight toward her. They seemed to enjoy watching her change paths to avoid them and, often, their laughter chased her down the hall to her next class.

Symphony didn't want revenge. She just wanted to find a way to make them stop. So one day, she dropped a note on Greg's desk at the beginning of Science.

Wouldn't Darla love to meet your mother?

She glared at him as he read it, watched his face change. That façade—that confident, well-rounded, upper-middle-class young man—seemed to fail him for a moment. It just fell away and left him with terror in his eyes.

*If they really knew you, I don't think you'd be President. And Darla Terry wouldn't be caught dead holding your hand, either.*

He must have realized that, somehow, Symphony had the ability to change his life. For the moment aggravating her seemed to lose its appeal.

Symphony was relieved. It was one less thing for her to worry about. One month ago, Elaine had been whisked away to St. Jude Hospital. No one had heard from her since. Life was beginning to return to normal but anxiety stood at attention, ready and waiting if the need arose.

⌘　⌘　⌘

One evening as Symphony finished cleaning the kitchen, someone rang the doorbell. Mama opened the door to a girl Symphony's age with long reddish-brown hair.

"Hi, Mrs. Weber," the girl said. "My name is Lilly. Is Symphony home?"

"Why, hello, Lilly," Mama said. "I heard you'd moved here. You're living with your aunt and uncle, right? Come on in." She turned to Leesa who had followed her to the door. "Would you let your sister know she's got company?"

Leesa took a deep breath and, standing right where she was, yelled, "Symphony! Some girl's here to see you!"

Mama tapped Leesa on the behind. "*I* could have done *that*. Now *go* tell her." Red-faced, Leesa stomped to the kitchen as Lilly stepped inside.

"So," Mama said, "what do you think of Titusville so far?"

"It's been a huge adjustment, you know what I mean? I've lived in New York my whole life, till now. This place is a lot smaller. Don't get me wrong. The people are nice and all, but I'm just used to more of 'em, you know? And my aunt and uncle have been great. They just want me to get out some. So I told them I knew Symphony from school and they said I should come over and say, 'Hi,' you know what I mean? So that's what I did."

Mama's eyes grew wide as she waited for Lilly to take a breath. When she finally did, all Mama could think to say was, "That's nice."

About then, Symphony walked to the living room, a dishtowel draped over one arm. "Oh. Hi, Lilly."

"Hey, Symphony. I was just thinking maybe you could come over to my aunt's house for a while, you know. I mean, if you've already eaten. Would that be all right?"

Symphony looked at Mama. "Can we go for a walk, instead?"

Mama nodded. "Not more than an hour. Okay?"

She handed the dishtowel to Mama. "Okay."

⌘　⌘　⌘

The girls left the Webers' and walked in the direction opposite Lilly's house. As they rounded the corner, Lilly pulled a cigarette from the back pocket of her skin-tight jeans and showed it to Symphony. It didn't have a filter. The ends were twisted.

"You smoke, right?" She lit a match and the odor of sulphur filled the air. Raising the flame to the end of the cigarette, she inhaled, holding the smoke in until a fit of coughing forced it out. "Here you go," she said, passing it to Symphony.

Symphony studied the cigarette before she put it to her lips. It was crushed and thin as if some of the tobacco had fallen out. *Probably squished out 'cause Lilly's jeans are so tight.* She took a drag. "God," she choked. The smoke tasted different. And it felt like it cut her throat. She coughed, expecting to see blood any minute. Within moments, her chest felt tired and lazy.

Lilly took another draw. Then, it was Symphony's turn. This time, her lungs seemed to accept the harsh smoke in a more civilized manner.

The two girls walked up one street and down another, passing their cigarette back and forth.

"I miss the city," Lilly said. "There's always something to do there. You know what I mean? There was a party or a sleepover at least once every weekend. It was nice. Got me out of the house, ya know. And that's good when there's always one of 'em lookin' for a reason to beat the crap outta you. It's all right here. But I had to leave my friends."

Lilly took a breath. "It's a lot warmer than it was in New York, though," she continued. "I like that. And I heard they're building a Disneyland in Orlando. That's just right up the road. That'll be cool. You know what I mean?"

Lilly rambled on and on, but Symphony's thoughts were coming so fast she didn't have time to listen. Her mind was a blur of what-ifs and why-nots. *What's Mack doing?* Just as she thought it, her dream floated in, his pale, blue eyes smiling at her. Then, she could almost feel herself rolling sideways down the hill in the soap barrel with Randy and Barry following. *Where could I find a barrel like that? If I had one, I'd take it to the dunes.* She thought of the last time she and Therese and Elaine had been at the dunes. Then, the dream of Elaine with curly grey hair flashed in her mind. *I saw her. But what if that doesn't mean anything?* She remembered the face of the girl at school who'd asked, "Do you think Elaine'll make it?" Then, she was in the hall. One second, Greg and Darla were glaring at her. The next, the hall was deserted and Greg had her by the arm, shoving her into a corner. "What do you know about my mom?" Suddenly, she was in the car with Roscoe Stanley again. Only this time, she was older. And she was alone. *What's happening?*

"—you know what I mean? Symphony?" Lilly moved over blocking the path. "Symphony?" She grabbed Symphony by the shoulders and shook. "Symphony! What the hell is wrong with you? I called your name about a dozen times. I thought you said you smoked."

They were standing on the side of the street, blocks from where they lived. In fact, they were right in front of Elaine's house and there, in the yard, was a for-sale sign.

"Oh, no!" Symphony said, beginning to cry. "Oh, no!" She backed away from Lilly and began to run.

"Wait," Lilly called, tearing after her. "What's the matter?" She caught up just in time to see Symphony standing, out of breath, at Therese's door. "Oh, shit!" she said, heading for the shortest route home.

⌘　⌘　⌘

"What happened?" Collette asked, ushering Symphony inside. "What are you so upset about?" She pulled Symphony to her with a hug. "What's that smell? Oh my gosh! Have you been smoking pot? Therese, come out here!"

"Pot?" Symphony said. "No. I went for a walk with Lilly and we smoked a cigarette. And when we stopped, we were in front of Elaine's and—They're moving. There's a for-sale sign out there and everything. Does that mean Elaine . . ."

Therese, who had heard enough to piece the conversation together, joined Symphony in looking to Collette for an answer.

"It means nothing, girls. Here, I'll prove it to you. Let's call the hospital in Memphis. Maybe we can find out something for sure. But first, I'd better let Maisy know what's happened and that Symphony's here."

So, Collette made things all right with Mama. Then, they called St. Jude's and found out that, although Elaine had been released, she was returning twice a week for treatment and tests. The nurse Collette spoke to gave them the hospital's address and promised to make sure Elaine received their letters. Before Symphony left, they wrote a quick note and stamped it for the morning mail.

By the time they finished, it was dark outside. "Therese, honey, I want to walk Symphony home. I'll be right back"

Symphony looked up at Collette, confused. "I'll see you in the morning, Therese," she said, stepping out onto the patio.

"Tell me about this Lilly person," Collette said as they started down the shortcut. "Is she the one who moved in with her aunt and uncle just around the corner?"

"Yeah."

"How well do you know her, Symphony?"

"Not very well. Today's really the first time I've done anything with her. Until today, I've just seen her at school. Why?"

"Because, when you got to our house tonight, you smelled like marijuana. Did the cigarette you smoked taste funny?"

"Maybe. But I really don't know. I've only smoked one other time."

"Look, honey. I know Therese's father and I let her get away with things other kids would get in trouble for. We let her smoke now, she can skip school occasionally, and at special dinners, we sometimes let her have a small glass of wine. But drugs are where I draw the line. If I thought you were using drugs, I'd have no choice but to tell your parents. You understand?"

Collette leaned over and looked into Symphony's eyes. "This new girl—Lilly. I think she may have given you pot tonight. So, be careful. Don't smoke anymore of her cigarettes, honey. If you want one, get it from Therese or me."

"Do you think that's why I can't remember walking to Elaine's?"

"Do you recall anything at all?"

"Yes. But it was stuff that was already in my head."

Before Symphony went inside to finish her homework, she thanked Collette for calling the hospital and promised to be cautious with Lilly. That night, she went to bed early. "I don't know why I'm so tired," she told Mama.

"Just go on to bed," Mama said. "That thing with Elaine's house really shook you up. Sweet dreams, sugar," she said with a kiss.

*I hope so.*

But the minute Symphony fell asleep, the dreams began and most of them were bad.

*She saw Mack's father kissing a woman who wasn't Mack's mother. Mama was sitting on the kitchen floor crying as Daddy stood over her, an angry look on his face. A woman carried a kicking and screaming child through a crowded mall. A group of young people shouted at men in suits, helmets, and masks. The men raised their guns and fired into the crowd. Thirteen fell. Lilly was inside the tent on Empty Island with Mack and Bo. Symphony was watching television. No one else was home. The doorbell rang. She opened the door to find David Terry standing there. At a football game, Greg Stanton grabbed her arm and forced her under the bleachers. "I know you can do this," he said. "Now, do it!" She watched as a tall thin man with a thick mustache let himself into a hotel room. "Come on, Janis," he called. "Everybody's waiting at the studio." On the other side of the bed he found a young woman face down on the floor, a syringe on the bedside table. Roscoe Stanley's face appeared. Daddy's scowl followed. Symphony felt as if she were falling, falling, then something took hold of her shoulder and she stopped.*

"Symphony," Dani whispered. "I just had a horrible nightmare. Can I sleep with you?"

Symphony rolled over and opened her eyes, relieved to be awake. "Thank you," she said.

"For what?" Dani asked.

"Nevermind." Eyes wide, she scooted over to make room for Dani, hoping she could stay awake until morning.

# CHAPTER EIGHTEEN

THE INTENSITY OF Symphony's dreams continued long after fear of sleep had painted the skin beneath her eyes grayish-lavender. She began to move slowly, as if she'd just awakened, not only in the morning, but all the time.

Mama took her to Dr. Hall twice. In his long white lab coat and his preppie black hair Brylcreem-ed to the side, he pushed an ice-cold stethoscope against her chest. "Is she getting enough sleep?" he asked, running his finger along the dark circles.

"She's going to bed at the same time she always does," Mama answered.

"Take a deep breath, Symphony," he said.

She breathed in and held, waiting for him to say she could release it, but the words never came. When her lungs felt as if they'd burst, she exhaled, taking her time, trying her best to be quiet so Dr. Hall could hear what he was listening for.

"How's her appetite?" he asked.

"About the same."

"Is she going to the bathroom as often as usual?"

*Sleep, eat, poop? That's all he's gonna ask?* Symphony was baffled. It didn't seem to her that Dr. Hall was acting much like a doctor.

"Let's step outside for just a minute." He motioned Mama toward the corridor.

The door to the exam room was closed and their voices were soft, but Symphony heard every word.

"You're a nurse, Maisy," the doctor said. "Leukemia isn't contagious. You know that."

"I know," Mama answered. "She's just been so tired."

"She is tired. But I believe that has more to do with her emotional state than anything."

⌘ ⌘ ⌘

Two weeks later, on her second visit, the purplish half-rings had darkened to brown, giving Symphony's eyes a sunken look. "Diabetes runs in my side of the family," Mama said. "I was wondering . . ."

So the nurse made Symphony pee in a cup. Then they strapped her arm down and drew some blood.

It turned out that diabetes wasn't the problem. To tell the truth, Dr. Hall couldn't find a single reason for Symphony's exhaustion. "She might feel better if she lost a little weight," he said. "But, for now, just keep a good watch over her and bring her back if the symptoms persist."

During that time, Symphony spent most of her weekends at Therese's. In the silence of their Florida room, she took naps, trusting her friend to awaken her at the first sign of dreaming. One morning as Therese and Collette watched, Symphony's eyes began to move rapidly under her closed lids. Collette gave her shoulder a nudge. "Symphony, honey," she said, "Why don't you get up for a minute."

Symphony sat up and stretched against the back of the couch. "Thanks."

Collette lit a cigarette, took a puff, and set it in the ashtray. "You know, I've been thinking. What if all this extra dreaming is a reaction to the marijuana? Have you asked Lilly about that cigarette yet?"

"No," Symphony answered. "I don't wanna accuse her of anything. What if it's all in my head?"

"What I smelled that night wasn't in your head. Besides, if these nightmares are related to the pot, then maybe, when it's all out of your system, your dreams will go back to normal."

Symphony put her forearm over her eyes. "I hope that's all it is. But what if it's not? What if I'm stuck like this forever?"

"Speaking of stuck," Therese said. "You know how moms are always tellin' their kids not to cross their eyes 'cause they might stay like that? Well my mom actually saw that happen to somebody. Tell her about that Paulie guy, mom."

"I'm sure Symphony doesn't want to hear about Paulie Powell."

"Yes she does." Therese winked at Symphony. "Don't you?"

"Yes. I do," Symphony replied, with a nod and a smile. "I wanna hear it." *Tell me anything you want, just change the subject. There's no way I'm askin' Lilly if that cigarette was marijuana.*

⌘ ⌘ ⌘

After almost a month, Symphony's dreams began to shrink to a number she could tolerate. When she was finally able to sleep through the night again, she celebrated. She stayed out of school and spent the next two days in bed, only getting up to eat, drink, or go to the bathroom. Mama came in at least once an hour and laid a worried hand on her forehead. "Do you hurt anywhere, sugar?"

"I'm fine, Mama," Symphony answered each time. "I'm just sleepy." Then she would turn over and close her eyes again.

By the time the weekend came, her energy had returned. "I don't want you doing too much just yet," Mama said. But when Therese called on Saturday afternoon with the promise of a "surprise," she gave in and let Symphony go for a visit.

When Symphony arrived, Therese was sitting at the dining room table with their first letter from Elaine. "I didn't wanna open it till you got here," she said. "Will you get me a butter knife?" Symphony pulled a knife from the silverware drawer and sat down next to Therese. Therese opened the letter and began to read.

> To my two best friends,
> This is to both of you.

Therese and Symphony looked at each other and smiled.

> I wish I was there. But if I was, I wouldn't know Alex.

"Who's Alex?" Symphony asked.

Just then, Therese discovered a snapshot still inside the envelope. "Oh my gosh! This has gotta be him." She held it up for Symphony to see.

"Let me see." Symphony snatched the photo out of Therese's hand. "He's got his arm around her. What else does she say?"

Therese held the paper up and began to read again.

> This is a picture of Alex and me. He's the really cute one
> with no hair. Honestly, he's the only person here who has
> less hair than me right now.
>
> Good thing I kept that ugly wig.

"Why don't you read the rest?" Therese said, handing the letter to Symphony.

"Are you sure?"

"Yeah. You know how much I hate reading out loud." Therese leaned back in her chair. "Now read, or I'll finish it myself."

Symphony cleared her throat. "Okay."

> They keep trying different things. One medicine works,
> but then it messes up something else, so they try another
> one. I don't feel too bad, though. Just tired.
>
> And bored! So, sometimes I explore. St. Jude's a huge
> place. One day I got lost and stumbled into this room full
> of cages. There were mostly rats and mice but there were a
> couple bunnies, too. I walked between the rows and they'd
> stand up like they thought I was gonna pet them or feed
> them or something. There was this one white rat with pink
> eyes. I wanted to hold him so bad. But I knew better. Plus,
> there was this huge wall of glass doors locked between me
> and the cages. I'm pretty sure it was the research lab.
>
> Part of me wished I could let them all out. But that
> would hurt a lot of people. Those cute, little rats were doing
> everything they could to help me get better. So I started to
> thank them, instead. But I didn't get to finish. Some guy

came in and yelled at me to get out. Jeez, you would have thought I was gonna burn the place down or something. Shouldn't they keep the door locked if no one's supposed to go in there?

Anyway, I should get some sleep now. Why don't you guys write me back and then I'll send a letter to Symmie. Don't do anything I wouldn't do.

XOXOXOXOXOXO

Elaine

As soon as they finished reading the letter, Therese got out some paper and they wrote her back. Neither of them mentioned the for-sale sign. They followed Mama's advice and just tried to help their friend stay happy.

⌘ ⌘ ⌘

Halloween came and went. Thanksgiving too. School got out for Christmas break but most of the time the streets of Overlook Terrace were deserted. It was too wet for visiting outside and too cold for kick ball. Three days before Christmas, a storm dumped two whole inches of snow on Titusville. That drew every kid in the neighborhood outdoors for a snowball fight. It lasted until all the snow had been balled up and scattered—about ten minutes. But that was long enough for Lilly to corner Symphony.

"Wanna come over for a little while?" she asked, her fourth offering since the cigarette incident.

Symphony shrugged. "I don't think my Mom'll let me do anything this afternoon." It was the fourth time she'd made an excuse.

Lilly put her hand on her hip. "If you don't wanna hang around with me, just say so!"

"That's not it. I've been super busy. That's all."

"Yeah? Too busy with everybody else." Lilly turned and headed for home.

"Wait," Symphony called after her. "How 'bout tomorrow?"

Lilly stopped and turned toward her, smiling. "Like two-o'clock?"

"I'll be there," Symphony answered. *I just won't stay long. And no walks.*

⌘ ⌘ ⌘

155

The next day, Symphony stood at Lilly's front door, surrounded by the aroma of baking chocolate-chip cookies. Her knock was answered by Lilly's Aunt Mabel who was an inch or so shorter than Symphony's five-foot-two frame. The tie of a red and white gingham apron divided her well-rounded figure in half at the waist. She appeared to be much older than Mama, with veins of white streaking her once-black hair. "You must be Symphony," she said. "Lilly's told me all about you. Come in." They started toward the living room, passing a silver Christmas tree. On the floor in front of it, a lamp with a rotating four-colored disk changed the tree from red to yellow, to green, to blue, and back to red again.

Symphony stopped, transfixed on the man-made beauty of it. "We always have a cut tree," she said. "This is pretty, Mrs.—"

"Mabel," the woman chuckled. "Just call me Mabel." She had a soft, happy voice, and an easy laugh. "Why don't we just have a seat here on the couch? Lilly will be right out."

Once Lilly joined them in the living room, Mabel excused herself and returned, moments later, with a plate of warm cookies. "Could we have some chocolate milk too, Aunt Mabel?" Lilly asked.

"Would we serve chocolate chip cookies without it?" Mabel giggled. "Not in this house. I'll be right back." And she was. Once she had delivered two tall glasses of chocolate milk, she left the girls alone with their cookies and a stack of magazines. The top one had a picture of The Monkees on the cover.

"The Monkees aren't a real band, you know," Lilly remarked. "They were just made up for television. And the Beatles . . ." She gave Symphony a sideways glance. "They're just a little too sweet. They're holding hands with their girlfriends while the Rolling Stones are spending the night with theirs. As far as the music goes, I've gotta vote for the Stones. But the Monkees and the Beatles are prettier to look at. For sure. What do you think?"

Symphony was stunned. For the first time since they'd met, Lilly was inviting her to speak. "Um . . . Um . . . I don't know. I guess I like them all. You're right. The Monkees are sweet and the Beatles are a little less sweet, and the Rolling Stones aren't sweet at all. But I don't care about how they look, either. I think it's more about *who* they are. I hate it when people judge me for how I look. So I try not to do that. Not even to people I'll probably never meet."

"Do you ever dream about any of them?" Lilly asked.

The curve of Symphony's lips dropped into a straight line. *Here we go.* "Like a regular dream?"

"No. The way *people say* you dream. About what could happen later and all. You know what I mean?"

"Can we not talk about that?" Symphony still hadn't decided whether to blame Lilly for the uproar of nightmares that had kept her awake since their smoking walk.

"Sure. We don't have to if you don't want to. I just mean I've heard about it. That's all. The way you sometimes warn people not to do stuff. Or *to* do stuff. You know, some people—not the really stuck-up kids but the regular ones—they appreciate it."

"Really?" Symphony asked. "Someone out there appreciates it? That's a shock. I try to tell total strangers how to stay out of trouble. The whole time, they stare at me like I'm some sort of weirdo. I guess they listen. I think I'd know if they didn't. But no one ever thanks me. They just whisper about me behind my back."

Symphony laid her magazine on the coffee table and began pacing. "You know, my grandmother calls it a gift. But there's only been two times when something really good happened because of it." She paused, remembering the time Daniel Munford fell in the Chattahoochee and the day Roscoe Stanley was taken away by the police. "Gift?" she said. She thought of the train of dreams she'd had over the last month. "It's more like a curse. As soon as I can figure out how to make it stop, I won't have this *gift* anymore."

"Okay," Lilly said. "So . . . you wanna talk about something else then?"

*You want me to talk?* Lilly's words always seemed endless. Symphony hadn't planned on having to say much. Besides, it was hard getting to know someone new. It was easier to be around Therese and Elaine. They already knew everything about her. She picked up a cookie and took a bite. "Yum. This is great. Does your aunt bake a lot?"

"Yeah. I think her chocolate chip cookies are the best, though." Lilly was quiet for a moment. She thumbed through the pages of a *Rolling Stone*. Without looking up she said, "Tell me about those guys across the street from you. The Westhills."

"Why?" Symphony asked, sending Lilly a suspicious glare.

"Woah," Lilly said. "I think they're cute. That's all. I thought maybe I'd like to get to know them better. But I would never move into your territory. Which one do you like?"

Symphony's cheeks burned with embarrassment. She opened a *Life* magazine and leaned into it. On the cover, a picture of the McCartney family blocked Lilly's view. Symphony had never even told Therese about Mack and the dream. No one knew about the ride in Freedom, either. She looked Lilly in the eyes. "Promise not to tell anyone?" she said. "I don't know how he feels about me yet."

Lilly stopped smiling and gazed back at Symphony. Her big, brown eyes softened. "I promise. It's the oldest one, isn't it?"

Symphony's face grew hotter. Her ears felt as if they were on fire. She nodded. "Mack." *There. I said it.* "Please don't tell anyone."

"I said I wouldn't. But what're you so worried about, anyway? I saw the way he was smilin' at you yesterday. I think he likes you. Want me to ask him?"

"No!" Symphony said, with a gnawing feeling in her gut.

"Why not? Back in New York we always did that for each other. When I was twelve, I was so crazy in love with this guy, Brad Lee. Isn't that just the coolest name? Brad Lee. Like Bradley. My friend Sandy asked him if he liked me and he said yes. So then, we went steady for a while, you know. But then, he broke up with me for nothin' so I started callin' him Bradley Lee but I said it more like lee-lee, you know what I mean? It sounded kinda like I was making fun of him. Like Brad-lee-lee. He hated me after that, but it wasn't long before Sandy asked Rick Mason if he liked me and when he said yes, I went steady with him for a while. But I never kissed either one of them, you know? I never kissed a guy until Manley Moore. Did you ever kiss anybody?"

Symphony couldn't hear a word Lilly was saying. She had just remembered the dream of Lilly in the tent on Empty Island. *What was she sayin' to Mack and Bo in the dream? What if she asks Mack if he likes me?* Her stomach twisted. *What if he says no?* She stood up. "I have to go. I told my mom I wouldn't stay long."

"But you just got here," Lilly whined.

"I'll stay longer next time."

"Come back soon," Mabel sang from the kitchen as Symphony walked to the door.

"I will. Thanks for the cookies."

⌘ ⌘ ⌘

Two days later, when Santa dropped off the Weber's presents, he left a most unusual gift for Symphony. It was a new game called a Quija Board. She and Dani set up the card table, read the instructions, and waited until it was dark outside before testing it out in their room behind a locked door.

Dani pulled her wavy hair into a clip behind her shoulders and got right down to business. "Who will I marry?" was her first question. They had agreed that whoever asked the question had to close their eyes but Dani kept peeking. S-T-E-V-E, the Ouija Board answered. Steve was the guy Dani talked about the most. "Wow!" she said, beaming at the board's reply.

"We should test it." Symphony suggested. "Let's ask it something we already know." She closed her eyes put her fingers lightly on the pointer. "I know. Where do I go to school?"

The planchette began to move across the letters, P-J-H-S.

"Parkway Junior High School," Dani squealed. "It's talking to us. Now let's ask who likes you."

"No," Symphony said with disgust. "Nobody does."

"It's just for fun. C'mon. Close your eyes."

So they tried it. The pointer hesitated at first, then moved quickly to the upper right corner and froze.

"That's weird," Dani said, moving the guide back to the starting point. "Let's try it again. Ask the question."

"Who likes me?"

After a pause, the planchette migrated, once again, to the same spot.

"You must be pulling on it funny or something," Dani said. "Let's switch places." They traded chairs and finger spots on the guide. "Now say it."

This time, Symphony said it with conviction. "Who likes me and what is his name?"

Finally, the pointer moved around the board, stopping three times— once at M, then at E, then W—before coming to rest in the same right corner.

"M-E-W?" Dani said. "That's not a name. It's the sound a kitten makes."

Symphony took her fingers off the guide and opened her eyes. "After all the times we tried, that's all it said? What did it do the first two times?"

"It went right where it is now," Dani said. "Maybe it's broken."

Symphony stared at the board. The planchette was aimed at the word NO. "It pointed to NO three times?" she asked.

"Yeah," Dani said. "But you know what I just thought of? M-E-W could be someone's initials. Try and think about who it could be. This is so exciting. Let's ask another it question."

But Symphony didn't want to know anything else. That board was a liar. Why else would it say, "No," about M-E-W? *Maxwell Edward Westhill.* "I don't wanna play anymore right now. Why don't I paint your toenails with that plum nail polish you got in your stocking?"

"You don't mind?" Dani asked.

That very night, the Ouija board was shoved to a shelf at the top of the closet where it stayed as a new year came and the days headed toward spring. Many letters were exchanged between Therese, Symphony and Elaine. Each time one arrived, Symphony was encouraged. After all, St. Jude Hospital and the cute little rats weren't giving up. *Maybe we shouldn't either.*

# CHAPTER NINETEEN

THERE WAS A sharp edge in the Weber household. Daddy was vigilant, ready to prove his authority—even in response to something as innocent as a questioning look from one of his own children. Although his behavior was not altogether unusual, it was almost unbearable by the end of every winter when their home seemed to shrink around them and the white terrazzo floors began to look gray in the winter light. This year it was worse. The house itself seemed to hold its breath, awaiting open windows and billowy curtains filled with sunny breezes.

One evening, near the end of February, the Webers sat around the crowded kitchen table finishing supper. The kids were talking to each other, the volume growing dangerously loud as it sometimes did. Then—

"Dammit!" Daddy slammed his glass down on the table. "Will you quiet down? Your mother and I are trying to talk."

Sudden silence followed.

"I could hear you," Mama said.

"Well I couldn't hear myself."

The hair on the back of Symphony's neck prickled. "I'm finished," she said. "May I be excused now?"

Dani stood up and reached for her half-full glass of iced tea. "Me too?"

Mama gave them a relieved glance. "Go ahead," she said. "In fact, why don't you all go watch television for a little while."

They left Mama and Daddy at the table and crossed the threshold into the living room where Jeanne closed the door and turned on *To Tell the Truth.*

"That guy's the real one," Joe said, pointing to a man in a dark grey suit and a skinny tie with diagonal stripes.

"You don't know that!" Jeanne snipped. "We just turned it on."

Joe shrugged.

Leesa looked up from the picture she was coloring on the coffee table. "He always picks the right one. Every time we watch it."

Dani, showed no interest whatsoever. She finished her tea then slipped out of the room and down the hallway until she was next to the kitchen. She placed the lip of her empty glass to the wall and rested one ear against the bottom of it, listening. When Symphony stuck her head into the hall, Dani, bug-eyed, motioned for her to come over.

"Does this really work?" Symphony whispered, reaching for the glass. "Let me try." But Dani wouldn't budge. Symphony leaned her head against the side of the tumbler trying to hear what her sister was hearing.

Between the occasional clatter of plates and silverware, Mama would question and Daddy would answer.

"I'm sick of the bullshit," he ranted. "Just when I get one office set up, they move me to another."

"Well, if they're asking you to train everyone," Mama said, "they must like the way you do your job. That's good, isn't it?"

"No, Maisy. Not when they don't pay any extra for the training. I still make the same goddamn commission as always but I have to work more hours to get it. If I'd finished college I'd be teaching right now and we wouldn't be worrying about this."

"If?" Symphony rolled her eyes. *Like you say, Daddy. If a frog had wings he wouldn't bump his rump every time he hopped.*

"Could you take the courses you need at night school?" Mama suggested.

"Can't afford it," Daddy answered. "Our money's stretched as tight as it'll go since we bought both those cars. There's no way we can pay for tuition and books, too."

Symphony grew tired of fighting Dani for the bottom of the glass. She moved over and peeked between the door and the frame.

"It's a shame," Mama said with a sigh as she picked up the plate of country fried steak and carried it toward the refrigerator. "You don't need many more credits, do you?" With her back to Daddy, she wrapped the meat in aluminum foil and put it away. Then, brightened, she turned back toward him. "What if I went back to work?" she asked carefully, as if her offering might hurt his ego. "Just two or three days a week. Don't you think it'd be worth it? In the long run?"

⌘ ⌘ ⌘

So Daddy signed up for night school and Mama won a battle she'd been fighting for years. She started working the three-to-eleven shift at the hospital each Monday, Wednesday, and Friday. And although she said she was exhausted, she began to smile more than she had in forever.

⌘ ⌘ ⌘

The first half of March heated up like mid-summer. Waxy white buds poked their heads through the ends of twiggy orange tree branches. They basked in warmth for a few days before opening, releasing a fragrance so fiercely beautiful, it hastened love where impatience thought it would never grow.

On one of winter's coldest days, Symphony had begun pretending she could feel Mack's arms around her. When she and Therese went to the movies, she would catch herself, lips moving, mimicking the lovers on the screen as she imagined what it would be like to kiss him. Still, even with the urging of the orange blossom, Mack held her only as close as his out-stretched arms would allow.

On the nights Mama was working, everybody's chores increased. Dani's after-school activities kept her out most weekdays until just in time for dinner. So, Symphony watched her younger siblings after school and got supper on the table. Dani was in charge of baths and homework problems. Jeanne and Leesa cleared the table and stacked the dishes by the sink for Mama to do in the morning.

These new responsibilities devoured most of Symphony's free time. Tuesday and Thursday evenings, she caught up on her homework. She was falling behind in her letters to Elaine, but still managed one a week. Here and there, she found a few hours to spend at Therese's. It seemed she was always apologizing to Lilly for not being able to go anywhere or do anything. But there was a bright side to the Webers' new lifestyle. At least once a week, Mama had to work *and* Daddy had a class. It was a perfect time to sneak away to Empty Island with Mack and *Freedom*.

⌘　⌘　⌘

Great nets of spider webs guarded the path to the camp. Mack always went first, slicing through them with a long stick, swinging it as if it were a machete. When they reached their destination, they sat in cushions of pine straw, resting their backs against the trees that marked the doorway to their squatter tent, smoking cigarettes and discussing the wrongs of the world: their fathers, grumpy siblings, bossy teachers, too much homework, and, as Mama called it, being on restriction. The list of rights was shorter: hard rock, a carton of cigarettes, cold cokes, the approach of summer, and *Freedom*.

"Tell me about your dreams," Mack said one night.

Symphony shivered in her flip-flops. "Maybe, one day."

"Just tell me one thing," he said. "Have I ever been in any of 'em?"

She looked away, picked up a twig, and drew a heart in the dirt. "No."

"Really?" Mack put his cigarette out on the bottom of his shoe. "Not even one?"

Symphony shook her head.

"That kinda hurts my feelin's." He rubbed his chin.

"It shouldn't. I don't decide what I dream about." She thought about Roscoe Stanley. "I wish I did."

"We should prob'ly go. C'mon." Grinning, he took her by the hand and pulled her back toward the lake.

The roughness of his calluses gave her goosebumps. She ran to keep up, not wanting to give him a reason to let go. When they reached the boat, he did anyway.

That night, as Symphony tried to go to sleep, she wondered what Mack's reaction would have been had she told him about the beautiful boy dream. She dozed off, thinking about the ride across the lake. She could feel the bounce of the boat as it moved through the peaks and valleys of water so the dream did not shock her at first.

*She was surrounded by darkness. She knew the rhythm of the lake. Her hands rested beside her on the wood plank seat as they always did when she crossed with Mack. "It's late," she thought. "And there's no moon."*

*"I'll get the rope." Those words were Mack's. He always said them when they got to either shore. But this wasn't Mack's voice. "Close your eyes for a big surprise," the man said. Symphony opened her eyes wider searching the blackness for a hint of where the man was standing.*

*"I said close your goddamn eyes you bitch or I let this rope go right now and you're on your own."*

*She closed her eyes and suddenly, Roscoe Stanley appeared before her in his clown suit, his feet on the shore, his hand holding the rope as she floated out in Freedom.*

*"Don't worry," he cackled, "I can't hurt you anymore. I can only scare you."*

*He yanked the rope and Symphony started to tumble backward. She gripped her seat and opened her eyes to the black night.*

*"See." He laughed. "Scared but not hurt. I just wanted you to know, when you were dreaming about me, I knew it. I could see you staring at me every time I got into my car to do something uh . . . well, let's just say something you wouldn't approve of. If I could have found you, I'd have put an end to those dreams, once and for all. Just think. If I can see you when you dream of me, there are other people who can see you dreamin' about them, too. But you have to close your eyes to find out who they are. Now shut 'em again like I told you."*

*Symphony closed her eyes. She was no longer on the lake. The rope was tight around her wrists and Roscoe Stanley was leading her through the halls of Parkway.*

*"You wanna see how they really feel about you knowing things that are none of your business?" He turned and walked into her, pushing his nose against hers. "Just close your eyes." He backed away again. "Look around."*

*The halls were jammed with students and teachers. Most people stared at her suspiciously, wondering what she knew about them. Others had questions which were more specific.*

*"Does she know about the fifty bucks I took out of the collection plate?"*

*"What if she tells John I kissed Brian?"*

*Greg Stanton passed. "Why do I see your face in my dreams? Leave me alone, bitch."*

*It was clear to Symphony that most people didn't see her as one of them. In her dream, she opened her eyes and the people faded away.*

*"Give me that damn rope," another man said.*

*She recognized the voice. When she closed her eyes, there was Uncle Gray.*

*"You've hurt her enough." He pushed Roscoe Stanley out of the dream entirely.*

*Gray looked into Symphony's eyes. "There's a way," he said. "You can stop the dreams if you really want to, honey. But it's dangerous. And if you can't trust the person holding the other end of the rope, dreaming might not be the only thing that stops. So try to live with it. I'll help you whenever I can. Now, open and close," he said.*

*She did as Gray told her and felt the bounce of the lake once again where she drifted into another dream.*

⌘ ⌘ ⌘

"Look here," Mama said, shoving the morning paper in front of Symphony as she ate breakfast. "That awful man died in prison."

"Roscoe Stanley?" Symphony asked.

"Ah-ha," Mama said, taking a gulp of coffee. "Day before yesterday."

⌘ ⌘ ⌘

One Saturday morning, three weeks before school got out for summer break, Therese appeared at the Webers'. "Can we go out back?" she said. "I feel like swinging."

Therese sat down on the swing set and rocked back and forth twisting her dark brown hair around her finger. "I hate my dad. And I just told him so."

Symphony gawked at her. "You've never hated your dad," she said. "What happened?"

"He applied for a transfer," she said, sniffling.

"A transfer?" Symphony said. "Where?"

"Back to Massachusetts where he's from," she sobbed.

"Are you sure?"

"He'll find out in August, whether it's approved or not. But he wants me and my mom to go up there for the summer. The whole summer, can you believe it?" She leaned her face into her hands.

"What does your mom say?"

"Nothing. I think she's up for it," Therese groaned. "Can I stay down here right now? I don't wanna go home yet. You should have seen his face when I said I hated him." She started to cry again. "But what did he think I'd do? Boogaloo through the house singing 'We're moving. We're moving?'" She pulled a tissue from her pocket and blew her nose. "I don't know anyone there. Not even my cousins. We haven't visited since I was eight."

"Maybe it won't happen," Symphony said. "Your dad's always changing his mind. Remember how he signed you up for Catholic school that one year?"

But, on the first day of summer, Therese and Collette left for Massachusetts. The girls promised to write twice a week and their mothers agreed to once a month phone calls.

Daddy decided to continue his classes over the summer and Mama, with her new job, wasn't eligible for a vacation. For the first time since they'd moved to Florida, the Webers cancelled their trip to Alabama. In relation to the other things going on in Symphony's life, not going to Granny's was low on the list.

In addition to writing to each other, Therese and Symphony still sent a letter to Elaine each week but near the middle of June, all correspondence from Elaine stopped.

Collette called Symphony one afternoon just after the Fourth of July. "I talked to St. Jude's today," she said. "The nurse told me there were complications, but that was all she could say. I'm sorry, honey. Are you okay?"

Symphony wiped her eyes. "I guess," she said. "Do you think her parents'll let us know if something happens?"

"I'm sure someone will write or call—just as soon as they're able to, honey. We'll just have to wait."

But it wasn't a long wait. At the end of July, a letter came from Memphis addressed to Maisy Weber. Enclosed was a copy of Elaine's obituary. Clipped to it was a note scribbled by her father.

We lost our Elaine last week.
Please tell the girls as tenderly as possible.

Therese and Symphony cried for an hour on the phone.

"I hate it here," Therese bawled. "I wish I was home so we could do something."

But there was nothing to be done.

"Come on," Mama said when Symphony got off the phone. I have an idea. Mama took her to a nursery. Together, they looked for something blue—Elaine's favorite color, finally settling on a Rose of Sharon. It didn't have blossoms yet, but the tag read *Blue Bird*. The next day, Mama and Symphony dug a hole and planted it in front of Elaine's still vacant house. The neighbor who was taking care of the lawn, promised to make sure it got enough water. Symphony went by as often as she could, watching for the blue to emerge. When the flowers finally came, they were purple and the bush was covered with them every morning. At night, they would close up and fall, a memory of beauty from the day before. But by sunrise, the bush was full of blossoms once again.

After the news of Elaine, Symphony, who was spending too much time alone in her room, began to look forward to Lilly's knock.

"You have to work too hard," Lilly would say.

And Symphony began to grow weary.

"When do you get to have fun?" Lilly would ask.

And within Symphony a seed of rebellion was nourished.

"You can never go anywhere," Lilly complained, "because your parents are always gone."

And Symphony tasted the bitterness of resentment.

"Come spend the night tonight," Lilly said.

And Symphony learned, on accident, how to quiet her dreams.

# CHAPTER TWENTY

L ILLY CLIMBED ON a chair and opened the cabinet above the stove. "Oh. I don't think I told you. Auntie Mabel and Uncle Will are gone for the weekend."

"They left you by yourself?" Symphony shifted in her chair. *What if my parents find out?*

"Sure." Lilly stepped off the chair in her hip-hugging, bellbottom jeans holding a bottle of vodka. "They trust me."

For a moment, Symphony was overcome with envy. Lilly's body was perfect. Her waist was small, but not too small, her hips just the right size, her stomach flat. The only parts of her anatomy that seemed out of proportion were her breasts. They were too big, if that was possible.

Lilly set the bottle down on the counter. "So, have you ever tried this stuff before? It's really good with orange juice, you know what I mean? And you have to like orange juice. This is Florida."

Symphony nodded.

"It's pretty good with lemonade, too, if you'd rather have that. Would you?"

"Doesn't matter," Symphony said.

Lilly set two glasses on the countertop and poured orange juice into each, leaving about an inch and a half for the vodka. "By the way, this other girl might come over. I met her at Aunt Mabel's church. She's pretty nice, but kinda straight. She's got her license, though, so maybe we won't be stuck here all night, you know what I mean? Did you bring your *wee-gee* board?"

"Yeah." Symphony got up and pulled the Ouija Board out of her pillowcase. "You can have it if you want," she said. "The stupid thing keeps fallin' out of the closet in the middle of the night."

"Why don't you put something on top of it?"

"We do. Monopoly and Checkers."

"So they fall, too? I bet that really pisses your ol' man off." Lilly opened the vodka and added the clear, harmless-looking liquid, filling their glasses almost to the brim.

"My parents keep yellin' at me." Symphony said. "But it's really their fault. They're the ones who got it for me. Last Christmas. Whenever it falls, my mom comes in to check where I had it. First time, it was on top of a blanket so I can understand why it fell then. But ever since, I make sure it's right on the shelf. I wonder what would happen if I put the iron up there to hold it down."

Lilly handed her a drink. "Symphony, Symphony, Symphony. You are soooo full o' shit. You're actin' like that thing is haunted or somethin'." She put her hands on her hips and stared at Symphony. "You tryin' to scare me, or what?"

"Nope." Symphony giggled at Lilly's posture. "I'm tellin' you the truth." She set the Ouija Board on the corner of the table and sniffed her drink. *I think this is what Daddy has when the Guttmans come over.*

"Cheers," Lilly said, clinking her glass against Symphony's.

Although the first swallow warmed Symphony's throat, it tasted like a rotten orange peel smells. "Yuck," she said, as Lilly grimaced.

"It tastes like really bad cough syrup," Lilly said. "I guess I should've stirred it." She pulled two spoons out of a drawer and handed one to Symphony. They mixed their drinks and toasted again. "To orange juice," Lilly said, just before they tapped glasses. "Let's take a couple more sips and put these in the fridge. I don't trust Debbie not to tell if she sees us drinkin', you know what I mean?"

"When my dad's been drinking, I can tell by his breath," Symphony said. "Don't you think she'll be able to smell it?"

"Not vodka. That's why my mom drinks it. She says no one can smell it so she doesn't get caught. Even if she has a little before work." Lilly walked to the stereo console, picked up a picture, gazed at it for a moment, then set it back down. "Anyways," she said, lighting a candle, "let's smoke and then play wee-gee."

Symphony stiffened. *The last time we smoked . . .* But she relaxed when Lilly reached for a brand new pack of Marlboros.

Lilly smacked the top of the pack against her palm a few times, then opened it and pulled out two cigarettes. She kept one and handed the other to Symphony. They puffed them in the candle flame to get them started and leaned back in their chairs.

"Watch this," Symphony said, blowing smoke rings just as Therese had taught her. But as it turned out, Lilly was a smoke ring virtuoso. She made fat, round rings and sent each one through the center of those before it. Symphony stared in awe. When they finished smoking, they put their cigarettes out and concentrated on the game board between them.

"I've never used one of these," Lilly said, running her fingers across the rows of letters and numbers. "Can I ask it anything?"

"Whatever you want."

They put the planchette just below the farewell mark and rested their fingers in the right spot, ready for action. Lilly closed her eyes. "Where's my ol' man?"

The spirit of the board refused to tell her.

"Is he still livin' with my ol' lady?"

Nothing shifted.

Before anyone could ask another question, a knock at the door interrupted the session.

"Shit." Lilly jumped up from her seat. "Who is it?" She dusted the ashes off the table and hid the ashtray.

"It is I," the person on the other side of the door answered.

"Debbie!" Lilly said, letting in a tall, blonde girl wearing white culottes and a crisp, melon-colored blouse. "You scared the bejesus out of me."

"You'll go to hell for talkin' like that," Debbie said.

Symphony started to laugh. Therese had said those words many times, but *she* was always joking.

"It's not funny." Debbie cocked her head at Symphony. "Hey, aren't you Daniele Weber's sister?"

Symphony panicked. "Do you know her?" She felt her face flush.

"Not really." Debbie opened the refrigerator. "Got any soda?"

"On the left. Bottom shelf," Lilly said. "We were just about to find the answers to some very important questions, weren't we, Symmie?"

Debbie opened her Coke and sat down at the table. "Eew! That's one of those witch boards, isn't it? Reverend Lord says they're bad."

"That's ridiculous," Lilly said. "It's just a game. Here, I'll show you. Turn out the lights."

Debbie flipped the kitchen switch, leaving them in candlelight.

Lilly placed her fingers on one side of the planchette. "Are we ready?"

"Yeah," Symphony answered, placing hers on the other.

"What's *her* name?" Lilly asked, nodding in Symphony's direction. Soon afterward, the guide began to move.

B-I-T-C-H

"Stop foolin' around, you guys!" Debbie said. "You're scaring me."

Lilly glared at the board, ignoring Debbie's remarks. "Who do you think you are, callin' my friend a bitch?"

R-S-T-A-N-L-E-Y

"Oh, come on!" Debbie blurted. "That's not even a real word. Nothing starts with RS." She stood up. "Did you invite me over just so you could make fun of me? I wish my mom hadn't promised Mabel," she muttered, storming toward the front door. Then, she stopped and leaned against the wall. "Which one of you is playing a trick?"

"No one," Symphony said, jerking her hands away from the board. "It's talkin' about that bad guy who died in prison the other day. Roscoe Stanley. Didn't you see it in the paper?"

"You read the paper?" Debbie asked.

"Someone left it open on the table one morning and I saw it." Symphony picked up the planchette and turned it upside down. "C'mon, Lilly. I don't wanna do this anymore."

Debbie began to pace from one end of the kitchen to the other. "Oh my gosh," she said. "Reverend Lord told us things like this could open the door for an evil spirit. This could be dangerous. We should burn it."

"Yeah?" Lilly said, sounding irritated. "Where we gonna burn it? There's not exactly a fire in the fireplace."

"The church parking lot," Debbie said, grabbing her car keys. "My youth group's having a get-together there tonight. They have a band and everything."

"Sounds like a blast," Lilly said in monotone, frowning. She grabbed her glass from the refrigerator and took a huge gulp. "You want some of your orange juice, Symmie?" she asked.

"No thanks," Symphony said. "I'll finish it when we get back."

Lilly went to the table and picked up the board and planchette. "Are you sure you wanna burn this?" she asked. "Didn't you say it was a Christmas present from your parents?"

"Yeah," Symphony said. "It's creepy, though."

"But there were a few more things I wanted to ask it. And you told me *I* could have it. Remember?" Lilly sat down again.

"I know. But maybe you should just get a new one. This one wouldn't move, no matter what you asked it."

"You're right," Lilly said, looking depressed. "I just wanna find out about my stupid parents," she mumbled, following Symphony and Debbie to the door.

All three girls slid into the front seat of Debbie's mother's metallic blue '68 Impala. Although Symphony was eager to get the Ouija Board off her hands, she chewed her nails the whole two miles to the church. *How did Roscoe Stanley get in there? How long was he in my closet?*

Their arrival at the church did little to relieve her stress. A band in the background played oldies but goodies. The parking lot was filled with teenagers doing everything from skating to arguing.

"We don't have to tell anyone why we're burning it, do we?" Symphony asked.

"Not if you don't want to," Debbie said. "Just as long as we get rid of it."

Three boys strolled toward them. "Hey, Debbie," a redheaded boy said. "Where'd you go? You missed a lot of fun."

"This is Lilly and this is Symphony. I went to pick them up," she explained.

"I'm David," he said, not bothering to introduce the other boys.

"Can you help us with this?" Debbie asked.

Lilly held up the Ouija Board.

"Oh yeah," David said. "We've already burned a couple of these tonight, and some Tarot cards, and a few *Lord of the Flies* and one *Tropic of Cancer*. Best thing to do is break it into chunks and then squirt on some kind of starter."

A blonde boy with glasses offered up his can of lighter fluid.

Within minutes, the board had been broken to bits and was fueling a tiny bonfire on the concrete. "So, whose board are we burnin?" David asked.

Symphony hesitated then waved her hand in front of her chest.

The boys acted like it was no big deal. All three of them seemed to have the attitude that they were doing the world a valuable service. They talked with Debbie, Symphony, and Lilly as the fire turned to a small heap of grey ashes. Although the girls seemed to be enjoying the conversation, they turned down the boys' invitation to stay, and were just leaving when a breeze came up and lifted the ashes away.

"Whoa," David said, pointing toward the pavement. "Look at that."

"What?" Debbie asked, turning to where the Ouija Board had been. "Eewww. Is that—"

"Yeah. A goat's head," he said.

"Where?" Symphony asked, inching closer. "Show me."

There, beneath the dim parking lot lights, Debbie and the redheaded boy showed her the sooty outline: two sharp horns atop a triangular head, with a small beard just beneath the goat's nose. There were even two oily grey spots where the eyes would have been.

Symphony shivered in the warm breeze. "What does that mean?"

"It's a sign of the devil," the redhead said. "Hey, everybody," he called to the crowd, waving them over. "You've gotta see this."

Teenagers rushed from all corners of the churchyard. "Who brought the board?" people asked. "Where'd she go?" Some turned to look.

Symphony slipped away from the crowd and headed straight for Debbie's car. About ten minutes later, Debbie and Lilly caught up with her, still jabbering about what had happened as if it were the plot to a movie they'd just seen.

Debbie unlocked the car and opened the back door. "It was a little crowded in the front seat on the way over," she said. "Why doesn't Symphony sit in the back this time?"

Symphony got in as Lilly went on and on. "You should have seen 'em, Symphony. All of 'em starin' at that mark on the concrete with their mouths open. It was pretty weird, though, you know? What would make a fire do something like that?"

"David told you, Lilly," Debbie said. "There was something bad inside that board. Something evil."

"Why'd you leave, anyway, Symmie?" Lilly asked. "It was cool. Everybody wanted to meet you."

*Yeah. They all wanted to meet the freaky girl who brought the devil in a game board.* "I was ready to go." Symphony fell back into quiet mode, wishing she hadn't seen the goat's head, hoping she wasn't in for more Roscoe Stanley nightmares.

Debbie stopped the car in front of Lilly's house. She turned around and looked at Symphony. "I need to talk to Lilly, alone for a minute. If you don't mind."

"Sure," Symphony said. She got out of the car and walked to the house to wait.

As Lilly unlocked the front door, Symphony asked, "What did she say?"

"That I should be careful of you," Lilly said, turning on the light in the dark kitchen. "She said you could be close to the devil and you could make me that way. Basically, she thinks you're a bad influence on me." Lilly took their drinks out of the refrigerator, set them on the table, and grinned. "Want a cigarette?"

For the first time ever, Symphony felt like she needed one. "Yeah." *Don't all bad influences smoke?*

They sat at the table sipping and smoking the night away as they tried to decipher song lyrics beginning with *Jumpin' Jack Flash.*

Symphony didn't notice the thickness of her tongue or the heaviness of her legs until she stood up. "Oh my gosh," she giggled. "I think I'm drunk."

"Really," Lilly said, wobbling on the chair as she reached to retrieve the vodka. "I'm ready for another. I'll fill you up again, too."

The girls stayed awake as long as they could, listing misheard lyrics, mostly the Rolling Stones and Creedence Clearwater Revival. When they got too tired, Lilly put on an album by Led Zeppelin, a band that Symphony had heard of but had never listened to. Lilly said they were hard rock, but Symphony's favorite song was *Babe, I'm Gonna Leave You.* It was soft, with beautiful guitar work and melancholy vocals that, for some reason, made her think of Mack. One moment, she was floating along on the song's flute-like melody. In what seemed to be the next, she awoke, head throbbing, her face against the page of lyrics she and Lilly had written down.

It was morning and she hadn't been troubled by a single dream.

⌘ ⌘ ⌘

The fight started over the phone bill.

"These goddamn long distance calls are gonna stop, Symphony. You hear me?" Daddy's eyes were bulging. He grabbed the bill and shook it in her face, as if his shouting wasn't proof enough of his outrage.

"But, Daddy," she said, "Therese is in Massachusetts this summer, remember?" Her whole body tensed trying to fight off the desire to yell back. "Mama said I could call *her* once a month and her mom lets her call *me* once a month." She could feel her teeth clench. Her jaw twitched.

"Don't you look at me like that!" He raised his hand.

She flinched, and glanced away, trying to forget what he was threatening. There, at the corner of the hallway, stood Jeanne, Leesa, and Joe, glowering at Daddy behind his back. She turned to face his dark, fiery eyes, her anger showing.

"If you've got a brain in your head, you'll wipe that look off your face right now."

She stared at her feet and let her shoulder's slump, remembering who had all the power. "Please, Daddy," she pleaded. "It's my turn to call her next week. I really need to talk to her." Tears gathered in her eyes. She willed them to stop in an attempt to retain at least a pinch of pride. "I won't talk very long, I promise."

"No!" He slammed the bill onto the desk. "When you start paying for things around here, then you can run up phone charges. Okay? Until then, use the goddamn postal service." He turned toward the hallway. Jeanne, Leesa, and Joe scattered into the kitchen to hide. "Don't make me tell you again."

The wrangling lasted only a few minutes, but anyone with open windows could have heard the details. By the time Daddy left for school, Dani was home. "I'll be back soon," Symphony said, heading out the front door.

She ran down the street and snuck up the driveway at the old Hightower house where she found Mack waiting.

"He didn't hit you, did he?"

"I was afraid he would," she said, pushing the toe of her tennis shoe into a diamond of the chain link fence. She swung one leg, and then the other, dropping both feet at once into the squishy mud on the banks of Empty Lake.

Mack took her hand to hurry her into the boat. "What'd he do?"

Symphony shook her head, afraid to speak. She had never let Mack see her cry.

"You can tell me," he said. "I trust *you* with stuff all the time." He pushed them off from shore and pulled himself into the boat.

"It's not that." Symphony's voice quivered. "He just hates me, okay. He hates the way I look at him. He hates the way I apologize for every little thing. He hates the way my clothes never fit. He hates the way I breathe." She paused to steady herself. "Maybe I should just stop."

For a moment, neither of them said a word. Mack took off his t-shirt and threw it next to his feet. "Stop what?" he demanded.

She watched him row, marveling at the muscles rippling in his arms and shoulders.

"What did you mean?" he asked, his voice softer now. "What do you think you should stop?"

Symphony stared at a clod of dried mud on the boat floor. "Nothing," she said, breaking it to dirt with her shoe. "I shouldn't have said that. I was just upset."

"Are you sure? You didn't mean you should stop breathing, did you?"

"I wasn't serious, Mack." She pushed her hair out of her face. "But I don't think he'd care if I did, that's all. Can we just forget about it?"

When they reached the island, Mack pulled the boat aground and helped her out. This time, he held her hand as they walked to the camp. Instead of sitting in their usual spots on the floor of the woods, he unzipped the tent and they went inside. He put his arms around her and they leaned against each other.

Being there with Mack, comforted Symphony, but as he kissed her shoulder, her neck, her ear, teardrops trailed down her cheeks. "Don't cry." He wiped them away. "No one can hurt you right now. You're with me."

Looking into her eyes, he kissed her bottom lip, her top lip and pressed his mouth against hers.

Every muscle in her body seemed to tremble and weaken. Mack must have felt it because he drew her closer and brushed his tongue softly against hers.

This kiss had played and replayed in her imagination many times. But, *Frenching!* She hadn't expected that. After waiting so long, Mack was finally kissing her. She wanted to kiss back, to show him how she felt. She pushed her tongue forward slightly, but lost her nerve.

Mack began to rub her back. His hand touched the skin just beneath the hem of her shirt and she froze. "Don't."

With a groan, he pulled away. "I need a smoke." In the corner of the tent, he found an almost empty carton stashed under the pile of blankets. He opened a pack, lit two cigarettes, and handed one to Symphony. They stepped outside and took their usual seats, staring up at the sky as curls of cigarette smoke disappeared against the forest ceiling.

The birds called back and forth across the island. Neither Mack nor Symphony paid them any attention.

Symphony closed her eyes and tried to recall the softness of his tongue against hers, the weakness, the trembling. She wanted to do it again. *But I made him stop.* She watched him and sighed, wondering if she would ever have another chance.

Mack finished smoking and moved under Symphony's tree, sitting cross-legged on the pine straw in front of her. "There's some stuff going on at my house," he said. "Something I have to talk to my dad about." His pale blue eyes seemed to turn grey. "I don't know how it's gonna go." He glanced away and ran a hand through his sand-colored hair.

"What kind of stuff?"

"I can't say right now. I just wanted you to know so you don't worry. I might have to go away," he said. "Just for a while, till my dad cools off."

Symphony's eyes filled with tears as she recalled the words to the Led Zeppelin song. *"I never, never gonna leave you, babe. But I got to go away from this place."*

That night, raised voices from the Westhill house kept Symphony awake until after Mama got home from work at almost midnight. The next morning, Symphony offered to weed the front flower beds. When that was done, she hosed down the porch, driveway, and sidewalks, hoping Mack would appear. About ten-thirty, Bo waved her over and they met in the middle of the road.

"Mack's gone," he said, his eyes red like he hadn't slept all night.

"Maybe he's at the camp," Symphony suggested.

Bo shook his head. "He's not. I checked as soon as the sun came up. When I got back, I found this under my pillow." He handed Symphony a sheet of notebook paper folded in half three times with her name on the outside. She opened it. In the center of the page, in small letters, Mack had written:

> Keep breathing.
> Mack

"Weird, huh," Bo said.

Symphony raised an eyebrow. "You read this?" She saw the pain in Bo's eyes and let it drop.

"Yeah," he answered. "You know what he meant?"

# *CHAPTER TWENTY-ONE*

LILLY STOOD IN front of the mirror fiddling with her hair. "Lucky for you, he's nice," she said to Symphony's reflection. "You know, some guys would've kept on till they had their hand up your shirt or down your pants."

Symphony's face was red hot.

"He's really cute too," Lilly said, grinning. "I might have let him." She turned around when Symphony didn't answer. "You okay?"

"I've gotta go."

"I didn't mean *I* would let him. I just meant if *I were you,* I might have. You know what I mean?"

Symphony opened the door. As badly as she needed to talk to someone about how much she missed Mack, she couldn't even force herself to say aloud that he was gone. "I'll see you later."

⌘　⌘　⌘

Sunday morning, after a late breakfast, Mama buzzed around the kitchen as Symphony cleared the table. "If you help me finish the dishes," Mama said, "I'll take you school clothes shopping. Just you and me."

"Okay."

"What kind of outfits do you want for high school?"

"I don't care. Jeans and t-shirts?"

"I think we can do a little better than that."

All of last year's clothes fit Symphony like a girdle. *Whatever it is, has to be loose.*

When the kitchen was clean, Mama picked up her purse and keys. "Daniele?" she called down the hall. Dani poked her head through the bedroom doorway. "Your father's watching television so just act like you're babysitting."

"Okay."

"Come on, Symphony. Let's go."

The air was so hot, if you stood still for long, you could hear yourself beginning to sizzle. The slight breeze didn't offer much relief but riding in the car with the windows down chased the heat away.

They drove past the junior high and turned right after the park. Just before they reached the high school, Mama pulled the car into a convenience store parking lot. She dumped a fistful of change into Symphony's hand. "Call Therese," she said, "I'll get us some cokes."

Symphony looked at the coins in her hand, then up at Mama. "You mean it?"

"I know you two miss each other."

Symphony deposited the change and dialed the phone. It rang four times before Therese answered.

"Hey, Therese."

"Symphony? I didn't think you were ever gonna call."

"I know. *Now* my dad says it costs too much. Mama gave me money to use the payphone down by the high school."

"Why's he always gotta be such a jerk?" Therese asked.

Just then, Mama walked over, handed Symphony an ice-cold can of diet cola. "Tell her I said hello."

For twenty minutes, Symphony and Therese talked, giggled, and planned for the next school year. Mama read a magazine in the hot car. By the time the coins ran out and Symphony returned, Mama was fanning herself with the magazine.

Symphony kissed Mama on the cheek. "Thank you so much."

"You're welcome, sugar." She set the magazine on the seat between them. "How's Therese doing way up north, anyway?"

"She can't wait to get back home."

Therese had shared every detail of her Massachusetts summer. In return, Symphony had spliced together drab descriptions of life going to and fro, cutting the most important events. She needed her best friend more than she ever had. She wanted to tell her about the kiss, to lament over Mack being gone. But, the truth was, Therese had never wasted any love on the Westhill boys. *She wouldn't understand.*

Mama touched Symphony's shoulder and smiled. "This phone call has to be our secret. Okay?" She backed out of the parking lot and turned toward the mall. "Now, let's go find you something cute to wear in tenth grade."

They returned home several hours later with four outfits; three loose-fitting tops—one of them tie dyed—two pairs of jeans, a pair of brown corduroys, a billowy blue dress that was mid-calf length, black high-top sneakers, leather sandals, and a crocheted shoulder bag that closed with a huge wooden button.

Symphony tried everything on, again and again, in front of the mirror, wondering what to wear on the first day of school. *Therese'll know.* But Therese never saw those clothes. A week later, she called to say her father's transfer had been approved. They were staying in Massachusetts.

Symphony pined away the remainder of the summer, gazing out the picture window, watching, in vain, for a sign that Mack was home.

⌘　⌘　⌘

The women of the neighborhood began to speak in low tones about Mr. Westhill. "Well, *I* heard he's having an affair."

"I guess that doesn't surprise me. He's always seemed flirty, don't you think?"

And people were beginning to ask, "Where's their oldest boy?"

One Tuesday afternoon, when Mrs. Guttmann was visiting, Mama called Symphony to the table. "You and Mack are friends, right?"

"Yes," Symphony answered.

Mama twisted around, giving Symphony a sideways glance. "When was the last time you saw him?"

"A few weeks ago." Acting unconcerned, Symphony opened the refrigerator and poured herself a huge glass of orange Kool-Aid.

"Thank you, sweetie." Mama turned back to Mrs. Guttmann. "The poor woman. Should we go check on her?"

Two days later, Mama and Esther Guttmann knocked on the Westhill's door, carrying a chocolate pound cake. Hours later, when Mama got home, her eyes were red like she'd been crying.

"What did she say, Mama?" Symphony asked from the table, resting her cheek on her open palm.

Mama handed her a bag of carrots, some potatoes, and the peeler. "It's not really something you should have to worry about, sugar."

Symphony slid the peeler down the first carrot trying to make a full-length strip. "But, is Mack okay?"

"I'm sure he'll be fine," Mama said.

When Symphony had removed all the peels, she rinsed the vegetables and left them in the colander to drain. "Do you need me to do anything else?" she said to Mama's back.

"No." But as soon as Symphony started out the door, Mama turned around. "Wait," she said, her eyes brimming with tears. "Will you make the salad, too?"

Symphony tore the lettuce into pieces and rinsed it.

"Has Mack ever said anything about his father?" Mama asked over her shoulder.

"Not really," Symphony lied. She finished pinching off pieces of lettuce and washed the tomatoes.

"I know your daddy yells a lot. And sometimes, he spanks harder than he means to. But he loves you. You know that, don't you?"

*Loves me? Yeah, right.* Symphony nodded as convincingly as possible. "Sure, Mama."

Mama gave a huge sigh of relief. "I can finish this up." She took the tomatoes from Symphony and began dicing them. "You've been a big help, sweetie. I'll call you when it's time for supper."

Symphony left the kitchen more curious than she had been. Whatever Mrs. Westhill had said, upset Mama. *I wish she'd tell me what she found out.*

⌘　⌘　⌘

One evening just before school started, Bo caught Symphony outside and met her at the edge of the yard. "I got a collect call this mornin' from Elmo Hazelwood."

When Bo grinned, he looked an awful lot like Mack.

"Who?" Symphony asked, wondering why Bo was so excited.

"Mack," he whispered. "He's goin' by Elmo Hazelwood now. He sounds okay. Got a job with the circus. You believe it? He said he might come home if my dad's still stayin' at the hotel."

"I hope he does," Symphony said, wishing she could scream it to the universe so Mack could hear her, too.

"I miss him," Bo replied, "but the old man's really pissed. That last night, he grabbed Mack by the throat. I thought he was gonna kill him. Bastard wouldn't let go till my mom threw the phone at him." Bo smirked. "Receiver hit my dad in the face. Gave him a black eye."

Symphony envisioned the scene. *Maybe he's better off gone.* Night after night, she waited, hoping for a dream that would tell her he was all right. As usual, her gift wouldn't cooperate.

⌘　⌘　⌘

Summer ended and tenth grade began. Kids from two junior highs joined the older students, squeezing through hallways, searching for classes, looking for a friendly face. To Symphony, all the students seemed familiar, an extension of the group she'd been through school with, just the names and faces were different.

"Let's go to the football game," Lilly suggested the first Friday after school started.

"I really don't know much about football."

"Neither do I. But it would be fun to walk around and see who's there. You know what I mean?" So Aunt Mabel dropped them off.

"I gotta pee," Symphony said after the first quarter buzzer sounded. But Lilly, who was busy getting to know a boy from her history class, wasn't going anywhere.

"I'll stay right here till you get back," Lilly promised.

Symphony wound her way around the stadium twice before asking somebody's mother where the restroom was. Afterward, unable to find Lilly near the field, she searched behind the bleachers. As she walked through a quiet area, Greg Stanton crossed her path.

"Well, whadda ya know? Weigh-big." He knocked a drink out of her hand, twisted her arm behind her back, and pushed her under the visitor stands. "Keep quiet," he said, the smell of alcohol on his breath. "Oh, what the hell? Make as much noise as you want. No one up there gives a shit about you."

She balled her fists. "What do you want?" she asked through gritted teeth.

His bloodshot eyes grew darker, fiery. "I just want to make sure you know I can call you any name I want, touch you anywhere I want, and when I tell you to do something, you better do it! Do you hear me?" He grabbed her breast and twisted.

She felt the sting of tears but fixed her glare, refusing to let them flow.

"Hey," a woman yelled from one of the seats above, "what's going on down there?"

"Better not forget," Greg said, laughing as he ran out into the crowd.

Symphony leaned against the metal frame, gathering the strength she needed to go find Lilly. What finally made her feet move was the fear that he would return.

Lilly was in the smoker's corner entertaining a group of people Symphony didn't know. With a sideways glance, she said, "Hey, Symmie. Where'd you go?"

Before Symphony could answer, Lilly turned back to her audience. "So I had saved the last one for a special occasion, you know what I mean? I was plannin' to use it when the Dead played the Fillmore East last year, but I had to come here instead."

Symphony stood next to her friend feeling more alone than she would have felt sitting in the bleachers by herself. Her breast burned. She couldn't get over the feeling that people were staring at her. Every few minutes, she glanced over her shoulder watching for Greg Stanton.

Lilly's story didn't sound at all familiar. *I wonder why she hasn't told me that one?* With bruised breast and battered ego, she wandered to the sidelines to watch the rest of the game, keeping the attack to herself.

With Therese, Mack, and Elaine gone, Symphony had relied heavily on Lilly to be there for her. Lilly didn't seem to be up to the task.

Symphony's fifteenth birthday came and went with the usual cake and ice cream. Therese sent her a Neil Young album. Each time she listened to *I Believe in You*, she was left wondering how Mack really felt. And although the song made her sad, she played it endlessly because it held him close to her.

One Wednesday evening, during the third week of school, a police car pulled up in front of the Westhills'. A policeman escorted a tan, thin Mack up the sidewalk and delivered him into his mother's arms. A short time later, Mr. Westhill showed up and the shouting began. He stood on the front lawn yelling at the house. "Send that little prick out here so I can teach him a lesson. I'm his father. He needs his ass kicked. He has no respect."

Although Mrs. Westhill opened the window and yelled at him to leave, it took a visit by the police and a citation, before Mack's father returned to his car and peeled off down the street.

Daddy's night school class had been canceled. He turned off the television so he could watch the Westhill show. "I wonder where the little bastard was?" Then, he flung his pointing finger at every female in the house. "You girls stay away from him, you hear me. He's trouble. I could tell that the first time I met him."

Symphony nodded her understanding, all the while fuming. *You don't even know him.*

Mack didn't leave the house for the rest of the week, but the next Monday Mrs. Westhill drove all three boys to school.

The school day dragged as Symphony hoped for a chance to see Mack that evening. Her afternoon chores went quickly, leaving her with idle time to resent. Supper seemed to take forever. She wanted to change her clothes and put on something she felt really good in. *Is Daddy ever gonna leave?* She cleared the supper table, trying to act normal, avoiding looking at the clock every two seconds. But she couldn't stop thinking about Mack. Every time she took a plate to the sink, she closed her eyes, imagining the warmth of his kiss.

Finally, when Daddy's car turned the corner, she mouthed "I'm gone," to Jeanne. As Dani guarded the front door, Symphony slipped out the back, across the yard, over the fence, and disappeared down the street behind the house.

Symphony had joyful tears in her eyes before she even reached the Hightower's old house. She ran for the chain link fence. He wasn't there. "Mack?" she whispered. "Mack?"

"Come here," he said softly from behind her.

She turned. He'd been there all along, hidden by the camellia bush. His jeans were worn and dirty. They only stayed on his hips with the aid of a suede leather belt. His feet were the only indication that the legs of his jeans weren't empty. His eyes looked huge against his bony face. His blonde hair had grown and was rubber-banded into a ponytail that hung between his shoulder blades. He put his arms out and, sobbing, she went to him.

"I missed you too," he said, holding her.

"I was afraid you wouldn't come back." She looked away, ashamed, feeling she'd said too much.

He touched her chin, lifted her face, and kissed her tears. "Let's go," he said. "Let's cross the lake."

"How did you get out tonight?" she asked. "I wouldn't think your mom would—"

"I promised her I wouldn't be gone too long. Between me and my ol' man, she's a fuckin' wreck. The son of a bitchin' bastard."

From her seat in the boat, she watched his sharp elbows as he pulled the oars. The muscles in his chest and arms had all but disappeared.

When they reached the island, Mack lit them both a cigarette and they walked to the tent. He opened the zippered door to the smell of musk and ammonia. A squirrel chattered a sharp warning from the corner where the blankets were stored. Mack and Symphony backed out and zipped the tent shut.

"Shit," Mack said.

They stared at each other for a moment, then began to laugh. When the laughter faded, he touched her face and gazed at her. She searched his eyes until he closed them and put his open mouth against hers. His body felt feverish, his tongue slipping, pressing. Not knowing how to kiss him back, she let him continue, grateful that he was here, feeling lovely that he wanted to do these things with her. His hands rubbed her back and she held him tighter. He kissed her neck and moved downward, nuzzling her breast. She pulled his face upward for another kiss.

"I almost forgot," he said, grinning. "I brought something home with me. I think you'll like it."

The twinkle in his eyes aroused Symphony's curiosity.

Mack reached into his back pocket, took out the cardboard center of a toilet paper roll, and bent it back into its natural cylindrical shape. From his deepest pocket, he pulled what seemed to be a wad of aluminum foil, tore off a piece, laid it over a small hole in the cardboard, and pressed a crater using his thumb. Next, he unfastened the safety pin that was holding his shirt closed, and poked tiny holes into the crater. When that was finished, he opened the foil ball, broke off a small piece of the golden chunk in the center, and put it in the crater. "There," he said, regarding his work as Symphony stared, mystified.

Then, he held one end of the toilet paper roll against his mouth. Covering the other end with the flat of his hand, he inhaled with the flame of his lighter against the golden chunk. After a moment, in another kiss, he blew the smoke from his lungs into Symphony's.

As soon as she exhaled, her chest felt lazy and her eyes got fuzzy. "What is that?" she asked.

"Hash," he answered. "Do you like it?"

"Thank goodness it's not pot," she said.

He laughed, lit the makeshift pipe again, and repeated. The third time, she coughed the smoke out right away. "No more," she said. "I can't—" She couldn't remember lying down, couldn't feel the forest floor against her back. For a moment, she got lost in flamingo-colored clouds of sunset, wishing she could reach out and touch them. Then Mack was beside her, rubbing his middle finger back and forth in the palm of her hand. He was talking to her, but each word seemed to stretch out and cave in on the next.

"Are you sure this isn't pot?" she asked. The words came out slowly and sounded wrong.

He kissed her, his tongue going deeper, licking harder against hers. His fingers teased her nipples and stroked her stomach. She felt them drift past the waist of her pants and dive down between her legs. What he did with one finger seemed to pluck a cord that rang through her center. She arched her back and moaned.

Then a picture flashed in her mind. "I've gotta go home!" She stood up quickly, rolling Mack onto his back. Dusk oozed into the clearing from between the trees.

"We've got plenty of time," Mack said. "Why don't you just try and relax?"

She looked at him. She didn't see the eyes of the beautiful boy anymore. The sparkle was gone. "I think he's home," she said, beginning to tremble.

He lit them each a cigarette, packed his pockets once again, and they headed down the path to the boat. They didn't speak as they crossed to shore. In silence, they climbed Hightower's fence and made their way past the camellia bush. As soon as Symphony got to the road, she could see her house. Daddy's car was in the driveway.

"Damn," Mack said, guiding her back behind the camellia. "What're ya gonna do?"

"I can't think," she said. And she couldn't. Thoughts were rattling in her head like they had the time she'd smoked with Lilly. "Are you sure this isn't pot?"

"I thought you were kidding," he said. "It's made outta pot, but it's stronger."

Symphony began to shiver—first her hands, then down into her legs and upward until her lips and eyelids were twitching.

"Concentrate," Mack said, pacing in a small circle.

"It's no use," she said. "This is what pot does to me."

He took her by the arm. "Look at me," he insisted. "Can't you say you were at your friend's house?"

"Therese doesn't live here anymore and Elaine died. All I have is Lilly and they went out to dinner." She sat down on the ground. "I have to stay here until I can figure out what to say. You may as well go home."

"Are you sure?"

The Mack she loved would never have left her there.

# CHAPTER TWENTY-TWO

MACK ROUNDED THE corner into the Hightower's front yard and disappeared.

Symphony lay down on the ground, closing her eyes. The smoke had affected her gift again. Scenes flashed behind her lids like a silent film. *A baby cried in the arms of a man wearing a black hat. A bride and groom danced on the edge of a cliff. Dani laughed as she took a bite of birthday cake. A young boy, wide-eyed but still, stared from underwater. Daddy's face drifted in and out of her thoughts. The only color image was his bloodshot eyes squinting in anger.*

"Breathe!" she reminded herself. The ground beneath her smelled like Granny's garden after a good watering. Its coolness clung to her and she began to shiver. She tried to recall the last time she had talked to Granny about anything important. Their relationship hadn't been the same since Gray died. *I wish she was here.*

Her predicament resurfaced, pushing thoughts of Granny aside.

*I could say I went to dinner with Lilly. No. I'll just wait at Lilly's till she gets home. She'll help me with a story.*

She opened her eyes and stood, brushing off remnants of leaves, grass, and dirt. The air felt thick. Alert to every sound and movement, she crept down the Hightower's driveway. When she reached the street, she ran, around the back side of the block, behind her house, then rounded the corner headed for Lilly's. There, she took a seat on the front stoop, waiting, chewing her thumbnail until it bled. She tasted copper, felt the sting, switched hands and began working on the other thumbnail. *I wish I had a cigarette. What's taking them so long?*

She stood, followed a pebble path to the backyard, and peered into Lilly's bedroom. It was dark, empty. The screen was off, leaning against the house. She tried the window. *Locked.*

Moments later, she retraced her steps and returned to the front stoop, fingers crossed. When stars began to stand out against the sky, she gave up and walked home, dragging her feet, dreading Daddy's wrath.

She put an ear against the front door, hoping to hear what he might be saying. The house was silent—*not a good sign.* The doorknob didn't make a sound as it turned. She tiptoed inside.

"It's about goddamn time," Daddy snarled, grabbing her by the front of her shirt.

Something ripped. She felt it. She heard it.

"Where the hell have you been?" The fire in his eyes turned her thoughts to ashes.

"I was—"

"Don't you lie to me, either, you little—" He glanced away and spat out, "Slut!"

She'd heard the word. Boys always said it with a grin, older girls with disgust. But no one had ever used it to describe her.

"You hear me?" he yelled, giving her shirt another yank.

"Uh, I went for a walk." She looked up, hoping he'd believe her if she said it to his face, but she couldn't stop her lips from trembling. "Then I went to Lilly's. I needed help with my homework."

He grabbed her arm and jerked her to attention. "I sent Daniele three times to see if you were there." He squeezed tighter and gritted his teeth. "No one's been home all night."

"I waited in their backyard, Daddy. Just for a little while. Then, I walked around some more. I went back a few times."

He snatched her close and sniffed her blouse. "You've been with that goddamn Westhill boy, haven't you?" He shoved her across the room. "You smell just like him. Cheap and dirty."

Symphony shook her head.

"You think I'm blind? I see the way you watch those boys. If you didn't eat all the goddamn time, maybe you could catch a boy who was worth a shit."

The shivering took hold of her again.

Daddy closed the distance between them. "Look at me when I'm talkin' to you."

But as soon as she raised her eyes, he slapped her, back-handed, across the face. She groaned and began to cry.

"I guess you've decided you're gonna be trash." He grabbed her arm. "Get out of here!" He tossed her down the hall toward the bedroom. "I can't stand the sight of you."

She opened the door, pushing an eavesdropping Dani aside.

"I'm so sorry," Dani whispered, sniffling. "I tried to find you so I could bring you home. Let me see your face."

"Daniele!" Daddy yelled. "Come out here and make me a goddamn screwdriver and then I want you all in bed for the night."

Since Mama had gone back to work, Dani had become a regular bar-maid, pouring vodka, measuring it by the length of her finger joints, and serving it without so much as a thank-you. She dried her eyes at his command. "I'll be right back. And I'll bring you a wet wash cloth. Do you need anything else?"

Symphony stared at the floor, shaking her head. After Dani left, she moved to the mirror to check for damage. She was relieved. *It feels worse than it looks.* School was tough enough without a handprint across your face.

Dani returned about ten minutes later with a cup of ice cubes, a cookie for each of them, and a report. "I promised the little sisters you were okay so they'd go to sleep. Joe wants a kiss."

Symphony tiptoed across the hallway to her brother's room. She helped him with his prayers, which consisted of "Now I lay me down to sleep . . ." and the "God-blessing" of everyone in the family. When he finished, she kissed him goodnight.

Dani was waiting in their room with two ice-packed washcloths. "Here," she said. "Put one on your lip. It's a little swollen. And the other can go on your right cheek. You might get a black eye." She grimaced. She didn't scold Symphony or ask, "Where were you?" She just hugged her and turned out the lights. They lay there, quiet in the darkness.

For Symphony, staring at the night was the equivalent of closing her eyes. The pictures began to flash again but she fought sleep, recalling how her dreams had accelerated when she'd smoked with Lilly.

She heard Mama come in from work, take a shower, and go to bed. Once the house was still, she slipped out of her room, went to the liquor cabinet, and took a few gulps of Daddy's vodka. It burned like a fire in her chest, but if that would stop the dreams as it had that night at Lilly's, she preferred the fire.

She slept through the night. By the time Dani's alarm went off the next morning, Daddy had already left for work.

Symphony checked the mirror. Her face was fine. She helped Dani get the younger kids up and ready for school, relieved that Daddy wasn't around to make the beginning of the day miserable. They let Mama sleep until it was time to go. She got up with a yawn and a smile, made a pot of coffee, and kissed them each as they headed for the bus stop.

"He must not have told her yet," Dani said as they walked toward the corner.

Symphony crossed herself as Therese had taught her. *Maybe he won't tell her.* If he did, wouldn't he have to include the jerking around? The hitting?

First chance Symphony got, she spilled the whole story to Lilly.

"Mack kissed you?" Lilly said, as if she were shocked. "And all that other stuff? Jeez, it sounds like you guys almost *did* it, you know what I mean. If you'd been there any longer—" Just then, Lilly's science teacher walked by. "Oh, Hi, Mr. Ottowa." She turned back to Symphony. "So, are you grounded?"

"My dad didn't say. Why?"

"I was just wondering. I ran into Bo at the mall yesterday. I know he's younger than me, and all, but he is *so* cute. He asked me to go to the island with him tonight. Will you be there too? With Mack?"

"I don't know," Symphony said, suddenly nauseous. "I want to see him really bad, but, even if I'm not in trouble, I'm afraid to push it. Ya know?" She thought about the situation for a moment. "How 'bout this? I could come to your house and we could go over your fence and walk along the lake to meet them. I couldn't stay long, though. Just for a little while."

"You're prob'ly right," Lilly said. "You shouldn't go. Maybe another time." She smiled and gave Symphony a serious nod.

That afternoon during lunch, Greg Stanton approached Symphony. "I need to talk to you." He pressed her into a corner. "Can you meet me after school?"

"No," Symphony said. "Leave me alone."

He pushed in closer. "People are always saying you know stuff."

"I used to," she said, wriggling free. "Now," she said with pride, "I'm just like everybody else."

"Think about it," he said.

She gave him an over-the-shoulder glance as she walked away.

By the time Symphony got home that afternoon, Mama had Daddy's version of the details. She didn't ask for Symphony's.

"You're never to see Mack again," she ordered in a display of urgency and tears that Symphony had never before witnessed. "I won't just sit here and watch you throw your life away. Do you hear me?"

Symphony nodded and looked at her feet.

Mama shook a pointed finger inches from her face. "You're on restriction! For at least two weeks, depending on your behavior. No friends, no phone, no television."

And so began the longest two weeks of Symphony's life.

The first few days, Mack walked up and down Overlook Terrace with Lilly and Bo, all three of them laughing, smoking, having a great time. Before the week was over, another girl had joined their party. She was a thin, long-legged, strawberry-blonde named Shelby who, judging by the way she leaned against Mack, was unable to stand on her own.

Symphony tried to pretend it didn't matter. After all, Mack would be hers just as the beautiful boy dream had predicted.

She concentrated on her chores and kept up with her homework. At night, when the rest of the family was sleeping, she tiptoed to the liquor cabinet and took a gulp of vodka. It was the only thing that could quiet her mind.

Each day, Greg Stanton appealed to her again, sometimes begging, other times threatening. One day he caught her in the hall between classes. "You have to do something," he said. "My brother is missing."

That night, Symphony passed on the vodka in hopes of dreaming some information that would help. Instead, she tossed and turned the night away, awakening in the morning with nothing.

On week nights, she ate dinner with the family, helped with the dishes, then went straight to her room. The weekends were the worst. Sometimes she and Dani would spend time just talking, or Jeanne would come in and visit for an hour or so. Mama wouldn't even look at her. On the most difficult days, Symphony wrote letters to Therese but tore them up before anyone else could read them.

Although school was the only place Symphony could socialize, Lilly began to distance herself, glomming onto Mack's new girlfriend who was also in tenth grade. By the time Symphony's two weeks were up, Lilly had completely turned away from her.

⌘ ⌘ ⌘

The evening of Symphony's first free day, Daddy had a class. After supper, she went straight to her room—a habit she'd been forced to acquire over the last two weeks. She brushed her hair until it was shiny and changed into her favorite outfit. When she heard Daddy leave, she went to the living room and stared out the front window, hoping for a chance to talk to Mack. He finally appeared with Bo and Lilly, walking—in a row of three—up the center of the street. Trembling, Symphony headed out the door, relieved that Shelby wasn't with them.

When she reached the lawn, Bo pointed at her. "There's Symphony."

Lilly's smile turned stiff. "Go on, Mack. Talk to her!" She nudged Mack's shoulder.

Grinning, he stepped forward. "Symphony," he called, motioning her over with a jerk of his head.

She quickened her pace, excited to see his smiling face, hoping for a hug. But Mack's expression seemed to change as she approached. "Hey," she said. "I missed you."

His pale blue eyes were intense. "What's this bullshit about you and me practically fucking?" he asked.

She felt her cheeks burn. "I'm sorry," she offered, glaring at Lilly. "I told her what happened."

Symphony nor Mack moved, but the distance between them grew.

"What you told her didn't happen. I shot-gunned you some hash, that's all. Either you imagined the rest of it, or you're an out and out liar."

Tears welled in Symphony's eyes.

"Don't you look in the mirror?" he asked. "You have a pretty face, but—the rest of you? Why would I be with someone like you?"

"Really!" Lilly said. She and Bo began to laugh.

Symphony stared at them in disbelief. A sob rose in her throat. She turned and ran home, away from everyone, back to her room where she was safe. She stretched out on the bed wishing she could sleep and forget what had just happened, but sleep wouldn't come. Nothing she did could stop the thoughts and images.

*Vodka.*

She opened the door a crack. Dani was in the living room on the phone, laughing. The others were playing out back. Creeping into the kitchen, Symphony opened the cabinet above the stove and found a new bottle of the clear, dream-killing elixir. It was cool against her skin as she slid it under her shirt.

Back inside the bedroom, she twisted off the lid, took her usual two gulps, and waited for the warmth to reach her toes. It didn't happen. She could still see the way Mack had looked at her. The bride and groom danced on the cliff. This time, the groom turned to face her. It was Mack.

She took two more swallows.

*Why'd he have to lie?*

The images flooded in. Mack was snickering. The fixed eyes of the boy underwater stared up at her. Lilly held Bo's hand as they yelled "Big, fat liar," and howled with laughter. The beautiful boy appeared before her, his smile turning to a sneer. Roscoe Stanley waved in his clown suit. The boy, Greg Stanton, ran out the door as his mother cursed.

Symphony turned the bottle up once again and swallowed vodka until her stomach ached. Her throat was an inferno. Still the visions flashed before her.

She drank again until she melted into a warm liquid. Her body disappeared and she glistened, like a lake in the sunlight. The visions faded into a transparency she could move through. She left them behind, flowing toward a blinding silver light.

Elaine was walking toward her. "Symphony?" she said. "What are you doing here?" She shook her headful of grey curls. "You can't stay."

Blackness and silence stretched out before Symphony. The warm liquid she was, began to turn cold.

A light burst through the center of the darkness. Elaine was back. "Hey. I forgot to tell you," she said. "Your dream about me—it was right.

After the last round of chemo, when my hair grew back, it was curly and grey. See. It still is." She shook her head and her grey curls bounced. "You're gonna be okay," she continued. "The doctors and nurses are taking care of you right now. Stay here where you are, Symmie. You've got lots more stuff to do. There's this one really amazing thing . . . and, let me tell you, you don't wanna miss it." Elaine kissed her cheek.

Suddenly, Symphony was no longer a liquid. She opened her eyes to find Daddy holding her hand.

"She's awake," he said, crying. "I'm sorry, sugarfoot. I am so sorry."

⌘　⌘　⌘

She recalled blinking once or twice, her throat aching from the tube they'd used to pump the alcohol out of her stomach. Somewhere, through the fog, she heard Daddy apologize.

Mama was working in surgery that night. She rushed in well after Symphony opened her eyes.

The doctor gave Symphony a stern glance over the top of his glasses. "You're a lucky, young lady," he said. "We caught it before there was any real damage."

Mama and Daddy followed him into the hallway and closed the door, but Symphony could hear them.

"I've set up an appointment for a psych consult," the doctor said in a low voice. "I don't think any of us want to see her back here again."

Mama broke down. "You think she was trying to . . ."

"Why else would she have done it, Maisy?" Daddy asked.

The doctor promised to check on her in the morning. Then, he walked away, his heels clicking down the long, empty hall.

When Mama and Daddy stepped back into the room, Symphony could see the "Why?" in their eyes. Daddy paced at the foot of the bed. Mama picked at her fingernails. Neither of them would look at her. She fell asleep knowing that everyone thought she wanted to die.

The next day, via red-eye Greyhound, Granny swooped in to gather up the truth. She didn't waste a second clearing the room. "You two look exhausted," she said to Mama and Daddy. "Why don't you go get some coffee?"

Mama shook her head. "No. I should stay."

Granny kissed Mama's cheek. "Take a step back, honey. I'll be right here with her."

"Come on," Daddy said, guiding Mama, his arm around her shoulders. "We won't be long."

By the time the door closed, Granny had moved to Mama's chair. She rolled her support hose down around her ankles and slipped off her shoes. She leaned back for a moment, sizing Symphony up. "You look better than I thought you would. A little pale but, all in all, pretty good." She bent forward and began finger-combing Symphony's tangled hair. "What happened, sugar? Your mama says you've been kind of blue lately."

Symphony thought of Mack and began to cry. "That's not why, Granny."

"Was it the dreams?" Granny asked. "They used to drive Graydon half crazy. He claimed that's why he drank every night." Her eyes filled with tears. "Lord, honey. You got your whole life ahead o' you. What dream was so bad you nearly killed yourself tryin' to make it stop?"

"It wasn't just *one*, Granny. Dreams kept waking me up. And there was too much real stuff happenin'. All I wanted to do was sleep and forget it all. But, no matter how hard I tried, I *couldn't* sleep."

"And you thought drinkin' would help?"

"One time my friend made me some orange juice with vodka. That night, I didn't have a single dream."

"Did you tell that to your mama?" Granny asked.

"No." Symphony put her forearm over her eyes. "They think I did it on purpose."

"Don't you worry, sugar," Granny said, wrapping her speckled, weathered hand around Symphony's. "We'll get this all sorted out. Now, try and get some rest. I'll sit right here and make sure no one bothers you."

"I love you, Granny."

"I love you more." Granny relaxed against the back of the chair humming *Amazing Grace*, until they both dozed off.

⌘　⌘　⌘

For months, Daddy side-stepped Symphony, only speaking to her when he had no choice. Gradually, she began to smile again. Little by little,

Daddy re-introduced scolding. Unwashed dinner pots and un-ironed hand-kerchiefs summoned his raised voice and soon, the household returned to normal. At least once a month he was out-and-out ugly to her. But he never again stooped so low as to belittle her about her weight or the people it kept away.

From vodka night forward, she gave Daddy plenty of reason to discipline her.

Once out of the hospital, she returned to school as "the girl who tried suicide but couldn't even do *that* right." A group of *unpopulars* took pity on her and she fell right into step with them. When they began passing joints around, Symphony took her share of tokes. By then, the effects were normal. There were no dreams to amplify. The vodka poisoning seemed to kill them. And with them went the old Symphony, or at least the part who cared whether or not she was a disappointment.

Membership in a group provided some protection. Kids who had tor-mented Symphony, now ignored her. But she was still tortured by Lilly's after school struts up and down the street with Mack and Bo. When spring arrived, their exaggerated laughter flowed in through open windows, reminding Symphony of what she had lost.

Just before eleventh grade all that ended.

Mrs. Westhill had allowed her husband a second chance. Within the year, he was gone again. Amid rumors of another affair, he moved out. Less than two weeks later, Mrs. Westhill took her boys back to Alabama.

That August, a tourist from New York snagged his fishing line on the remains of a boy in the Indian River just outside of Titusville. By the time authorities jailed Greg Stanton's mother on suspicion of murder, Greg was safely tucked away at his father's house in Tennessee. No one had ever reported his little brother missing.

With Lilly's laughter subdued and Greg Stanton gone, eleventh grade was almost as easy as breathing. Life at home wasn't so bad, either. Daddy didn't act like he hated Symphony anymore.

He mostly left her alone.

# PART TWO

(Eight Years Later)

# CHAPTER TWENTY-THREE

DADDY SAT IN a chair by the window staring out into the night. "The weatherman didn't say a word about lightning." A flash of silver-blue split the darkness. "Lord, Lord." He shook his head and glanced above him as if searching for Jesus in the hospital's white ceiling tiles. "I wish your mother'd hurry up and get here."

As he held his upward gaze, Symphony noticed the bald spot on top of his head. *Wow! And when did his hair get so grey?*

He twisted around, catching the look of surprise on her face. "Are you sure you're all right?"

"I'm fine, Daddy. I promise."

Still, his brows crowded together, crumpling the forehead between them.

*What's he so worried about? It can't be the labor room. He and Mama did this five times.* Then, she realized. What was keeping Daddy stirred up had nothing to do with the baby. *I almost died last time I was in this hospital.* She glanced over, hoping to catch his expression, but he had turned back toward the window. *He was the only one with me when I woke up that night.*

She studied him for a while. She'd spent her whole childhood trying to avoid his wrath, wishing she was good enough in his eyes, wondering when he would just hit her and get it over with. He was different these days: soft against the storm—far from the angry man who had stolen her confidence.

Her kiss with death had changed all that.

Tonight, as Symphony's labor progressed, Daddy turned away, watched the storm, moved around the room. His expression, when she could see it, reminded her of back then, back when his avoidance proved he didn't care. *Look at me. Please.* She wanted to see his face; see if she could understand him without the mask of blame that had always come between them.

He turned around, as if he'd heard her. "You still okay?"

What she needed was in his eyes. She had been so fragile. *He didn't know how to keep from crushing me back then. He still doesn't know.*

The stiff, white sheets scratched her back where the hospital gown parted. Quietly, she slid down in bed, careful to keep the blanket pulled over her, hoping a change of position would ease her somehow.

Daddy was next to her in no time. "What's wrong?"

"I'm fine," she said with a tired smile.

He cocked his head and gave her an "Are-you-sure?" look. "I wish your mother'd hurry up," he said again. "Of all nights for her to work late."

"I'm sure she'll be here any time," Symphony said. But she was beginning to wonder.

Daddy touched her forehead as if testing for fever then turned back toward his chair. "I can't believe it's storming like this. Not as cold as it is outside."

A silver-orange flash lit the night sky, followed by a sizzle and boom, which left the hospital in darkness.

"Lord, Lord." He pressed his forehead against the window. "That one had to hit something. Sounded like a transformer. And since the power's out . . ."

"I thought it was quiet in here before," Symphony said. "But now it's—" Thunder crashed outside. As if guided by the storm, Symphony's belly stiffened. A belt of muscles squeezed all the way around her back. At first, she tightened her grasp on the bed frame. Then she remembered Granny's words. "Won't do a bit of good to fight it. Don't waste your energy." She took a breath and counted to ten as she exhaled. Her body began to relax.

"Don't worry," Daddy said, still watching the storm. "They'll have it back on soon." Within seconds, a dim light over the bed flickered twice, then stayed. "See. I told you. Generators."

"Daddy?"

"What, sugarfoot?"

"Would you mind seeing how much longer Mama's gonna be? And what about the doctor?" Symphony asked. "When does he come?"

"Oh, they won't call him till you're almost ready. Your mother'll know. I wish she was here." He patted Symphony's hand and smiled reassuringly. "Let me go get the nurse for you. I'll only be a minute." He bolted for the door like an animal released from captivity.

Symphony rolled her eyes. *You'd think he was afraid of me.* She picked up the phone and called Dani.

"Hey, Dani. Guess where I am?" She moved the receiver away from her ear in anticipation of Dani's squeal.

"The hospital?" Dani squealed. "How long have you been there?"

"About three hours. And Mama's been assisting in surgery the whole time. Daddy's so fidgety he's about to drive me crazy. I know it's gettin' late but is there any way you can come down?"

"Oh—my—Gosh! You should've called me earlier. You need anything? Want me to bring anyone else?"

"No. Just you. Jeanne and Leesa are in Orlando."

"What about Joe?"

"Don't call him. He has to work at six in the mornin'. I have to go," Symphony said, her abdomen tensing again. "I need to concentrate on getting this baby out of me. And it'd sure be nice to have you here to help take care of Daddy."

"Say no more," Dani said. "I'll be right there."

Symphony hung up the phone. She hated to complain about Daddy. His patience over the last few months had been a surprise and a relief.

A nurse holding a clipboard walked into the room. "I need to check you Sym—is it Symphony?"

"Yes. Like the concert."

"What a beautiful name," she said, stretching a fresh glove over her hand. "I need to see how far you're dilated." She pushed her fingers inside Symphony. "Hmm. You're making some progress. Three and a half, almost four centimeters."

*That hurt.* "How many centimeters do I have to go?"

"Can't push till you're at ten. I'll be back in about an hour. Use your call light if you need me before then."

"Ten?" Symphony asked with a heavy sigh.

The nurse gave a sympathetic smile over her shoulder as she left.

In an instant, Symphony's excitement deflated. She felt alone, just as she had in Pennsylvania, with Quinton.

⌘　⌘　⌘

She had met Quinton when she was a freshman at Auburn University.

He wasn't on the dean's list, but schools don't usually grade students on their ability to party. Quinton majored in having a good time. He made Symphony laugh although, sometimes, he used artificial means to do so.

They married two and a half years later, a week after his graduation, and headed straight for Quinton's hometown—Carlisle, Pennsylvania. Each day, Quinton took Symphony's car to work at his father's upholstery shop, leaving her in a tiny one-bedroom rental that seemed to shrink around her.

"Can't I take you to work?" she pleaded. "I wanna look for a job during the day."

Quinton would just give her that half-smile of his and wink. "I don't want you to work," he insisted. "I want you to stay home and have babies."

*Babies?* She hadn't planned on having kids so soon. But as the months went by, and her first drink of the day got earlier and earlier, she softened on the idea. *A baby.* Then, her pill prescription ran out and Quinton just didn't "like doing it with a rubber."

"If it happens," he said with that same half-smile, "then it's meant to be."

She knew from the nausea. The stench of frying bacon sent her running for the bathroom. Pine oil cleaner made her head spin. Her breasts felt bruised. She peed constantly, not because of the pregnancy, just in search of the period that wouldn't come. She stopped her occasional use of drugs and limited her drinking.

Quinton was thrilled. He called his parents first. Then, with a "Let's celebrate," he pulled Symphony to the car and drove to the nearest Italian restaurant, ordering, "A bottle of your best wine." As the waiter poured them each a glass, Quinton shared the news. "I'm gonna be a daddy." He told everyone—the patrons at the adjoining tables, the people they passed as they walked to the movies two blocks away, the boy in the ticket booth, the usher.

Two months later, when Symphony began to bleed, he didn't believe her. She had to show him the proof. Although he'd roughed her up every night for a week, he demanded to know what she'd done to cause it. All she could do was cry.

Symphony wasn't ready but the second pregnancy came as soon as her body had re-established its equilibrium. This time she stopped all partying, aside from those nights Quinton insisted she join him. She made it one week longer before she miscarried.

Quinton began staying out late. He pushed her away, wouldn't talk to her. Only the phone calls from Therese kept her sane until her husband warmed up once again.

⌘ ⌘ ⌘

Dani rushed into the room. "I'm here," she said, pulling off her coat, balancing a dripping Auburn Tigers umbrella in the corner. "Any news?"

Symphony chuckled. "No. Still waiting. Did you see Daddy?"

"I caught him at the nurses' station and sent him to the cafeteria for awhile. They said Mama ran home to take a quick shower. She'll be right back. So tell me . . ." Dani scooted a chair next to the bed and sat down. "Does it hurt?"

Symphony studied her sister's face. She thought of the nightmares that had brought a scared Dani to her bed so many times when they were growing up. *Her imagination always makes everything so much worse.* She wanted Dani and Phil to have a baby one day. "It's really uncomfortable," Symphony said. "More like pressure. But I can tell you one thing for sure. It was a lot easier getting it in there than it's gonna be to get it out."

"Ew!" Dani wrinkled her nose. "That's gross."

After that, Dani didn't ask any more pregnancy questions. She launched into a series of diversions that succeeded in taking Symphony's mind off of labor—at least until her body reminded her. "You know, the houses on the eastside are all twinkling with Christmas lights and as soon as you get to Barna Avenue there's nothing. Not even traffic lights. Three weeks till Christmas and downtown is completely dark."

"Yeah. The power's out here too. Daddy said the generator kicked in."

Dani settled in her chair and began filing her nails. "Tonight reminds me a little of the hurricane in Mobile. Do you remember that?"

"Oh, yeah!" Symphony said. "I haven't thought of it in a long time. I wonder how Miss Ida Stalls is doin'. Maybe after things get back to normal, we can go see her."

"That'd be fun. How's Therese?" Dani asked. "Have you called her yet?"

"No. I'll call her when I have something to tell her."

Dani pulled her long curls into a silver clasp at her neck. "I'll bet she comes down here."

"She can't. She just started back to college. I know she won't come for Christmas and there won't be another break till spring."

"That's too bad," Dani said. She picked up her half-a-cow-sized, leather bag from the floor and reached elbow-deep into its innards. When her hand resurfaced, it was wrapped around a camera. "We'll just have to send her some pictures." She grinned and turned on the flash. "Maybe I should take one now. Why don't you push back the sheet so we can remember your belly?"

Symphony yanked the covers up to her neck. "Don't you dare!"

"Come on. Just one?"

"I'm serious, Dani. Put it away. Please!"

Dani slipped the camera back into her purse and picked up her emery board. "Hey, you'll never guess who I ran into the other night." She cracked her knuckles and began filing her nails again. "One of Phil's co-workers invited us to a party and Darla Terry met us at the front door, only her name's not Terry anymore. She's married to the guy who was having the party. She said to tell you, 'Hi'. Her brother was there, too. You remember him, right? David? He's still a hunk. Said something about veterinary medicine. I didn't catch it all. It was really loud in there. Besides, Phil thought David was being kind of flirty so we moved across the room to talk to someone else. You're sweating really bad. Can I get you anything?"

Symphony was counting down a contraction. As soon as it subsided, she nodded to Dani. "A cool washcloth sounds good. And maybe a little ice. There's a cup on that tray."

Dani wet a cloth in the bathroom sink and wiped Symphony's face. "The kids'll be mad they weren't here tonight." She snickered. "The kids! I'm trying not to call them that anymore. Joe gets all bent out of shape when I do. But I didn't stop calling Jeanne and Leesa 'the little sisters' till after they started community college." She handed the cup to Symphony. "I think *the kids* is an improvement."

Symphony watched another bolt of lightning flash outside the window. "Will you do me a really big favor?"

"Sure. That's why I'm here."

"Will you make sure the newspaper doesn't put this in the birth announcements? If Quinton finds out about—"

"I'll have Phil call his friend at the Sentinel first thing tomorrow morning. He'll make sure they pull it. Don't worry about that right now. Let's talk about something else."

But it was too late. Symphony's thoughts had already drifted back to Quinton.

⌘    ⌘    ⌘

The instant Symphony suspected she was pregnant again, she began stuffing every dime she could into the pocket of her winter robe at the back of the closet. She rinsed the empty brown beer bottles and guzzled cold water from them so Quinton wouldn't notice she'd stopped drinking. Whenever they were together, she measured her words and movements, careful to smile at the right time and nod when it was called for. And she never disagreed, but tried not to be overly agreeable either. It only saved her a punch here and a blow there but that must have been enough. Six months ago, she had appeared on Mama and Daddy's doorstep, bruised, broken, and still pregnant.

From that day forward, Daddy officially changed Quinton's name to "Thatsonofabitch." Every time he said it, his fists balled up. "Thatsonofabitch had the nerve to call here today. I told him I'd file charges if he bothered you again. Thatsonofabitch better never darken our door. If Thatsonofabitch knows what's good for him, he'll leave you alone."

⌘    ⌘    ⌘

The girdle of labor gripped Symphony once again. This time, something seemed to shift. Her hip bones ached and her legs wanted to spread.

She bent her knees and rubbed the bottom of her feet back and forth along the sheet until the pressure slacked. *This isn't so bad. And when it's over, I'll have my own little person to love.* She took a breath and relaxed for a moment, hoping she was close to the end of it.

She looked up. Dani was staring at her, mouth agape, eyes filled with terror.

"Okay," Symphony said. "So what do you wanna talk about?"

"Jeanne and Leesa," Dani answered. "It's the middle of the week. What are they doing in Orlando?"

"Don't say anything to Mama or Daddy yet."

"Okay."

"They both had second interviews at Disneyworld." Symphony smiled. "Isn't that hilarious?"

"I don't even want to know this," Dani whispered. "Daddy'll be furious. They just have three quarters to go. Tell me they're not dropping out."

Symphony shook her head. "They're gonna finish x-ray school. It's just for next summer. Leesa wants to work with concessions but Jeanne's trying to be one of the characters. Do you believe it?"

"Jeanne's always been a character," Dani said. "They probably won't even make her wear a costume."

They were both laughing as Mama walked into the room. "What did I miss?" She kissed Dani's cheek then moved straight to Symphony. "Hey, sugar," she said with a peck to the forehead. "How we doin'?"

"Hang on a minute." Symphony turned on her back, inhaled, closed her mouth and blew out slowly through her lips. She took another breath and repeated. "Not too bad. I just hope it's over soon."

Mama patted Symphony's hand and, in the soft light of the generator, got out her knitting.

⌘ ⌘ ⌘

Five hours later, as Daddy and Dani waited in the hall outside the delivery room, the doctor gave Symphony a local anesthetic and an episiotomy. "So you don't tear," he said from behind his green mask.

Mama whispered into Symphony's ear, "Next time you have a contraction, sugar, you push, just as hard as you can."

Assuming Mama knew what she was talking about, Symphony grunted and gave it her all.

The baby shot out so fast the doctor had to play wide receiver.

Right away, the room was filled with the newborn's welcome to the bright, cold, world—the gasp for air followed by that soft baby shriek that seems to grow louder with each breath.

"You have a daughter," the doctor announced.

*My little girl.* Symphony's eyes streamed tears as she reached for the baby. She wanted to touch her, to see all of her, to marvel at her fingers, to count her toes. But the nurse whisked her away.

"I need to take a few measurements. Then you can have her," she said. "Did you pick out a name yet?"

"Choral," Symphony answered.

"That's pretty," the nurse said. "It sounds like the little girl of a Symphony."

"Doesn't it?" Mama said, looking over the nurse's shoulder at her rose-colored granddaughter. She moved to the bed and kissed Symphony's cheek. "She's beautiful. You did real good, sweetie."

For a short while Symphony rested, but the ache seemed to be building once again.

"You need to push one more time," the doctor said.

Symphony's eyes widened. *There's another one?*

Mama caught the look of concern on her face. "Everything's fine," she said. "You just have to deliver the placenta."

"Oh."

When that was over, the nurse handed the doctor a syringe. He gave Symphony a shot. Then, with a curved needle and what looked like a set of needle-nosed pliers, he began to repair the episiotomy. "After we get you all stitched up," he said, "you'll get your daughter back."

⌘ ⌘ ⌘

When new mother and daughter were clean and covered in soft, white blankets, the nurse placed the baby in Symphony's arms where the two saw each other for the first time.

At that very moment, the lights came back on.

# CHAPTER TWENTY-FOUR

MAMA SAT IN Symphony's bedroom staring into the bassinette as Choral slept. "I remember when you kids were babies. Seemed like, as soon as I got you to sleep someone would say, 'Let me hold her for a minute.' knowing it was sure to wake you up." With a dull chuckle, Mama reached over and patted the baby's behind. "Well, I've turned into one of those people. Hasn't she slept long enough?"

"Mama!" Symphony said in a raised whisper.

"I know." Mama rubbed Symphony's shoulder. "You're tired." She stood up and began folding diapers still warm from the dryer. "I tried to get you to rest while you had the chance. But you just had to have that job at the nursing home."

Symphony turned toward the laundry basket and grabbed a wad of diapers. "I was trying to take care of myself—my family."

And she had, for a while. But when Symphony's huge belly and tired back made her nursing assistant work difficult, Sandstone Flats put her on maternity leave.

During the last six weeks of pregnancy, she had grown accustomed to the golden Florida mornings: rising at her leisure after everyone left for work or school, lounging past noon—book in hand, watching soap operas until time to help with dinner. Those lazy days had done nothing to prepare her for motherhood: the sore-like-a-boil nipples, cramping, episiotomy stitches that throbbed and itched, the never-ending need for rest, and a baby who woke just as its mother dozed off.

The first week was hard. As Symphony began to lag, she would notice Mama watching.

"Is there anything I can do?"

But Symphony felt the baby was her own responsibility. "I promise, Mama. I'll ask if I need help."

⌘  ⌘  ⌘

Mama emptied the laundry basket and tucked the folded diapers into the top dresser drawer. "I don't have to work tomorrow," she said. "Have you thought about training Choral on some formula? She's over a week old and I haven't even gotten to give her one single bottle." Her pale brown eyes almost pouted.

Symphony gazed at Choral. "What if it upsets her tummy?"

Mama shook her head. "Every one of you survived it."

"But what *if?*"

"Then I'll bring her right to you, sugar."

Symphony tossed the thought back and forth for a moment. "Are you sure?"

Mama nodded, repeatedly. "Yes. I'll set up the playpen in the living room. She'll be fine. That way you can catch up on your sleep."

The next morning, as Choral began her five-thirty opus, Symphony, eyes half closed, felt her way to the bassinette.

Mama slipped between Symphony and the baby, an already warm bottle in her hand. "I've got her." She carted Choral off to the living room where she fed, burped, changed, and rocked her, grandma style. As the sun rose to the rocker creaking against the cold terrazzo floor, Mama petted the downy hairs on the baby's head. When Daddy's alarm went off, Mama put Choral down for her first nap of the day and made a pot of coffee.

One by one, the household awoke. Jeanne and Leesa grabbed toast and hurried off to class. Mama cooked breakfast and sat down to eat with Daddy and Joe. By the time she pushed them out the door at seven forty-five, the little one was awake again. Mama settled her down, stretched out on the couch with a yawn, and closed her eyes.

⌘  ⌘  ⌘

Symphony awoke peacefully. A strip of sunlight stole between the drapes turning dust to glitter as it crossed the room and wrapped over the top of her blanket. For a moment she lay still taking it in, not wanting to disturb this masterpiece of particles. Then, the tightness of her breasts reminded her. Her nipples tingled and began to leak. She leaned toward the bassinette and reached for Choral. *She's gone.* In her mind, she saw Quinton. She gasped and jumped to her feet just as she remembered. *Mama has her.*

In the living room, Mama had stopped mid-diaper and turned Choral onto her stomach.

"I thought she needed an airing-out," Mama said with a grin as Symphony hurried into the room. "She's so beautiful. And just look at that precious little bohunkus." She gently tapped Choral's behind then touched a spot on her right hip. "Have you noticed this birthmark?"

"I thought it was a freckle."

"Nope. Your granny says it's a family thing. Papa had it, Gray had it, you have it, and now Choral has it."

"I have it?"

"Right in the same spot. I can't believe you haven't noticed it. Quinton never—" Mama caught herself and looked at Symphony's wet shirt. "You're overflowing." She turned the baby face up, pinned a dry diaper around her, and handed her to her mother. "You may as well nurse her out here," Mama said. "None of the men are around and I'm gonna start supper."

"Supper? What time is it?"

"Almost three-thirty."

"You're kidding."

"I told you, you needed to catch up on your sleep. We're having ham tonight. Would you rather have potato salad or sweet potatoes?"

"Slaw."

"Sweet potatoes it is," Mama said, walking away.

Symphony pulled up her t-shirt and raised the baby to her breast. Choral turned and latched on with fervor. "Ouch!" Symphony grimaced. Soon, the baby settled down to a softer suckle and the pain dulled. *No one ever tells you it hurts at first.*

Mama was a modern woman. All she knew about nursing was what other mothers had told her. Symphony and her siblings had been bottle-fed.

"You'll get used to it," Granny told Symphony over the phone. "I think the most it ever took me was two weeks. Soon, someone could step right on one of them things and you wouldn't even know it."

Granny was right. It didn't hurt the way it had for the first three days. But from the time the baby latched on until the moment the pain let up, Symphony still wondered if Mama hadn't had the right idea.

She leaned back in the rocker and hummed, first "Summertime," then "Shenandoah." Somewhere along the way, Choral fell asleep. Symphony put her in the playpen and sat back down watching, in awe, the rise and fall of each breath. It soothed her. She stood, one breast empty, one breast full, and headed into the kitchen to help Mama.

There was a knock at the door. She turned back to answer it but, feeling damp-shirted and a bit lopsided, she decided to peek out the window first.

There stood Quinton with a brand new haircut, wearing a business suit and shiny brown shoes.

Symphony froze.

He knocked again.

Mama started toward the door but, seeing the look on Symphony's face, stopped.

Joe, just home from school, caught a glimpse of their visitor and slipped up the driveway to the back door. He made his way through the kitchen. Although just a few months shy of seventeen, his sisters still referred to him as their "baby brother." Right then, he couldn't wait to get his hands on the man who'd used Symphony as a punching bag.

"Take Choral to the bedroom," he whispered.

Symphony didn't hear a word Joe said. Her thoughts were filled with memories of Quinton's rage, his tepid day-after apologies, his broken promises of "Never again." *What if he knows?*

He knocked again. "Candygram," he said, imitating his and Symphony's favorite Saturday Night Live skit.

*He's trying to make me laugh.* He'd always used laughter to bridge their differences, to break her down when he was ready for a fight to end. As if entranced, she took a step toward the door.

Joe touched her arm.

She flinched.

"Come on, sis." Joe guided her down the hall by her shoulder. He left her in the bedroom and went back for Choral. "I'm locking you in," he said, placing the baby in her bassinette. "Whatever you do, keep her quiet." He closed the door and checked to make sure it was locked.

Choral stretched and changed position but she didn't wake up.

Symphony watched her. *The only part of your daddy I ever wanted you to have was those light blue eyes.* She shrugged. *You got his nose instead.* "Why was he so dressed up?" she wondered aloud.

⌘　⌘　⌘

She and Quinton had met at a block party her third quarter at Auburn. Each time he went to refill her plastic cup with beer, he planted a kiss on her cheek—right in front of God and everybody. When the party began to fizzle out, he draped his arm over her shoulders. "Just stay at my place tonight. You're way too drunk to drive home." He stood there, looking innocent in the soft glow of the streetlamp.

Symphony paused, waiting for a danger signal to flash. If it did, she was too drunk to see it. "All right."

Back at his apartment, he made his best attempt at seduction.

"I just met you tonight," she said, getting up to leave.

"I'll stop," he promised. And he did. He pulled a blanket from the closet and curled up on the couch.

She slept in his bed, fully clothed, a firm grip on the covers.

He was cute and smart and funny, but on top of it all, he had kept his word. That was his best selling point.

Now, he stood at the front door, wearing the same expression that won her over back then. She sighed and sat down on her bed.

⌘　⌘　⌘

Joe remembered the playpen just as he got to the door. He carried it to the dining room and shoved it under the table.

Mama stood at the edge of the kitchen wringing her hands. "What if he gets violent?" she asked. "I wish your father was here. Should I call the police?"

"Don't you worry, Mama," Joe said, flexing his muscles. "I've got this one." With a snort, he went to deal with their company.

⌘ ⌘ ⌘

Symphony pressed her ear against the door but couldn't hear a thing. *Oh my God. What if Joe hadn't been here? I would have let him in.* Confused, she sat on the side of the bed, biting her fingernails. *But I don't trust him. I don't know why I trusted him as long as I did.*

⌘ ⌘ ⌘

"Gonorrhea," the nurse at the clinic had said, handing Symphony a card of antibiotics. "Take this for ten days. No sexual intercourse until you're rechecked."

Symphony was horrified. "I have—"

"Gonorrhea," the nurse repeated. "And we need to see the person you got it from, if you know who that is."

"Of course I know!" Symphony stumbled out of the clinic in a daze. *How am I gonna tell Quinton?*

Quinton didn't take the news well. He grabbed Symphony's wrist. "The fuckin' clap? I better not get it," he snarled. "Who else have you been with?"

"You're the only one," she said, flushing. "And the nurse says it won't just go away. You have to take the medicine."

He let her go and turned to leave, muttering, "Don't tell me what to do you fat slut." Then, he slammed the door as he left.

They'd been together for almost two months.

*Why did I stay after that?* She closed her eyes and stretched out on the bed, hoping Quinton would leave without a fight.

⌘ ⌘ ⌘

Joe opened the door with a smirk. "Why hello, Quinton." He crossed his arms and blocked the doorway. "What the hell can I do for you today?"

"I- uh-just-um," Quinton stammered.

"What's a matter, buddy? You didn't get all nervous when you were beating the shit out of my sister, did ya?"

"I-I don't know what she's told you, but I didn't—"

"Oh, I see," Joe said, raising his hand. "*Now* you're gonna make things a hundred times worse by calling Symphony a liar? You're not the smartest guy I've ever met. Tell you what. I'll just step outside and see if I can make you a little smarter." He tore off his shirt and threw it onto the rocking chair.

Just as he stepped onto the front porch, Daddy's car pulled into the driveway. Daddy hopped out like his pants were on fire and slammed the door so hard the window cracked. "Just a minute, Joe," he called, sprinting across the lawn. "Let's see if we can handle this like gentlemen."

He reached the porch and grabbed the lapel of Quinton's sports coat. "You get the hell off my property right now," he said, through gritted teeth.

The three men fixed a glare on each other. The air swelled with hot sweat and testosterone.

Daddy gave the lapel a jerk. "Having the police take you to jail's the *best* thing that could happen right now. You hear me?"

Quinton didn't budge.

"I said, 'Go!' You've done all the damage you're gonna do to this family."

Joe moved closer, his fists balled up, ready to fire. "You heard him. Go!"

Quinton backed a few steps away, then turned and walked toward his car. "She wants me back and you know it," he said over his shoulder. "This isn't finished."

The last phrase ignited Joe. "The hell it's not." He bolted after Quinton.

Quinton jumped into his car and started the engine. Joe got there just as he pulled away from the curb.

"Asshole!" Joe shouted, pounding his fist on the trunk. He chased the red Falcon halfway down the block before returning to Daddy in the front yard. "If the car'd been locked, I'd've had him."

"Yep," Daddy agreed. He shook his head and put his arm around Joe. "I haven't seen you without a shirt since last summer. Your arms and shoulders sure are gettin' big."

"I reckon old Quinton thought so, too," Joe said, beginning to chuckle.

"That son of a bitch moves pretty fast when he's scared. I don't think he'll be back. Do you?" Laughing, the two of them went inside.

Mama met them at the kitchen with a frown. She couldn't seem to find any humor at all in the situation.

⌘ ⌘ ⌘

Inside that locked room, Symphony's strength had begun to falter. She was heavier than she ever had been. And now, she had a baby. The mirror loomed before her like an approaching enemy. *Who's gonna want me?* For a moment, she cried, sure that Quinton was the only man who would ever love her. Hadn't he suffered for weeks when they lost the first baby? *He's Choral's daddy. Shouldn't I let him see her?* Choral stirred. Symphony picked her up and studied her face. *But what if he treats you like he treats me?* She put her hand on the baby's chest wanting to feel her heartbeat. For the first time she noticed that, although Choral's heart was much faster, it beat in rhythm with her own.

Joe knocked. "He's gone, sis. Are you all right?"

Symphony unlocked the door and opened it. When Joe hugged her, she crumbled, beginning a sob that continued off and on throughout the night.

That was the day, the girls stopped calling Joe their "baby brother" and Daddy was forced to realize he was not as young as he used to be.

For the next week, Symphony trembled at any sudden sound or movement. She thought about leaving town, going somewhere Quinton couldn't find her, but she couldn't even work yet. *And if I move, who'll take care of Choral while I work? I've gotta stay here.*

⌘ ⌘ ⌘

Choral's first Christmas—a baby toy extravaganza—came and went. The Weber household seemed to be adjusting to the infant's schedule. Although no one complained about Choral ruining their sleep, when she finally slept through the night, the whole family celebrated. After that, coffee consumption decreased considerably.

Then, the phone calls began—long distance, collect—for Symphony. The two times she accepted the charges, the caller would breathe for a moment, then hang up. When the collect calls stopped, but the hang-up calls continued, Daddy contacted the Chief of Police in Carlisle, Pennsylvania.

"I've known the Bolins for years," Chief Radsdorf said. "I even met your daughter before she left. Seems like a nice young woman. I see Quinton around, usually at the upholstery shop. He's back in college, now, going for his Masters. Is there a problem?"

"Not as long as he stays in Pennsylvania," Daddy answered.

"I can't promise you anything, but I can tell you I saw him earlier in the week. If that helps."

⌘　⌘　⌘

Symphony spoke with an attorney about divorce, but the matter of Choral came up so she let it drop. There was no rush.

When Choral was three months old, Sandstone Flats called Symphony back to work. "Do you have an evening shift available?" she asked.

She and Mama had already discussed how they would handle the baby when Symphony returned to her job. The nursing home was right next to the hospital where Mama worked the early shift. She got off at three-thirty in the afternoon. Symphony's shift began at four. Mama caught a ride to work in the morning. Symphony brought her the car and the baby in the afternoon.

Symphony's first night back to work was brutal. There were three new patients sent over from the hospital. One of them was a very sweet woman who'd just had a hip replacement and couldn't find a comfortable position. Her call light stayed on all night.

They moved a thirty-eight year old lung cancer patient into the last room on the hall. Although his breathing was slow and irregular due to morphine, each short, shallow breath jolted his body. Every so often, his hand would move back and forth from his lap to his mouth and he pursed his lips as if he were still smoking a cigarette.

The third, a woman Mama's age, had been diagnosed with cirrhosis. If she wasn't hurting, she was itching. She scratched her swollen abdomen raw. Both arms were striped with blood. "Make it stop. Dammit! Please. Make it stop."

221

The nurse did what she could for the itch and the pain, but nothing seemed to touch it.

Finally, the doctor called with an order for a new shot. The tension seemed to leave the woman almost immediately. The lines and creases in her face smoothed. Symphony studied her. Something about this woman seemed familiar. *But I don't know a Margaret Browden.*

Symphony checked on her every twenty minutes. She was resting quietly until the last hour, when the frantic whispering began.

"I'm sorry, Margaret. I can't hear you." Symphony leaned over, putting her ear next to the woman's mouth.

"He's gone."

"Who, Margaret? Who's gone?"

The woman's eyes flew open filled with anger. She grabbed Symphony's arm with a strength no one would have believed. "He's out there alone."

Symphony stared back at her.

Margaret relaxed her hold and closed her eyes. "Find him," she whispered.

# CHAPTER TWENTY-FIVE

MOST NIGHTS, SYMPHONY rode home from work with Junie, a clerk from the East wing of the nursing home. Junie was an even five feet tall. Her frosted hair was always short, teased, and sprayed into the biggest possible style. The thirty-seven year old mother of three boys—a transplant from Trenton—was one of those women who felt comfortable wearing leopard skin pants and spike heels to work. She would have looked great in mechanic's coveralls. Nothing in her figure hinted at the fact that she'd been through pregnancy and childbirth. There was, however, no mistaking her Jersey accent.

Every ride home began the same way. "Since my boys started school, I never see 'em anymore. I just don't know what I'm gonna do if the boss won't let me go on days. Then, even if I *am* exhausted, at least I can see 'em at night. Jeez!"

Symphony's response was always the same. "Did you call personnel to see when the next opening'll be?" But Junie never answered. By then, she had drifted to her second favorite subject: the people who lived at Sandstone Flats.

Each evening after dinner, as the nurses and medical assistants helped patients and residents settle in for the night, Junie studied their charts and histories. If you caught her with her nose in a file, she'd say, "Hey. I'm gonna be a writer one day," or, "The biggest thing I've learned on this job is that no one's life is boring. Not if you know how to dig."

Each night, during the fifteen-minute drive from the nursing home to Symphony's house, Junie discussed the patients' lives. "This is the kinda stuff that gets someone a best seller. You can't begin to know how interestin' everyone is. And I mean everyone. For example, Mrs. Wagner in E43. You'll never guess what she did. A magician's assistant. For thirty years. In Vegas. Catch her on a good day and she'll tell you how every trick is done. But sometimes, all she can say is 'Yes. We have no bananas.' Poor thing."

Sometimes, Symphony was so tired she glazed over, tossing in an occasional nod just to be polite. But tonight, Junie's patient histories kept her wide awake and wondering about the people she took care of. She knew that Mr. Patrick's kids never came to visit, not even on his birthday, which was coming up next week.

"I think I'll pick him up some argyle socks," Junie said. "Something snazzy, maybe. With a little red or yellow."

She'd finish discussing one patient and, without so much as a breath, move on to the next. "Did you know E55 has over thirteen documented personalities? All of them with different names. I never know what to call her. How does somethin' like that happen? One of 'em's a guy who curses like a sailor and, consider yourself warned, he spits, too." She stopped at a red light and turned to look at Symphony. "She'd make a really good story. I mean, you can't make up anything more interestin' than that, can ya? But all the psychological research would probably kill me."

"I've never even met her," Symphony said.

"Well, she mostly stays in her room after lunch. I forget. They like to keep *you* with the critical patients. You don't getta spend much time with the people who live there year round." The light changed. Junie turned the car into Country Club Estates and headed toward Overlook Terrace. "You know who's a real trip is that woman, Margaret, down in E7. I don't know how you take care of her. I've been in that room twice since she came. Gives me the heebie-jeebies with all her whispering to ghosts."

"She's lookin' for someone. Him. That's all I've been able to figure out." Symphony opened her wallet and put a five on the seat next to Junie. "This is for gas."

"Thanks. You know, it's really sad." Junie sighed. "Her son died." She stopped the car in front of the Weber's house. "And her chart says she's been tryin' to off herself ever since. Sometimes, when the aide on graveyard shift comes in to check on her, the pillow's right over her face."

"I wish you wouldn't call it graveyard." Symphony paused, staring out the window at the almost dark neighborhood. "That's weird," she said, turning back to Junie. "Margaret's hands are tied to the bed rail at night. Doctor's orders."

"Ew. Then how does the pillow get over her face?" Junie shivered. "Anyway, she's one of *those* patients. You know, the kind you hope goes sooner than later."

Symphony knew what she meant. All you could wish for some patients was for their battle to end. Ron, the lung cancer patient, struggled forever before finally letting go. Symphony had spent months trying to keep him comfortable, easing his mind, reminding him he wasn't alone. Then, he passed on her weekend off.

That Monday, she'd returned to find a new patient in Ron's bed. Chet, the new guy, said whatever came to mind. His jokes made her uncomfortable but she smiled a lot and tried to ignore his love songs to her "big butt and bazooms." *Ron would've thought Chet was disgusting. But he would've laughed anyway.* The thought made her miss Ron less.

⌘　⌘　⌘

Symphony opened her door to get out. "Junie?"

"Yeah-huh."

"You wouldn't really write about 'em."

"The residents? Oh, hell no!" Junie pushed herself back from the steering wheel. "I love these guys. You know that."

Symphony smiled and got out.

Junie leaned toward to passenger side of the car and looked out at Symphony. "I should be more careful what I say, huh? My dad useta tell me I had diarrhea of the mouth."

Symphony laughed. "I need to ask you a favor."

"You name it."

"Well, I haven't had time to look at Margaret's history. Do you remember anything else important? Somethin' I should know?"

"Why? You gonna be a writer, too?"

"No." Symphony rolled her eyes. "If I can find out why she's upset, maybe I can figure out how to calm her down."

"You're so much nicer than me," Junie said.

"No. I'm just nicer than you want people to *think* you are. See you tomorrow. And don't forget to call about days."

"G'night, kiddo."

Symphony stood at the end of the driveway watching Junie's car pull away. *If she wants to work days why doesn't she apply for days?*

Across the street, in the Westhill's old house, a light flickered and went out. She thought of Mack. That part of her heart—the part she'd let him break—began to ache for the beautiful boy he was back then. *No matter how many years . . .* She shrugged it off and headed toward her front door.

Something in the air tensed. Tiny hairs on the back of her neck stood at attention. She turned toward the street, scanning the neighborhood. "Don't be ridiculous, Symphony," she whispered, continuing her trek to the house. *It's all that talk about Margaret and ghosts.*

Once inside, she relaxed. She put the breast milk she'd pumped at dinner break into the refrigerator, checked on Choral, then took a hot shower. A late evening rainstorm had cooled the house, leaving her room just the right temperature. She put on a cotton gown and curled up on the bed watching Choral breathe. *She's gettin' so big. I'm gonna have to get her some new outfits.*

At midnight, Choral awoke ready to eat. Within fifteen minutes, her tummy was full and she was sleeping again. Symphony turned the light out and dozed off, feeling like the luckiest person ever.

Around three o'clock, she felt a hand on her shoulder and sat up with a gasp.

"Shhh. It's me," Joe said. "Did you hear that?"

"What?" Symphony whispered, reaching for the lamp.

Joe blocked her arm. "Don't," he said. "Is your window open?"

"No."

"Someone's out there."

Symphony stood over Choral. Joe crept to the window and peeked behind the curtain.

At that moment, Daddy walked in. "You see me chase him off?"

"You went after him?" Joe turned around looking disappointed.

"Yep. He was about six inches taller than me. But not so big he wasn't scared of this." Daddy held up a long metal flashlight as if it were a club. "Wish I could've gotten a good look at him."

"Shouldn't we call the police?" Symphony asked.

"I'm pretty sure he's gone," Daddy said. "But if he comes back, this gun in my pocket's sure to shake him up more than the flashlight did."

Symphony was terrified.

"Don't worry," Daddy added. "He's not comin' back tonight."

*Yeah. Right! Just cause you said so?* As soon as Symphony was alone, she double-checked her window locks. She could hear Joe and Daddy as they went from room to room making sure the rest of the house was closed up tight.

The fact that Symphony couldn't open the windows made the room seem at least twenty degrees hotter. She lay down sweating, wishing for a fan, tossing and turning until the frustration of not sleeping was what kept her awake. Only after nursing Choral at five-thirty, was Symphony able to fall asleep once again.

The next day Mama called on her lunch break. "Does Junie wait until you're inside the house?"

"Not usually."

"Tell her what happened last night. I'm sure she won't mind waiting."

"Okay, Mama. I'll ask her," Symphony said.

But after that evening, everything was fine: no hair standing on end, no one caught roaming around the backyard. By the end of the week, Mama had convinced Daddy to put the gun out of reach, high on its shelf in their bedroom closet.

⌘　⌘　⌘

September came. Jeanne and Leesa left their summer jobs at Disneyworld and returned to X-ray school.

Joe had been employed full-time at the machine shop since he graduated from high school. He loved working with his hands. There wasn't a machine he couldn't decipher. Rather than continue his education, he decided to apprentice at work.

Daddy was disappointed. "You have the grades to go on to college, son."

"I just don't see the need, Daddy. Mr. Bertram's gonna pay me eight dollars an hour plus a percentage of what they charge the customer."

So, Joe rented a small garage apartment across town and moved out.

When Choral was eight and a half months old, she got her Uncle Joe's room—painted pink, of course—with a daisy border. After work, Symphony would sit for hours watching, wondering if Choral could feel her there.

The peace of the night often pulled Symphony's thoughts back to more difficult times. Trials of the past gave rise to worries of the future. *What if Choral has dreams?* She watched the baby, aware of each nocturnal expression. *Is she dreaming right now?* As Symphony's eyelids grew heavy, she convinced herself that Choral was different. *She's not gonna have them. Not like I did.* Most nights, that's how she was able to sleep.

⌘ ⌘ ⌘

"What do you think?" she asked Granny on the phone one afternoon.

"Just have to wait and see," Granny said. "Stop borrowing trouble. Just let it be."

⌘ ⌘ ⌘

One morning, as Mama was leaving for the hospital at six forty-five, the phone rang.

"Symphony," Mama called. "It's work. Something about a patient."

Symphony shuffled down the hallway where Mama handed her the phone with a kiss.

"I'll see you this afternoon, sweetie."

Symphony yawned and rubbed her eyes. "This is Symphony Weber."

"Hello," a deep, male voice said. "Detective Spano with the Titusville Police Department. I'd like to ask you a few questions about one of your patients. How soon can you get to Sandstone Flats?"

"Not tili this afternoon," Symphony answered. "There's no one to watch my daughter. Is everything okay?"

"We can discuss that when you get here. Go ahead and bring the kid. On second thought, that's probably not the best idea."

"I'll try to find someone to stay with her." Symphony searched for a pen and paper. "What time do I need to be there?"

"Twenty minutes would be ideal."

"I don't know if I can do that," Symphony answered. "I'll do the best I can." She hung up and called Dani.

"I'm sorry," Dani said. "I have to be at work by eight. I could watch her at lunch. That's twelve thirty. Would that help?"

"He wants me there in twenty minutes," Symphony said. "He doesn't seem to care that I have a baby."

"What about the sisters?" Dani asked.

"They've both got clinical today. They can't miss or they fail. And Joe has to work, too."

"Just call that detective back and tell him he'll have to wait till I get off for lunch."

Symphony began to worry. "I tried to put it off till this afternoon. He won't let me. I don't know what to tell him."

"Tell him he's a jerk," Dani said. "Better yet, give me his number. I'll tell him."

"You're kidding, right?"

"Maybe a little. Why don't you try and catch Mama at work. See if she has any ideas."

"Okay. I'll call back if I need you at lunch. Thanks, sis. Love you."

Mama hadn't clocked in at the nurses' station yet. "Please have her call home before she sits down for report," Symphony said. But there wasn't time. A few minutes later, someone knocked.

Symphony peeked out the curtains to find a navy blue car parked in front of the house. A woman with an olive complexion waited just outside the door, her long, black hair braided and wrapped into a bun on back of her head. Her police uniform was snug, revealing a few extra pounds around her middle. Symphony buttoned her blouse, put Choral in her car seat, and stepped outside.

"I'm Officer Rodriguez," the woman said. "Detective Spano sent me to pick you up." "I'm glad he told me to take *his* car." She smiled at Choral. "No way I'd put a baby in the backseat of a squad car."

"I was planning to drive," Symphony offered.

"You may as well ride with me, since I'm already here."

Choral began to wail as soon as Symphony put her in the car. "Sorry. She's a little cranky. We don't usually go out this early."

"Babies don't bother me. I'm the second of ten," Officer Rodriguez said. "I feel like I've already raised my share, though. I'm not sure I want any of my own."

⌘　⌘　⌘

At Sandstone Flats, police cars blocked the front parking lot. Rodriguez found a spot on the street.

"Where's Detective Spano?" Rodriguez asked the officers guarding the entrance.

One of them stared straight ahead, expressionless. The other took a gulp from his disposable coffee cup and pointed down the hall. "E7," he said. "Second left, last room on the left."

*Margaret's room.* Symphony rushed ahead leaving Rodriguez behind. Choral was dozing, her head on Symphony's shoulder, when they passed a policeman in the hall and walked into E7.

Margaret was diagonal in the bed, her wrists tied to the bedrails. Her eyes, open. Her lips, purple. A pillow stood on the floor, leaning against the frame beneath the point where her head hung over the side. On the pillow, someone had written, "AGAIN," in black.

"Oh, no," Symphony whimpered.

A man took hold of her arm. "Ms. Weber? You'll have to leave now."

"Oh, no," she said again, eyes fixed on the body.

Slowly, he guided her toward the door.

"Dammit, Cates," he barked at the policeman in the hall. "When I say no one goes in, I mean no one! Got it?"

"Yes sir, Detective Spano. I glanced away. It was only a second and—"

"Don't let it happen again."

Officer Rodriguez caught Symphony as she backed into the hall. "Here," she said, scooting a chair close and reaching for the baby. "Let me take her. What's her name?"

"Margaret, um, Browden," Symphony answered.

"No," Rodriguez said. "The baby's name."

"Oh." The scene repeated in Symphony's mind. "I guess I'm not used to having her here at work." She gulped and trembled. "Choral," she answered, handing the baby to Officer Rodriguez.

Choral slept from her mother's shoulder to Rodriguez'. "Pretty name," the officer said. "How old is she?"

"Uh . . . nine months."

"She's beautiful."

"Thanks," Symphony said, staring at the blank wall opposite her.

Detective Spano finished with Officer Cates and moved across the hall toward Symphony. He smoothed his black hair into place and tucked a clipboard under his arm. "So, Officer Rodriguez, where were you when Ms.—ahem—Weber was in the room with our dead body?"

"I knew you had Cates at the door, sir. I assumed *he* would stop her."

Spano tilted his head and looked up at Rodriguez, who was a good six inches taller. "You know what they say about assume, officer. It makes an ass of you and me. Do I have to remind you? A slip up could be costly."

He leaned in and peeked at Choral who had just opened her eyes. "Sorry, baby. I just said the 'a' word." She smiled at him. He turned to Symphony. "So, you managed to get into the room all by yourself."

"I was worried about Margaret." She pointed toward E7. "How could someone do that?"

"That's what we're here to find out." He pulled the clipboard out from under his arm and opened a copy of Symphony's employee file. "Tell me Ms.—ahem—Weber, why do you continue to use your maiden name when you're married?"

She looked at the floor. "My husband and I are separated."

"But your legal name is still Bolin. Is that correct?"

Symphony nodded.

He stopped writing and tapped his pen against the clipboard. "Is there anything else you'd like to tell me?"

Her eyes flashed fire, just as they had at Daddy during her growing up years. "What do you mean?" She glanced away, trying to get the fire under control.

"For instance, did you touch anything while you were in the room?"

Symphony looked up. "I don't think so."

His dark brown eyes stared back. "It's a simple question." He rolled up his sleeves, pulled a chair directly in front of Symphony, and sat down.

"You think I took something from Margaret's room?" She stood, put her keys on the chair, and began pulling each pocket inside-out. "Well, if I did, I don't remember. And if I have something, where is it?"

"Exactly," the detective replied.

Rodriguez motioned him aside. "She was in there less than a minute. Do you really think she could have taken something?"

Detective Spano grinned. "You're questioning my discretion?"

"I'm just sayin'."

He turned to Symphony. "Could you have misplaced something under the baby's blanket?"

"I really think I'd remember that." Symphony unwrapped the blanket, took Choral from Rodriguez, and handed her to Spano. "If you could just hold her for a minute . . ." She shook the blanket and a tiny pink sock fell out.

The baby looked up at the detective, babbled some baby talk at him, and smiled again.

"Stop it, kid. You'll have everybody around here thinking I'm love-able." He glanced across the hall at Cates who was grinning. "What're you starin' at? You better be makin' sure no one else gets in that room."

"I'll take her back, now," Symphony said. "I really don't think I touched anything in there."

Spano handed Choral back to her mother and began writing on his clip-board once again. "Do you recall anything unusual about last night? Were there more than the average number of visitors? Someone who stayed later than they normally do?"

Symphony squeezed her eyes shut, thinking. "Unusual? Nothing I remember. And I was here a little bit late last night 'cause Junie, the woman I ride home with, had to leave early. I had to call a taxi."

Spano began writing. "But you clocked out at the regular time."

"At eleven, I finished my rounds. Then I called for a ride and waited in the visiting room till he got here."

"And did anyone see you in the visiting room?"

"Probably not. The patients were asleep. The swing shift people had left—all but me—and the night shift was looking over charts and new doctors' orders and stuff."

"Okay. I guess we're finished here. You'll be around if I have anymore questions?"

"Yes," Symphony said. "I work this afternoon." She looked at Margaret's room and shivered. "Will she still be in there? Like that?"

"No," Spano answered. "We'll have it all cleaned up in the next hour or so." He turned to Rodriguez. "You can go ahead and take them back home."

"Thank you, Detective." Rodriguez looked at Symphony. "Ready?"

"Yeah," Symphony said. She took three steps up the hall and turned around. "Detective Spano?"

He looked up from his conversation with Cates. "Yes, Ms. Weber?"

"What do you think he was saying? I mean, with the pillow?"

"With the pillow?" Spano walked toward her.

"Again," she said. "What do you think he meant?"

"I don't know what you're talking about."

"You've been in there, right?" Symphony asked.

Spano, Rodriguez, and Cates stared at her, looking confused.

"Didn't you see it? What he wrote on the pillow?"

Spano's brow furrowed. "No," he said.

"Again?" It was written on the pillow. The one on the floor."

"I was in there right after they found the body this morning," Spano said. "There's nothing on that pillow but a plain, white case. C'mon. I'll show you."

# CHAPTER TWENTY-SIX

DETECTIVE SPANO ESCORTED Symphony toward Margaret's room. "You sure you've got the stomach to go back in there?"

"I'm okay, now that the shock is over," Symphony said. "But I don't really want Choral in there again."

"I'll hold her," Rodriguez offered. Her expression softened as Symphony handed her the baby. She looked into Choral's eyes. "You're such a sweet girl."

Back inside Margaret's room, Symphony gawked at the plain white pillow. "It was there."

"Probably trauma," Spano said. "We get that reaction all the time. People are so upset, they think they see something they don't. Or worse, they forget something they *did* see."

"I guess," Symphony mumbled. *I know what I saw.*

He touched her shoulder. "Are you ready to go home now?"

She moved toward the door. "Yeah. I'd like to spend a little time with Choral before work this afternoon."

"Well, thanks for coming down," he said, motioning to Rodriguez." I'll contact you if I have anymore questions."

"Okay."

Rodriguez handed Choral back to her mother. "She really is such a great baby. Is she always this good?"

"She's a happy girl," Symphony said. "I've gotta get her home, though. She didn't get her cereal this morning."

Just then, Junie walked toward them. "Symphony? What are ya doin' here? And, oh look, ya brought the baby. Hey sweetie." She put her cheek next to Choral's. "Smoochie, smoochie." Junie widened her eyes. "When they told me to come in I thought I was gettin' fired or somethin'. Ralph got this call last night sayin' my sister had been in a real bad accident. I took off outa here like Secretariat. Come to find out it was a prank call. My sister's fine. She didn't even leave her house last night. Who would play that kinda joke on someone? Sick. They just have to be sick. Did you hear about Margaret?"

"Yeah."

"Well of course ya did. That's why you're here. I wonder—"

Spano walked over, interrupting. "June Radabach?" he asked.

"That's me," Junie answered.

"I'm Detective Spano. Would you mind stepping over here?"

"Sure. Pleased ta meet ya, Detective. I don't think I've ever met a real detective before."

Symphony walked away feeling sure that when the detective finished questioning Junie, she would know more about the detective than he would know about her. The thought made her grin but only for a flash. The image of Margaret's body swept away any thought that tried to surface.

At home, the phone was ringing as she unlocked the front door. It stopped just as she picked it up.

Choral was getting fussy, so Symphony nursed her, changed her, and put her in her high chair for lunch: half a jar of creamed spinach diluted with baby cereal. *Yum, yum.*

The phone rang again but before Symphony could get there, the caller gave up.

Bath time gave way to nap time. Soon, Choral was asleep and Symphony stretched out on her bed hoping to rest until time to go to work. But the phone rang again. This time, she caught it on the third ring. "Hello."

No one said a word.

"Hello," she said again.

Still nothing.

"Hello!"

"Do you know who this is?" He was almost whispering.

"No. Who is it?"

Click.

On her way back to bed, the phone rang again. Symphony hesitated but picked it up anyway. "Hello."

"Hi." The same almost whisper. "Please just talk to me for a minute."

"Who is this?" she demanded.

Click.

She paused, then headed down the hallway but stopped when the ringing began again. She ran to the phone, grabbed it, and put it to her ear. "What?" she shouted. "Either talk or stop calling!"

"Hello," a man said. "This is Detective Spano. Could I speak to Symphony Weber, please."

"Sure." Symphony tried to disguise her voice. Embarrassed, she placed the receiver on the table and took a few deep breaths. Then she picked up the phone once again.

"This is Symphony."

"Hello, Ms. Weber," Spano said. "We just finished with the crime scene. Could you meet me downtown at the station on your way to work? It'll just take a minute. We need a sample of your writing."

"Why?"

"Oh. It's all part of determining who was in the room yesterday."

"But you already know I was in the room."

"I'll see you at the station. About three fifteen?"

"I'll be there."

After Spano's call, a nap was impossible. Symphony stretched out on the bed once again, but couldn't unwind. Soon, she just got up. Before she left for the police station, the kitchen was spotless and two loads of clothes were clean, dry, and folded.

Detective Spano wasn't available, but had left instructions with Rodriguez, who grinned and reached for Choral. "Do you mind if I hold her while you write this sentence?"

"Thanks." Symphony handed the baby to Rodriguez. "By now, she's probably starting to think you're family." She picked up a pen from the desk. "What do you want me to write?"

⌘ ⌘ ⌘

237

Although the Administrator of Sandstone Flats sent out a memo forbidding any employee discussion of Margaret's death, Symphony's shift was a deluge of stories and rumors. Some of the more alert patients, having caught bits and pieces of staff conversation and television news, began asking questions. The families of three residents had already made arrangements to move their loved ones to a "more secure" facility.

Brian, a new medical assistant, began work that afternoon.

"Why don't you take him tonight, Symphony?" the charge nurse offered. "You've had a rough day," she said, sounding as if she were doing Symphony a favor. "Besides, there's a new patient in E7 and she seems to need a little extra TLC."

"What?" Symphony asked. "There's already someone in Margaret's room?"

"A patient died, Symphony. It happens. You've been doing this long enough to know that. And when there's an empty room, we fill it. That's how we get paid." The nurse turned and walked away.

Symphony stood there for a moment, surprised at the nurse's callousness. Then she remembered Brian. "Sorry," she said. "She's not usually so blunt. Is this your *actual* first day, or have you done this before somewhere else?"

"I've never done anything like this," Brian said, blushing. He pulled his shoulder-length brown hair into a ponytail.

Symphony smiled. "Well, let's start with the linen closet," she said, readying herself for a long shift.

⌘　⌘　⌘

"I don't really care for guys with long hair," Junie said on the way home that night. "But Brian's kinda cute. Don't ya think?"

"I guess," Symphony answered.

Junie was beaming. "So? Whadda ya think? I asked him straight out. He's single."

Symphony rolled her eyes. "Well—I'm—not—lookin'."

⌘　⌘　⌘

Symphony awoke at three in the morning with "Babe, I'm Gonna Leave You" playing in her ears and Mack on her mind. For a moment, she was back with him on Empty Island, in the tent, his beautiful boy smile sending warm currents through her body. Then she remembered how he'd walked away and left her to face Daddy, how he'd lied about what happened between them.

*I hope Choral didn't kick her covers off again.*

Standing up, she moved toward the door but froze when something shadowy passed outside her window. Catlike, she crept over and peeked out the side of the curtain.

*Just my imagination. Maybe I should be a writer.*

Symphony put her palm on the baby's back, feeling the rhythm of her breathing. "God, I love you," she whispered, kissing Choral on the cheek. Then, tucking her in, she went back to bed and snuggled under her own covers, trying to sleep.

⌘　⌘　⌘

Morning came early, but Symphony was glad. Choral had outgrown nearly every outfit she had, not to mention her shoes. And she had to have shoes. It was starting to get cold outside. As much as Symphony dreaded the mall, it was time.

By ten thirty, she was strolling the long terrazzo aisles, checking the stores that sold baby shoes. Searching for sales.

People gazed at Choral in her stroller. "What a beautiful little girl," they would say as Symphony glowed. *Why do I hate the mall?*

By noon, Choral was famished. Symphony snuck into the ladies' room to nurse, knowing it was only a matter of time before the baby needed something more solid. The car was in the lot at the other end of the mall so she headed back down the terrazzo, glancing into each store as she passed.

A poster in the bookstore's new release section snagged her attention. She stopped. On the shelves, a dark grey book with a clown on the cover seemed to mock her. *Where have I seen this?* She picked one up from the display. *Psycho the Clown—The Life and Times of Roscoe Stanley.*

The trembling began in her hands and spread to the rest of her body. She turned the book over and read. "After twenty-five years of performing as a clown, Roscoe Stanley was arrested in Titusville, Florida on kidnapping and murder charges. He is believed to be responsible for the disappearance of more than thirty children."

Symphony looked at the front of the book again. Roscoe Stanley had been a clown in some of her nightmares. A small part of her wanted to buy the book, but Roscoe Stanley and his dream had already stolen too many of her nights. *No.* She just wanted to go home and feed Choral. She returned the book to the display and reached for the stroller.

Choral was gone.

She spun, hoping she had pushed the stroller behind her. *Where is it!* "Oh my God!" she wailed. "Choral." She ran toward the register. "Where is my baby? Did you see her? She was right here. In a stroller. A pink and yellow plaid stroller."

"I'll call security ma'am," the teenaged boy behind the counter said.

"She was right here," Symphony screamed. "Oh my God! I have to find her." She ran out of the store. There was one exit straight ahead, two on either side.

"Help me!" she screamed into the congested mall. "Someone took my baby. Please. She was in a pink and yellow stroller. A plaid stroller. Oh my God. Choral!"

Symphony raced toward the nearest exit and outside. She scanned the parking lot. "Please help me," she screamed, hoping the world would hear. "Have you seen anyone with a baby in a pink and yellow stroller? Someone stole my baby. Someone just took her. Please, she's hungry. I have to take her home and feed her." She began to sob.

A man hurried up from the parking lot and put his arm around her. "Come on now," he said. "I'm Ed. What's your name?"

"Symphony." She pushed him away. "I have to find her!"

"Okay," he said. "But it'll be better if we work together." Ed turned to the small group of people who had stopped to watch. "Someone call the police," he ordered. "Tell 'em we have an emergency. And grab a couple security guards. Hurry." He guided Symphony to a concrete bench and sat down with her. "Now tell me what happened."

Symphony stared at the walkway beneath her feet. "Someone just took her. Who would do that? Why would someone take Choral?"

"Where was she, Symphony?" he asked.

"At the bookstore. Right in front. I just turned my back for a second. She was right there."

A middle-aged woman pushed her way through the gathering crowd. "Sir," she said, breathing hard. "I found this in the parking lot." She glanced up at Symphony. "I'm sorry." She stepped aside, revealing a pink and yellow plaid stroller. It had been crushed by a car.

Symphony stood and staggered to the edge of the group. As her eyes met theirs, they grew silent and turned their faces away.

Symphony's world faded to black.

She folded into a heap on the sidewalk.

# CHAPTER TWENTY-SEVEN

DETECTIVE SPANO SAT at his desk.

In a chair directly across from him, Rodriguez sorted through a stack of files. "I can't find a thing here on Symphony Weber or Symphony Bolin. There were a couple of domestic disturbances called in by her neighbors in Pennsylvania. But, the reports never mentioned her. Just her husband."

"Okay," Spano said. "She went to college in Alabama. Did you find anything there?"

"A fix-it ticket for a bad tail light's all." Rodriguez grinned.

Spano clicked the button on his pen. "You really don't think she had anything to do with this, do you?" He stared at Rodriguez. "Then why did she know what word the killer left behind?"

"She said it was on the pillow, little brother."

He leaned forward toward Rodriguez. "Look, Connie. I don't mind you calling me 'brother' around here, but little brother? C'mon, Sis. I'm a detective and I'm the newest guy here. If I'm gonna be effective, people have to respect me. What's the timing on your transfer?" He put the pen on the desk and leaned back in his chair, losing his balance for a moment before regaining it.

Rodriguez shot him a disapproving look.

"Don't you say a word," Spano warned.

"I'm not sayin' a thing. If you tip over, I'll just let one of your staff take you to the hospital. I'm sure that'd go a long way toward your gettin' some respect."

He sat up straight. "Maybe it was a bad idea for me to move here. We can't even finish a collective thought."

Rodriguez rolled her eyes. "I'm sorry, okay? All I'm tryin' to say is, she knew the word the killer had written, but she didn't know where he wrote it. Maybe she's got some sort of—"

"And all I'm sayin' is," Spano leaned back in his chair again, "she either wrote the word on that little white piece of paper, or she saw that piece of paper and thought it was a pillow."

"There always has to be a logical explanation for you. You don't believe in—"

The phone rang. "Spano," he answered, sounding irritated. "What? Miracle City Mall? Where's the mother? And no sign of— It was crushed. Okay, who's down there right now? Do what you can with the witnesses but don't touch anything. I'll send a crew."

He hung up and dialed another number. "Any chance you and Leland can meet me over at Miracle City? There's a kid missing. Yeah I know it's not a homicide and I hope it stays that way. But my gut says it's connected to the Browden case. I'll get there as soon as I can."

He hung up the phone and threw his keys to Rodriguez. "Let's go," he said. "You drive this time."

She caught the keys in mid air. "The mall?" she asked, starting for the door.

"The Medical Center," he said. "Symphony Weber's there. Someone took her daughter."

Rodriguez stopped, stunned. "That sweet baby?"

"Yeah," Spano said. "Come on. We gotta go."

⌘　⌘　⌘

Police officers and security guards peppered Miracle City Mall. Yellow tape was tied from the bookstore, down the hall, and through the exit Symphony had used. More was strung from that area to the parking spot where the stroller was found. Officers took pictures of anything that might be evidence but nothing had been touched. Nothing, that is, but the stroller, and that couldn't be avoided. Luckily, the woman who found it picked it up by the cloth seat and not the handles.

The officers on the scene interviewed employees and customers who were in a position to see the kidnapper. They questioned the crowd outside, taking down names and phone numbers of those with possible information. Everyone who was not a witness was encouraged to go home. However, most of them stayed. As word of the kidnapping spread, more people came.

When the volume of the crowd reached a dull roar, a man with a megaphone stood on a bench and shouted over them. "I know you all want to help," he said, "but we have to keep it down. That baby could be right next to us and none of us would hear her. Now, instead of standin' around, maybe we should split into two or three groups and check out the area. There are some people in the crowd handing out whistles. If you find something, it is imperative that you do *not* touch it. Just blow your whistle."

The crowd separated. Some searched in, under, and around the cars in the parking lot. Others walked the grounds that surrounded the mall. All of them were quiet, listening for the sounds of a baby.

⌘ ⌘ ⌘

"I know this is hard," Spano said, standing next to Symphony as she lay on a cot in the Emergency Room. "Just take your time."

She sat up and stared ahead as if she were seeing it again. "It was so stupid! I was looking at that book. Then when I reached for the stroller, it was gone—Choral was gone." Her eyes widened in terror. "Oh, God!" she screamed. "What if *he* has her?"

"Who?" Spano asked.

"They said he died. But what if he really didn't? Oh my God. If he has her—"

"Ms. Weber?" The detective leaned over and looked into her eyes. "Who do you think took Choral?"

"What if he escaped? He's already taken over thirty children." Symphony scratched her arm until it was bleeding. "What if he didn't die? What if he just escaped and they didn't want us to know?"

Spano looked at Rodriguez. "Tell them to get somebody in here."

Rodriguez slipped out through the curtain.

245

"He followed me to the bookstore. He had to. He knew I would look at the book. He used to know when I was dreamin' about him. I didn't tell you that, did I?"

The detective touched Symphony's hand. "What was his name again?"

"You know who he is," she snapped, jerking her hand away.

"You may have said it but I didn't write it down."

"Roscoe Stanley. He took her . . . to pay me back." She flopped down onto the cot, sobbing. "If it wasn't for me, you never would've caught him."

Spano softened his voice. "Why's that, Symphony?"

"There was a man and he was mad," she sang. "Then, Poof!" Her breathing accelerated. "I saw him at the park." She put her hand over her heart, panting. "I made Mama call the police."

"Roscoe Stanley?" Spano asked.

"That's why he's so mad," she said. "That's why he took Choral." Her eyes were wild. "I have to get her. He'll—" She threw her legs over the side of the cot.

The curtain slid open and a doctor in green scrubs appeared, a nurse in tow. Rodriguez stood in the opening, watching with pain in her eyes.

"Could you lie back down for me, Ms. Weber?" the doctor asked. "I'd like to examine you again."

Symphony swung her arms at the doctor and tried to stand. "Where do you think he took all those other kids?" she asked, her eyes fixed on Spano who shifted his weight from foot to foot.

"Ms. Weber," the doctor said, "I'm giving you something to calm you."

The nurse handed Symphony a small white cup with a pill in it.

Symphony batted it away. As the pill tapped and skittered across the floor, she turned and glared at Spano. "I said tell me where he took them. I don't want Choral there. He can't have her."

The doctor turned to the nurse. "We'll have to give her a shot."

"I'm one step ahead of you." The nurse pulled the cap off a syringe. "This may sting a little," she said. She held Symphony's arm and stuck the needle in.

"Don't," Symphony screamed. "I have to find Choral. Take me out there where he hides them. Roscoe Stanley has her. He wasn't dead. They just . . . they just . . . they . . . ." She relaxed against the cot. Within seconds, her eyes closed.

"Are you keepin' her?" Spano asked.

"Yes," the doctor said. "At least until she can be evaluated. Seems like she's had a break of some kind."

Spano shot the doctor a dirty look. "A break? Someone just took her kid!" He handed the nurse a card. "Please have someone call me when she wakes up." He turned to Rodriguez. "Let's get over to Miracle City."

⌘ ⌘ ⌘

On the way, Rodriguez called the station. "Hey, Rose. It's Connie. Detective Spano wants an officer outside Symphony Weber's room until he says otherwise. Family only. Get a list of 'em from the precinct, okay? Thanks."

"Hey, sis," Spano said. "Do you know anything about that guy she was talkin' about? That Roscoe Stanley?"

"Name sounds familiar but I'm not sure why. Soon as we're done here, I'll do some research." She settled back in her seat, looking out the window. "Hey. I just wanted to say, you were really sweet to her back there at the hospital. The way you defended her to that doctor. Made me proud to be your sister."

Spano smiled and shook his head. "Remember how Mom used to send me to that Quickie Mart on the corner?" His smile faded. "I was always beggin' her to let me take Paulie and Sam. When she finally let me, I felt so grown up, you know? Well, Paulie wandered off that day. God! I thought I was gonna die. I kept callin' to him, but he didn't answer. I remember thinkin' 'the one time Mom treats me like a big kid, I lose Paulie.' In all the years since then, I don't think I've ever been that scared."

"But you found him," Rodriguez said.

"Yeah. I was lucky."

Rodriguez watched him for a moment. "If we weren't working, I'd give you a hug, right now."

Spano glanced at her and grimaced. "Don't you dare. I mean, I love you and all, sis, but we can't keep working together. They need to finish up with your transfer."

Rodriguez smiled at him and looked back out the window as they pulled into the Miracle City parking lot. "Jeez," she said. "Look at all these people."

Spano and Rodriguez spent the next three hours talking to witnesses but no one had seen the person pushing the stroller away. Symphony's hysteria was all anyone recalled. The security cameras didn't cover the entire mall, and the guard who was supposed to be watching the footage was no help. He was on the phone with his girlfriend when Choral was taken.

⌘ ⌘ ⌘

"Maybe it's a coincidence," Rodriguez said as they headed back to the hospital. "It doesn't make any sense. Why would someone murder one of Symphony's patients *and* take her baby?"

"Someone who wanted to hurt her, maybe?" Spano answered. "Like an ex-husband, an old boyfriend, someone who thinks she hurt them?"

"Yeah, that would work if we were only talkin' about the baby. But Ms. Browden was a patient. Not someone Symphony was close with. Ya know? It just doesn't add up."

⌘ ⌘ ⌘

Mama and Daddy sat at the hospital in a private visiting room, waiting for Symphony to wake up. The powder blue walls weren't doing their job. No one in the room was calm.

Detective Spano knocked before entering. "I'm sorry Mr. and Mrs. Weber. There are no solid leads yet," he said, after introducing himself. "But Officer Rodriguez is doing some research right now into something Symphony said to us this afternoon.

"Well, what'd she say?" Daddy asked. "Maybe we can help."

"Roscoe Stanley."

Daddy looked confused, Mama, horrified.

"We were there the day that awful man was arrested," Mama said. She clicked the nail of her index finger against a tooth.

Daddy's brow wrinkled. "Is that the guy who ran right up to the car when you were at the little market that time?"

Mama bit her lower lip and nodded.

"For some reason," Spano continued, "your daughter believes he's still alive. That he's paying her back for something. If he was alive, would he have reason to blame Symphony for his arrest?"

Mama looked at Spano and shook her head. Her body language said, 'no,' but her eyes said something else.

Spano cocked his head. "Are you sure?"

She chewed her nails. Tears formed in her eyes. "There's more to it," she said, turning to Daddy. "I'm sorry I didn't tell you this before."

Daddy reached over and took her hand. "Go ahead."

Spano listened, putting pen to clipboard.

"Symphony was nine then, and we were on our way to the shoe store when we passed Boynton Park. Well, Symphony started havin' a fit, beggin' me to pull over. She never acted up like that, so I stopped. She pointed to a car and told me she'd been dreamin' about it since she was in nursery school. Since she was five. She knew what that man looked like and what he was wearing. That the seats of his car were pale green. I walked past him and she was right. About everything. But there was something else. She said, in the dream, she and her sister were in the car with him. She was afraid he was here to take them away. So I locked the kids in the car, went to the payphone on the corner, and called the police."

"Maisy! And you never thought to tell me?"

"I didn't know what to think about it. My whole life, Mama's been tryin' to tell me those dreams run in the family. That day, I knew she was right, but I still didn't wanna believe it. I just wanted Symphony to have a normal, happy life. So I didn't say anything."

"Oh, God, Maisy. And it never occurred to you that this may have had something to do with her tryin' to kill herself? Maybe it wasn't *just* because I was such a jerk all the goddamn time. And now, that son of a bitch could've taken Choral?"

Mama started to cry. "It can't be Roscoe Stanley," she said. "He's dead. He died in prison."

Daddy stood, pacing for a moment. "I just can't believe . . ." He walked to the door. "I'm gonna go sit with Symphony for awhile."

Mama watched him leave.

Spano handed her a tissue. "I'm sorry, Mrs. Weber. I'm just trying to get all the information I can." He sat across from her. "Is there anything I can do?"

"Find Choral," she said. "Just find our precious baby."

"A current picture would help. If we could get her face on the news, you know?"

Mama handed him a picture from her purse. "This one was taken last week."

Joe blasted through the door. "I just got the message Jeanne left at work. Have they found her?"

Spano reached out to shake Joe's hand. "I'm Detective Spano," he said. "I want you to know we're doing everything we can. If anyone in the immediate family comes up with any information that might help, please let me know right away." He picked up his briefcase. "Excuse me, Mrs. Weber. I need to make some calls." He turned to Joe. "I'm glad you're here. Your mother could use the company."

Daddy's chair was still warm when Joe sat down. He put his arm around Mama and leaned his head on her shoulder. "They'll find her," he said.

And Mama fell apart.

⌘　⌘　⌘

As Symphony began to break through the medicinal fog, she called out for Dani. With bloodshot eyes, Dani moved to the bedside and stood over Symphony.

"I had a really bad dream," Symphony said. "I dreamed I had a baby and someone took her."

Dani couldn't speak at first. Then she grasped Symphony's hand. "I had the same dream. And I'm scared. Can I get in bed with you?"

Symphony turned on her side and moved over. She closed her eyes and was asleep again.

"Can't we just keep her like this till we find Choral?" Dani said. "Then she won't have to feel it."

"We can't," Daddy said. "It's like lying to her. Besides, what if she knows something that'll help the police?"

"Like what?"

"I don't know but she needs to talk to Detective Spano." He rubbed Symphony's shoulder. "Will you stay with her, Daniele? I left your mama alone and I need to get back."

Dani nodded. "How's Mama doin'?"

"Don't worry about your mother. I'll take care of her. You concentrate on Symphony. If you get a chance to use the phone, why don't you call Jeanne, Leesa, and Joe. Symphony's gonna need all of us when she wakes up. I'd better call your granny, too." Daddy pulled some change out of his pocket and walked down the hall toward the pay phone.

⌘　⌘　⌘

After the last traffic light in town, the man took off the baseball cap he was wearing at the mall. Tossing it onto the back seat, he turned left onto Highway One and headed out of Titusville toward Mims, driving hard, adrenalin pushing the accelerator. Beside him, in a brand new car seat, sat Choral.

She'd cried for the first five minutes. Now, every time he looked at her, she watched him, her dark eyes wide, but calm, as if she were trying to understand.

*Kid gives me the creeps!*

He pulled the car into an orange grove, deep enough to be hidden from the road. He turned off the engine and stared at her.

*What am I doin' with a fuckin' baby?*

# CHAPTER TWENTY-EIGHT

JEANNE AND LEESA went straight from their final exams to the hospital where Symphony had just been re-sedated. Dani, ready for a break, left them in charge while she went to eat, call Phil, and talk to the police.

For two hours the little sisters held Symphony's limp hands as she slept, whispering soothing words in her ears.

"They'll find her soon, sis," Leesa said. "You'll see."

"Try not to worry," Jeanne added. "Everyone's lookin' for her. On the way over here, the DJ on WRKT was asking people to watch TV or buy the newspaper so they could see Choral's picture. By now, I'll bet everyone in Florida knows her face."

When Dani finally tiptoed back into the room, she scolded them. "Maybe you should talk about something else," she said. "Tell her about school, or about your test, or anything to get her mind off all of this. Jeez! I don't want her to get so upset she tries to . . ." Dani covered her mouth and stared at them. "I'm sorry," she said. "Have you talked to Mama yet?"

"No," Jeanne answered. "We wanted to see Symphony first. Then when we got here, I had to run all the way back to the car to get my purse. The cop guarding the door wouldn't let me in without ID. What's that about anyway?"

"I'm sure it's nothing. Ask Mama and Daddy, okay? They're in a visiting room across the hall, three doors down. Joe's there, too."

Jeanne and Leesa crossed the hall to see Mama, Daddy, and Joe, leaving Dani alone with Symphony once again.

Dani kissed Symphony's forehead. "They'll find her," she said. "Try not to worry." She sat down, opened "All Things Wise and Wonderful," and began to read.

⌘ ⌘ ⌘

"Why is there a policeman guarding Symphony's door?" Jeanne asked first thing.

"You know," Joe said, "I was wondering the same thing. There's only two reasons they'd do that. One is if they think the person who took Choral still wants to hurt Symphony. The other is to keep Symphony from runnin' off, which makes no sense whatsoever. Either way, I'll have to talk to that Detective what's-his-name. Did he leave a card, Daddy?"

Mama's eyes opened wide. "Oh no," she said. "With everything that happened today, I forgot."

"Forgot what, Mama?" Leesa asked.

"One of Symphony's patients passed away night before last. The police must have been suspicious about it because they called yesterday morning and insisted Symphony meet them at the nursing home. She had to take Choral down there with her." Mama's face froze in a horrified expression. "You don't think that could have anything to do with this." She stared at Daddy, mouth open. "Do you?"

Now, Maisy," Daddy said. "We've got enough to worry about. Don't let your imagination make it worse." He rubbed Mama's shoulder.

Her body relaxed. "You're right. It just struck me as strange. That's all."

⌘ ⌘ ⌘

Rodriguez closed the last file in the stack she'd been studying for three hours. She unwound the bun in her hair and let the black braid hang down her back. "It's almost ten," she said, looking at the station clock. "You want more coffee, or should we call it a night?"

Spano stacked the paper coffee cups scattered across his desk and tossed them into the trash. "Tell me what you found, then we'll decide."

She straightened the piles on her desk. "Well, Roscoe Stanley was a real sicko. The case files say they found him guilty of the abduction and murder of thirteen kids. Boys and girls. But the book that just came out, the one Symphony Weber was talking about, claims he murdered over thirty. He died in prison—the Marion facility. Heart attack. Only served a couple years. If you ask me, he got off easy. Did you find anything else about the Browden case?"

Spano raised his eyebrows. "You know, Margaret Browden spent a few years in Lowell Prison for murder."

"Really?"

Spano gathered the paperwork from his workstation and moved it to one corner. With the sleeve of his shirt, he dusted the crumbs from his desk to the trash. "Lowell's practically next door to Marion. I wonder if they could've met. Nah. That's crazy. Anyway, her attorney introduced new evidence and the case was reopened. At the retrial, the jury found her guilty of," he flipped open the file on his desk, "involuntary manslaughter. They sentenced her to time served and sent her home. Tomorrow I'll talk to the crew that went through her house."

Rodriguez picked up her purse and pulled out her keys. "Did you hear anything from the lab?"

"Yeah. No fingerprints on the note the killer wrote." Spano stood and pushed his chair in. "That means whoever murdered Margaret Browden was very careful."

Rodriguez tilted her head. "That's easy. There's a box of gloves in every room at Sandstone Flats. Have you talked to the hospital tonight? I wonder how Symphony's doin.'"

"I called half-an-hour ago. She's still out. I just wish we had good news for her. Maybe something will open up tomorrow."

"Come on, brother. Let's go home. We can't fix anything tonight."

⌘　⌘　⌘

"Go on home," Mama told the rest of the family. "Symphony'll sleep for at least another eight hours. And if she wakes up asking for you, I'll call."

As soon as the nurse found out Mama was staying all night, she brought in a guest cot. Mama was comfortable enough, but her thoughts wouldn't settle. Each time Symphony mumbled in her sleep, Mama watched her expression.

For the first time, Mama wanted Symphony to have a dream, one that would tell them where to find Choral.

⌘ ⌘ ⌘

The phone rang around three in the morning. Jeanne stumbled down the hall half asleep and answered, "Hello," just as Daddy raced up in his skivvies.

"I'm sorry, Symphony," a man said, his voice just above a whisper.

"About what?" Jeanne asked, still in a fog.

"For what I did."

Jeanne jolted to attention. "Who is this!"

Daddy grabbed the phone. "Who is this? And why are you calling in the middle of the night?"

There was a click on the line.

Daddy slammed the phone down. "What did they say?"

"It was a man," Jeanne answered, beginning to cry. "He thought I was Symphony. He said he was sorry for what he did. You don't think Choral's—"

"We better call the police," Daddy said.

Leesa, heavy sleeper that she was, didn't even twitch.

⌘ ⌘ ⌘

Mama awoke at six the next morning as the police guard stepped into the room. "There's some people in the hall. They're not on the list. Your mother and brother?"

"Thank you," Mama said with a yawn. Stretching, she stood, folded the cot, and rolled it out of the way. Leaving Symphony sleeping, she stepped into the hallway to find Granny and Austin waiting.

"Let's go over here where we can talk," Mama said, pointing to the visiting room. They stepped inside and closed the door behind them.

Mama sat down. "I don't want to be gone too long, but I don't want to talk in front of her. Who knows what she can hear? And I don't want her to wake up yet. She just can't handle what's happened."

"No, Maisy," Granny said. "*You* can't bear that she *has* to handle it. But hard as it is to see her hurt like that, she needs to be here. I hate it, sweetheart, but we have to let her wake to it."

"Why did this have to happen?" Mama sobbed. "Symphony was just starting to feel good about herself. And Choral. She's our joy. We have to get her back. But, what if . . . ?"

Austin sat down next to Mama and put his arm around her. "I hope you don't have to find out, Sis."

Granny stroked Mama's hair. "I'm so sorry, sugar. Maybe you should sit here for a spell. Have a good cry."

Mama looked up. "I need to be in there with Symphony."

"You're no good for anybody if you don't take care of yourself. I'll go stay with her, sugar. You do what you need to do. When you're done, come on across the hall."

Granny shuffled over to Symphony's room and pulled a chair close. As Symphony began to stir, Granny took hold of her hand, gripping it as if her touch could siphon off some of the pain.

⌘　⌘　⌘

Across the hall, Mama had herself a good cry, sobbing her secret fears against her brother's solid chest. When the tears stopped and all she could feel was the tremble of the unkown, she apologized. "I'm just so tired of being strong. For some reason, with the two of you here, I feel like someone else can be the grown up. At least for little while."

Austin held her tight and patted her back. "I'm just glad we got here before everyone else this morning. Is there any news?"

⌘　⌘　⌘

"Here, brother," Rodriguez said as she walked into the squad room. "I brought you a strong cup of coffee." She set a cup on Spano's desk and one on hers. "Is it me or did we just leave here?"

He smelled the coffee and smiled. "Strong. Just what I need. Be glad I didn't call you at three-thirty."

She pushed a bag of donuts across the desk to him. "Two of those are for you. And, this time, try and eat them in at least two bites. What were you doin' up at three-thirty?"

"The Weber's had another one of those phone calls in the middle of the night. Some guy apologizing. Said he's sorry for what he did."

"Like he's the one who took the baby? Can the phone company—"

"I had 'em put a trap on the line. If he calls back at least we'll have the number he's callin' from." Spano shoved half a maple bar in his mouth and washed it down with a sip of coffee. "Have you heard anything from the inquiry you did on the husband?"

Rodriguez shook her head as he finished off the first donut. "The sheriff's office checked about eight last night. He was at home. They talked to him. Told him it would be in his best interest to stay put."

⌘　⌘　⌘

Symphony opened her eyes. "Granny," she said, and closed them again. "I didn't know you were coming." She half-smiled and drifted back to sleep.

Granny sighed and waited.

The next time Symphony opened her eyes, she said, "It's true. Isn't it?"

"What's true, sugar?" Granny asked. "Tell me what you remember."

"Somebody took Choral," Symphony answered, her voice flat from the drugs.

"That's right."

"She'll be back, though. Won't she?" She nodded off again.

A tear escaped Granny's eye. She turned her head, hoping Symphony missed it.

⌘　⌘　⌘

Choral had been screaming since she woke up.

*She has to be hungry. And wet. I don't think she messed.* He found a deserted country market and pulled the car into the trees behind it. "Okay, baby," he said. "I'll be right back." He locked the car, paused to tuck his shirt in, then hurried around to the front of the building.

He entered, winking at the clerk, a bleached-blonde in her forties.

"How's your day?" she asked, popping her gum.

"You tell me," he said, stepping to the counter with a swagger "My sister and her ten-month-old are in town for a visit."

"That's nice," she said. "Boy or girl?"

"Huh?" he asked, scanning the display rack for a newspaper.

"The baby? Boy or girl?"

"Girl," he answered.

"How sweet."

"Yeah. She's pretty cute, all right." He smiled. "The problem is, my sister gave me a list of what to buy and I lost it. So here I am. The baby has nothing to eat or drink, no diapers or clean clothes . . . nothing." He tried to look helpless. "I don't have any kids. Can you help me?"

The blonde crossed her arms. "That sister of yours must've left home in a real hurry."

"Their bags were put on the wrong plane."

"That happened to me once. Almost ruined my trip, too. Well, let's see." She walked down a side aisle swinging her ample hips. "Here's all the baby stuff I've got. You say she's ten months old?"

"Yeah," he answered, following.

"We don't carry any clothes, but I can help you with most of it. Hang on while I get a box outta the back room."

She returned a few moments later with an empty orange box and began to fill it with disposable diapers, powdered formula and rice cereal. She carried a baby bottle and some jars of baby food to the counter. Then, with an "Oh yeah," she trotted to the back of the store and returned with a bunch of bananas. "This should get you by for a few days," she said.

The certainty in her voice made him feel he was doing the right thing.

"I haven't seen you around here before," she said, punching the price of each item into the register.

"Just bought the old Smith place." He winked again. "My sister came to help me get moved in."

"Smith place?" She tilted her head a gazed at the ceiling. "Is that out by the lake?"

"Yeah," he answered. "That old lodge out there." He walked through the store picking up other necessities: a box of crackers, a jar of peanut butter, a bottle of distilled water, two candy bars and a soda. "Do you have today's paper?"

"Around here we only have a weekly. Where y'all from?"

"Uh, Tennessee," he said.

"Will that be all, then?" She popped her gum and grinned.

"Yeah." He handed her three twenties. "Thanks for all your help."

She gave him his seven dollars and thirty-two cents change. "I can carry some of that out for you."

"No thanks." He shoved the change into his pocket. "I've got it." He balanced the box on one hip, picked up the brown sack with his free hand, and headed out.

The clerk watched him struggle with the door. When he got it open, he turned right.

She shook her head. "Men."

⌘ ⌘ ⌘

Choral stopped crying when he opened the door.

He sped down the highway behind the store and pulled off onto a logging road. There, he read the instructions on the formula box and made Choral a bottle with the cold water.

*This stuff stinks.*

But Choral drank it in what seemed like seconds.

He popped the lid off the strained peaches. *Dammit. No spoon.* He held the jar to her lips like a cup. Choral sucked the peaches down one sip at a time.

*Now for the hard part.* He opened the huge box of diapers and pulled Choral out of the car seat she'd been in for almost twenty-four hours. "Okay, baby," he said, ripping off the disposable she was wearing. The stench of ammonia burned his eyes. Her bottom was scarlet. Digging through the glove box, he found a napkin. "I'm sorry," he said. "I didn't mean to hurt you." He wet it and washed her off. Then, he put a new diaper on, destroying three before he got it right. After tossing his trash on the ground outside, he pulled back onto the highway heading north.

Choral was asleep within minutes.

They traveled for almost an hour before coming to a town with a mom and pop grocery store. He stopped just long enough to use the pay phone.

⌘　⌘　⌘

Uncle Austin was exhausted from driving all night. He followed Jeanne and Leesa home where they fed him sandwiches and made a bed for him on the couch. He stretched out and went right to work snoring.

"Come on, Leesa," Jeanne called down the hall. "I'll meet you in the car." When she opened the front door to head back to the hospital, there was Quinton.

"The police came to see me last night," he said. "That baby has to be mine. Symphony must have been pregnant when she left. I should never have let her go."

"You didn't let Symphony go. She let herself go." Jeanne said, squeezing her fists so hard her fingernails cut into her palms. "Judging by the way she looked when she got here, if she'd stayed with you, Choral might have ended up another miscarriage."

"Don't you talk to me like that!" Quinton said through gritted teeth.

Jeanne raised her fist. "You just couldn't stop hitting her, could you?" She took a swing and missed.

Quinton jumped back a step. "Hey. Who the hell do you think you are?"

Jeanne swung again. "Now you show up here—"

This time, Quinton caught Jeanne's arm. "Look. I have every right to know about that baby. I want to see Symphony. Right now!"

"You can't see her." Jeanne jerked away and tried to close the door.

Quinton shoved it open again. Jeanne lost her grip. The door pounded against the wall, leaving a hole where the doorknob hit.

"You Weber girls must all be bitches," he railed. "Now go get Symphony or *I* will!"

"Get outta here," Jeanne yelled.

"Symphony is still my wife. And I'm gonna see her. Right now. Don't try and stop me or I'll—"

"Or you'll what?" Uncle Austin asked, stepping between Quinton and Jeanne. His arms were crossed, but he used the same tone he might use at the supper table.

261

"I need to see her," Quinton said. "She's my baby, too."

"That may be so," Austin answered, continuing with his southern politeness, "but believe me when I tell you, you're not gonna see her. Now you best leave here 'fore I get as mad as you are."

Quinton did his best to stare Austin down. When he realized Austin wasn't going to back off, he walked to his car and drove away.

Austin patted Jeanne on the head. "Nice swing, there. Who do you think you are? Some red-headed Muhammad Ali?"

Jeanne crossed her arms and glared at him.

"Seriously," he said. "You did good."

She relaxed and the corners of her mouth turned upward.

Austin grinned. "And just so you know, they *do* have a federation of women boxers. Maybe you should check 'em out?"

"Jerk!" Jeanne said, exaggerating a swing at him.

He laughed all the way to the couch, where he stretched out once again.

Jeanne shook her head and walked out the door.

⌘　⌘　⌘

Leesa walked in carrying a small blanket and pillow. She had changed into jeans and a sea foam green cotton blouse. "What's all the noise about?" She glanced around the room and shrugged. Austin was sleeping. Jeanne was gone.

Just then, the phone rang. She picked it up. "Hello?"

"Symphony?" a man said.

"Symphony's not here right now. May I take a message?"

"Tell her I was watching her. I watched as long as I could."

Leesa snapped her fingers trying to get Austin's attention, but he was already snoring again. "Who's calling?" she asked.

The caller answered with a click.

She stood there dazed until Jeanne blew the horn, jolting her back into the moment.

"Hold your horses," she scolded, running out the door.

⌘　⌘　⌘

Spano hung up the phone just as Rodriguez walked up to her desk. He looked at her and scratched his head. "Preliminary autopsy results are in on the Browden case."

"Oh, yeah?" Rodriguez responded. "What'd the coroner say?"

"No petechial hemhorrages in the eyes, so she dug deeper. Apparently, cause of death was internal bleeding. Probably a complication of liver failure." He leaned back in his chair, arms crossed, staring up at the ceiling.

Rodriguez sat down, shaking her head. "So. Natural causes? Then how did the body get in the position it was in? Did she say anything about that?"

"Said it could've been a seizure. Something about toxin levels in the blood."

"I don't believe that for a second," Rodriguez said. "Besides, if she died without anyone's help, what about that little piece of paper with 'AGAIN' written on it? If you ask me, someone wants us to think it was murder."

Spano set all four legs of his chair on the squad room floor and looked straight into Rodriguez' eyes. "That doesn't make any sense."

She shrugged. "No. I guess not." The phone rang and she picked it up. "Rodriguez. Really? Here. Lemme let you talk to Spano." She handed the phone across the desk. "It's Dunn. The Webers had another phone call."

Spano put the phone to his ear. "What'd the guy say?"

"That he'd been watching her for a long time," Dunn answered.

Spano scrawled a note on a yellow pad. "About what time?

"Her sister thought it had been half an hour."

"Who did he talk to this time?"

"The younger sister, Leesa. She was pretty upset about it. That and the fact that Symphony's ex showed up at the house."

"Okay. Thanks," Spano said. "I'll be right down." He hung up the phone and looked at Rodriguez. "He talked to a different sister this time. Sounds like he may have been stalking Symphony Weber. I'll head over to the hospital and question the sister while her memory's still fresh. Call the phone company. See what number came up in the trap."

"Sure," Rodriguez answered. "I'll let you know what I find out. Anything else?"

"Yeah. Quinton Bolin, showed up at the Weber's today. Track him down. I wanna talk to him before the day's over." He shoved the notepad into his briefcase and grabbed his keys. "Oh, and let's take a look at the family members of Sandstone Flats' employees and patients. See if anyone has a connection to Margaret Browden." He started out the door.

"Is that all?"

Spano stopped and turned around. "Thanks."

"You got it," Rodriguez said.

⌘ ⌘ ⌘

Symphony turned on her side, eyes closed, wishing she could have a dream that would lead her to Choral. She'd been faking sleep for over an hour. She needed to stretch, go to the bathroom, but she didn't want to see anybody—especially Granny, who had told her all along the dreams were a gift. *And I couldn't wait to make them stop.* She pushed the thought aside and listened to the conversation around her.

"Why don't you run home and catch a nap, Maisy," Granny said. "I'm sure you didn't sleep at all last night."

"When's Daddy supposed to be done at work?" Dani asked.

"I talked to him a few minutes ago," Mama answered. "He said he'd be another hour or so."

Dani shook her head in disgust. "You'd think they could do without him at a time like this. I'll take you home, Mama."

"Go on, Maisy," Granny said. "And I'll get my nap after you get back. Besides, it may be a good idea for someone to stay at the house in case another one of those calls comes in."

"Austin's there," Mama said.

Granny looked up and Mama and smiled. "Have you forgotten? Your brother could sleep through a train wreck."

"You're right." Mama picked up her purse. "If Symphony asks for me, tell her I'll be right back, okay?" She kissed Granny's cheek. "Love you."

"See you later, Granny." Dani turned to Mama on the way out. "Are Jeanne and Leesa still with that detective?"

They crossed the hall to the visitor's room. "Let's see," Mama said, pushing the door open.

They found Jeanne and Leesa alone, brows furrowed, so engrossed in conversation they took their time looking up.

"What's going on?" Mama asked. "Did the detective have anymore news?"

"No, Mama," Leesa said. "But we told him about Quinton and how bad Symphony was beat up when she got here."

"Symphony needs to file a restraining order," Jeanne said. "I hate it that Quinton's in town. Detective Spano said he's not supposed to be. The police told him to stay in Pennsylvania. But he didn't."

"So why don't they make him go home?" Dani asked.

"Because nobody filed anything with a judge," Leesa said.

"Yeah." Jeanne stood and walked toward the door. "That bastard can go anywhere he wants to."

The room grew silent. Under normal circumstances, Mama would have acted shocked and scolded Jeanne for her language. Instead, Mama hugged her. "I'm going home to get a little rest," she said. "Symphony's been awake for awhile but she's pretending to be asleep. I think she needs some time alone with your granny, so don't go in there for a while. Okay?"

"How could Choral just disappear?" Jeanne said. "Someone had to see something." She stood and picked up her keys. "Maybe we should be out there driving up and down the streets. At least then, it would feel like we were doing something to help."

⌘　⌘　⌘

Granny leaned forward in her chair. "Come on, honey. I know you're awake. You've been awake for a while."

Symphony rolled onto her back. "I wanna sleep, Granny. Why can't everyone just let me?"

"Doesn't do a bit of good for you to lay around pretendin' you're asleep. I bet what's goin' through your mind's a lot worse when you don't share. Tell me what you're thinkin', sugar."

Symphony pushed her legs over the side of the bed and sat up. "Okay. I'm thinkin, if I hadn't turned my back for that second, I'd be home with my daughter right now. I'm thinkin' why did I have to go to the mall? I'm thinkin' on most days, I'd wanna get up and stretch my legs, go to the bathroom, look out the window, listen to the birds, and play with my baby.

And since I can't play with Choral, I don't want to do any of those other things, either."

Granny looked Symphony straight in the eye and nodded. "Uh-huh," she said.

# CHAPTER TWENTY-NINE

SYMPHONY WAS RELEASED from the hospital five days after Choral's kidnapping. Her family clustered around her, giving whatever comfort they could, but nothing helped. After a few days, Granny and Austin went back to Alabama.

Every time the phone rang, Symphony jumped, both hoping and fearing it was news of Choral. To make matters worse, she never knew when a reporter would knock at the door in search of an interview.

One night, when no news people were around, Symphony took a small piece of luggage and escaped to Joe's apartment where she remained hidden for a month and a half.

⌘ ⌘ ⌘

Symphony sat up on the pink overstuffed sofa that almost filled Joe's living room.

*Choral.*

She picked up the calendar on the coffee table and wrote the number forty-nine in the next open box then stumbled to the tiny kitchen wearing yesterday's dirty clothes. After putting on a pot of coffee, she sat on a stool at the pink Formica bar that divided the two rooms.

From her seat, she eyed the bare branches of a knotted, old oak. Morning was over. It was afternoon. She could tell from the light. But it didn't matter what time she got up. Since the police had exhausted their leads, the days just ran together. Choral was gone. Life was a nightmare. And she'd learned long ago how to handle nightmares. *Vodka.*

She stood to check the coffee. While she was up, she stuck her hand in the cabinet above the stove, feeling all the way to the back. *I know there was more. I saw it yesterday.*

A key turned in the lock. Joe stepped inside and caught her in the middle of her search. "If you're lookin' for that other bottle, you're wastin' your time."

She stopped searching and poured a cup of coffee. "Where'd it go?"

There was a knock at the door. "You finished it last night. But you prob'ly don't remember, do you?" He peeked out the window and closed the curtains. "Shit!" he whispered. "You better hide for a minute. I tried to be careful but fuckin' reporters must've followed me from Mama and Daddy's."

Symphony stood staring at the door as the person outside knocked again.

"I'm serious," Joe said. "Hide!"

With a glare, she handed him her mug and tiptoed to the bathroom.

He took a sip of her coffee and opened the door. "May I help you?"

Two women stood on the landing. "Are you Symphony Weber's brother, Joe?"

"Look," Joe said. "I'd really appreciate it if you ladies would leave before you get me kicked out of this apartment. My landlord doesn't like much attention."

"I'm sorry Mr. Weber. The public wants to know how Symphony is doing. Was she able to identify the clothing they found this morning?"

Symphony walked out of the bathroom. "What's she talking about, Joe? The pitch of her voice was sharper, louder with each word. "What did they find?"

The reporter looked at Symphony. "You didn't know? I'm sorry."

"Know what? What happened?" she screamed.

"Please step back." Joe said softly. He closed the door and locked it. "It doesn't mean anything, Symphony. Just sit down here on the couch for a minute and I'll tell you."

"No, Joe! You tell me now. Is my baby all right?"

"They didn't find Choral, sis. They just found some clothes that match the ones you said she was wearing that day."

Her eyes widened. "Her little lavender sweater? Oh, God," The fear grew in her heart. "Why would he throw her clothes away unless . . ." She began to tremble. "Oh, God. Oh, no!" She chewed her fingernails.

Joe helped her to the couch. "Detective Spano wants you to come to the station to see if the clothes they found are Choral's. Do you think you can do that?"

Symphony stared into space. "Mama knitted that sweater for her," she mumbled. "Choral's skin is so pretty in that color."

Joe walked to the window and pulled the curtain back just enough to see the landing and the driveway below. "The reporters are gone. I can drive you, sis. Do you want Mama and Daddy to meet us there?"

"No," she said. She walked to Joe's truck, still wearing the clothes she'd slept in.

⌘ ⌘ ⌘

The door of the convenience store chimed as he slipped inside. He scanned the aisles. As far as he could see, there were only two other people in the store and they were both at the counter. One was the clerk, a woman in her early twenties. With her long blonde hair and copper hoop earrings, she stood facing a man with dark, curly hair, who looked to be her age. His curls bounced as he talked, emphasizing whatever he was saying. Neither of them looked up.

Not wanting to attract their attention, he moved, with a casual stride, down the center row, headed for the wine at the back of the store. He picked a bottle, running his fingers up and down the neck as if it were a lover. His posture changed—relaxed. He was no longer alone. He tucked it inside his green army jacket. Putting the neck in his armpit, he kept his elbow bent, cradling the bottle to keep it in place.

Even the fall afternoon sun couldn't shake the chill that had taken hold of him as he'd slept on cold earth last night. *Maybe this'll help.*

The clerk and her friend were louder now. "Why can't you just tell me where you've been? One day you wanna get married and the next, you go to Bert's and you don't come home for three weeks?"

"Look, if you don't trust me," he said, curls bouncing emphatically, "then we prob'ly shouldn't get married."

"Great!" The clerk turned away from him so fast her blond hair spun out, almost hitting him in the face. "That's just great!"

The wine bottle was beginning to slip. The quiet man stopped behind a high shelf to adjust it, watching the huge, corner mirrors to see if there were any pointed in his direction. When the bottle was snug again, he walked toward the door, trying to appear ordinary—like a guy who had just bought a soda and was on his way out.

The clerk began to cry. "Well there's something you don't know."

"What?" the dark-haired man asked, and then his voice softened. "Don't cry. What don't I know?"

"Forget it," she said, storming back behind her cash register. "Why don't you just go. Take another three weeks! Or better yet . . ."

The door chimed. The quiet man exhaled when he was safely outside the store.

He crossed the street to Boynton Park, where he fished through the trash for a bag to hide his wine in. After he used the pay phone, he wandered through the grounds until he found a secluded bench drenched in afternoon sun. He sat, drinking his wine, hoping to warm himself before evening's chill caught him sleeping on the ground once again. He reached into his pocket. *It's gone!* With a panicked look, he set the bottle on the bench and checked the other pocket. *Oh. Here it is.* He sighed and unfolded the disintegrating square of white napkin. *I need to write this on something else.* After examining the numbers he had scrawled on it weeks ago, he put it in his pocket, leaned back in the sun and closed his eyes.

⌘ ⌘ ⌘

Spano hung up the phone at his desk. "Boynton Park again. That's the only phone he's used all week."

"Did he say anything different this time?" Rodriguez asked, opening the Weber file, pen in hand.

"No. Same old crap. He's sorry. By the time the phone company gets back to us with his location, he's already gone. God! I wanna catch this guy."

"Maybe they'll get him this time," Rodriguez said. "Symphony Weber's on her way down here to look at the baby clothes the highway patrol brought in. Part of me wants to leave before she gets here." She shook her head. "I just can't stand to see what this is doing to her. And if *I'm* wonderin' if we'll ever find her Choral, I don't even wanna think about what goes through *her* mind."

⌘ ⌘ ⌘

Children played in the warm sun, jumping rope, throwing footballs, chasing each other from yard to yard. Symphony stared out the car window in a daze, seeing only splotches of color and light. Her mind was a jumble of incomplete thoughts.

"I know you're havin' a hard time, sis." Joe rubbed her shoulder. "But I have to tell you, I'm worried about how much you're drinkin'."

Symphony turned her dull eyes toward him.

"I was young when you almost died, that time. But I remember how scared I was. I thought I was gonna lose you. And when I see you drink like this, I've got that feelin' all over again."

She stared at him for a moment, then turned back to the window.

"No one really talked to me about it. It was an accident, right?"

At that moment, Symphony's vision cleared. They passed a little girl who seemed to look right into her eyes. *Yeah. I almost died and the dreams stopped. Now I can't have 'em back.* Her sight blurred again and did not clear until they parked at the police station.

"C'mon, sis," Joe said, helping Symphony out of the car. He put his arm around her as they walked inside. At the front desk he asked for Detective Spano.

An officer came from behind the counter. "You'll have more privacy in one of the interrogation rooms," he said. "Follow me."

They walked up a short flight of stairs and took a turn to the left. The landing opened into a huge room, the center of which was cluttered with desks and chairs. On the right side of the area were several small rooms, each with its own observation window. The policeman opened the door to the third room. Joe and Symphony followed him. Inside, a table and chair were bolted to the floor. In the far corner was one more seat. "Let me grab something for you to sit on," the officer said. "I'll be right back."

⌘　⌘　⌘

"They got some guy at Boynton," Rodriguez said. "He was carving something into one of the benches with an old screw. Drunk. Bottle of wine on him was almost empty. No ID. They're bringin' him in."

"Good," Spano said. "I can't wait to meet him." Spano's phone rang and he picked it up.

"The Weber woman is here," a man said.

"Yeah. Okay. Thanks." He hung up and turned to Rodriguez. "Symphony's here." He grabbed a plastic evidence bag. "They're taking her to three. You coming?"

Rodriguez paused for a moment. Sadness washed over her face. "Yeah." They walked side by side toward the interrogation rooms.

"Dammit!" Spano whispered. "I don't want to do this."

⌘　⌘　⌘

"I'm sorry you had to hear it on the news," Mama told Granny, "but I wanted to wait till we knew for sure. Maybe it's not Choral's outfit. Joe's headed down there with Symphony right now."

Mama chewed on the nail of her index finger. "She's still staying at Joe's. But Joe seems a little more concerned every time I talk to him. He can't keep his liquor cabinet stocked."

"Joe's too young to have a liquor cabinet," Granny responded.

"I'll deal with that later. Right now, Symphony's drinking again. A lot. Joe's worried and so am I." Mama crossed her legs and began to tap her toe in the air.

"If there's any chance of the dreams comin' back, she needs to stop that." Granny cleared her throat.

"Could you try and talk some sense into her?" Mama asked.

"I'll do my best, Maisy."

"Even if the dreams don't come back, she can't be drinkin' like this. She'll be back at Joe's later. Will you call me and tell me what she says?"

⌘  ⌘  ⌘

Neither Symphony nor Joe moved until the policeman came back with two chairs.

"Detective Spano will be with you shortly," he said, and excused himself, closing the door as he left.

Symphony's heart was pounding. She stood and walked to the window. "Do you see that man out there?" she asked, "The one in handcuffs?"

Joe went to the window. "Sis, this is a mirror," he said. "I can only see you and me." He cocked his head at her, puzzled. "Are you all right?"

"I don't know," she said. "Look out the door. See if you know him."

Joe glanced out. "There's no man in handcuffs. Just people sitting at desks." He turned back to Symphony.

They went to the table just as Spano and Rodriguez walked in.

Symphony saw the evidence bag Spano was carrying. "Oh, no!" she screamed. "That's the little sweater Mama knitted. Oh, God!" Her knees went weak. Joe caught her and guided her into a chair. "She's not gone." Symphony was almost breathless. "She can't be. I'd know, wouldn't I?"

Joe squeezed her hand.

Rodriguez sat across the table from Symphony. "There was no indication of trauma, which is a good sign."

Spano looked into Joe's eyes and nodded.

"Can I touch them?" Symphony asked. "See if they smell like her?"

"I'm sorry," Spano answered. "They have to stay in this bag to be processed. This is evidence, now."

Symphony reached out and touched the bag, closed her eyes and waited. *Come on. Come on. I promise I'll never complain about the gift again. Please!* But nothing came to her. When she opened her eyes, the others were staring.

"You ready to go, sis?" Joe asked.

Crying softly, Symphony stood to leave.

"You know she's staying at my house right now?" Joe put his arm around her once again. "You have my number?"

Spano nodded. "I'll call if anything comes up."

They stepped into the hallway. Across the room, a policeman had just reached the landing with a man in handcuffs. Symphony froze. Joe stood beside her, waiting for her to move.

"C'mon, sis," he said. "We should go home now."

She didn't budge. She was staring across the room at the man in handcuffs.

Joe looked up with a puzzled expression. "Is that the man you were asking about before?"

She nodded. Slowly, she turned to Detective Spano. "Who is that man?" she asked, pointing.

Spano seemed surprised. "Do you know him?"

Symphony's eyes grew wide. "Mack?" she yelled across the room.

The man in handcuffs looked right at her.

The picture of the beautiful boy flashed in her mind, then she remembered the tiny lavender sweater. "Why are you here?" she screamed. "Did you hurt my baby?"

Mack stood there with his mouth open. "No, Symphony. I tried to help. That's why I've been calling. But no one ever lets you talk."

Symphony couldn't breathe.

"Grab a chair," Joe yelled.

Spano slid a plastic orange chair under Symphony just as her legs gave way again.

"You think I should take her to the hospital," Joe asked?

"I don't think so," Spano answered. "She should be okay in a minute." He wiped his brow with the back of his hand. "I wanna get over and talk to this guy. Do you know him, too?"

Symphony's breath was beginning to have rhythm again.

"Mack Westhill," Joe said. "He used to be our neighbor. He and Symphony were friends. He's the one who's been calling?"

"Looks like it. I want to talk to him as soon as possible. We'll let you know what we find out."

"Thanks." Joe turned back to Symphony. "You gonna be all right?" he asked.

As Rodriguez and Spano crossed the room toward Mack, Symphony regained her strength.

*I saw him. Before he was here? The gift?* There was one sure-fire thing that would tell her right away. She looked up at Joe and whispered, "Do you know where I can get some pot?"

He glanced at the roomful of officers and rolled his eyes. "Let's get you home."

# CHAPTER THIRTY

THE NEWS OF an arrest blared from Daddy's desk radio. He left work early and headed home.

"They arrested someone," he yelled into the empty living room, slamming the front door behind him. After he called Detective Spano and discovered the name of the man in custody, he launched the phone against the far wall. "Goddamn son of a bitch."

Mama ran in from the kitchen drying her hands on a dishtowel, her eyes wide. "What happened?"

"Those goddamn Westhill boys happened. They picked up the oldest one. They think he's our caller. Detective Spano says they don't know if he took Choral or not."

"Mack?" Mama muttered. Slumping onto the couch, she began unraveling the fringed edge of the dishtowel. "No. I can't believe that. Why would Mack take Choral? It just doesn't make any sense."

Daddy crossed his arms and stared out the front window. "Out of the blue, some crazy bastard takes our sweet baby girl." He turned to look at Mama, his eyes welling with tears. "Not a damn particle of it makes sense, Maisy. Only way it'll ever make sense is if we lose our minds completely."

⌘ ⌘ ⌘

"I don't wanna hear anymore about it," Joe said, when Symphony brought up marijuana on the ride home.

"But, you don't—"

"No!" He gave her a sad smile.

"Just let me expl—"

"Look, sis. For the last few weeks you've done everything you could not to think about Choral. Your drinkin' is way over the top. Now you're gonna start smokin' pot? I feel like I'm losin' you, too. And before I let that happen, I'll turn this car around and carry your ass straight back to Mama and Daddy's."

Symphony grinned at him. "Are you finished?"

"If *you* are," he answered.

"Well, I'm not," she said. Her voice was awake, alive. "For the first time since this happened, I feel like I can help. If I move fast enough, maybe I'll be able to find Choral."

"How?"

"Well, if you'd let me get a word in . . . I know. Let's stop and grab a cheeseburger and I'll tell you. But you have to promise to hear me out before you say a word."

So, at Bronco Bill's Diner, over two cheeseburgers and a huge tub of chili fries, Symphony told Joe about her gift. Beginning with Roscoe Stanley, she narrated through the pitfalls and triumphs. Then, she moved on to Lilly and the accidental joint, Mack and the kiss that had filled her lungs with hashish smoke. Joe sat across from her, head tilted in attention as she told him how those incidents had caused the dreams to accelerate. How she could no longer sleep through the night. How she discovered that alcohol slowed them down. She picked at her fingernails, avoiding eye contact with Joe as she told him the story of why, at fifteen, she'd guzzled so much vodka it almost killed her.

When she finished talking, the chili fries were limp, cold, and greasy. Neither of them had eaten their cheeseburger.

Joe gazed at her for a moment, silent. Then he shook his head. "It seems to me, sis, that the last thing you need to be doin' is drinkin'."

"I know," Symphony said. "I haven't had a dream in years, But with what happened today at the police station, I don't know what to expect next."

"Do you think it's back, for real?" Joe asked. "'Cause if it's back, I'd be willin' to step up and help. But you've got to stop the drinkin'. I'm serious about that. C'mon. Let's go home." He picked up his cheeseburger and took a bite. "And on the way I'll stop at DJ's."

⌘　⌘　⌘

Spano ate a hoagie at his desk, glaring at the window of the interrogation room where Mack Westhill waited.

Rodriguez was digging through a box of files. "Thanks for taking that call from the Webers." She smiled, showing her perfect, white teeth. "I owe you one."

"Just one?" Spano said. "I thought Symphony's dad was gonna lose it. Apparently he didn't like Westhill when they were neighbors. I'm not sure why, but I'll bet you ten it has something to do with Symphony." He took another bite of his sandwich, swallowed it whole, and tossed the rest into the trash. "I didn't tell him Westhill refused to talk to anyone *but* Symphony. Keep calling her brother's house. They've gotta get home at some point."

"Still no answer." Rodriguez turned to look at Mack through the window. "That guy," she said, shaking her head. "It's hard to believe he escaped from prison."

"There's a helluva difference in escaping prison and walking away from a work crew," Spano quipped. "He's an idiot. He was almost done with his sentence. Now, he's got escape charges and who knows what else."

Rodriguez called Joe's phone again. She grimaced and hung up. "Now it's busy," she said. "Well, at least we know somebody's home. Should I take a ride over?"

"Yeah," Spano said. "Better yet, I'll go with you. It may take both of us to convince Symphony to come back down here. Hey, Richards," he called to an officer at the next desk. "You're on floor for the next couple hours, right?"

Richards was on the phone. He nodded.

"Keep an eye on our guy over there in number five, will ya? We have to pick up a witness."

Richards flashed an okay sign.

Stars were beginning to pop into view as Rodriguez and Spano drove toward Joe's house.

"I hope they haven't left again," Rodriguez said.

"Me too." Spano sighed. "I'm afraid if we don't get something out of Westhill soon, he won't talk at all."

⌘　⌘　⌘

"Do you mind if I call Granny?" Symphony had asked when they got back to Joe's apartment. "I'll pay for the long distance." She plopped down on the couch and dialed.

Why? You gonna ask her if you should smoke DJ's pot?" Joe asked.

"No!" Symphony rolled her eyes in disgust. "She told me somethin' once. I just—"

"Hello?" Granny answered.

"Hi, Granny. It's Symphony."

"Well hey, sugar. You doin' better today?"

"A little." Symphony paused for a moment. "Granny, I saw something. Before it happened. And I know it wasn't a dream but do you think the gift could be comin' back?" She chewed her fingernails, waiting for the answer.

"Well, honey, I've never heard tell of that happenin'. But I reckon the best way to find out is to stop all that drinkin' you been doin'."

Symphony glared at Joe. "Who said I was drinking?"

Joe shook his head and mouthed, "Not me."

"I'm not drinkin' anymore." Symphony crossed her legs and jittered one foot. "I want the dreams. They could help me find Choral."

"Now, sugar," Granny said. "Even if you do get your gift back—and that's a real big if—the old rules still stand. You can't expect to use it for yourself."

Symphony closed her eyes and leaned her head against the back of the couch. "I know, Granny. But do you really think this would be considered—"

"I don't know, baby. All I know is those rules keep the gift from becomin' a bad thing. You understand?"

"Yes ma'am, but—"

"Give the dreams a chance to start up again. They might not tell you about Choral, but—"

Symphony's eyes began to tear. "Well, then I'll just keep tryin' till I *do* get something about Choral. I can't just lay around and wait anymore. There has to be a way for me to find her."

"Study everything you see. And trust yourself," Granny said. "Call me later, sugar. I love you."

"I love you, too."

Joe perked up as Symphony hung up the phone. "What'd she say?"

"She says not to expect too much. That, even if my dreams start up again, I might not dream about Choral."

"And did she tell you to quit drinkin'?"

"You know she did! What I wanna know is, who'd you tell?"

Joe grinned and pulled a joint from the top left pocket of his plaid cowboy shirt. "So, you ready to fire this bad boy up?"

"Wait!" Symphony said.

Joe slid the joint back into his pocket, which turned out to be a good thing. When Symphony opened the door, there stood officer Rodriguez, fist up, ready to knock. Detective Spano was behind her. Symphony gave them a confused stare. "Hi."

"Can we come in for a minute?" Rodriguez asked.

"Sure," Joe answered. Uncomfortable, he moseyed into the bathroom where he locked the door and hid the contraband.

"Is there news?" Symphony asked, motioning them toward the couch.

"Nothing new," Spano answered. He remained standing as Rodriguez and Symphony sat down. "Unfortunately, we can't get a word out of Mack Westhill. You're the only one he'll talk to." He fixed his eyes on Symphony's. "I know you've had a rough day, but we were hoping you'd come back to the station."

"Why didn't you just call?" Symphony said, grabbing her sweater from the back of the couch. "I would've met you there."

Joe emerged from the bathroom. "Where you goin'?"

"To the station," Spano answered. "We want her to talk to Mack Westhill."

Joe looked at Symphony. "You don't have to do this, sis."

"Yes, I do," she said. "I'm the only one he'll talk to."

Joe put his arm around her shoulders. "Then, I'm comin' too," he said. "We'll be right behind you."

They followed Spano's car to the police station where an ambulance was pulling out of the parking lot. Officers were scouring the outside of the building with flashlights and search dogs.

As Joe stepped out of the car, someone shined a light in his face and yelled, "Halt!"

"He's with me," Spano shouted. "What happened here, Richards?"

Richards hurried over. "Could I talk to you inside, Detective?"

"Who was in the bus?"

"Carter," Richards answered. "They think he had a stroke."

"Shit!" Spano shook his head. "He was retiring too. Three months out, right? Well, I'm back now. Why don't you see if the captain'll let you go on to the hospital?"

"He said I have to talk to you first," Richards answered.

"Well, you and I are done," Spano said. "Go on down to the hospital and check on your partner. I've got someone who may be able to get at word or two out of our suspect."

"That's what I need to talk to you about, Detective Spano."

Spano's gaze turned to a glare.

"Westhill said he had to take a leak," Richards began, "so I took off his cuffs and shut him in the john. Next thing I know, Carter makes this weird sound and hits the floor. So, I yell for Soo to call an ambulance. Then I grab the emergency kit off the wall and run over to help. The whole time I was with Carter, I had my back to the bathroom. Soo finally came up and took over with Carter, but by that time, Westhill was gone. Like into thin air. No one saw him."

Spano looked away. "Shit!"

"I know I broke procedure," Richards said. "But my partner was down."

"Fill out the paperwork on Westhill and get to the hospital."

"I'm sorry," Richards said. He stood there for a moment longer, then turned and jogged into the building.

Spano met Joe and Symphony halfway across the parking lot. "Westhill's gone."

Symphony looked alarmed. "In the ambulance? What happ—"

"No," he said. "One of our officers had a medical problem and Westhill managed to sneak out." He sighed. "I'm sorry to drag you down here for nothing."

Rodriguez squeezed Symphony's hand. "We'll call you as soon as we hear anything."

Joe and Symphony walked back to the car. They'd only driven a block when Symphony sat up straight and gasped.

"What?" Joe demanded. "You okay?"

"Yeah." Symphony turned away from him and stared out the window in silence.

⌘  ⌘  ⌘

"You comin'?" Rodriguez asked, starting into the station house.

"I better wait a while," Spano answered. With his flashlight, he helped the other officers search the perimeter. Fifteen minutes later, with his frustration under control, he walked into the squad room.

As Rodriguez opened folder after folder, Spano sorted through a stack of pink messages, avoiding the usual chatter. When he had finished returning phone calls, she spoke to him from across the desk.

"You know, brother, I decided to search for crime reports in the Weber's neighborhood around the time Mack Westhill lived there. Turns out, we picked him up as a runaway and took him home—twice. Looks like his father was a real jerk. We were called out more than once to settle *him* down. Other than that, there were a few drug charges at a few different houses, including one at the suspect's. But that's just about it." She handed him a file.

He leaned back in his chair, studying it. "Hmm," he said, sitting upright. "Here's one you didn't mention."

"Really? What?"

"Well, there were four boys picked up in the middle of the night out by that man-made lake behind the Westhill's house. According to the report, an anonymous caller said the boys were throwing kittens in the water as alligator bait and swimming to the island in the middle. But that was before the Westhill's moved in."

"That's disgusting," Rodriguez said. "Were they convicted?"

"Well, sort of. They were charged with curfew violations. Looks like they spent a few days in detention."

"How old were they? Are their names listed?"

"Expunged." Spano stretched and yawned.

"I wonder if Symphony remembers when that happened?" Rodriguez sat back, a faraway look in her eyes. "You know what history says about people who hurt animals."

⌘ ⌘ ⌘

Symphony decided to wait on the joint.

She insisted Joe go to bed as soon as they returned home from the police station. Now, the house was black dark. She lay awake on the couch, fully dressed, waiting for Joe's confounded snoring to begin. As soon as she started to doze off, his grinding, nasal roar woke her. Bending over, she picked up her shoes and tiptoed toward the front door, aiming for floor-boards that wouldn't squeak. Just before she turned the knob, she paused. *Okay. I have my coat, purse, keys, flashlight, lighter, and there's a blanket in the trunk.* Satisfied, she slipped out into the night.

The moon was hidden by clouds. Symphony could feel the coming rain in the cold air's grip. She shivered as the wooden stairs groaned with her descent. *I'll be fine.* Her hand tightened around the flashlight. Where she was going, it may be her only friend.

She glanced up then down the street. The whole world was asleep. She got into the car, started the engine, and pulled away from the curb, hoping Joe had slept through her departure. At the end of the block, she turned the headlights on. Not because she needed them. She could have felt her way.

The car seemed to fly through the empty streets on autopilot. So quickly, she was there.

She pulled to the side of the road and parked. Once outside, she grabbed the blanket and, careful not to slam the trunk, wandered off behind the Hightower's old house. With her flashlight, she searched the brush beyond the fence. *Of course it's not here. Freedom probably rotted years ago.*

As she turned to leave, something heavy splashed and plunked into the water. She jerked around, shining her light toward it. *Alligator!* Panting, she hurried toward the path. Then she stopped cold. Something rustled in the brush behind her. *Another one?* She ran a few steps but slipped, dropping her flashlight. The rustling was nearer. Heart pounding, she tried to move, but her feet slid out from under her. She landed face-down in the water.

Every attempt to stand put her back in the same position. Dazed, on hands and knees, she tried to feel her way toward the land. Instead, she found herself even deeper in the lake.

Splash. Plunk.

*Maybe if I don't move.*

A hand wrapped around her arm and dragged her out of the water.

"I knew you'd come," a man whispered.

# CHAPTER THIRTY-ONE

"I'M TELLING YOU," Rodriguez said, "there's something else connecting these two cases. There's no way Symphony Weber's the only link. We've missed something."

Spano was inching his way toward the door but Rodriguez wouldn't stop talking. Turning, he walked back to his desk. "Fine!" He picked up the phone. "Eileen, this is Detective Spano. Officer Rodriguez will be down shortly. She wants to sift through the evidence on the Browden case. Yeah. Thanks." He hung up. "See you at six AM."

"You're not gonna stay and help me?" She gave him a pouty face, hoping.

"Not tonight. I'm gonna go home, microwave some lasagna, crack a few beers, and watch television." He threw his keys up in the air and caught them. "Call me if you find something that won't wait till morning," he said with a smirk. Then he was gone.

Rodriguez shrugged. Margaret Browden's house was a hoarder's dream. The police had taken very little evidence. Then, since there was no family, they had bolted the doors and wrapped yellow tape around the perimeter. She took the elevator to the evidence room, hoping to find something that would convince Spano to open that house again.

Eileen was filing her nails when Rodriguez got off the elevator. She pressed a clipboard toward Rodriguez. "Here, sign the sheet," she said. "I set the box on the first table. There's gloves on the counter by the door."

"Thanks." Rodriguez said. After gloving up, she headed straight for the box. Inside, there were two plastic bags. One was marked "Sandstone Flats." The other held mostly pictures of the interior of the Browden house. She sat down and examined the photos one by one, looking at every object in each picture before moving to the next. She went through them once, twice, three times, before she saw it. There, amid the clutter and disarray of Margaret's house, was a vase of cut flowers. They had to be fresh. They weren't the least bit wilted.

She closed up the evidence bags, walked to Eileen's window, and signed herself out. "Thanks."

"Did you find anything new?" Eileen asked.

"Yeah. Actually I did." Rodriguez walked away smiling. As she entered the elevator, she mumbled to herself, "Something far too new."

Back at her desk, she wrote a pink message to Spano and taped it to his coffee cup.

⌘  ⌘  ⌘

Symphony didn't recognize the man's voice. He was whispering. But the hand squeezing her upper arm reminded her of Quinton. She twisted away and shrieked. He grabbed her by the back of her shirt and cupped his hand over her mouth. "Quiet," he hissed, hot lips against her cold ear.

By the arm, he led her through squishy mud for what seemed like forever. Then, he stopped. "Here it is." He murmured, "Don't scream," and let her go. He took her hand and pulled, guiding her forward until her palm was against a hard, vertical surface. "Feel this?" he asked. "I need you to push with both hands when I say." She could feel him move away from her. Then, from a few feet, he said, "Now."

She pushed and the object gave way so fast she almost fell forward. There was a scrape against mud, a flutter in water. *A boat.*

"I'll hold it still but you're gonna have to feel your way. As soon as you have both feet in, sit down."

For just a flash, the moon found a break in the clouds. He turned toward her. There were Mack's beautiful boy eyes—but they weren't the same. They were hurt, tired, maybe even angry.

"Don't waste the light," he demanded. "Use it to get in the boat."

286

She was shivering. Not just because she was wet and cold. "What do you know about my baby?" she asked, afraid to speak any louder than the ripples on the lake.

"Soon," he said. He pushed the boat farther from shore and jumped in. As he rowed, the black water gurgled softly beneath them. In the moonlight, Symphony could see the outline of Empty Island.

⌘　⌘　⌘

The baby didn't complain much. She just stared at him, those dark brown eyes sizing him up as if, inside her little body, was a wise old person. Sometimes, under her gaze, he would second guess his decision to take her. After all, he had wanted a boy. But he was adjusting to her and she was getting used to him. She didn't seem to miss her mother.

Probably because he had promised her a new mother. A better one. One who wouldn't let her get taken. One who would keep her safe.

He hadn't planned on doing this alone. But her new mother never came. After a while, he got better at diapers. Oh, there were times, mostly with the stinky ones, that he put off changing them for as long as he could. And some days, he let her crawl around naked. Then, he'd have to mop, if he ever got around to it. Now she was trying to walk. When she made it two or three steps, she would laugh the whole way. Like she couldn't believe she was doing it.

She loved to eat, too, even though sometimes he couldn't get the right food. But, if all they had was money for cupcakes, that's what they ate. And she was drinking regular milk now. At first she had diarrhea every time she drank it. Now she was fine.

She had quite a few teeth, but not really chewing teeth. If he couldn't get baby food, he just mashed up whatever he was eating. She loved eggs. And she'd eat beans and rice as long as they weren't too spicy. If he gave her something that didn't agree with her, she'd let him know.

He'd never really taken care of a baby before.

*How hard can it be? Animals do it and they don't have half the brain I do.*

The only time he worried was when he had to work. He couldn't take her. So he'd push the bed into a corner—fence her in. And he'd get back just as soon as he could. No matter what, he had to hang on to her. When her new mother got here, she wouldn't think about how he'd brought a girl instead of a boy. She'd see this baby and know that he got it for her.

To replace the one she'd lost.

⌘　⌘　⌘

The moon was hiding again. When they reached the island, Mack got out and pulled the boat onto land. Empty Island was the same mucky mess the other shore had been.

Mack set out walking, pulling Symphony by the arm as she slipped and slid trying to keep up. The farther into the island they went, the more solid the earth felt.

Symphony managed to put one foot in front of the other, but her mind was wild. *Is Choral here? Or does he know where she is? Did he bring me here to hurt me?* She couldn't imagine her life past this moment. Her heart fluttered, then began pounding again. She reached into her pocket. Her car keys were still there. So was the lighter. Once, someone had shown her how to use her keys as a weapon by weaving them between her fingers, pointed end out. That memory, and the lighter in her pocket, reassured her. Breathing hard, she continued along until Mack stopped.

"We can talk here," he said. "Why don't you sit on that log?"

"Where? I can't see anything." She pulled the lighter from her pocket and shook the water out. It flamed on the third try. Circling around, she found the log and sat down. Mack threw some pine needles and twigs into a small rock pit filled with ashes. He reached for the lighter and Symphony jerked it away.

"My matches got wet," he said. "Don't you wanna warm up?"

Shivering, she handed it to him.

The twigs caught. Gradually, Mack stacked larger pieces of wood on top, crisscrossing them so the fire could breathe. When he was done, it roared.

Symphony moved closer.

"I'm sorry I scared you earlier," he said, placing the lighter in her hand. "But I can't go back. Not yet."

He sounded more like the Mack she knew.

"Just tell me where Choral is," she demanded, "and take me back across the lake. No one has to know. I just want my baby."

Mack stood near the flame, rubbing his hands together. In the firelight, his face looked older than it should. "I was in jail," he said. "I stole a car. Sold it for drugs. I was a mess. I ain't been right since I turned my back on you."

Symphony's heart stalled for a moment. She looked away from him.

"It was like something ugly started to grow inside me that day. Like the way they talk about cancer, only I could feel it in my heart. And it wouldn't kill me. I just had to hurt from it. I'm not complainin'. I deserved it. And one day, a couple of months ago, I realized I had to find you. I had to tell you. It was fucked up, what I did to you. I came back from the circus all wired up. Black beauties. I was just a stupid fuckin' kid. And you were so different." He rubbed the lines in his forehead. "I needed time where I didn't have to fight anyone. Some time just to be accepted. For life to be easy. Next thing I hear, you're in the hospital."

"I don't wanna talk about this," Symphony said. "Just tell me where Choral is."

Mack didn't seem to hear her. "I'm so sorry, Symphony. You deserved to be treated so much better." He walked over to her and touched her face. "I didn't know till way later that what I felt for you back then was love. And I've never felt it for anyone since. So, that's what I came back here to tell you. Every night I hid behind that orange tree in your front yard trying to get up the nerve to talk to you when you got home from work. I thought about knocking on your window. But I knew if your daddy heard me, I'd never get to tell you. So I took a car and started following you."

He turned away from her and paced in a circle around the fire. "I was there that day, at the mall. I saw that guy push the stroller away. I almost caught him, too. But I tripped over a goddamn mop bucket. He musta turned and went out another door, 'cause by the time I got to the parking lot, he was miles away. I saw him. He was taking your little girl out of her stroller, putting her in this dark green Malibu. I ran, but I couldn't get there. He drove right past me, though. I got his tag number. But the weird thing is, I got this feeling when I saw him. Like Déjà vu almost. Like I should know who he is."

Symphony's mouth gaped. She stared in disbelief. "You've known all this time?" She stormed over to him "You knew who took my baby the day it happened?" She slapped him so hard he almost stumbled into the fire.

"Don't," he said, grabbing her hand. "I've been calling you for over a month." He turned to face her. "I know it was wrong to wait. But the longer I waited the harder it was to figure out what to do. I couldn't go back to jail before I told you how I felt. And if I went back to jail, then maybe I couldn't help find your little girl."

The clouds broke and the moon shone into the clearing. Mack glowed a silver blue that was almost the same shade as his eyes. "Soon as the fire dies down, we'll go back across," he said. "You can take me to the police. I'll help you figure out who took her."

By the time the flames were gone, it was beginning to get light. Mack and Symphony slipped across the lake. In the dawn, muddy prints from the night before showed them where to leave the boat. They tiptoed through the Hightower's old backyard and out to Symphony's car. The sky was grey and fluffy with clouds. Soft rain fell as they drove toward the police station.

Mack gazed at her. "I was afraid people would look down on me for being with you." He shook his head. "I was an idiot."

Symphony was too exhausted to look at him. Still damp and caked with mud, she led Mack into the police station, delivered him into the hands of the desk sergeant, and headed back to Joe's apartment.

Joe jumped up from the couch as she walked in. "Where the hell have you been?"

"What are you doing up so early?" she asked.

"Trying to decide whether I should call the police or the coroner. I got up to take a pee and you were gone. What happened? Are you okay?"

"Oh yeah," she answered, avoiding eye contact. "I just need a quick shower."

He stared at her, mouth open. "And then you'll tell me where you were?"

"After I get back from the police station," she agreed, putting off an argument. *He's gonna be furious.* She grabbed some clean clothes and headed straight for a hot shower.

⌘ ⌘ ⌘

Even after her late night of research, Rodriguez beat Spano to work. She was beaming when he arrived. "Westhill turned himself in. They put him in a cell this time."

"When?"

"About an hour ago," she said. "Symphony Weber dropped him off."

"I can't wait to hear that story." Spano picked up his coffee mug and read the pink note Rodriguez had left him. "Why don't you give Sandstone Flats a call? Get the number for their swing shift clerk. What's her name? Genie?"

"Junie?" Rodriguez answered. "I think that's it. I'll ask her to come in this morning."

Junie arrived around seven AM in a tight pink sweater and black pants. Huge hoop earrings dangled from just below a giant hairdo. "Wow! I've never been called in for questionin' before. I feel like I'm on a TV crime show. Don't ya wanna swear me in or somethin'?"

"I don't think that'll be necessary, ma'am," Spano said with a grin. "Since Sandstone Flats has instructed you to cooperate with our investigation, we thought you might answer a few questions about their policy regarding visitors."

"Okay," Junie said, adjusting her hair. "Well, visitors are allowed from ten in the morning till eight at night. And they're all supposed t' sign in and out, if that's what you're askin'."

He crossed his arms and leaned back in his chair. "That's exactly what I'm asking. Now what about private items going into patients' rooms?"

"Oh, you mean like flowers and stuff. Well, if flowers come, we're supposed to keep a log of who delivers them and who they go to. See, some patients can't have flowers. Depending on the equipment in their room or if they're allergic or somethin'. We hafta be careful about that sorta thing."

Spano tapped a pen against his thigh. "So, do you remember? Was Margaret Browden able to have flowers in her room?"

Junie cocked her head and stared up at the ceiling. "Sorry," she said. "I don't think so. But I can't say for sure. I don't recall seein' any flowers in her room. But I was only in there a few times. She was always talking to some invisible guy. Gave me the creeps. Made me feel like there were ghosts in the room."

Spano shifted in his chair and looked at Rodriguez. "Do you have anything to add Officer Rodriguez?"

Surprised by the offer, Rodriguez stood and walked over to where Junie was sitting. "I do," she said. "I was wondering, if you recall what sort of things Ms. Browden would say to this invisible guy. And, to the best of your knowledge, did anyone ever visit her?"

"Symphony or one of the other swing shift nursing assistants could tell you what she talked about. Evening was the time Margaret talked the most. And as far as I know, she never had visitors. Poor thing. Is that all?"

Rodriguez looked at Spano.

"For now," Spano answered.

"I'm just sorry I couldn't be of more help," Junie said, turning to leave. "Wait a minute." She slapped her hand to her forehead and turned around. "I just remembered. One night, kinda late for a delivery, this really cute guy comes in with flowers for her. When I tell him she can't have 'em in her room, he gets irritated. Then, he does somethin' really weird."

"What'd he do?" Rodriguez asked.

"Well, I guess it's not that weird. Unusual, I should've said. If a patient can't have flowers, most delivery guys'll leave 'em at the desk. What else are they gonna do with 'em, right? But this guy took 'em with him."

"Would you be able to find an entry in the log for that day?" Spano asked.

Junie shook her head. "I didn't really have anything to log so I can't tell you the day. But it musta been cold out 'cause he was wearin' a jacket."

"You think you could identify him from a picture?"

"Definitely," Junie answered. "Like I said, he was really cute."

Spano walked over and shook Junie's hand. "Thanks for your cooperation," he said.

"Oh, you're welcome. Just call me if you think I can do anything else. Oh, by the way, that guy you arrested. Do you really think he's the one who took Choral?"

Rodriguez touched Junie's shoulder and walked her down the stairs to the front door. "Unfortunately," Rodriguez said, "We can only *ask* you for information. We can't *tell* you anything."

"It was worth a shot," Junie said. "Have a good day."

# CHAPTER THIRTY-TWO

THE JOINT REMAINED hidden in Joe's bathroom. Symphony had plenty on her mind without it.

As soon as she was out of the shower, she made a pot of coffee.

Joe glared at her. "*Now*, will you tell me where you went last night?"

"Just, don't get mad, okay."

Joe looked at her hard. "I'm not promisin' anything."

With one of those big sister stares, she said, "I went to the lake to see if Mack was there." She breezed past him, sat down on the couch, and put her shoes on.

He crossed his arms and followed her. "Our lake? The one across from Mama and Daddy's?"

"That's right," she said.

"I just had a feeling . . ." She crossed her arms back at him. "And I'd do it again if I had to."

Joe leaned down and looked her in the eyes. "What were you thinkin'?"

"I'll tell you what I was thinkin'." Symphony put her hands on her hips. "I was thinkin' about how my baby's been gone for almost two months. About how, for the last few weeks, I've been layin' around here drinkin', feelin' sorry for myself instead of lookin' for her." She glanced down at the floor.

Joe touched her shoulder. "You should've taken me with you, sis. What would you have done if you found him?"

She stood up straight. "I'd've made him tell me what I wanted to know. And then I'd've taken him to the police station."

"Yeah," Joe said. "And he was just gonna come along peacefully, was he?"

"Yep." There was a bounce in her step as she walked to the kitchen. She poured herself a cup of coffee. "That's exactly what he did, too."

Joe's eyes bugged. "You shittin' me?"

"Nope. He told me what I wanted to know and then I dropped him off at the police station on my way home. They said it'd take a while to process him so I came home to get cleaned up."

Joe stared at her. "You're either lucky or nuts. Maybe a little o' both."

"That's how it happened." *Well, almost.*

Joe glanced at his watch. "It's nearly seven-thirty." He grabbed his jacket from the back of the couch. "I'll take you down there. Let me just call work and tell 'em I'll be late."

"No." Symphony walked over and kissed his cheek. "You've missed enough work, little brother. I can do it this time."

"When did you get so tough?" He studied her face for a moment, then picked up his keys. "All right. But if you need me, call work. I'll ask Annette to find me right away."

"I'm sure I'll be back here by the time you have your first break. Call me and I'll tell you what I find out."

Smiling, Symphony watched him drive to the end of the street. *One day, some girl's gonna be lucky to catch him.* She unplugged the coffee pot and put on her sweater. By eight, she was in her car heading back to the station.

⌘ ⌘ ⌘

As soon as Detective Spano got in that morning, he called the jail requesting that Mack be moved to interrogation room five. For a while, he stood at the two-way mirror, glaring, unseen, at the prisoner. Rodriguez joined him there with a cup of coffee. He glanced at her and returned his acidic stare to the window. "All this time, that son of a bitch had information that would've helped us find Choral Weber." He exhaled and shook his head. "He didn't have to turn himself in. He could've called." He threw his hands up in the air. "Christ, he could've put a note in a bottle and thrown it into the Atlantic. Anything would've been better than what he did . . . which is not a damn thing."

"We need to get in there and talk to him," Rodriguez said in a soft, soothing voice. "He's tired. I don't think we'll have to fight too hard for information."

"I'm trying to get myself psyched up to go in there." Spano stretched his arms and cracked his knuckles. "Right now I hate that guy. I used to see this kind of crap all the time back home. I should be used to it, but I can't help wondering what kind of man puts himself above a baby?" He sat down at his desk just as Symphony walked in.

She waved at him and started over.

"I'm glad you're here," he said, motioning to a chair. "I wanted to talk to you about last night."

She stood, staring through the window at Mack. "Has he told you anything?"

"I haven't talked to him. I'll go in there after we're done here. Why don't you sit down for a minute?"

She heard him this time and sat.

"Look," Spano said, "I know you're worried. And it must seem like this is taking forever. But what if you'd been hurt last night? Or something worse?"

She looked at the floor. "I knew he wouldn't."

"Next time, call me, okay?" He handed her his card and wrote his home number on it. "If they can't reach me here, call me at home. But don't go out on your own like that. There's too much at stake."

She nodded. "He knows what the kidnapper looks like. And he got his tag number."

Spano handed Symphony a notepad. "While I'm in with Westhill, why don't you make a list of everything he told you. We've got an artist comin' at eight-thirty so if you stick around . . . Well, you should see the composite when it's done. If you finish with your list, the diner across the street's got great coffee. But if you plan on waiting here, you should move to the lobby. The seats are more comfortable." He stood and picked up a file. "Oh, yeah." he said and sat right back down. "I wanted to ask you something."

Symphony looked at him. His hair was shorter than he usually kept it. She decided he was better looking when it covered his ears. "What?" she asked.

"I was wondering. Back when you were in junior high something happened out on the lake behind Overlook Terrace." He studied her face for a reaction. "It was late at night." He waited. "Involved a group of boys?"

Symphony grimaced. "Swimming to Empty Island and back," she said. "They were throwing kittens in the water to distract the gators. I could never understand how someone could—" She glanced at Spano.

He was listening with his head tilted, a strange look in his eyes. "How did you know all that?"

"Um." She turned away for a moment. "Probably heard it at school."

"I just wanted to see if you were associated with any of the boys involved."

"David Terry," Symphony volunteered. "His family lived in that huge house out where the airport is now. Back then, there were orange groves all around the place."

"Thanks," Spano said. "I'll see you in a while." Before he entered the interrogation room, he stopped and whispered something to Rodriguez.

She left the window and went straight to her desk. "You doing all right this morning, Symphony?" she asked, opening a file and picking up a pen.

Symphony was bewildered. "Why did Detective Spano ask me about junior high?"

"Last night I was checking out the arrests during the time Mack Westhill lived in your neighborhood. That was one of the reports that showed up. The records were expunged so we couldn't get the names of the boys. But since you remember, we'll just do a little investigating. So one of them was David Terry. Do you recall any of the others?"

"He's the only one I saw—uh, knew," Symphony answered. David Terry's eyes flashed in her mind. The terror of that night grabbed her all over again. *He loved that he could scare me.* She shivered. "You don't think that has anything to do with Choral, do you?" She thought of the joint in Joe's bathroom and hoped for a deluge of dreams.

⌘　⌘　⌘

For the first few minutes of the interrogation, Detective Spano thumbed through a file.

Across the oak table, Mack waited, tracing the wood grain with his finger.

"So now you're ready to talk," Spano said. The break in silence was so abrupt Mack jerked, startled. When he looked up, Spano nailed him. "Why didn't you come forward sooner?"

"Why do you think?" Mack asked.

Spano stared at him, one eyebrow raised. "You could have helped that little girl."

"I care about Symphony's baby. But how was I gonna help find her if I was back in jail?"

Spano turned away, mumbling "Son of a bitch," under his breath.

"I got the guy's license plate number. It was in my pants pocket. Didn't you get it?"

"Yeah," Spano said. "A month after we should have had it. And it was written on a napkin. By the time I got it, it was pretty much dust. What did the car look like?"

"It was a Malibu. Not rounded like the new ones. More square. And it was that dark green color some of 'em had right when they started makin' 'em." For the first time, Mack sat up straight. "Oh yeah," he said, looking Spano in the eyes. "I still have that number. I scratched it into a bench at the park with a loose screw," he said. That's what I was doin' when they picked me up."

Spano opened the door. "Rodriguez? Could you step in here for a minute?"

"At Boynton?" He looked at Mack.

Mack nodded.

"Which bench?"

Rodriguez opened the door. "Yes, Detective?"

Spano gave her a stern look. "Westhill here, says he carved the kidnapper's tag number into one of the park benches at Boynton."

Mack looked up at Rodriguez. "The tan one," he rushed. "Way back in the corner. Near the bathroom."

"By Pearl and Hawthorne?" Rodriguez asked.

"I think so."

Spano stepped outside with Rodriguez. "Were you able to find anything on the kitty killer?"

"The file's still open on my desk," she said. "We can talk about it after I get back." She put on her jacket. "This shouldn't take long."

"Make sure you take some pictures," Spano said, before re-joining Mack in the room.

⌘　⌘　⌘

After Rodriguez left, Symphony finished her list then stood at the window of the interrogation room watching Mack and Spano. In the light, Mack didn't look at all like the boy she'd known. At twenty-three, life had already carved creases into his face. He seemed to avoid eye contact with Spano. His hunched shoulders gave him the appearance of someone who had lost more than his share of battles.

Symphony despised the part of him that had held back information about the man who took Choral. But, somewhere inside her, she felt sorry for the beautiful boy who had drifted through her dreams. She sighed. *I need coffee.*

She exited the front door of the precinct house, crossed the street, and entered the diner. Other than a few brunchers, the tables were empty. She took a window seat. Outside, people walked up and down the sidewalk. Inside, patrons talked, laughed, ate, and drank. Everyone around her seemed to be living.

The ache in her heart left her breathless.

A petite young waitress in a pink uniform with a white apron, arrived. "Good morning," she said, perky exuding from every pore. She handed Symphony a menu.

"Good morning," Symphony replied. She opened the menu and studied it. *I need more than coffee.*

"Could I bring you some coffee while you decide?" the waitress asked. Then her voice became a deep, coarse growl ". . . Weigh Big?"

Symphony glanced up, relieved to see the shiny, tan face of the young waitress. "I'd love some coffee, thanks." She turned her focus back to the breakfast items but, for the moment, lost her appetite. *What just happened?*

⌘ ⌘ ⌘

Joe stood in the office at work, talking on the phone, eating peanut butter crackers between words. "I chewed her out for not takin' me with her," he said. "It's like she finally woke up or somethin' and she wants to make up for all the time she couldn't help. Did she ever talk to you about her dreams?"

"What dreams?" Dani asked.

"Didn't she ever tell you about that Roscoe Stanley thing?"

"Ewww. Isn't he the guy who was arrested when we were at the convenience store that time?"

"Yeah. She told me she'd been dreamin' about him. For years."

"That's what she tried to tell me, but I didn't believe her." Dani said. "I wasn't the best listener back then. If I apologized every day for the rest of our lives, it still wouldn't make up for some of the stuff I did to her."

"I'm sure that's not true, Daniele. But I gotta go. My break was over at ten. Listen, don't tell Mama or Daddy about last night, okay?"

"I won't. But you know they'll find out."

"Yeah, I know."

"Talk to you later." Then, "Mwah," she blew him a kiss through the phone and he hung up.

⌘ ⌘ ⌘

The floor had been cold the last few days. Against the wall, he folded a stack of blankets for the baby to sleep on. He patted her head and pushed the bed into place, trapping her in the triangular playpen-like structure. A newspaper slipped from between the mattresses. He picked it up, ensnared by a picture on the back page and the words beneath it.

Still reading, he dropped to the floor in a moan that crescendoed in a guttural scream. "Your new mother's not coming."

The baby shifted her feet, moving around the edges of the fortress. She watched him, her dark eyes calm, attentive.

"She wanted to," he sobbed, "but she can't. She's gone."

He rose from the floor and went back to the child. "I shoulda let him walk with me. It was almost dark. And he was so little." Squatting, he looked into her eyes. "I would never let *you* walk alone in the dark like that, baby. If you can't see where you're goin' maybe you can't see the water down there. If your new mama will just come, I promise I won't ever let you near the water."

He picked up the obituary page where it had fallen and talked to the picture. "I told him to leave me alone. I told him to go home but he didn't listen."

He pointed at the baby. "And your first mama—she could've helped, but she wouldn't."

Covering his face with his hands, he cried. When he stopped, he wiped his eyes with his sleeve.

"That's okay. Now everybody'll see. Nothin's gonna happen to this baby. You're just fine. Aren't you?"

He picked up his car keys and jacket. "Don't go anywhere," he said with a chuckle.

He walked out and closed the door.

⌘　⌘　⌘

Rodriguez got out of her squad car and headed for the northwest corner of Boynton Park, searching for the bench where Mack had carved the tag number. Throughout the first half of the grounds, all the benches were painted dark green. As she neared the restroom, a tan bench caught her eye. She hurried forward as a grey-suited city employee covered it with a coat of dark green. "Stop," she yelled, running toward him. But it was too late.

"What?" he asked, setting the bucket of paint down. "My supervisor told me to have this finished before lunch."

Rodriguez sighed. "Do you have a cloth?" she asked.

The painter handed her an old t-shirt. She wiped off the area he'd just finished.

"What the hell are you doin'?" he asked with disgust.

"There was something carved here," Rodriguez said. "Some letters and numbers."

"I'm sorry. I sanded it off. Was it important?"

"Yeah." She shrugged. "It was a license plate number for a vehicle used in commission of a crime." Shaking her head, she turned to leave. "You may as well finish your painting."

"Wait," he called to her. "Let me see if I can remember. You got a piece of paper?"

"Rodriguez pulled a notepad and pen from her pocket.

The painter sat down at a picnic table and closed his eyes. He scratched out three letters on one side and two numbers on the other. "I'm sorry," he said with a grimace. "That's all I can say for sure."

⌘  ⌘  ⌘

Rodriguez was back at her desk by the time Symphony stepped onto the landing. "Great timing," she said. "The artist should be just about finished. How was your coffee?"

"Actually, it was pretty good. It woke me up, anyway."

"It's strong. Makes our coffee here taste like hard water."

"Did you find the tag number?" Symphony asked.

"Well, most of it," Rodriguez answered. "Right now, we're running it through the state databases."

Spano opened the door and came toward Symphony and Rodriguez. "How'd it go at the park?"

"Just perfect," Rodriguez answered. "The city picked the last two days to sand and paint the benches. Luckily, one of the workers was able to remember some of the digits. So Data is searching for possibilities. How's the drawing of our suspect?"

Spano kept the tablet close to his chest. "Westhill was pretty good with his description. Hopefully someone'll recognize the guy. I just wish he hadn't been wearing that baseball cap. I have to get this downstairs. What time is it?" He glanced at his watch. "Oh good. Not quite eleven. We should make the deadline for tomorrow morning's paper. And I'm sure the state and local stations'll pick the story up right away. Let's hope for something quick." He took two steps toward the stairs.

"Wait," Symphony called to him. "Can I see it first?"

"I'll show it to you, but I can't let you touch it until I make copies."

"Okay." She moved to the chair next to his desk.

Spano turned the picture around.

Symphony gasped. "Oh my God." Covering her face with her hands, she began to sob, rocking back and forth. "This is my fault," she said. "This is my fault."

"You know him?" Rodriguez asked.

301

But Symphony couldn't hear.

Rodriguez touched her arm. Nothing.

Spano squatted down and put his hands on her shoulders. "Don't do this," he said. "This is not your fault. Tell me who this guy is." Symphony stared, her eyes empty. "C'mon, Symphony," Spano prodded. "Who is it?"

She looked at him and mouthed, "Greg Stanton."

"Call her brother at work," Spano ordered.

# CHAPTER THIRTY-THREE

AS RODRIGUEZ QUERIED the DMV for records, Spano read through files on his desk, making inquiries by phone. He had just finished up with the school district offices when Rodriguez returned with a copy of a driver's license. "Looky here," she said, pushing the paperwork under his nose.

"Hmmm," he grunted, reaching for the page. "So that's our kitty killer." He scratched his chin. "He looks enough like our drawing to warrant a chat. Don't you think?"

"Oh, yeah. Here's what I've got, so far." Rodriguez said. "He dropped out of veterinary school two years ago. As you can see, his last DMV address is out by the airport."

"Let's get him in here." Spano picked up the phone and pushed a button. "Do we have a team available to pick up a suspect? Great. David C. Terry. 537 Groveland Way." Spano hung up.

A few minutes later, a meaty policeman with a kind face lumbered over. "Good to see you, Detective Spano, Rodriguez. Dispatch says you've got a pick up?"

Spano nodded. "Thanks, Owens." He handed the officer a copy of the fax Rodriguez had shown him. "This is David Terry. Just need to ask him a few questions."

"Wow," Owens said, looking surprised. "I went to school with this guy."

"Really?" Spano looked up at the young officer. "So did you know Symphony Weber, too?"

Owens smiled shyly. "Yeah. Back in junior high I considered myself her bodyguard. But I was ahead of her so when I started high school, we sort of lost touch. I feel real bad about her daughter. You don't think David Terry has something to do with it, do you?"

"Possible lead," Spano said. "Bodyguard? Who were you protecting her from?"

"What was his name?" Owens glanced up at the ceiling. "Greg something. That guy was always shovin' her, or grabbing her, or trying to pin her against a wall. Heard he left school early. Sometime in tenth or eleventh grade." He stared at the picture for a moment. "Hey, you know who else was always after her? This guy's sister, Darla. Mostly it was just mean girl stuff. But, you never know."

"You're taking your partner, right?" Spano said.

Riley Owens nodded. "Yes sir, she's getting' the car." He started toward the door.

"Owens?"

"Yes, Detective?"

"Do you remember David Terry being in trouble when you were in school?"

"Nothing comes to mind," Riley said.

"That's all then. Get him back here as quick as you can."

When Riley left, Spano turned to Rodriguez. "Something tells me Symphony Weber didn't find out about David Terry and the lake incident from school gossip." He studied the paperwork on his desk. "You know, I asked the school district to check their graduation records for a Greg Stanton. But Owens says he didn't graduate. I wonder if their files'll show where his records were forwarded." He picked up the phone and called them back.

⌘ ⌘ ⌘

It took some convincing, but Joe returned to work. "I'm fine," Symphony said. "I just need a few hours sleep."

Before he agreed to leave, he made her curl up on the couch.

"Now, close your eyes," he said, tucking her in under one of Granny's softest quilts.

But as soon as his truck pulled away, Symphony's memories turned on her. Her mind stuck on the dream of Greg Stanton, the part where his mother sent him out into the night, warning, "Don't come back without him."

She began to cry softly. For the first time, she understood what the woman was really saying. Symphony, herself, wanted to scream, "Bring my baby home right now!" and be able to expect it. She cried harder. *None of this would have happened if I'd helped.*

She rolled over, hoping for sleep, but couldn't quiet her thoughts. The first remedy she thought of involved vodka. Her second choice was a call to Granny. She opted for Granny.

They stayed on the phone for over an hour.

"Being different was so hard," Symphony said, after filling Granny in on the details of Greg Stanton's brother. "So I lied. I told him I didn't have the dreams anymore." Symphony broke down again. "Why didn't I just help?" she sobbed. "And why didn't I tell anyone his brother was missing?"

When Granny spoke again, her tone was firm. "Now, sugar, all this cryin' you're doin' ain't helpin'. Not one little bit." She paused. When she continued, her voice was softer. "You were just a girl then. A young'un with grown up things to worry about. You can't go through life lookin' backwards at what could or shoulda been. If you do, you miss all that's worth seein'. And sometimes you trip over the big stuff 'cause you don't know it's comin'. So you're just gonna have to get hold of yourself. You hear me?"

Surprised by Granny's sternness, Symphony took a breath and blew it out before answering, "I'll try."

"No, you won't just try! You're a grown woman. You'll *do* it. Because you have to."

Symphony stiffened. *Why's she bein' so hard on me?* She felt anger moving to the surface, but pushed the feeling back down.

"This time," Granny said, "if the dreams come, you're old enough to sort them out. Trust that they're not here to hurt you. You have to study the details. Figure out exactly who needs your help and how best to help 'em. Now, stretch out. Get yourself some rest. And call me later."

Symphony lay on the couch trying to concentrate on what Granny had said. Instead, "Don't come back without him," echoed down the corridors of her brain and back again. She shivered and pulled the quilt up over her face so she was almost in darkness. As she began to relax, a picture flashed before her—Choral wearing the tiny lavender sweater.

Symphony cried herself to sleep.

⌘　⌘　⌘

David Terry raised a verbal storm as he walked into the station house. He threatened jobs left and right, finishing with the Mayor, himself. The Terry family attorney, Jack Baker, showed up just minutes later.

"So, what's this all about?" the attorney asked.

Spano showed him the drawing. "Look familiar?"

"Oh, come on," David said. "I don't even own a baseball cap."

"What is your connection with Symphony Weber?" Spano asked.

"Oh my God!" David stood up. "I don't *have* a connection with her. And it's been years since I did. What? You can't find any decent leads so you're hauling in her old enemies? Great strategy."

The attorney touched David's shoulder. "Sit down, son."

David flinched him away and remained standing. "This better not be about what happened at the vet school. Those records are supposed to be private."

"David!" the attorney warned.

"Actually," Spano said, "someone mentioned your name in connection with an incident that happened when you were a juvenile."

"Expunged," the attorney said.

"You've got to be kidding." As David spoke, tiny particles of foamy spit attached themselves to his most emphatic words. "That bitch! All these years she keeps her mouth shut and now—"

"Are you finished with my client?" the attorney asked.

"For now," Spano answered.

"You're finished, all right. I'll see to that," David promised as he turned to leave.

He and his attorney were on their way down the stairs when Rodriguez looked at Spano. "Jeez. What a hot head!"

"Yeah, I can't wait to find out what happened at vet school. Whether he's our guy or not, I'll be keeping an eye on him," Spano said. Picking up the phone, he began again, searching for a trail that would lead to Greg Stanton.

⌘   ⌘   ⌘

*Symphony stood on the outside of a house peering through a hole in the curtain. On the floor next to a chair sat a bottle of whiskey. Her heart began to pound as the woman in the chair leaned over, picked up the bottle, and took a long pull.*

*Symphony stifled a groan. It was cold, dark. She wanted to go inside. There was something she needed to tell this woman, but fear held her just outside the door.*

*She reached for the doorknob, but paused, waiting for the courage she needed. Her hands seemed strange, felt odd. Her fingernails were dirty, chipped. Her shoes were scuffed, brown, untied. There was a rip in the knee of her jeans.*

*These aren't my clothes.*

*Back at the window, she searched for her reflection, but she was gone. The only face there belonged to a boy. Greg Stanton.*

Drenched in sweat, Symphony sat up on the couch in complete darkness. *I must have been sleeping for hours. No moon tonight?* She reached for the lamp next to the couch and turned it on. Nothing.

*The air reeked of rotten trash and something else. Ammonia? A fury was building inside her. It began with a sob and ended with a scream. She felt herself rise, walk, twist a doorknob, and pull. Then, she turned. As if her eyes had just opened, she saw Choral playing. The toddler was fenced into a triangular area by a twin-sized bed turned on its side and shoved against a corner. Symphony studied her strange hands as they closed the door and locked it with the key.*

*She found herself in a yard, surrounded by woods. The nose of a pine green Chevy Malibu peeked out from beneath the overhang of an ancient rose thicket. She walked toward a paint-camouflaged pick-up. Once inside, she turned the key and drove off down a road pocked with huge, mud-filled craters.*

*It seemed forever before she reached pavement. At the asphalt, she made a right turn into the path of another car. The other driver laid on the horn. She leaned to the right, opened the glove box, picked up a revolver, and placed it on the floor beneath the seat.*

*The scenery flew by. Miles upon miles of orange trees lined the road as a fine mist coated everything. She turned left into a long shell driveway where an elderly woman walked through the yard toward a large white house. Symphony parked the truck and got out, waving at the white-haired woman. When the woman went into the house, Symphony felt herself walking toward the barn. There, she picked up some tools and carried them out toward the orange grove.*

*"Stan," the woman called.*

*Symphony stopped and turned around. The woman was standing on the front porch. "Yes, Mrs. Whitaker?"*

*Symphony's words were deep, scratchy.*

*Not my voice.*

*She blinked her eyes, trying to get her own sight back but it didn't help.*

*"I think the Hamlins are just about ready to pick," the old woman called across the lawn. "See what you think."*

*"Will do." She waved at Mrs. Whitaker. "Oh yeah," she said in that low voice. Walking back to the truck, she picked up the revolver, put it in her pocket, and continued into the orange grove.*

⌘ ⌘ ⌘

"The school district found the transfer for Greg Stanton," Spano told Rodriguez. "They have the address he moved to in Tennessee. What's the fastest way to find out who lives at that address? Or at least who lived there."

"I'll see what I can do," Rodriguez said. Twenty minutes later, Spano was on the phone with a very inebriated man who said he was Terry Stanton, Greg's uncle.

"Is Greg all right?" the uncle asked.

"Just some background information for a case we're working on," Spano said. "Is he currently living with you?"

"Oh, no. I ain't seen him since that whole thing happened up in the woods. But Harlan didn't press charges. So why you callin' here?"

"When did you see him last?" Spano asked.

"Been about two months. You can't blame him for what he did. His daddy's a mean son of a bitch. Always has been," the uncle said. "I guess Greg just finally had enough of it. Put Harlan in the hospital. Nearly killed him."

"And that was back in August, September?"

"I'm tellin' ya, it was just payback. Harlan beat the hell outta Margaret for years 'fore she left him. Beat the hell outta Greg, too. And when Greg come back here to live, it started all over again. I know Harlan's my brother, but I'd say he's about due. Now, why'd you say you was callin?"

When Spano got off the phone, Rodriguez was staring at him. "You're not gonna believe this. The school district just faxed over Greg Stanton's records. And—"

"I know," Spano said. "Margaret Browden was his mother."

"Captain's been calling," Rodriguez grimaced. "Wants to know if you're done with Westhill."

"Tell him, no. I'm still not sure he wasn't involved somehow in the kidnapping."

"Okay. I'll let him know. So tell me what Stanton's father said."

Spano rubbed his chin. "It was his uncle. Okay, so here's my guess-timation. In August or September, after being beaten up his whole life, Greg Stanton assaults his father bad enough to put him in the hospital. We should see if the hospital filed a report with the locals. After that, Stanton disappears. What I think happened, is that he came here to see his mother. He sneaks in one night to see her and finds her dead."

"So he has some sort of break," Rodriguez said, nodding. "Makes sense so far. But how did Choral get caught up in this?"

"If we tell Symphony what we've found, I'll bet she can help us find the connection," Spano answered.

"After the way she fell apart this morning, I'm not looking forward to asking her anymore questions."

Spano picked up a cold cup of coffee and drained it. "I'm not either, sis. But if it helps us find Choral . . ."

Rodriguez glanced at the clock. "It's almost two. Maybe she's had a chance to rest. I'll call her." With a frown, she picked up the phone.

⌘　⌘　⌘

*The sweet, musty smell of long-wet mud filled Symphony's nostrils. Scattered throughout the waxy leaves, in great, heavy clumps, were hard, dark-green balls— oranges that wouldn't be ready for months. She could feel his legs move, arms swinging* as he walked through the slippery, man-made jungle, stepping mostly in the grassy areas. Finally, a left turn revealed a row of trees with ripening fruit. She felt an orange in his hand, felt him squeeze, felt the fruit give under the pressure. Then, with a twist, he released it from the tree.

His large hands broke the orange apart. He took a bite right from the center.

Sour.

Mouth puckering sour.

"Maybe another week," he mumbled, tossing the rest of the orange under the nearest tree.

At the end of the orange-green row, he turned a corner. The grove gave way to an open field, a pond in the center. He walked to the edge. From the surface of the water, the grown up Greg Stanton stared back at her. He reached for his pants pocket. He grasped the hard cold shape of the gun. Through his eyes, she watched his reflection as he raised it to his temple. She strained to move her arm, his arm. She tried to scream. But a vice seemed to tighten around her. Then everything went black.

Click.

There was a sigh, breathing. Then slowly, the pressure of the barrel eased.

Once again, she could see the water. Greg pointed the gun at his reflection. "Next time," he said. "You worthless piece of brother-killing shit."

# CHAPTER THIRTY-FOUR

T HE PHONE RANG.

The reflection in the pond failed and Symphony was in the dark again. She dragged her hand along the bumpy grain of Joe's pink sofa. *I'm back.* But her sight wasn't. She felt her way to the phone. "What?" she yelled into the receiver, irritated that the phone had interrupted her vision.

"Symphony?" Officer Rodriguez said.

Symphony's face burned. "It's me," she said. "Sorry. I was asleep."

"Oh. I didn't mean to wake you, but this is important. There are some developments on the Greg Stanton thing and we can't move forward without your input. Would you mind coming back to the station? We've sent an officer to pick you up. He should be there shortly."

"Okay," she said. "I'll see you soon." *Not that I'll actually be able to see you.* She hung up the phone and sat down, heart pounding. *What if I stay like this?* She blinked repeatedly, hoping to regain the vision that would tell her where Choral was. Neither the vision nor her sight returned.

Someone knocked.

"Just a minute," she called. Under normal circumstances, she'd peek around the curtain to see who was knocking. But normal had run, screaming from her life. "Who is it?" she called.

"Officer Owens," he answered. "From the Titusville PD."

"I'll be right there." At that moment, Symphony realized she was in her socks. "I'll just be a second." She got down on her hands and knees and crawled around, feeling for her shoes. "Sorry. I'm almost ready."

After several minutes, the officer knocked again.

"Are you all right in there?"

"Yes. I'm looking for my shoes." Again, using the couch to navigate, she crawled toward the front door, stood, and let Officer Owens inside. "Can you help me? For some reason, I just can't find them."

"What do they look like?" he asked.

"Aqua sneakers," she answered, her frustration obvious. "I usually keep them right in front of the couch. My brother must have moved them."

"Here they are," he said.

"Where?"

"Right by the door," Owens said. "Funny how you can look right at something and not see it. Here you go." He picked up the shoes and handed them to Symphony.

As he waited, Symphony felt her way through putting them on. Then, standing, she started toward the door. Missing it by a few feet, she slid along the wall to the left until her hand found the doorknob. "My keys," she said as they started out. "They should be on the counter near the kitchen. Do you see them?"

He picked up the keys. "Got 'em." Pausing, he glanced at the locket attached to the key ring. In the center was a picture of Choral.

"I'm sorry," Riley said, as he helped her down the stairs.

"About what?" Symphony asked.

"You know. That comment about not seeing what was right in front of you."

"It's true."

"Maybe so," he said. "But I never would have said it if I'd known you couldn't see."

"Oh," she said. *And if I told you it just happened, I'd be in an ambulance on my way to the hospital, wouldn't I?*

"Well at least now I'm not insulted that you didn't recognize me," he said.

"I know you?" Symphony asked as she bumbled her way into the front seat.

"We went to Parkway together." He shut the door.

*Junior High? Owens!* By the time he sat down in the driver's seat, Symphony was beaming. "Riley Owens?"

"At your service," he said, starting the car.

⌘ ⌘ ⌘

Joe called the apartment on his two–thirty break, but hung up after the third ring. "I hope I didn't wake her up," he muttered, looking around for a quiet place to cool off. As he ate an apple, his expression went from curious, to perplexed, to worried. He threw the core in the trash and walked to the office.

A brunette in her mid twenties looked up from her paper-sorting as he entered. "Hi, Joe. What can I do for you?"

"I just wanted to make sure I haven't had anymore calls since the one this morning."

The brunette gave him a stern look. "Joe Weber. Didn't I say I would come get you if there was another call about your sister?"

"Well, yes, Annette, you did," Joe rubbed his hands together. "And I wasn't doubting that you would." He shifted his weight from leg to leg. "I just tried to call her and there was no answer so I thought I'd double check."

Annette batted her blue eyes. "I was just teasin' you," she said. "I know how worried you are. And I'm sure everything's gonna turn out just fine."

"Thank you," Joe said. He backed out of the office, closed the door, and headed straight for the phone in the corner of the breakroom. Still no answer at his place.

No one was at Mama and Daddy's house either.

He hung up the phone and walked away. Moments later, he was back, calling another number. "Is Mr. Weber available? Yes, ma'am. This is his son." Then, he waited.

A moment later, he lightened his load of worry.

"Daddy," he said. "I need to tell you what all's going on with Symphony. But don't get mad at her, okay. She's just really mixed up."

⌘ ⌘ ⌘

For a few minutes Symphony and Officer Owens made small talk. About halfway to the police station, they turned onto a sunny street. Symphony's sight began flickering between bright light, blackness, and orange trees. Soon, the bright light won out. She squinted.

Officer Owens glanced over as she raised her hand to shield against the stream of sunlight. He pulled the squad car to the curb. "All right, Symphony. What's going on?"

"I was hopin' you wouldn't notice." She felt her face burn with embarrassment.

"You can see, can't you?" He turned his head to look at her.

Symphony turned toward him. She hadn't seen him since junior high. He looked the same, only bigger. "If I tell you the truth, you won't believe me."

"Try me."

"Well, you know how people used to talk about me? How they'd say I knew things I shouldn't?"

"Yeah. But I never paid attention to any of that."

"Some of those stories were true, Riley. But in tenth grade, something happened—"

"I know. You almost died, right?"

Symphony stared at the sidewalk. "From too much alcohol," she said. "And then, for some reason, that part of me didn't work anymore. But since I saw Mack Westhill yesterday, it started coming back in bits and pieces."

She paused, studying Riley's eyes. "When I got back from meeting with Detective Spano this morning, I fell asleep. One minute I was dreaming about Greg Stanton when he was a boy. The next thing I knew, I was seeing through his eyes. I could see Choral. She's all by herself, trapped in the corner of some sort of cabin in the woods. I watched him drive to work at an orange grove. And then, he pulled a gun out of his pocket and put it to his head. But he changed his mind at the last minute."

She sighed. "When Officer Rodriguez called, it must have forced me back to where I was. But, at first, I couldn't see anything but black. Not till just a minute ago."

Riley watched her for a moment then, nodding, pulled the car back into the street. "Okay," he said. "I better get you to the station."

When they reached the landing, Spano was at his desk, deep in conversation with a white-haired man.

"I'll see you later," Riley said, leaving her with Rodriguez.

"Thanks for coming," Rodriguez said, leading Symphony to a small room with a large round table. Moments later, Spano and the white-haired man joined them.

"This is Dr. Reynolds, Symphony. He'll be listening in on our meeting today to see if he might shed some light on the situation."

Smiling, Dr. Reynolds shook Symphony's hand and sat down. On the table in front of him, he opened a notebook and rested a pen on the top sheet. He leaned against the back of his chair and crossed his arms as if waiting for something. He watched Symphony for a moment, then turned to Spano and nodded.

"Well, Symphony, to make a long story short," Spano began, "this morning, due to some information revealed by Officer Owens, we were able to track down Greg Stanton's uncle. Apparently, about two months ago, Greg had a serious altercation with his father. His uncle hasn't seen him since. That's probably when he came to Titusville. So we investigated further. And, at this time, we don't believe Stanton came here with the intention of kidnapping Choral. We believe he came to see his mother, Margaret Browden."

Symphony groaned and gripped her forehead. *Again. That's what he meant. He blames me. Once for his brother. Again for his mother.*

Spano and Rodriguez glanced at each other, then at Symphony.

Dr. Reynolds sat up taller. "Did you know Greg Stanton's mother was in prison for murder?"

"Yes." Symphony put her hands in her lap. "For her youngest son."

"And did you know that Margaret Browden had been in prison?"

"No," Symphony answered. "All I knew about Margaret was that she had a boy who died when he was little."

"How were you able to deduce that but remain unaware that Margaret Browden was Greg Stanton's mother?" Dr. Reynolds asked in a condescending tone.

Symphony was puzzled. "What do you mean? How did I find out her son died? It was in her chart."

"I see," the doctor said. He looked at his notebook, running his finger down the lines as he read. "Is there any reason Greg Stanton may see a connection between you, the death of his brother, and the death of his mother?"

"You know what." Symphony scooted her chair away from the table. "I'm startin' to feel like you're accusing me of somethin'."

"Now, Ms. Weber, no one is accusing you of anything." He looked at his notebook again. "Sometimes when a person feels any sort of remorse—"

"Remorse?" Symphony stood and glared at Dr. Reynolds. "My daughter has been missing for over six weeks. Are you saying *I* did something to make Greg Stanton take her?"

"Dr. Reynolds," Spano said. "Maybe we should take a break."

"Was Stanton angry with you about something?" Dr. Reynolds prodded.

Symphony shook her head.

"What was that, Ms. Weber? I didn't hear you. Did Greg Stanton have reason to be angry with you?"

"He hated me, okay. From the first day he saw me till he left in eleventh grade. Ask anyone. He did anything he could to make me miserable. Maybe that's why he took Choral. To make me miserable."

"You don't really believe that." the doctor said. "Greg Stanton took your daughter for a reason. And I believe you know what that reason is."

The door burst open and Daddy walked in catching the last part of the doctor's statement. He pointed at Dr. Reynolds. "You use that tone with Symphony again and Officer Rodriguez here's gonna have to lock me up for assault."

"I'm sorry, Detective," Riley said. "Mr. Weber insisted on seeing Symphony."

"What the hell's going on here?" Daddy demanded. "It looks a little like my daughter's on trial." He turned to Symphony. "You okay, sugarfoot?"

Symphony walked over to Daddy and gave him a huge hug.

⌘　⌘　⌘

Annette found Joe in the grinding room.

"Your daddy just called," she yelled over the noise.

Joe parked the machine and took out his ear plugs. "Sorry. Now what?"

"Your daddy called. He's with Symphony. She was back at the police station."

Joe exhaled hard. "Thanks, Annette."

She smiled and batted her lashes before shutting the door.

He put his earplugs in and turned the machine back on.

⌘  ⌘  ⌘

Symphony and Daddy stood outside the conference room. "You really don't have to stay," she said. "I'm fine now."

"Yeah. Now that Dr. SOB's out of the room. I'm not going anywhere, sugar. You go ahead and say what you have to. I know all about your dreams."

She stared at him, bewildered. "How?"

"Well, your mama's not comfortable talking about it. So I asked your granny."

"When?"

"While you were in the hospital last time," he said.

Owens stepped into the open doorway. "Are you ready to start, Symphony?"

Symphony frowned. "We better go back in."

Daddy put his arm around her shoulders and guided her to a seat. Then he sat down next to her. His presence in the room seemed to expand. "Now," he said, tapping the table with his open palm, "let's get all this laid out here. Doesn't matter how we get Choral back, as long as we do. Right?"

Spano nodded to Rodriguez.

Rodriguez slid her chair closer to Symphony. "Okay." She put her elbows on the table and rested her chin on her hands. "There have been a few times during this investigation, that I've wondered how you knew something significant. Something no one could have told you. The first time was when you saw 'again' written on that pillow in Margaret Browden's room."

Symphony glanced around the table, but her eyes came to rest on Daddy's.

He took hold of her hand.

"That wasn't written on a pillow like you said," Rodriguez continued. "It was on a tiny piece of paper on the nightstand." She stopped and looked at Symphony for a moment.

Symphony felt the heat of the officer's stare and met it.

"Then," Rodriguez said, "your mom told Spano about how Roscoe Stanley came to be arrested."

Symphony shifted, suddenly uncomfortable in her chair. Daddy squeezed her hand.

Rodriguez looked at Spano and he nodded. "Now, we're wondering how you knew about the David Terry incident when other people in the school had no idea it happened."

"Now wait a minute," Daddy said, turning his chair at an angle to see Symphony's face. "I haven't heard anything about this David Terry person."

"I'll tell you later, Daddy. I promise."

"Then, there's the matter of Mack Westhill," Spano added. "Just how is it that you were able to find him and deliver him back here?"

Symphony looked across the table at Spano and grimaced.

"Yeah," Daddy said, raising an eyebrow. "I know about that, too. I nearly had a stroke when your brother told me."

Symphony covered her eyes and sighed.

Spano took over. "I promise you, Symphony, whatever you say in here won't leave this room. But you have to be completely honest with us."

"If I tell you, you'll send me straight to the psych ward."

"No," Spano said. "I give you my word, it's off the record. That's why we're in this conference room. It's sound proof." He stood up and began to pace. "Look, Symphony. I'm not the most open-minded person in the world, but I've seen this sort of thing before. What you have may be our best chance to find Choral."

"Tell 'em, sugar," Daddy said. "You've done nothin' to be ashamed of."

"Yes I have, Daddy." For a moment, Symphony forgot about the others. She told her story to the only one in the room who mattered.

"It was around the time when the dreams were really bad. I'd started sneaking a little of your vodka every night, just so I could sleep. Greg Stanton had always been mean to me. And he'd done things I was too embarrassed to talk about."

"Like what, sugar?"

"It doesn't matter anymore. The important thing is, I was afraid of him. But I hated him, too. So when he asked me to help find his brother, I told him I didn't *know things* anymore." She buried her face in her hands. "I told him I couldn't help. And now, he's got Choral."

Daddy pulled her closer and she cried against his chest.

"I just wanted everybody to leave me alone," she sobbed.

"We've all made mistakes, sugarfoot," Daddy whispered. "You forgave mine. You have to forgive yourself."

She sniffed and gazed up at him, filled with a sense of wonder. A new strength flowed through her. Once again, she glanced at the others. "I need to tell you all what happened to me today. Maybe, between us, we can figure out where Choral is. First of all, there's someone named Mrs. Whitaker, living in a big white house on an orchard with a pond. . ."

⌘ ⌘ ⌘

When all had been said, Daddy headed back to work.

Spano instructed Officer Owens to take Symphony home. "Stay for a while," he said. At least until her brother gets there."

A little after four, Riley walked Symphony up the stairs and waited on the pink couch until Joe got home.

"Thanks," Symphony said, when Riley left. "I think I'll try and get some sleep."

He pulled the squad car around the corner, watching the stairs to Joe's apartment.

# CHAPTER THIRTY-FIVE

SPANO ATE CHINESE food out of a carton as he studied the map on his desk. "It would have been nice if Reynolds had been able to hypnotize Symphony today," he said between bites.

"Well, yeah," Rodriguez answered. "But after the way he treated her . . ."

Spano handed her the half-empty carton and the chopsticks. "Want the rest?"

"Yeah," she said. "I haven't eaten since breakfast." She took a bite and swallowed almost without chewing. "So what's Dr. Reynold's problem anyway? I thought he was supposed to have experience in special abilities."

"Yeah. I know," Spano answered, looking through a magnifying glass at the map. "You should've heard him talkin' this afternoon before Symphony got here." He looked up at Rodriguez, crossed his arms and straightened his spine imitating Dr. Reynolds. "With the mind, anything is possible." He rolled his eyes and bent over his desk. "It's pretty clear, he doesn't really believe that."

"Have you found anything?" She took another mouthful of chow mein.

"Not really." Spano rolled up the map. "The description Symphony gave us could be in any rural area where they grow oranges. How's the search for the Whittaker lady?"

"Nada," she said. "I'm looking through zoning records for anything agricultural attached to a Whittaker. It's tedious. I've got the green car figured out, though."

Spano raised his eyebrows. "Oh, yeah?"

"I'm pretty sure it's the one that was registered to Margaret Browden back in sixty-eight. Stanton must have taken it when he dropped off the flowers."

Spano sat down at his desk and tapped his fingers. "I'm surprised the thing started. All I know is, it's gettin' later and later and we're still stuck." He leaned back in his chair and gazed at the ceiling. "What's this guy thinkin'? And where the hell is he?"

⌘ ⌘ ⌘

"Hello, baby," he called, stepping inside.

Usually, she was standing by the time he put his keys down. She didn't move.

"Mrs. Whittaker sent us some food."

She was asleep on the stack of blankets.

Something caught inside his chest. He set the plate on the floor. Taking hold of the bed frame, he scooted it out of the corner and turned it right-side-up.

She didn't even flinch.

He stooped next to her. "Baby?" He touched her. Her skin was hot. With a gasp, he picked her up.

She was limp in his arms.

*Water. Water will cool her off.* Trembling, he sat on the edge of the bed and held her in his lap. He stared down into Choral's flushed face. But, this time, when he looked at her, he saw his little brother. "No. No water, Markie." He raised the baby to his chest and hugged her. "I won't let the water take you this time."

⌘ ⌘ ⌘

David Terry threw his head back and swallowed a shot of scotch. "You should've seen the way that cop was looking at me today. Goddamn

322

Symphony Weber. Fuckin' bitch. I don't know who the hell she thinks she is, Darla. Bringing up what happened in junior high."

Darla rolled her eyes. "Are you drunk?"

"Wouldn't you be? I mean if someone accused you of something you didn't do? They fuckin' insinuated I had something to do with that fuckin' kidnapping. Can you believe the balls on that fat bitch?"

"I know you're upset, David, but I don't think—"

"Upset? You think I'm upset. I'm fuckin' furious." He poured himself another shot of scotch.

Darla took the bottle from him and set it on the counter. "The police found the report while they were looking for something else." She inspected her fingernails. "They asked Symphony about it. That's what Jack told Mom, and he was right there with you. He said there was nothing to worry about."

"Yeah? Well, we'll see who has something to worry about." David leaned back and laughed.

Darla glared at him. "You know what? I've heard enough." She picked up her purse and walked to the door. "Why don't you call me later, when you've sobered up. When we can have an intelligent conversation."

⌘ ⌘ ⌘

Symphony paced the floor of the apartment. She'd tried taking another nap but her eyes were wide open. "Okay," she said, stretching out on the couch again. "The sun's going down. Maybe that'll help."

Joe pulled a quilt over her and tiptoed to his room.

Ten minutes later, she was knocking on his door. "Maybe it's time to try the joint thing. I have to get back in his head."

Joe opened his door and sat down on the side of the bed. "Smoking that joint won't help, sis." He wouldn't meet her gaze.

"It might. I know it's not the same as dreaming but—"

"No. That's not it, Symphony. It won't help because, when I got it, I didn't really understand."

She crossed her arms and scowled at him. "What do you mean?"

"It's oregano," he said, staring at the rug beneath his feet. "You were drinking so much. I was afraid it was just another . . . I'm really sorry."

323

"Great." She turned and stomped away. In the living room, she picked up her purse to leave. When she got to the street, she remembered her car was still at the police station. *Shit!*

"Hi."

She jumped, startled, as a police car pulled up next to her. "Riley. Have you been here all this time?"

"Just patrolling the area," he said with an unconvincing grin. "Need a ride somewhere?"

"Yeah. To get my car. I left it at the station."

"Get in. I'll take you down there."

⌘　⌘　⌘

Jeanne and Leesa had quietly finished x-ray school the week after Choral disappeared. They put their celebration on the back burner. Both of them were now employed, pending the receipt of their certificates. As soon as they got their test results, they rented a two-bedroom apartment three miles from home.

Mama and Daddy sat at the dining room table as the all-grown-up-little-sisters carried boxes through the front door and put them into Jeanne's car.

"We're stayin' the night at the new place," Leesa said.

"What are you gonna do with all the peace and quiet?" Jeanne asked, blowing her parents a kiss as she walked through the door.

"Enjoy it!" Mama said sternly. But the expression on her face would have led anyone to believe otherwise.

Leftover fried chicken was reheating. The aroma wafted in from the kitchen and Mama got up to make a salad. "I don't know if I'll ever get used to this." She sniffled.

"Symphony and Choral'll be back soon." Daddy walked over and stood next to her. "I know you don't like to talk about her dreams, but you should have seen her today. I was so proud."

"I was never ashamed or embarrassed by what she could do," Mama said, looking into Daddy's eyes. "It's just that I didn't want to encourage it." She diced a tomato in her hand and threw it into the salad. "The whole time I was growing up I could see what it was doing to Gray. I just didn't want that for Symphony." Mama handed the bowl of salad to Daddy and pulled a cookie sheet out of the oven. "But, look at her now. Despite everything that made her stick out. Despite the mistakes we made. Just look at her."

She put the rest of their meal into serving dishes and set them on the table. "Well," Daddy said, looking at the huge salad, the eight pieces of chicken, the six baked potatoes Mama had set out. "Eating by ourselves is sure gonna take some getting used to."

A car door slammed outside. They looked at each other and smiled.

"Jeanne and Leesa?" Daddy asked.

Mama stood and wiped her hands on a napkin. "Maybe they'd like to stay for supper. We have plenty." She made it to the door just as a car sped away. By the time she stepped outside, it had already disappeared around the corner. Jeanne's car was nowhere to be seen. "I guess not," Mama said. As she started to close the door, a flash of red caught her eye. There on the stoop was a large heart-shaped box. "Candy!" she exclaimed. "How sweet!" She picked it up and carried it inside. Beaming, she turned to Daddy, "Look what the girls—" Suddenly, her smile faded, her eyes bulged. She shivered and dropped the box. "There's something moving in there."

As it hit the floor, the lid of the box opened a crack. A snake slid its triangular head through the opening.

Mama shrieked and the snake coiled, knocking the top of the box away. In a flash, it turned toward Mama and opened its mouth.

"It's a damn cottonmouth!" Daddy yelled. Eyes glued to the snake, he stepped away. He grabbed the broom from beside the refrigerator. "Behind me, Maisy. Get the trashcan."

Mama was frozen.

"Maisy!" Daddy pushed the box against the wall with the broom. "The trash can!"

Mama seemed to wake up. She backed her way across the kitchen, all the while staring at the snake. When she reached the trashcan, it was full. She dumped it onto the kitchen floor. "Here," she said, setting it next to Daddy.

"Okay," he said. "Now go in the living room."

Mama stood behind him, terrified to move.

He turned the broom around and shoved the handle at the already irritated cottonmouth. The snake hissed, jolting its head toward the wooden pole. After a few more pokes, Daddy rested the broomstick near the snake, giving it a chance to calm down. As soon as it straightened and began slithering toward the living room, Daddy pushed the broomstick up under it, lifted it, and dropped it into the bottom of the trashcan.

"Why don't you give the police a call," he said, shaking the trashcan, "while I find something to keep this little bastard from getting out."

Mama looked at the empty heart-shaped box as she stumbled to the telephone. In the bottom, there was a piece of paper that said, "Weigh Big."

⌘　⌘　⌘

Mrs. Whittaker was brushing her teeth in front of the bathroom mirror when she thought she heard a door slam. She tilted her head, listening with her best ear for another sound.

"Mrs. Whittaker," he yelled, as he went from room to room searching for her. "Mrs. Whittaker?"

"Stan?" She stepped out of the bathroom and cocked her head at him. "What's a' matter? I thought you went home." Then she saw the little one in his arms. "Well, who do you have here?" She moved closer, pushed back the blanket. Her posture relaxed. Joy filled her heart, until she touched the child. "This baby's burning up!"

"I know," he said. "What's wrong with him? He was fine this morning."

"Well, I don't know, Stan. But we need to cool him down. I'll run a tepid bath. If that doesn't work, we'll have to call the doctor."

"No water," he said. "He can't go near the water."

"I'll tell you what," she said. "Let me get the thermometer. Then we'll at least know how hot he is." She walked down the hallway into the bathroom. It took her awhile to find the thermometer. It was in its case behind everything in the top cabinet. She rinsed it off with cool water. "All right," she said. Shaking the thermometer, she stepped into the living room.

Stan and the baby were gone.

⌘　⌘　⌘

Daddy pressed a baking sheet against the top of the trashcan. "It doesn't have to be Spano or Rodriguez. Tell 'em that, Maisy. And tell 'em to send someone who knows how to handle snakes. I want this thing outta here."

"They're on the way," Mama said, hanging up the phone. She reached for the box the snake had come in.

"Don't," Daddy said. There may be fingerprints or something they can use to figure out who it came from."

"There's a note in it. It says 'Weigh Big.' What do you think that means?"

Daddy's face flushed. "Son of a bitch!"

"What?" Mama's eyes grew wide.

"That's what Stanton called Symphony all through school."

Mama began to cry. "That awful man was here? Choral was in the car with that snake?" She covered her face with her hands and began to sob. "That means she was right outside. Just a few minutes ago."

"Aw, Maisy, don't cry," Daddy said. "I can't let go of this snake container right now. And you know I can't stand for you to cry."

⌘ ⌘ ⌘

The phone rang at Spano's desk.

Rodriguez watched him pick it up, hoping it was the call they were waiting for.

"What?" He asked, nodding in her direction.

Her heart pounded. She listened, wishing she could hear what the caller was saying.

"Wait. Say that again." He paced halfway around his desk then back. "And she said it was a boy, not a girl? Uh-huh. But he fits the description of our guy." He doodled on a yellow pad as he talked. "Her name wasn't Whittaker, was it?" He glanced up at Rodriguez and nodded again.

Rodriguez stood and did a little dance.

"What's her address?" Spano asked, adding the information next to the design he'd drawn. "Thanks."

He hung up the phone and grabbed his jacket. "C'mon, sis. We're going for a ride."

327

As they left the building a group of officers had gathered at the front desk. "No shit!" one of them said. "A snake in a box of chocolates? Jesus! That guy's not gettin' any for awhile."

⌘ ⌘ ⌘

On the way to the station, Riley's police radio screeched out the call to Overlook Terrace.

"Oh my God," Symphony said. "That's my parent's house. What happened?"

Riley grimaced, turned, and headed for the Webers'. "Something about a snake."

⌘ ⌘ ⌘

When Joe remembered Symphony didn't have her car, he raced downstairs after her. He scoured the streets and alleyways, then checked the apartment again. She was nowhere. When dusk had come and gone, he drove to Mama and Daddy's house, hoping she was there.

He stopped just past two police cars parked at the curb.

"What's going on?" He asked a female officer on the stoop.

"Do you live here?"

"No. But my parents do." He walked through the unlocked front door. "Daddy?" Glancing to his right, he saw garbage scattered all over kitchen floor. The odor of onions and wet coffee grounds stuck in his nostrils.

"Over here, son." Daddy called, motioning Joe into the den where Symphony sat on the couch next to Officer Owens. "Everything's fine now," Daddy said, "but someone delivered us a valentine candy box with a damn cottonmouth in it." He paused. "Young one, too. Still had all its markings, yellow tail and all."

Joe crossed his arms and looked at Symphony. "Where's Mama?"

Symphony opened her mouth, but Daddy answered before she could get the words out. "I sent her to lay down," he said.

"Who would do somethin' like that?" Joe asked.

"I don't know, son."

Joe squinted his eyes at Symphony. "Next time you wander off, I'd appreciate if you'd let me know."

Symphony raised one eyebrow at him.

He shrugged and turned back toward the kitchen. The empty trashcan was by the front door. He filled it with the pile of garbage and took it to the large can outside. After sweeping and mopping the kitchen floor, he headed down the hall to check on Mama.

⌘ ⌘ ⌘

"Would you like a cup of coffee?" Mrs. Whittaker asked when Spano and Rodriguez were seated.

"No, thank you." Spano answered.

Rodriguez looked up and smiled. "I've had way too much coffee already."

Mrs. Whittaker sat down, smoothed the creases out of her skirt, and folded her long delicate hands in her lap. "I felt bad callin'. I don't want to cause Stan any trouble. He's been good to me. But that child was burning up with fever and he just didn't seem to know what to do."

"How long have you known Stan?" Spano asked.

She patted the fine, white curls covering her head. "He just showed up one day, beginning of last month, lookin' for work." She pulled a tissue from her skirt pocket and blew her nose. "He's always been sort of quiet. And always polite around me. But when he rushed in with that baby today, something just felt out of place." She looked at Spano. "I mean, he eats supper with me every day he works. Not once has he mentioned having a son. And he's not married. In fact, he's stayin' in our old superintendent's house just up the road. One room with a bathroom. There's no one but the two of us out here for miles. So who's been watching that baby while he's here? That's why I called," she said, "I'm worried about the little one. I want to make sure he gets to the doctor."

Detective Spano held up a picture. "Is this Stan?"

"Why, yes," Mrs. Whittaker answered. "Why do you have a picture of Stan?" She aimed her pale blue eyes at her visitors.

Spano looked at Rodriguez.

Rodriguez glanced around the living room. "I see you don't have a television in here. How do you get your news?"

"Oh, I pick up a paper whenever I go into town," she said, pointing to a stack by the fireplace. "But my eyesight's gotten so bad, and with Teddy gone . . . Mostly I listen to the radio. Teddy and I never saw the need for television. We used to read to each other."

"So you're alone," Spano said.

Rodriguez shot him a look. "How long has your husband been gone?"

"A little over a year," Mrs. Whittaker answered. "The cancer took him."

"I don't want to upset you," Rodriguez said, "but Stan is not really Stan. His name is Greg Stanton. And we believe he may have kidnapped a little girl, Choral Weber."

"Oh, no. That baby on the radio?" Mrs. Whittaker put a hand over her mouth. "I didn't make the connection. Maybe 'cause Stan said he was a boy." She frowned and shook her head. "I can't believe he'd do something like that."

Spano held out a picture of Choral. "Does this look like the baby he had today?"

Mrs. Whittaker took the picture and studied it. "Could be," she said. "But the baby Stan had was bigger. And asleep. It's hard to say for sure."

Rodriguez stood to go. "Thank you for calling, Mrs. Whittaker."

"Yes, thank you," Spano said, squeezing the white-haired woman's hand.

Once in the car, Rodriguez radioed ahead for backup, the woman in dispatch muttering something about jurisdiction. They followed Mrs. Whittaker's directions, which led them straight to a clearing in the woods.

Detective Spano pulled his unmarked car onto a muddy path just off the highway. "There." He opened the door, leaving the engine running. "No one can see us unless they turn in here. Stay behind me until the troops arrive," he said.

They stole through the trees until they found the old superintendent's house. "There's the truck," Spano whispered, glancing around. "That has to be the rose overhang Symphony told us about. The Malibu's gone. With the APB, maybe someone'll spot it." He turned to Rodriguez. "I think we're safe to assume he's gone."

"You know what they say about assume," she said. "What if he *is* in there? With Choral? Let's wait."

"That was the right answer, sis. We don't know how Stanton'll react if he sees us. And we *sure* don't want to be in the house if he comes back."

It took six sheriff's deputies in three cars, seven minutes to arrive and vanish into the woods. Spano and a deputy went to the door. Rodriguez and another stood guard at the only window.

The deputy knocked. "Brevard County Sheriff's Department." They waited. He tried again. "Sheriff's Department." After two minutes of silence, Rodriguez peeked through the window. The bathroom door was open, there was nowhere else to hide. Aside from the bed, the room was empty. "Clear," she yelled.

Spano tried the knob. "It's open," he shouted, throwing the door wide. *Ammonia.* He buried his nose and mouth against the inside of his elbow and made his way across the room. The bed was in the middle, a plate of food on the floor next to it.

Rodriguez passed him, going straight to the corner where the blankets were stacked. The floor in that area had been stripped by the breakdown of the baby's urine. She studied the blankets, Choral's imprint. "Look," she called to Spano. "You can see where she slept." Using her finger, she drew Choral's shape in the air above it. "And I wonder . . ." she said, squatting to examine a crusty substance on the blanket where the baby's head had been. "She may have a bad ear infection."

Spano spotted a piece of paper on the floor by the bed. He called one of the deputies over. "Would you mind baggin' this for me?" he asked. "I had to promise not to touch anything until we had approval from your department." He turned to Rodriguez. "Look at this." The deputy held up the evidence bag.

### Once Again AGAIN

Spano reached for the baggie but caught himself. "I'd like to send one of our evidence teams out to help go through this mess. Any chance you can keep your guys off it until I get that okayed?"

The deputy nodded. "I'll let you know."

"Here's my card. If you hear anything, please call me. I've got a missing baby somewhere out there. And now she's sick. Come on, Rodriguez. Let's head back. Why don't you radio in. Tell them to contact Officer Owens. We need Symphony back at the station."

⌘　⌘　⌘

"I'll call you in a little while," Symphony promised, kissing Daddy's cheek. Her head was beginning to ache as she said goodbye. *It's probably the stench in here.* "You smell that?" she asked Riley as they passed through the kitchen on the way out.

"Well," he said. "they had to dump the garbage to have something to put the snake in."

"That's probably all it is." She stalled for a moment. "I know the note said Weigh Big, but, for some reason, I don't think it was Greg Stanton who left that snake."

"Who else called you that?"

She shook her head. "Nobody. To my face. But he made sure everyone knew I was the one he meant when he said it."

In the patrol car, the radio chattered. "Number twenty-three, what's your ten-twenty?" Riley picked up the mouthpiece. "Twenty-three, 3112 Overlook Terrace."

The radio buzzed for a moment, then the voice said, "Number twenty-three, fifty-four calling for ten-nineteen."

"Twenty-three, ten nineteen," Riley answered. He looked at Symphony. "Spano wants us back at the station."

He did a u-turn and followed instructions.

Symphony felt a pain in her right hand and glanced down to find it bleeding. When she looked up again, she was somewhere else.

⌘　⌘　⌘

Joe ordered pizza at Mama and Daddy's and ate with them in the den. Mama couldn't bring herself to go anywhere near the kitchen. After they'd had enough, Joe put what was left in the refrigerator, then called the police station to inquire about the snake.

"They haven't run the fingerprints from the box yet," Joe said after he hung up the phone. "But the snake's gone. Some guy from St. Cloud came to pick it up. Something about anti-venom. They called him a serpentologist."

"Okay," Mama said, shivering. "I'm just glad it's not in my house anymore. Now, no more talk about snakes."

⌘   ⌘   ⌘

"She's not home," the deep, strange voice said just before Symphony felt the glass in the front door crush against her fist and slice through the top of her hand. She looked down. It was bleeding. She reached through the broken window and untwisted the door lock. Still, the door wouldn't open. There was a contraption around the doorknob. Something with a combination. Looking around, she found a red brick and used it to even the edge of jagged glass around the door's window. Then, she climbed through the opening and into the living room, landing, face first, on the small rug in the entryway.

For a moment, she was stunned but her breath returned in short gasps then leveled out. Sitting up, she looked around. Where is Choral?

The house looked the same as it had through the hole in the curtain. She felt herself stand, body aching from the fall. Moving around the room, she passed a mirror. The scrapes on Greg Stanton's face were weeping blood. He wiped them on his sleeve and walked through the house, stopping at a room where a small bed stood in the far corner. He opened the chest of drawers and pulled out a pair of pajamas. Blue flannel, with cowboys riding horses all over them. "I'm sorry, Markie," the deep voice said. Then, a ripple began inside her, as if she were filled with a billion tiny ponds that a billion little boys had just thrown a billion miniscule stones into. The ripple built into a shiver, the shiver to a tremor, the tremor to a tremble.

Then, her legs were moving.

She was at his mother's chair, collapsing into it, giving in to quaking knees. Here, she reached across the end table and picked up a photograph. On the back, someone had written

Greg and Mark, 1966.

She turned it over. Through his eyes, she gazed at the front. Greg was holding his baby brother.

That was sixth grade.

An overwhelming sadness flowed into her like cement. The heaviness felt like it had always been there, would be there forever. Even breathing was difficult.

She felt her body slide down in the chair. He's giving up. She felt the gun in his hand. He put it in his lap, cocked and ready. He picked up a pen from the end table, found a white spot on a magazine advertisement. The pen wouldn't work. He dipped the point of it into the blood on his hand, writing: Once, Again, AGAIN.

*"Okay, Weigh Big. First it was Markie. Then it was Mom. Now, here's your third." He picked up the gun and stared at it for a moment, then, put it to his temple.*

*Symphony tried to move, tried to pound against his inside walls, hoping to shake the gun out of his hand. But nothing she did caused him to move. She tried to scream. His mouth only worked for him.*

*In a flash, she realized her only chance. She gathered every bit of strength within her. She concentrated on the words she wanted him to hear. She aimed for his heart.*

*I AM SO SORRY.*

⌘　⌘　⌘

"Tell me what you've tried so far," Spano said, staring at Symphony's catatonic-like figure.

"I shook her, tapped her face, yelled at her," Officer Owens said. "And then I did them all again in different combinations."

"It was the phone that brought her out of it before, right?" Spano asked.

"Yeah."

"Then let's get her inside." Spano pulled her right arm as Riley took her by the left. Then, standing tall, they carried her into the station house. The phone rang. People shouted from one end of the room to the other, but nothing stirred Symphony.

"I have an idea," Rodriguez said. She ran down the stairs and across the street. Minutes later, she returned with a cup of ice. "I'm sorry, Symphony," she said, dropping a handful down the back of Symphony's shirt.

Immediately, Symphony gasped and opened her eyes. "Where am I?"

"At the station," Owens said. "See. This is what she did last time. She couldn't see for awhile."

"Riley?" Symphony said. "Who else is here?"

"Rodriguez and Spano."

"Greg Stanton's at his mother's house," she said. "But he doesn't have Choral. I tried to stop him," she said. "But he's got a gun. He's gonna shoot himself if we don't do something." She moved her head as if she were scanning the room. "Oh, God. Where's Choral? What did he do with my baby?"

⌘　⌘　⌘

Two nurses huddled around a baby in the emergency room. The redhead rubbed the back of her hand against the baby's face as it slept. "What was Dr. Hall doing in the ER, anyway? I thought surgeons were too—"

"C'mon, Sandra," the blonde nurse said. "He's a good guy. I've never seen a doctor give a baby medicine like that. He was really sweet to her. Now I just have to clean the gunk off her ear and she's almost good as new. Bless her heart."

"Can you believe her father just left her here like that?"

"I know," the blonde said. "Social services should be here any minute to take her. Until they can find a relative."

At that moment, Dr. Hall stuck his head through the curtain. "I've got the damndest feeling," he said. "Did either of you see the man who dropped this little girl off?"

"No," the redhead answered. "He handed her right to Rennick at the front desk."

"Thanks," he said. "Don't let this little girl go anywhere. Not with social services. Not anyone. Not until you talk to me." Then, he was gone. A moment later, he popped his head through the curtain again. "I would appreciate it if one of you would stay with her. I'll take over when I get back."

"I think I'm in love," the redhead said.

The blonde rolled her eyes. "You're so fickle."

⌘ ⌘ ⌘

"Maisy," Daddy called. "It's Dr. Hall."

"Really?" She stretched and walked to the phone. "I wonder what he wants this late. Hello?"

"Ah-huh. Yes. Ah-huh. He just left her there? Well, did you call the police? Did Rennick recognize the man from the picture on the news?" Mama wilted into the chair next to the phone. "You're staying with her? Okay. We'll be right there."

Daddy had moved closer as the conversation went on. By the time it ended, he was standing right next to Mama. "What was all that about?" he asked, eyes wide.

"Dr. Hall," Mama said, dazed. "He treated a baby in the ER a few minutes ago. He thinks it might be Choral."

"Now, Maisy," Daddy said. "Don't get your hopes up."

"Too late," Mama said. Standing she reached for her coat, purse, and keys. "For the first time in weeks, they're up."

⌘ ⌘ ⌘

Darla Terry had dreaded calling her mother, but the threat in David's voice had left her uneasy. "Mom, I'm just telling you what I think. David needs help. I'm afraid he'll do something to Symphony Weber. If he hasn't already."

"Trust me, Darla. You're overreacting," Mrs. Terry said. "And before you come down on your brother, you best remember some of the things you've done."

"You're right, Mom. I *have* made mistakes. Plenty of them."

"Exactly," Mrs. Terry answered.

"Ah-huh. But you see, Mom, here's the difference. I've learned from the things I've done. And David, well, you just keep bailing him out. He hasn't learned a thing. He's still trying the same stunts he tried in junior high."

"What do you mean? I don't bail him out anymore than I bailed you out. I don't know what you're—"

"Yes you do! You've been covering for him since before the Empty Island incident."

"I'm just about sick of this conversation, Darla. That was a perfect example of boys being boys."

"He was feeding kittens to alligators, Mom! Then, there's the episode with the vet's office in Vermont. That one cost you a bundle. And then you turned around and paid his way through vet school, knowing his history."

"Sometimes I wonder how you sleep at night. After what he did to those animals at the shelter. And, instead of getting him help, you bought his way out of trouble again."

"I'm his mother," Mrs. Terry snapped. "I don't know what you expect." Then the hardness of her voice broke. "He's my only son." Her voice cracked and she sniffled. "I can't send my own son to jail. Can I?"

"I'm sorry you're upset, Mom," Darla said. "I know it's hard because he's your son. But if you don't stop hiding what he's doing, who's gonna protect the rest of us from *him*?"

⌘ ⌘ ⌘

Four patrol cars, an ambulance, and a hostage specialist surrounded Margaret Browden's house. Greg Stanton was inside. Symphony sat with the specialist, still unable to see anything but black. She was waiting for when they needed her.

"What happened with Markie wasn't your fault, Greg," the negotiator said, over the speaker. "You were just a kid with grown up things to worry about," he said. "No matter how this turns out, you can't bring Markie back. We need you to put the gun down and come out, Greg. We need you to tell us where the baby is."

"He thinks Choral is his brother," Symphony whispered.

"I brought Markie back," Stanton screamed from behind the front door. "And I didn't let anything happen to him this time. I left him at the hospital."

The man nodded. "So you took your brother to the hospital?"

Symphony's heart thumped in her chest. *Choral's at the hospital!*

"Yeah," Stanton answered.

"When?" The negotiator asked.

"Before he got in the water. I need to get out of here," Greg said, "but someone put a lock I can't open. Can you take it off?"

"If you drop your gun out the door, we can do that."

At that point, Stanton stopped talking. Moments later, there was a gunshot.

⌘ ⌘ ⌘

Mama and Daddy raced into the Emergency Room. "Hi, Rennick," Mama said, almost breathless. "What room is Dr. Hall in?"

"I'll page him, Maisy. You know the rules. You can't go back there."

Mama walked past her, Daddy right behind. "Dr. Hall?" she asked, knocking on the wall between every exam room with a closed white curtain.

Finally, he peeked out. "Come on in. God, I hope I'm right," he said. "I just had the strangest feeling."

Inside the room, Choral was awake. Her eyes met Mama's and she reached out. Mama scooped her up, and held her until she'd been re-christened with laughter and tears. Daddy stood like a soft mountain, his arms wrapped around them both. On occasion, he glanced at Dr. Hall, who was wiping his eyes.

⌘　⌘　⌘

Inside, Greg Stanton stared at his image in the bullet-fractured mirror. "Greg? Greg!" the hostage specialist called from outside.

But Stanton was silent.

⌘　⌘　⌘

Detective Spano ran over to Symphony. "Rodriguez is calling the hospital. I'll let you know when we find her. Are you getting anything from Stanton?"

"He's still alive," Symphony answered. "I can feel him breathing."

Spano looked at the specialist. "Should we go in?"

"I think we should keep trying."

⌘　⌘　⌘

"Greg? Talk to me," the negotiator's voice rang from the street. "You said you wanted to come out. If that's gonna happen, I have to keep my officers safe. You have to give up your gun."

After a moment, Greg Stanton turned away from the broken mirror and walked toward the door. He uncocked the gun and dropped it onto the landing.

"Now, Greg," the specialist said, "I need you to hold your hands out where we can see them, and we'll have you out of there in no time."

He held his hands through the broken window as a policeman moved the gun, then used bolt cutters to remove the lock box. When they opened the door, Greg came out, still holding his hands in front of him.

On his way to the ambulance, his eyes met Symphony's. He tilted his head, a blank look on his face.

"We got her, we got her," Rodriguez yelled, tearing across the road toward Symphony. "I just got word. Your parents have Choral. They're on their way to the station."

The surrounding officers and the small crowd of spectators cheered.

As Officer Riley Owens helped Symphony back into the car, her sight returned.

⌘ ⌘ ⌘

The precinct house was a rolling wave of reporters and officers. Everyone wanted to talk to Symphony, and all Symphony could think about was getting to Choral. "She'll talk to you later," Riley told them, as they made their way through the throng of people.

Inside, the crowd parted, showing Symphony the way to Choral.

Choral reached for her mother, with tears that stopped only when she was in Symphony's arms. As Choral wrapped her tiny arms as far as they would reach around her mother, applause thundered through the station.

Symphony sat down next to Mama, resting cheek to cheek with her baby as the noise of the police station faded into the background.

⌘ ⌘ ⌘

That night, they both slept in Symphony's bed at Mama and Daddy's house. Choral's crib was out of the question. For now, she needed the constant embrace of her mother.

⌘ ⌘ ⌘

The next day, they made a trip to the station to sign paperwork.

"Well, hello, pretty girl," Rodriguez said, holding up a beautiful pink sweater. "I couldn't resist." She smiled. "Choral is the baby who made me rethink my decision not to have kids. I will love her forever."

"Thank you." Symphony removed Choral's sweater and slipped the pink one onto her short arms. "It's perfect."

When Rodriguez left, Riley came by. He stood by Symphony as she read and signed the stack of papers on Spano's desk.

"I was wondering," Spano said. "Would you consider helping me out on a case or two every now and then?"

"Really?" Symphony asked. "I'd love to. I think."

"And I was wondering," Riley said, "if maybe, after things settle down a little, you'd think about going to dinner with me."

Symphony looked up at Riley and smiled.

At that moment, Mack walked by in handcuffs, on his way back to prison. He nodded at Riley, then turned toward Symphony and Choral, flashing that smile that made his eyes crinkle. Symphony smiled back. There was still a seed of that beautiful boy inside him. *I hope he can find it again.*

She stood on her tiptoes and kissed Officer Riley Owens on the cheek.

Spano grinned. "I think that's a yes." His phone rang and he picked it up. "Spano. Oh, yes. The snake." He paused. Raising his eyebrows, he picked up a notepad and began to make notes. "Tell me. What makes you think your brother had something to do with it?"

# *THE END*

Made in the USA
Lexington, KY
06 July 2012